Dedicated to Harry Chapin
"There only was one choice . . ."

More praise for
William Bernhardt
and *Extreme Justice*

"Captivating . . . An excellent and very believable murder mystery. As good as the puzzle is, what makes the book so entertaining is the characters Bernhardt introduces along the way."
—*Oklahoma City Oklahoman*

"Compelling courtroom scenes, realistic characters, good plotting, just enough plot twists to foil most armchair detectives with die-hard jealousy, sexual obsession, and cold-blooded murder thrown in for good measure."
—*Cheyenne Tribune-Eagle*

"William Bernhardt fans familiar with his previous novels like *Double Jeopardy*, *Cruel Justice*, and *Naked Justice* are in for something even more thrilling with *Extreme Justice* . . . His best work to date."
—*Tulsa World*

"William Bernhardt remains on a roll with his latest book, *Extreme Justice*. The seventh in the *Justice* series continues the saga of Tulsa criminal attorney Ben Kincaid, who has become disillusioned with his law practice. . . . Bernhardt has penned an excellent and very believable murder mystery . . . a well-written, well-researched, and captivating novel."
—*The Daily Oklahoman*

"Master of the legal thriller."
—*Abilene Reporter-News*

Please turn to the back of the book for
an interview with the author of
EXTREME JUSTICE!

EXTREME JUSTICE

William Bernhardt

BALLANTINE BOOKS • NEW YORK

A Ballantine Book
Published by The Ballantine Publishing Group
Copyright © 1998 by William Bernhardt

www.randomhouse.com/BB/

Library of Congress Catalog Card Number: 98-96399

ISBN 0-345-42481-6

Manufactured in the United States of America

First Hardcover Edition: February 1998
First Mass Market Edition: January 1999

10 9 8 7 6 5 4 3 2 1

The greatest thing in the world
is to know how to be one's own self.

—MICHEL EYQUEM DE MONTAIGNE

* Prologue *

She has never looked more beautiful than she does right now, completely naked and absolutely forever still. He cannot take his eyes off her, cannot part with the sight of her chocolate brown skin, her proud high cheekbones, her smooth velveteen neck. His eyes scan her immaculate body, radiant in the light of the twelve candles encircling her. She is an impeccable creation, a masterpiece; and now, he supposes, she is *his* masterpiece.

She is not as young as she once was, he thinks, then chastises himself for having such an unkind thought. Still, he cannot block out the unbidden image of the girl who once inhabited that body—young, fresh, innocent. Time is a cruel master; it keeps no secrets. And yet he is struck by how well she has held her beauty, how her deepening lines suggest character and grace more than age. Surely maturity is as valuable as innocence. Perhaps more so. Or perhaps he is simply being romantic because, no matter how much he tries to deny it, he cares for this woman deeply.

He is amazed that she can remain so rivetingly attractive with her eyes closed. Wasn't it Shakespeare who said the eyes are the doorways to the soul? The eyes, more than any other feature, are what make a woman lovely. And yet here she is, those vivid brown eyes concealed, and still every bit the beauty. Her face is still *the* face—it may not have launched a thousand ships, but in its own way, it moved men to commit acts even more extreme, even more dangerous.

He wonders: would it be in bad taste to take a picture?

1

He decides to do it—he is the arbiter of taste here, now. He takes his Polaroid and snaps the shot, the flash turning the tiny room inside out, making it an X-ray reversal of what had been before. The square photo juts out suddenly, vulgarly, urging to be released.

He checks his watch and waits as the requisite minute passes and the photo develops itself. His eyes return to the woman lying before him, like wayward puppies making their way home. He loves the way she cut her hair. Short in the back and on the sides, but full in the front, creating a peekaboo effect as the long bangs dangle flirtatiously over one side of her face. A touch of glamour, a hint of mystery. Now that he thinks of it, he realizes that describes not just her hair but her. Her persona in a nutshell. Her elusive charm.

The photo is finished, but it is awful. It does not do justice to her splendor. It is too dark in here, and the candles made everything look greenish-yellow and grainy. He tosses the snapshot aside. It seems film is of no help to him on this occasion. He will have to remember everything himself.

He approaches her quietly, gently, as if afraid he might disturb her peaceful sleep. She is so beautiful! As he draws close, he is overwhelmed by a sudden surge of energy; it courses through him like an electric shock, like a frisson of passion and memory.

Did he dare touch her? Did he dare not? he answers himself. This is his last opportunity; he cannot let it pass untaken.

Gently he lowers his hand. His fingers trace the lines of her face, the soft sensual pout of her lower lip, her elegant neckline. He feels the old stirrings, just as he did before. The old affection returns to him; or perhaps it never left.

His hand moves onward, brushing over her collarbone, tracing the mounds of her shoulders, drawing a line down the tender valley between her breasts. He bends down and kisses them, unable to restrain himself any longer. It is a sweet, cold kiss—just as he remembers it. He can see the soft push of her ribs under her skin, see the soft curve of her hips below a nearly nonexistent waist. God, how he wants to pull her close, how he wants to press himself against her, to roll her over and brush his lips against her back, to curl one leg between hers, to feel the soft cushion of her backside against his groin.

It is becoming too much for him, not just the yearning, but the sorrow, the heartbreak. How had it come to this? They had made beautiful music together, and he didn't mean that just as a cliché—they really had. But that was all past now. All gone. And all that remained was, well, what he saw before him now, in the fierce glow of candlelight.

He casts his eyes one last time upon her perfect face. It is almost as if he had set her in stone, sculpted her, preserved her visage for all eternity. The only thing missing was her smile. She had such an infectious, vibrant smile. It warmed his heart every time he saw it.

Yes, the smile is important, he realizes. He would have to add the smile.

Almost without thinking, he bends down and presses his lips against hers, presses hard. He is kissing her for all time now, kissing like there is no tomorrow, which of course for her there isn't. Sweet angel, he thinks, squeezing her tightly. Now you can be in heaven where you belong. Where you have always belonged. One more kiss, this time a chaste address to the cheek, and then he pulls away.

He stands over her for a moment and then ritualistically extinguishes each of the twelve candles, leaving the room in darkness. It is time to get on with it. He has much work to do.

He presses his fingers to his lips and blows her a kiss, casting it out into the black void.

Farewell, angel, he says aloud, even though he knows she cannot hear. I love you so much. I always have. I wish I hadn't been the one who had to kill you.

But I was.

ONE

* *

Just Another Night
in Babylon

* 1 *

Ben Kincaid was playing the piano and singing with such enthusiasm that he neither saw nor heard the man sitting at the foot of the stage desperately trying to get his attention.

" 'I know I'm going no-oh-where . . .' " Ben belted out his song in a high-pitched adenoidal voice that seemed part Bob Dylan, part Sonny Bono. " '. . . and anywhere's a better place to be.' "

Unfortunately, the man offstage couldn't stand it any longer. He stood up and barked, "Stop!"

Ben did not hear him. " 'I come back with my pa-ay-per ba-a-ag . . . to find that she was gone . . .' "

The man slammed his fist down on the nearest table, rattling two beer mugs and a centerpiece candle. "*Stop* already!"

Ben froze. He stopped singing. He stopped playing. For a moment he even stopped breathing. "Earl? Were you talking to me?"

Earl Bonner let out a sigh of relief. "I was."

Ben nervously fingered the sheet music propped up before him on the piano. "But . . . I'm not finished yet."

Earl pulled a white handkerchief out of his back pocket and wiped his brow. "Not finished? You've been compin' chords for somethin' like ten minutes already!"

Ben swallowed. "It's a long song."

"That ain't no song, son. That's more like an opera."

Ben scooted to the end of the piano bench. "It's a story

song, Earl. It takes a while to lay out the plot, develop the characters—"

"What're you talkin' about? Plot? Characters?"

"See, it's a Harry Chapin song—"

"Harry *who*?" Earl ambled to the foot of the stage. "Ben, did you happen to notice on your way in what the name of this here club is?"

Ben cleared his throat. "Uh ... Uncle Earl's Jazz Emporium?"

"Right. And what do you suppose the most important word in that name is?"

Ben looked down sheepishly. "Jazz?"

"You bet your sweet mama's pajamas. *Jazz*." He pronounced the word as if it had about sixteen syllables. "Now what in the name of Thelonius Monk does what you were cuttin' have to do with jazz?"

"Variety is the spice of life."

"Maybe in vaudeville, but not in Uncle Earl's Jazz Emporium." He reached out. "C'mere, Ben. Walk with me."

Ben pushed himself to his feet. "Should I bring my music?"

"Definitely not."

Ben jumped off the stage and allowed himself to be swallowed up by the huge black man's right arm. Earl steered him toward the exit doors on the east side of the club. They stepped out into the sunlight of a bright April day.

The club was located on the North Side of Tulsa in the heart of Greenwood, the city's jazz district. Several clubs, studios, shops, and bars flanked Uncle Earl's on all sides. In one direction, just a few blocks away, Ben saw the time-honored Mt. Zion Church, a cherished historical icon for the black community in North Tulsa. In the opposite direction, he could see the skyline of the ultramodern, spanking fresh campus of Rogers University. Quite a contrast.

"Now you look here," Earl said, spinning Ben around like a top. "I know you can play jazz. You've been handlin' yourself real nice these past few months, 'specially considerin' you've got the only white face in the combo. You've got a smooth two-hand rhythm style; you know how to make that piano sing like a canary. So what was that all about?"

Ben shrugged awkwardly. "I just thought if I was going to audition for a solo spot, I might try something . . . different."

Earl peered at him with eyes like daggers. "You mean somethin' that means a little more to you than jazz?"

"No, no," Ben answered, a bit too hastily. "I love jazz. I do. I mean—"

"Some of your best friends are jazz players?"

"Well—yes, they are."

Earl laid his hand firmly on Ben's shoulder and squeezed hard enough to turn grapes into wine. "Look here, Ben. I like you, so I'm gonna take a minute to tell you what's what. Savvy?"

Ben nodded.

"Jazz ain't somethin' you do jus' 'cause you can, or 'cause you need work, or 'cause you like hangin' out in clubs. If you want to be a jazzman, you got to feel it deep down, in the core of your soul. In the marrow of your bones."

"I could feel that."

Earl grinned. "I don't think you're listenin' to me, son. It ain't somethin' you *could* do. It's somethin' you do 'cause you ain't got no choice. It's a part of you, like an arm or a leg. You got to listen to that jukebox thumpin' away inside your chest. I mean, really listen!" He paused, licking his broad lips. "Look, son, I don't know what you did before you came to my club, but I bet it wasn't playin' jazz licks."

"True."

"Personally, I never thought no white boy had any business playin' jazz anyway. Some of you do a pretty nice imitation, but it ain't the same, you know? It ain't the truth. To be a real jazzman, you got to suffer. You got to hurt. You got to hurt so bad you got to work your axe just to send all the pain away for a little while."

"Maybe I should've worn a cast to the audition."

"I think I'm not makin' my point." Earl swayed when he talked, as if he was speaking to the beat of some unheard syncopated rhythm. "Let me ask you a question, Ben. Do you understand the *meaning* of jazz?"

"What?"

"You heard me. Do you get it?"

Ben squirmed awkwardly. "Mmm . . . well . . . maybe you could explain it to me."

Earl held up a finger. "Now you see, that's the problem. It's like ol' Satchmo said, 'If you gots to ask, you'll never know.' "

"Not even a hint?"

"I wouldn't know where to begin. Sure, it's about sufferin', but everyone suffers. It's more than that. It's about findin' the answers, findin' some peace within yourself. It's about knowin' who to trust, who's lookin' out for you. It's about harmony, about findin' out what really matters in the cosmic scheme of things. It's about learnin' to believe." He shrugged his shoulders. "Look, it ain't somethin' I can explain. It's somethin' where you just wake one morning, and all of the sudden you know."

"Look, Earl, I can learn any piece of music you give me—"

"I know you can, Ben. Like I said, you got a real nice way with that keyboard. You remind me of some of the all-time great piano professors—Tuts Washington, Huey Smith, Allen Toussaint, Art Tatum. But that ain't the point. If your heart tells you you'd rather be playing this . . . this . . . Harry . . ." He wiped his brow again. "Oh, hell. What do you call that stuff anyway?"

"Folk music."

"Folk music?" Earl began to laugh, a deep hearty bowl-full-of-jelly laugh. "Well, blow me over. That's one I ain't heard in a while." He tried to suppress his grin and get serious, although Ben could see it was a struggle. "So

anyway, if your heart says you should be playin' this . . .
folk music, that's what you got to do."

"This isn't exactly a renaissance period for folk music."

"It don't matter, son. Listen to me. It don't matter what
the other folks are doin'. It don't matter what they want
you to be. You got to be who you are." He jammed his
handkerchief back in his pocket and steered Ben toward
the club. "Your problem, if you don't mind my sayin' so,
is that you ain't figured out yet who you are."

Ben tried to smile. "Thank you, Uncle Sigmund."

* 2 *

By the third time he had dropped the corpse, he was ready to call it a day. Nothing could possibly be worth this much trouble. Could it?

It wasn't as easy as it looked. He had learned that the hard way. When she was still alive, even just barely, when he stripped her clothes and put her on the bed within the circle of candles, he had no trouble moving her. But something happened to bodies once that last vestige of life trickled away. Once the fonky cat played her last note and Gabriel's horn started beckoning, the body changed. It became heavy, unmanageable, all loosey-goosey. It flipped, it flopped, and it weighed a ton.

Getting her down the stairs had been the worst. He should have just rolled her down, but at the time, that had seemed a bit callous. Her natural beauty would undoubtedly have been marred by a deadweight run down two flights of stairs. Of course, now it was apparent that her natural beauty was fading fast, stairs or not. By tonight, by the time of the big show, he expected she would be something altogether gruesome.

Anyway, she was down the stairs, but he still had to get her into the van and into the club. He had to set the stage carefully to produce the desired effect. He needed some way to contain her, some way to make her more manageable.

He laughed. Not that she had ever been particularly manageable—even when she was alive. She had always had the upper hand. But now that she was dead, dead, dead, he had a distinct advantage.

He noticed the area rug in the center of the living room. Hadn't he seen that in a movie once—rolling a corpse up in a rug? It seemed like it would work. It would keep her tragic deterioration from prying eyes, and it would hold her together so he could get her where she needed to go. It would require some alteration of his cover story, but so what? With all the hustle and bustle surrounding the anniversary show, he was certain no one would take much notice.

He bent down, placed one hand against her back and the other against her buttocks, and pushed. Fortunately, the hardwood floor had been recently varnished; she scooted along smooth as Red Tyler's fingertips. Soon he had her positioned on the rug, and a few minutes after that, he had the rug wrapped tightly around her.

He stood and marveled at his work. She was completely invisible. As long as he didn't give any indication that the package was heavier than it looked, no one would ever suspect that this innocent rug was a nightmare meat enchilada. It was perfect.

Getting the package onto his shoulder was no piece of cake, but he managed it. Hell of a lot of work, but it was worth it. He had big plans for this victim.

A grin spread across his lips. This victim—and the next one.

On his drive home, Ben tuned in to KVOO with Andy O'. It was, admittedly, a country music station, and he had been trying to force himself to listen to jazz, but Andy O' was a favorite, as was Steve Smith at KBEZ, who had just signed off. The antenna on his van could sometimes pick up the Oklahoma City DJs like Bob & Josh, his personal favorites, but it was too late in the day for their on-air hijinks. KWGS was great for news, of course, but there were times when Ben just wasn't in an NPR mood.

Ben loved his new car. After his Honda Accord had

bitten the dust, he'd been forced to select a new means of transportation. He chose a Ford Aerostar, a minivan. Although he had no kids to tote, he'd always wanted to drive a van, to have the feeling of something big and powerful surrounding him. And it was very useful for gigs, hauling sound equipment around. He and the band were planning to tour during the summer; when that happened, the van would be invaluable.

Ben parked the van on the street and hoofed it to the rooming house where he lived. It might not be one of the swankiest neighborhoods in Tulsa, but it was close to Earl's club, barely a ten-minute drive. He just wanted to change clothes and get a bite to eat before he returned for the anniversary show.

As he approached the house, he saw his landlady, Mrs. Marmelstein, puttering in her front garden. She was facing away from him, digging up mounds of soft loamy soil with her trowel.

"Bit late for tulips, isn't it?" he said, hovering over her shoulder.

Mrs. Marmelstein glanced up at him and smiled. "Late? Why, Benjamin Kincaid, you don't know a thing about gardening, do you?" She was wearing a print dress, blue with a white blossom pattern. She had lived eighty-two years, and Ben suspected she'd had that dress for at least eighty-one of them. "They have to be planted in the fall if you want tulips come April."

"But, Mrs. Marmelstein"—he leaned closer and whispered—"it *is* April."

"April? But we only just had Halloween." She frowned. "Benjamin, are you playing a trick on me?"

No, he thought sadly, you're playing a trick on yourself.

It had been like this for the last six months. In September, she had suffered two heart attacks, one right after the other. Although she had recovered, she was not the person she'd been before. Sometimes the change was so profound it frightened Ben. It was like talking to an entirely different person.

Her speech gradually returned, but the blow to her health had advanced her Alzheimer's with a vengeance. Granted, she had been a bit dotty for as long as Ben had known her, but during the past few months she had become increasingly senile. Ben tried to help where he could; he ran errands, paid the bills, collected the rent. But he knew his efforts were just a tap dance against time, and it broke his heart.

"I'm sorry, Mrs. Marmelstein," Ben replied. "You're the gardening expert, not me." And he could always buy blooming tulips at a nursery and plant them in the garden. She'd never know the difference.

Mrs. Marmelstein glanced at her watch. "It's a bit early for you to be home, isn't it, Benjamin? I don't think your bosses will appreciate your taking the afternoon off."

"Mrs. Marmelstein." He drew in his breath. What was the nice way to handle it? He could barely remember anymore. "I haven't worked at the law firm for years."

She sniffed. "Well, I'm not surprised. Coming home in the middle of the afternoon. Honestly." She started back at her gardening, then stopped. "By the way, you have a visitor waiting in your room. A *female*." She could not have put more disapproval in her voice had she been saying "she-devil from hell."

"That would be Christina, I assume?"

"Who else?" She eyed him with profound suspicion. "Benjamin, you know I don't approve of my gentlemen boarders receiving females in their rooms without a chaperone."

"Mrs. Marmelstein, we're just friends. And coworkers. Were, anyway."

"I don't care if she's your long-lost sister. I don't like it."

"Listen, what if I ask Christina if she'd like to go to the flea market with you this Saturday?" Tulsa had one of the best flea markets in the country, a weekly event at the fairgrounds. And Mrs. Marmelstein had decorated most of her building in flea-market kitsch.

"Well," the elderly woman said slowly, "I suppose that would be all right."

"Good. I'll tell you what she says." He started toward the front door. "Don't stay out in the sun too long. Remember, it's still awfully hot for—er—whatever month this is."

He bounded up the front steps to the porch and opened the mesh inner door. A glance up the stairs told him Joni Singleton, one of his fellow boarders, was not in her usual afternoon spot. He had to remind himself that she was taking classes at Tulsa Community College this semester. A child development major, if the gossip he got from her twin sister, Jami, was to be believed. Joni's brief stint as nanny for Ben's nephew, when Ben's sister had parked the kid with him, seemed to have had a profound impact on her.

He took the steps two at a time till he reached his room. He cracked open the door and peered inside.

Christina McCall was sitting on the sofa reading. Whatever it was, it was holding her attention. Her eyes were glued to the manuscript pages.

Manuscript pages? Wait a minute—

Ben burst through the door. "What do you think you're doing?"

Christina brushed her long strawberry-blonde hair back behind her shoulders. "Hi, Ben. Good to see you, too."

Ben stomped across the room. "I don't recall saying you could read this."

"That's because I didn't know it existed. Of course, if I had known it existed, and I had asked if I could read it, you would've said no."

"Damn straight."

"So I saved us both a lot of bother." She grabbed Ben by the shoulders and grinned. "Ben, you wrote a book!"

He shrugged awkwardly. "Well . . . I've had a lot of spare time on my hands."

"True crime. Just like Darcy O'Brien. Very classy. And it's about one of our actual cases. This is so exciting!" She beamed. "You know, television loves these based-on-real-events things. Maybe you could get a movie of the week!"

"Well, that would be the be-all and end-all, wouldn't it?"

"I love the title. *Katching the Kindergarten Killer.* I think it'll sell billions."

"Only if my mother buys all the copies." He snatched the manuscript back and stuffed it in his desk. "What say I find a publisher before you negotiate the movie rights?"

"I can't help it, Ben. I think this is tremendous. Here I thought you were wasting all your time plinking on the piano and pretending you weren't going to practice law anymore—"

"Pretending?"

"—and it turns out you're writing a book! I'm so proud of you."

"Well, now my day is made." Christina was the best legal assistant he had ever worked with, but sometimes she could be downright irritating.

She ignored him, sweeping around the sofa with unrestrained enthusiasm. "You told me you'd been contacted by some professional ghostwriter and that he was going to write up one of your cases. What happened to that?"

"What happened was he finished it and it was godawful. So I got rid of him. He played fast and loose with the facts. Took a serious serial murder case and turned it into an episode of *Starsky and Hutch.*"

"Really?" Her eyes lit up. "Was I Starsky or Hutch?"

"Neither. You were the useless female who was only around to scream and be rescued."

"Then I'm glad you got rid of him." She frowned. "If I couldn't be smart, I hope he at least made me pretty. Did he say I was pretty?"

Ben covered his smile. "Radiant."

She plopped back down on the sofa. "Well, this is better, anyway. They're your cases. No one knows them better than you. You should be the one who tells them. Have you sent the manuscript to any publishers or agents?"

"Dozens."

"What do they say?"

" 'Get lost.' But nicely."

"Well, don't stop trying. You'll get published. I know you will."

"Thanks, but you still didn't have any business reading my manuscript."

"I saw it there on your desk. How could I resist? You should be grateful I come here at all. Your landlady glares at me like I'm a call girl, and your cat tries to kill me."

"I guess they're just protective of me."

"Well, so am I, but I try not to go overboard." She bounced off the sofa and jabbed him in the side. "Enough banter. Let's go up on the roof."

* 3 *

Joe Willingham huddled in the parking lot across from the bus station at Third and Cincinnati. He used his high-powered Ricoh binoculars to scan the motley collection of passengers who stepped off the latest arrival, watching for the right one.

It was a talent he had developed over the years—an art, really. He could tell at a glance if a person would be susceptible to the scam. Of course what he ideally wanted was someone who would not merely fall for it, eventually, given much time-consuming effort and persuasion, but someone who would fall for it with great aplomb and enthusiasm, someone who could not only be pushed but would tumble head over heels into the abyss. And someone who, in the unlikely event the ruse fell apart, would not be in a position to put up any opposition. The perfect patsy—that was who everyone working the con hoped for. And Joe Willingham knew how to find him.

He continued scanning the passengers until he saw exactly what he wanted. The instant the black kid in the bib overalls and straw hat stepped off the bus, Joe knew he'd found his mark. It was not even something he had to think consciously about. Years of experience had made it instinctive. Truth was, Joe thought, he was the best scam artist in Tulsa—probably the best in the whole damn state. Perhaps his self-estimation was immodest, but facts were facts. He was the best.

He eased out of his crouched position and started slowly across the street. Judging from the rube's garb, he was

19

from some hick town west or south of Tulsa—Henrietta or Poteau or some backwater burg like that. Probably saved up his money all year long so he could treat himself to a weekend in the big city—see a show, go to a bar or club, maybe transact a little business with one of the hookers on Eleventh Street. One of the first things Joe had spotted through his binos was the fat wallet in the back pocket of the kid's overalls.

Joe smiled. The kid was perfect. Just the way Joe liked them—unsophisticated, gullible, and loaded with cash. This would be easy pickin's.

He waited until the kid walked a fair distance from the bus station. Better to ply one's trade on the anonymous and unpopulated downtown streets. It was after five; all the lawyers and bankers had gone home. The sun was setting. Soon they would be able to have a conversation in near seclusion and relative darkness.

Just after the kid crossed Main Street, Joe began shouting. " 'Scuse me! 'Scuse me!"

The black kid in the overalls slowed. He glanced back over his shoulder, checking out the source of the commotion. He did not stop walking.

"Hey, wait!" Joe shouted again. "You! In the overalls!"

He could hardly pretend he didn't know he was being accosted. He stopped, but his expression made it clear that he did so only with extreme reluctance.

"I don't want any trouble," the kid mumbled, obviously nervous.

"Neither do I," Joe said as he panted up to his prey. "But I've sure got it."

"Well, I'm sorry . . ." The kid tried to slip away, but Joe jumped in front of him, blocking his path.

"Please, sir. You've got to help me." Joe brought all his acting talents to bear, slathering on the sincerity and earnestness. It was a flawless performance—really, he ought to be up for an Oscar. "I'm in a desperate situation."

Something about what he said or the way he said it caught the kid's attention. These country boobs were all the same. Mama raised them to be good Samaritans and all that hogwash. "What happened?"

"I gave my friend all my money," Joe said. He reached into his pockets and pulled them out, showing that they were empty.

"And he spent it?" the kid guessed.

"No, man, he's still got it. He's waitin' for me. I just ain't got no way to get to him."

The kid began shaking his head. "I don't have a car. I came in on the bus."

"It ain't transportation I need," Joe said, leaving the important part of the sentence unspoken. "He's holed up at this country club, Utica Greens. It's clear across town. I got no way to get there. Plus, they ain't gonna let me in dressed like this. Hell, I hear they won't let anyone in unless they cough up a hundred bucks at the door."

"A hundred bucks?" The kid swallowed.

"That's right. Sad, ain't it?"

"Maybe you could call him. Get him to meet you somewhere else."

"Don't you think I thought of that already? No can do." Joe shoved his hands dejectedly into his pockets. "He's not near a phone. And they don't take messages for nobodies like me."

"Gee," the kid said. Joe could detect the slow sashay of his feet moving away. "That's tough, but . . ."

"Please." Joe grabbed the nearest bare arm poking out of the overalls. "You've got to help."

The kid shrugged him off. "Don't touch me."

"But you've got to help me. I don't have any money. I don't have anyplace to stay."

"I'm sorry, but—"

"Do you know what it's like, living on the streets? The bums, the thugs, the cops. They might murder me in my sleep."

"I don't see what I can do."

"The police might arrest me as a vagrant. Can you

imagine? Here I've got ten thousand bucks just waiting for me, and I get arrested as a vagrant."

The kid paused. "Ten thousand—"

Joe nodded. "That's what my cut is. Me and my buddy, we won big down at the Remington track in OKC. I just need a way to get to my money!"

"And you say you've got ten thousand—"

"Hell of a note, ain't it?" He stopped suddenly and put that glassy-eyed I-just-got-a-brilliant-idea look on his face. "Hey, I just thought of something. If you could lend me some money—"

"Oh, I don't know . . ."

"It would only be temporary. Till I get my stash."

"But I've got plans—"

"Look. Here's what I'll do. You give me a little stake—say, two hundred bucks—so I can get my money, and I'll pay you back five hundred."

The kid's eyes widened. "Five hundred?"

"Right. For your trouble. Hell, what do I care? I've got ten thousand. I can afford to be generous."

"Well, I don't know . . ."

"C'mon. Think of it. You can turn two hundred into five hundred in just a few hours. Maybe less. And there's no risk. If you don't trust me, you can come to the country club."

The kid squirmed. "I'm not sure . . ."

"Please, I'm beggin' you. You're my last hope."

The kid pressed his lips firmly together. "No, I don't think so." He whirled around abruptly and started walking away.

Damn! Joe thought. What did he do wrong? He thought he had this one hooked and reeled. He raced after his quarry. "Wait! Don't go!"

The kid continued walking, accelerating his pace. "Leave me alone."

Joe reached out and grabbed the kid by the arm. "Please stop! You've got to listen!"

The kid whirled around. "I told you not to touch me!"

Joe squeezed all the harder. "But you've got to help me!"

All of the sudden the kid screamed. "Oh my God! You touched my blood!"

"What?" Joe looked down and saw that his hand, tightly gripping the kid's arm, had rubbed off a large Band-Aid covering what appeared to be an open sore. The red, mucousy surface of the wound touched his thumb.

"Wh-what's that?" Joe asked. His voice began to tremble. "Come on, tell me. What is it?"

"It's the *plague!*" the kid shouted. "I got the plague!"

Joe became paralyzed with fear. "You don't mean—"

"Worse! I got that thing from Africa, you know. That Ebola virus!"

"No!" Joe vaguely remembered hearing something about that on television. "But . . . I thought you came from a farm—"

"Farm? I just came in from Africa. And I've got the *plague!*" His eyes widened, filled with panic and fear. "And now you've got it, too!"

Joe's mouth went dry. He could barely speak. "B-b-but there must be some mistake."

"There ain't no mistake, man. I'm dying! My internal organs are meltin'! My whole body is turnin' into a big mess of flesh soup!"

"Th-there must be something you can do—"

The kid shook his head gravely. "Maybe if they'd caught it earlier. But it's too late for me now."

Joe's face went wild. "But it ain't too late for me. I just got it! What can I do?"

The kid continued shaking his head. "It's hopeless. There's an antidote, but by the time you got to a doctor—"

Joe could feel his joints stiffening. It was getting harder to breathe, harder to think. Damn but this thing worked fast! "Where can I get the antidote?"

The kid looked away. "I've got one vial left, but I'm savin' it for myself."

"For you? Why?" Joe's eyes were watering. He was having a hard time focusing. Everything was beginning to spin around in dizzy circles. He knew he didn't have much time. "You're already doomed, you said so yourself!"

The kid looked away. "Still, it cuts the pain—"

"Please, I'll do anything." Joe ripped his wallet out of his inside jacket pocket. "Look, I'll pay you."

The kid frowned. "I thought you didn't have any money."

"I lied, okay? How much do you want?" He started ripping bills out of his wallet. "You want two hundred? Here it is! Or make it three."

The kid eyed the wallet carefully. "Looks more like you've got five."

Joe threw the wallet into the kid's hands. "Fine, take it all. Just give me the antidote!"

The kid hesitated. "I shouldn't do this."

"Please!" Joe could feel his heart weakening, his lungs collapsing. *"Please!"*

The kid took a deep breath. "All right." He removed a small vial containing a purple liquid from his top bib pocket. "Here."

Joe snatched the vial away. "Oh, thank you. Thank you." He removed the cork and downed the contents in one swallow.

It went down smooth, with a pleasant grape flavor. He could feel the liquid coursing through his veins, calming his heart, strengthening his body. Slowly but surely he felt his old self returning. It had been a narrow escape, but somehow he had managed to survive.

"Thank you," he whispered, leaning against the side of a building. "You don't know how grateful I am." His breathing began to normalize. Thank God, he thought, he was going to make it. Now he needed to get his cash back. "Look, about the money . . ."

He turned, then stopped abruptly in mid-sentence.

The kid had disappeared.

About a quarter of a mile away, in a dark alley behind the remains of the old Mayo Hotel, the kid counted his loot. His eyeball estimate had been conservative. There were more than seven hundred dollars in this wallet. And now it was all his.

He tossed the wallet, credit cards intact, in a nearby Dumpster, and took his own wallet from his back pocket. He removed the shredded paper he had put in to make his pocket bulge, inserted his newly acquired cash, and shoved it back in his pocket. It felt good in there. Nothing cushioned the tush quite so sweetly as other people's money.

Tyrone Jackson grinned, congratulating himself on another successful scam. He laughed when he thought about the boys he had grown up with, the North Side Hoover Crips, the gang that had first taught him how to work a con. Back then, they had preyed on innocence and kindness, exploiting people's desire to help and backing it up with the threat of violence. He had never liked that, and now that he had split from the gang, he didn't do it.

It was much more satisfying to scam the scammers. He never felt a trace of remorse, much less regret. And as it turned out, con artists were the easiest people on earth to fool. They'd gotten so accustomed to thinking of themselves as the most clever dudes on earth that it never occurred to them that someone might try a little flimflam at their expense. They'd lived so long in fantasy they'd lost their grip on the real world. Who else would believe the dreaded Ebola virus could be cured by Welch's grape juice? He'd been working this con for four months now, and it had worked almost every time. Dress up like a country boy, get off the eastbound bus, and watch the patsies fall at his feet.

Tonight's killing was an absolute record, though. Most con men carried a fair amount of cash to sustain them through emergencies, like making bail, but he had never scored anything like this before. With seven hundred smackers, he could live high and happy for days. He could get some new clothes, maybe get a good meal at the Polo Grill. He might even treat himself to a little North Side entertainment. Jazz. That was his favorite. He was learning to play sax, and he loved nothing better than to hear the pros play.

It was only natural that he would gravitate to jazz. He was kind of a jazz artist already, playing his riffs on the streets of the city. The only difference was, his improvisations were making him rich.

* 4 *

With his last bit of strength he managed to propel the rolled-up rug into the back of his van. It landed with a heavy thud, reminding him of its fragile contents.

"Sorry about that," he gasped as if the corpse might actually hear. "Couldn't be helped."

Bracing himself against the van for support, he turned around . . . and jumped almost a foot into the air.

There was a man standing directly behind him, someone he'd never seen before. He was white, middle-aged, and entirely bald. As soon as they made eye contact, the man plastered a smile on his face so earnest it was almost vomit-inducing.

"Charlie Conrad," the man said, jabbing his hand forward. "Friends call me Chuck."

Seeing no escape, he took Chuck's hand and shook it.

"Just moved into the place next door," Chuck explained. "Been meanin' to come say howdy to the neighbors, but hadn't gotten around to it. Then I saw you out here haulin' this rug and thought, Well, Chuck, maybe this is the time. Maybe you ought to go do the right neighborly thing and give the man a helpin' hand."

So that was it. Of all the damned luck.

Chuck bounced from one foot to the other, filling the awkward emptiness created by the other man's failure to speak. "So . . . what kind of work do you do, anyway?"

He cleared his throat. "I'm in . . . consulting."

"Consulting. Oh, well. I see." Chuck continued his annoying bouncing. "Must be interesting work."

"Yes, it is." He started to turn away.

Chuck stopped him with another question. "What exactly does that mean—consulting?"

He took a deep breath. "It means other people bring me their problems and . . . I try to solve them."

"Oh. I see." Chuck began to fidget with his hands. "Well, that must be—must be damned interesting work."

"Yes, it is."

Chuck pointed toward the interior of the van. "So what've you got in there?"

"It's nothing. Nothing at all."

"Looks like a rug." Chuck pressed forward, inching toward the van.

"Yes, that's what it is."

"You know, my grandmother had a rug like this." Chuck reached forward to touch it.

The man slapped his hand away. "Stop!"

Chuck drew back, startled. "But—"

"It's—it's very dirty."

"Oh."

He reached for the back van door. "If you'll excuse me—"

"You've got a stain on your rug."

He turned slowly around to peer into the van, fearing the worst. His fears were not misplaced. A dark black stain was seeping through the bottom of the rug. Blood.

He glanced back at Chuck. His expression had changed. His smile had disappeared.

Slowly, with no great movement, the man slid his hand inside his jacket and touched the long silver serrated knife tucked inside its sheath.

Chuck cleared his throat. "Is that stain what I think it is?"

The man gripped the hilt of the knife. He could have it out in a second, he calculated. He could have it out and slit this fool's throat before he knew what was happening. "And what do you think it is?"

Chuck shook his head. "Coffee."

The hand on his knife relaxed. "Coffee?"

"Yeah. Coffee stains are the worst. You just can't get them out. I suppose that's why you're hauling it away."

The man tried to smile. "That's it exactly."

"Do you have more to carry? I could help—"

"No, that's all there is. But thank you."

"Oh, not at all. Just bein' a good neighbor. That's what it's all about, right?"

The man watched as Chuck lumbered back to his own domicile. That good neighbor would never know how close he came to being a dead neighbor.

He closed the back of the van, slid into the driver's seat, turned over the ignition, and switched on the tape deck. Dr. John's *Gris-Gris*. It had some moving parts. The good doctor was not bad at all, for a white boy.

He smiled contentedly as he pulled into the street, pounding the steering wheel in time with the pulsating jazz rhythm streaming out of the speakers.

Almost showtime!

* 5 *

Some time ago, Christina had discovered that an access panel in the closet of Ben's bedroom opened up onto the roof. Many a day, and even some nights, they had crawled up there to get away from it all, to find a quiet nook to talk or just relax. And on one occasion, the passageway had saved her life.

Ben was stretched out on one end of a flat narrow section of the roof wedged between two gables. Christina was on the opposite end, sitting in the lotus position, catching the setting sun directly in her face.

"Are you meditating?" Ben asked.

She hesitated a moment, eyes closed, as if deliberating whether she really wanted to answer. "If you must know, I'm communing with my angel."

"Oh, please."

She opened her eyes. "What? What's so unbearable about talking to angels?"

"Honestly, Christina. Do you have to jump on the bandwagon for every New Age fad that comes down the pike?"

"Angels are not a fad." She closed her eyes and turned away. "You can be so intolerant."

"Intolerant? I don't think so. I tolerated your digression into past lives. I made no comment when you plunged into the wonderful world of crystals. I remained altogether silent as you charted your course through holistic medicine and when you read *The Celestine Prophecy* eight times, marking key passages with a yellow highlighter. But *angels*?"

"Angels are not a fad," she repeated. "They've been around forever." She looked down her nose at him, which was quite a trick, since her eyes were still closed. "They're in the Bible, you know."

"Actually there are only four angels mentioned by name in the whole Bible, and one of them is Lucifer. I assume you're not communing with him."

"Angels aren't just guys with wings and harps," Christina informed him. "Angels are all over the place. Some of my best friends are angels."

Ben raised his eyebrows. "Am I an angel?"

"I'd have to say you are at best an angel in training. Still trying to fight your way through cynicism and a sort of neurotic crabbiness so you can earn your wings."

"Shades of *It's a Wonderful Life*."

"But the good news is, you don't have to do it alone. You have a guardian angel, you know. We all do."

"Mine must be on vacation."

"Don't joke. It's true. Your angel is always watching you."

"Like, when I'm picking my nose? Going to the bathroom?"

"Would you be serious for a minute? If you communed with your angel on occasion, you'd be better off." She raised her head, letting the bright rays beam down upon her. "Do you miss him?"

"Miss who?"

"Oh, stop pretending. You know perfectly well who. Joey. You kept him for almost six months. Your life must be a lot different now that he's gone."

"True. I only go to bed once a night now, as opposed to six or seven times. I haven't had to mind-read what a crying baby wants. And I haven't had the supreme thrill of changing dirty diapers."

"Once again, you've skillfully managed to avoid the question. Don't you miss him?"

Ben shrugged. "Now and again." He shook his head. "Julia doesn't deserve a kid like Joey."

"Face facts: parenthood isn't a merit-based appointment. Heard anything about him?"

"You know how things are between Julia and me. She's not likely to phone with an update. Especially after all those nasty remarks she made when she took him away." He paused. "I don't know how these things happen. There was a time, when we were little . . ." He let out a slow sigh. "I remember when Julia and I were the best two friends in the world. When she—" He stopped abruptly. "It seems like only yesterday."

Christina laid her hand gently on his shoulder. "Did I tell you your mother called?"

"What? *Mother?*"

"Would you stop acting like that's so bizarre? Mothers have been known to call their sons on occasion. Especially when their sons have a tendency to forget to call them."

"What did she want?"

"Apparently she read about tonight's anniversary show in *The Daily Oklahoman*." Ben's mother lived in the upscale, elite Nichols Hills section of Oklahoma City, about two hours from Tulsa. "She was thinking about coming down."

"Why?"

"To see you, you blithering idiot. It's not like you ever invited her to come hear you play."

"My mother doesn't know anything about music, much less jazz."

"That's beside the point."

"She'd be miserable."

"I doubt it."

"I hope you didn't encourage her."

"No, but I did give her directions."

"Christina!" Ben rolled over on one side. He wanted to complain, but what was the point? Christina obviously did what she thought was right; nothing he said was going to change her mind.

After several minutes had passed, Christina broke the silence. "I'm sorry the audition didn't go better."

"How did you know?"

"If you'd gotten the gig, you would've mentioned it already."

Christina had a habit of startling him with her understanding of matters she had no business understanding. Her instincts were uncanny. It was almost as if she were a mind reader. Which, given all the other weird stuff she was into, was not altogether impossible.

"You must be disappointed."

He shrugged. "Not really. I never expected to get it. I'm all right playing with other musicians—Mike when we were in college, the guys in the jazz band these past months. But I'll never cut it as a soloist."

"Don't sell yourself short. You're the best pianist I've ever heard.'"

Ben laughed. "Remind me to take you to a Van Cliburn concert."

"But I don't think jazz is your forte."

"Yeah, well, people expect folk music to come from a guitar, not a piano. And there aren't a lot of folk music clubs in town."

"Maybe you should start one."

He laughed again. "You're dreaming."

"True. Wish I could get you to do the same."

"You can't start a club playing music people don't want to hear."

"Ben, do you know what your problem is?"

"I suspect I'm about to."

"You always try to please other people. Which is commendable, but there are limits. You don't start playing a kind of music just because that's what other people want to hear. At some point in your life, you have to be who you really are."

"You know, this is the second time today I've heard this speech, and frankly, I'm tired of it."

"Then listen for a change!" Her words poured out with unexpected force. "Do you think I'd be telling you this if it wasn't true?"

Ben turned away. "I don't need other people to tell me who I am."

"Evidently you do!" She threw up her hands. "And this is all a symptom of this ridiculous business of pretending you don't want to be a lawyer anymore."

"I don't."

Christina didn't respond.

"I said, I don't."

She remained silent, impassive.

"I *don't!*"

She turned her head slightly. "Methinks he doth protest too much."

Ben rolled his eyes and edged toward the access panel.

"You know, Ben, just because your last case turned out badly—"

"I do not want to discuss this!"

Christina drummed her fingers. "I stopped by to see Jones and Loving today."

"Please don't start with that again, all right?"

"They need you."

"They do not. Jones is a top-notch legal secretary and office manager, and Loving is a relentless investigator with great business connections. They don't need me for anything."

"They feel abandoned since you closed your law practice."

"I didn't close my practice. It was blown to smithereens."

She made a tsking sound. "Excuses, excuses. Think of all that time you spent at OU getting your degree."

"So what? Is it written somewhere that I have to be a lawyer forever just because I spent three years at the best law school in the state?"

"Tulsa has a perfectly good law school," Christina interjected.

Ben stopped. It was true, of course, but since when did she become the defender of TU's law school? "The point is, I don't have to be a lawyer. I'm doing just fine."

"Right, living off the proceeds of your big case. It won't last forever, you know."

"I make an income as a musician, too."

"Not enough to pay the rent, but money isn't the issue. I know you'll eventually learn to be who you really are." She paused, staring up at the sky. "I'm confident you will. In time. I just get tired of waiting. So do Jones and Loving. They need you."

"Oh, would you stop with the guilt trip already? They do not need me. I'm sure they're staying perfectly busy on their own . . ."

Jones leaned back, aimed carefully, and propelled another wad of paper toward the trash can. It came in high, bounced off one office wall, ricocheted off the other, and dropped just outside the rim.

"Blast!" Jones said, swinging around in his black swivel desk chair. "I had eleven baskets in a row and I blew it!"

"That's so excitin'," Loving said, looking up wearily from his magazine. "I'll alert the media."

"Yeah, well, at least I'm not wasting my time reading some idiotic magazine for the third time through. What is that, anyway?" Jones walked over to Loving's desk and snatched the magazine out of his hands. "*UFO Newswatch*? Give me a break. How can you read this junk?"

"It ain't junk," Loving said, snatching it back. "It's serious journalism."

"This is one step removed from the *National Enquirer*," Jones replied. He scanned the cover of the magazine. " 'What Really Happened at Roswell? What—or Who— Is Hidden in Hangar 18? Elvis and JFK Alive in Andromeda?' Sheesh."

Loving jumped to his feet. "You shouldn't make fun of things you don't understand."

Loving was a huge man, muscled from head to toe, and he outweighed Jones by about two hundred pounds. Jones, however, knew him well and wasn't intimidated in the least. "Don't you think if aliens had really landed it might have made the front page of *The New York Times*? Or at least the *Tulsa World*?"

Loving slapped the cover of his magazine. "These guys print the news the surface media is afraid to cover."

"Afraid?"

"Everyone knows there's been a cover-up. Vested interests are makin' sure the truth don't come out. People in the know know aliens have been abductin' earthlings for decades."

"Is that right?" Jones said, heading back toward his desk. "I guess that's what happened to all our clients."

Jones scanned his calendar, mulling unhappily on all the empty untouched squares on the Day-Timer. When Loving first opened this office in Warren Place, using his share of the loot Ben made off his last case, Loving had a stream of clients who needed his private investigator services. After about two months, though, the work had dried up. With some reservations, Loving had asked Jones to share the office space (and the rent), and Jones had agreed. Unfortunately they'd both been virtually idle ever since. Although they had enough in savings to hold out for a few more months, they both knew they couldn't last forever without more business.

"Have you heard anythin' from the Skipper?" Loving asked, his face buried in the magazine.

"No. Christina keeps saying he'll come back."

Loving grunted. "Wish he'd hurry."

"Yeah, well, you know how he is." Jones put a goofy expression on his face and raised his voice an octave. " 'Yes, I could practice law, but should I? Is it the ethically appropriate thing to do? Is it the best use of my journey on Spaceship Earth?' "

Loving dropped his magazine and guffawed. Jones was a talented mimic. He could do dead-on impersonations of other people's voices, even after having heard them for only a short time. And of course he had heard Ben Kincaid's voice a lot.

"Well, this is incredibly boring," Jones said, returning to his own voice. "I'm going online."

Loving shook his head. "You're gonna go broke on that Internet crap."

"Brilliant minds crave stimulation," Jones replied, as he triggered his modem to connect. "Sherlock Holmes had cocaine. I have the Internet."

There was a short succession of beeps, then a growling mechanical hiss that told him he had connected with his Internet carrier. He clicked on his desktop icon for Netscape and started browsing the Web, but it didn't hold his attention for long.

There had to be something more stimulating.

He glanced over his shoulder. Loving was back in his magazine; he didn't appear to be paying any attention.

Quietly Jones closed his web browser and clicked the icon to open his IRC client software. He chose the University of Oklahoma's undernet site and logged on.

A moment later, a blue-bordered window told him he was connected. A click after that, the program began scanning and automatically listing the names of all the chat rooms.

Once again, Jones marveled at the vast array of chat rooms—over three thousand, according to the toolbar at the top of the screen. And for some perverse reason, the program always loaded the ones whose names began with exclamation points first. Exclamation points were a tip-off that this was a chat room your mother wouldn't want you to be visiting, like *!nastytalk* or *!!!perversex* or *!!!!!!!!!!barnyardfun*.

Well, it was a little early for that sort of thing. Jones drummed his fingers and waited patiently while the rest of the channels loaded.

He knew many of the rooms would be empty this early (before midnight), but there were some exceptions. There were a few chat rooms in which participants played quiz games, but he wasn't in the mood to display his superior intellect. There were always stacks of people in the rooms to discuss sci-fi shows like *Star Trek* or *Babylon 5*. But he needed something more challenging to liven up his dull existence.

Like music. After all, the Boss (sadly enough, he still thought of Ben that way) wasn't the only music lover around. The Net was full of them. He clicked on the Music subheading, then MusicLovers. A long list of subtopics filled the scroll bar on the right side of the screen. Scanning the channels, he saw rooms devoted to the life and works of Patti Smith, four for Elvis, a couple for John Lennon.

His computer screen blipped and the picture momentarily disappeared. This happened sometimes; the Internet was far from infallible. One random surge of electricity, and you could be anywhere.

He scrolled down the channel listings, trying to figure out where he was. Something caught his eye—a room labeled THE WILD SIDE. Good, he must still be in the music subsection; that was obviously a reference to the works of Lou Reed. "Walk on the Wild Side" had always been his favorite Reed tune.

Jones clicked the Join button, which allowed him to enter the room using his online moniker Fingers. A second later, he was in. He was pleased to see there were more than a half-dozen people "chatting." Their "conversation" began to appear on the text portion of his screen:

COBBLEPOT>Welcome, Fingers.

Jones smiled and sent his fingers into action.

FINGERS>Welcome back at you. And a bluesy good evening to one and all.

He smiled. A clever inside Lou Reed reference these aficionados would be sure to pick up on.

MADMAX>Glad you could be with us.

PAUL89>Ditto.

PILOTBOB>I'm Bob. Fly me!

Well, this seemed like a friendly bunch. Jones felt better already.

FINGERS>So, what are you folks talking about?

PAUL89>Well, now that you've arrived—you.

This was typical chat-room behavior. Even in cyberspace, folks wanted to get to know you a bit before they included you in the conversation.

FINGERS>How flattering. What would you like to know?

PILOTBOB>Well, for starters, I'd like to know if your fingers are girl fingers or boy fingers.

Jones stopped typing. Now that was a bit unusual.

FINGERS>And may I ask why you want to know?

PILOTBOB>(snicker) Well, if they're girl fingers, I might invite you to let your fingers do the walking over to my cockpit.

Jones pushed himself away from the computer. *Yuck!* Who was this pervert? And what was he doing in a perfectly respectable music chat room?

PILOTBOB>Still no answer? C'mon, baby. I'll let you play with my stick shift.

FINGERS>(indignantly) For your information, they're boy fingers. So back off.

COBBLEPOT>LOL. Way to put that horny devil in his place, Fingers.

MADMAX>Cut the guy some slack. We've been in here for half an hour waiting for a woman to show up. But so far, it's just us guys.

Jones frowned at the screen. He was beginning to get the impression he had made an error regarding the subject matter of the Wild Side chat room.

PILOTBOB>Are you sure you're a boy, Fingers?

FINGERS>Absolutely positive. Have been all my life. Wanna see some ID?

COBBLEPOT>Bob is just being thorough. Sometimes when women log on, they pretend to be men. At least until they get the feel of the crowd.

And Jones could see why, too.

PILOTBOB>Sorry, Fingers, but for some reason, you make me suspicious. People do log on as the opposite sex. I've seen it many times.

FINGERS>Well, the longer one goes, the less one knows.

PILOTBOB>No offense intended, Fingers. What brings you to our room tonight?

FINGERS>I was hoping to find a discussion of music.

PILOTBOB>Music! (Explosive noises) Are you trying to show your sensitive side? Despite your protestations to the contrary, I think you are a she-male. Wanna go to a private room and let me look up your dress?

Jones drummed his fingers on the keyboard. He'd had just about enough.

FINGERS>Well, it's been fun, all. But I'm out of here. So
    we'll go no more a-rovin' . . .

PAUL89>Wait! Don't go!

Jones stopped just before his mouse clicked on the Exit
button.

PAUL89>Please don't go. I'd like to talk with you some
    more. I mean . . . if you don't mind.

FINGERS>Sorry, Paul, but this room is not what I ex-
    pected. I thought we'd be discussing music.

PAUL89>Really? So did I! Please stay!

FINGERS>Sorry, no. I'm outta here.

PAUL89>Please don't go.

Jones paused. And a few seconds later, he read:

PAUL89>I have a confession to make. I'm a lurker.
    (Breathless pause) Truth is—I'm actually a woman.

PILOTBOB>Whoa-ho-ho! The femme unmasked!

COBBLEPOT>Paul! Who'da thought it!

PAUL89>Actually . . . my name is Paula.

Jones let go of the mouse. He couldn't resist exploring
this turn of events. His curiosity was definitely piqued.

FINGERS>Why were you pretending to be a Paul?

PAUL89>Need you ask? You saw how these lugs came on
    to you.

FINGERS>Then why log on at all?

PAUL89>I don't know. I just wanted . . . someone to talk to.

Jones stared at the words at the bottom of the screen. He could have written them himself.

FINGERS>I can understand that.

PAUL89>Please don't leave me to these heathens.

PILOTBOB>Who are you calling a heathen?

FINGERS>I should probably go back to work.

PAUL89>Later then. I'd really appreciate it. Maybe I'm crazy, but—you seem . . . different somehow.

Jones's lips parted. Had someone finally recognized and appreciated his innate superiority?

PAUL89>I just wanted someone I could talk to. About music, I mean.

PILOTBOB>Hey, baby, I've got lots of music for you. I'll play you like a violin. You'll hear the angels singing.

PAUL89>(shivering with disgust) Fingers, will you join me tonight in a private room? So we can talk? Alone.

Jones stared at the computer screen. He knew he had to decide fast. And he knew agreeing to join her would probably be a mistake. And he knew if Loving found out about it, he'd give him no end of grief. But she just wanted someone to talk to . . .

FINGERS>All right. Channel 365. Tonight at midnight. I'll restrict admission to everyone but you.

PAUL89>I'll be there! :)

"What is this, some kind of on-line romance novel?"
Jones almost jumped out of his seat. Loving was standing right behind him, hovering over his shoulder. And reading the computer screen.

"Uh . . . right. Yes. Exactly." Jones reached forward and switched off the power to the monitor, darkening the screen. "Man, that World Wide Web is really not all it's cracked up to be."

"Yeah. But I notice you're glued to it all day long."

"Well, I had to do something. At least until the aliens return our clients."

"Ha, ha." Loving smirked, then walked back to his desk.

That had been close, Jones thought. He would have to be more careful in the future.

He picked up his pen and made a note on his calendar. At last, his Day-Timer for the month of April was not completely bare. At the bottom of the column for the day, he penciled in:

1200AM—CHAT, CH. 365. PAUL89EXCL.

He thought about it for a moment, then added:

BE THERE.

* 6 *

Ben stood on his tiptoes and stretched up to adjust the center stage light. He had to stand on the piano bench to reach it. The overhead light was about the same width as the baby grand Ben played. It was flat and square and, thanks to some rusty wheels that did not easily roll down the guide track, a real pain in the butt to move. Unfortunately, it was the only overhead on center stage, and it always seemed to be shining down somewhere behind and to the left of the piano, which was not a heck of a lot of help to Ben when he needed to read his set notes.

He placed both hands on the closest edge and tried to yank the light toward him.

"Ben, stop that!"

It was Earl, and he was scowling. He'd been pacing maniacally, and it was still more than an hour before the club opened and the anniversary show began. "Ain't I told you not to mess with that!"

"Ain't I told you to buy another light?" Ben shot back.

"Can't afford another light. 'Less you want me to take it outta that chump change I'm payin' you."

"How can I possibly play when I can't even see what my fingers are doing?"

"You don't watch your fingers play, boy. You jus' let it happen. You let the music take over."

"Well then, why don't we turn out *all* the lights, and we can *all* just let the music take over?"

Earl turned about-face without replying.

Ben felt a hand on his shoulder. It was Denny Bachalo—

Dr. Denton on the marquee. He played drums in the combo. "Hey, Ben baby. Chill already."

"Easy for you to say. The drum set is always lit."

"Cut the bossman some slack, okay?" Denny had long jet-black hair. He always seemed to be wearing the same pair of torn blue jeans and the same NO FEAR T-shirt. "Can't you see he's seriously stressed?"

Ben glanced back over his shoulder. Earl had been on edge, pacing and mumbling and generally acting as though the world were coming to an end at any moment. "I don't get it. He's had the club for a year and he's never acted like this before."

"Yeah, but tonight's gonna be something else again. Ain't it, Scat?"

The tall, lean older man idly fingering his saxophone nodded. His actual name was Ernie Morris, but on the club circuit, he was the Scatman. Scatman Morris could run his fingers up and down the sax stick so quickly it was like a scat singer free-falling through the scales.

"Major to-do tonight," Scat answered, never removing his eyes from the sax. "All the cards on the table. Make-or-break time for this club. Earl's been in honeymoon land till now. But tonight they're gonna expect him to show what he can do."

"Who's this *they*?" Ben asked. "You think someone will cover the show?"

Scat nodded. "Major press tonight. The *World. The Oklahoman.* Word is John Wooley's going to be out. Maybe James Watts. Maybe even some of the TV babes. Karen Keith. LeAnne Taylor."

Ben's head tilted to one side. "Karen Larsen?"

Scat shook his head. "Didn't hear the name. Why?"

He suddenly looked embarrassed. "Oh, no reason."

Denny let out a snort. "That's the third time I've heard you mention her name tonight. Have you got a thing for this Larsen woman?"

Ben turned away, his face flushing. "Don't be ridiculous."

Dr. Denton and the Scatman exchanged a long look, followed by a hearty chuckle.

"Where's Gordo?" Ben asked, changing the subject as nonchalantly as possible. "If he's late for rehearsal again—"

"Speak of the devil!" The voice boomed out from the back of the club. A moment later, they saw the youngest member of the combo, their lead guitar and sometime bass player, emerging from backstage. "Did ya miss me, Benji?"

He did not smile. "My name is Ben. Benji is a trained dog who appears in sappy children's films. And you're late."

"Sorry, pal. Had a little trouble at home." Gordo Grant was a punk from the deepest, poorest part of the North Side who had somehow managed to pull himself up and out, send himself through two years at TCC, and teach himself to play guitar licks like nobody's business. "Gimme a second and I'll be ready."

"Fine," Ben said. "Maybe I can use the time to shed a little light on the subject. You guys wanna help me move this stage light over?"

"Not particularly," Denny said. "Why?"

"Well, you know what they say. Many hands make lights work." After checking to make sure Uncle Earl wasn't watching, he stood up on the piano bench and began grappling with the huge overhead, trying to bring it closer to the piano.

Eventually Gordo was unpacked and Ben had a sliver of light, so they began to play. The first number in their set was their own version of "Sweet Georgia Brown," mostly arranged by Scat. What began slow and almost balladic gradually picked up steam until, by the final stanzas, it was a full-blown jazz spectacular. They led with it for a reason; it was their best number.

Usually. Tonight, however, it reeked. Denny was dragging the tempo, Ben was botching the syncopation, and even Scat, who was normally flawless, missed a few notes. The song limped to its concluding riff.

"Well," Gordo said, smiling amiably, "that stank on toast."

"What's wrong with us tonight?" Denny called down from the drums. "My grandma plays better than that."

"It's nerves," Scat pronounced, pushing his sunglasses up. "I've seen this before. Uncle Earl's jitters are infectious. S'like some kinda virus."

"Now wait just one cotton-pickin' moment." Ben looked down and saw Earl, his considerable girth winding its way through the tables on the club floor. "Don't be pushin' your load off on me. I didn't have nothin' to do with that pathetic noise I just heard."

"But you're the bossman," Scat answered.

"When you're good, I'm the bossman," Earl said. "When you suck gas, you're on your own."

Ben grinned. "Scat thinks you've infected us with your anxiety about the anniversary show tonight. The reviewers and TV people and all."

"Aw, hell." Earl made a little hip-hop and parked his rear on the edge of the stage. "I don't give two good goddamns about no reviewers or TV people."

"Then—"

"I got my own reasons." He paused, obviously debating whether they needed to know any more. "I'm expectin' a visitor."

"What's this?" Denny stepped out from behind his drums, pushing his long hair behind his shoulders. "Would this visitor by any chance be . . . a *woo*-man?"

A chorus of oohs and hubba-hubbas drifted across the stage.

"Calm down, you horny devils." Earl acted casual, but Ben suspected he was anything but. "It ain't nothin' like that. This here's a special woman. From the old days."

"The old days?" Gordo asked.

"That's right." Earl smiled. "The good ol' days. Back when the jazz scene in Tulsa was really happenin'. Back when Ol' Uncle Earl still worked his sax. Back when I was tourin' the wide-open chitlin' circuit, playin' juke joints and chicken shacks, roadhouses east to the Carolinas, along the Gulf Coast from Tampa to Galveston, then up to Monroe, Jackson, Shreveport, Texarkana, Dallas, OKC, Tulsa, and of course, that cruelest of all mistresses, New Orleans."

This was news to Ben. "How long ago was this?"

Earl shrugged. "Oh, 'bout a million and five years. Back when I was makin' magic with the one and only Professor Hoodoo."

Professor Hoodoo? Ben had heard the name bandied about before, but he didn't know anything about him. "Was he a jazz musician?" Ben ventured.

"Was he a jazz musician?" Earl shot back. "The boy wants to know if Professor Hoodoo was a jazz musician. You tell him, Scat."

Scat cleared his throat. "He was *the* jazz musician. He was the man what put us all to shame. Until the day he laid down his sugar stick for the last time, he was the king."

" 'Fraid I don't know much about this funksterator myself," Gordo said. "What's his story?"

Earl closed his eyes. "Professor Hoodoo was a giant. He towered over the rest of us, leavin' us in the wake of his mighty strides. When he played, everybody listened—like they had no choice. His music commanded attention. He could take a two-bit tune by some Tin Pan Alley hack and make it burn like lightnin'! He could make it somethin' it never was, somethin' better than anybody'd ever thought it could be, because the music came from inside him. He was one of the special ones, one of the men who's born with it, one of the chosen few who's got music burnin' in their brains and no holes in their souls." He paused, wiping his brow. "When Professor Hoodoo played, you heard the truth, and you heard it from the man who knew, 'cause he'd been there. He'd lived it."

Earl leaned against the stage, his eyes still closed. " 'Course that was twenty-plus years ago. It's all jus' a memory now."

"What happened to him?" Ben asked.

Earl drew in his breath, then released it all at once, in a heavy sigh. "The world happened to him, son. Like it always does to genius. Other people's petty needs and ambitions came weighin' down on his shoulders. Some folks didn't care for a black man doin' so well. Some wanted to take him out of the clubs and move him up—give him hotel gigs and TV spots. Make him the white man's bebopper." Earl paused meaningfully. "Sometimes he got his heart broke. 'Course, that happens to everyone. But when the Professor's heart broke, it was like he felt the pain of every broken romance in the world, like he could feel all our pain. Small wonder he needed salvation. Small wonder he began to develop . . . bad habits."

"You mean—"

"By the time I played with him, he was a man carryin' many burdens. His color. His habit. And his genius. All of them burdens, all of them things this old world treats none too kindly. Any fool could see he couldn't carry that load forever. Eventually, somethin' had to break. But through it all, the Professor played like an angel, like the angels wish they could play. Small wonder they called him home. I expect that celestial choir never heard licks like the ones Professor Hoodoo brought with him."

"Then he's—"

"Yeah." Earl slowly opened his eyes. "He's gone. And the sad part is, he never made a recording. We've got no record of what that man could do. Except the record a few of us keep locked up in our memories. And in our souls. Right, Scat?"

Scat nodded gravely. "That's right, Earl."

Earl pushed off the edge of the stage. "But you boys ain't so sorry yourself. You just ain't in the groove yet. You've let too many other things distract you from the truth. Remember that's all you got to do when you're up there playin'. Just make your music, and make it the truth."

His head dropped, and Ben could swear he saw traces of moisture glimmering in the corners of Earl's eyes. "So you play that number again, you hear? From the top. But this time, you let the Professor's spirit guide you. You play it for him. 'Cause when you play for Professor Hoodoo—you got no choice. You got to play the truth."

The truth was, he was too old for this kind of work.

Or felt too old, anyway. He dropped his bundle onto the floor, just outside the club. He was dripping with sweat; his hands were so wet he could hardly hold on to the rug.

Man alive! Next time he thought up some elaborate fonky-monkey business, he'd think again. Simple was good, he reminded himself. Like in jazz and geometry—the straight line is best.

He peered through the window of the double doors in the front of the club. It was mostly empty. A couple of the band members were on the stage, but he could tell they were finishing up. Soon the coast would be clear.

Since he was alone, he took the opportunity to roll down the rug a bit and take one last look at his once-glorious bundle.

There was something wrong with her face; it only took him a moment to recall what it was. Of course—he'd forgotten her smile. He had meant to address this earlier; the smile was very important. But with all the trouble he'd had moving her, he'd almost forgotten.

After checking to make sure no one was watching, he pulled his long serrated knife out of its sheath. She was long dead, so there would be no bleeding; that was a relief, anyway.

He took a deep breath. The first incision was the hardest. Best to get it over with.

As he laid his knife against her icy flesh, he found himself involuntarily squinching his eyes shut. What do you know? he thought to himself. After all he had done, he still had some sensitivity. He could still be squeamish. Especially when it came to her. *Especially* when it came to her.

But enough of this foolishness. He had work to do.

He closed his eyes and began to carve.

* 7 *

"No, no, no!" Uncle Earl leaned across the piano, his fists clenched. "Slow down already. That ain't no damn typewriter you're playin'!"

Ben pursed his lips. Earl had been trying to help him whip this new number into shape so they could use it tonight as an encore piece, if required. It wasn't coming easily. "But this is supposed to be lively, right? We're still playing jazz, aren't we?"

"We're playing the blues, son. There's a difference."

"Yes, I know, but—"

"Only a fool plays the blues like Machine Gun Kelly. This ain't no race, son. You're makin' music. You got to let your instrument sing. You got to caress it slow and easy, like a woo-man."

Ben flushed. "Let's not get too passionate here."

"And why not? What do you think the blues are, Ben? What do you think music is? It's the language of love, son. The one and only international language of love." He grabbed Ben by the shoulders. "Your problem is, you need to loosen up. Don't be so pent-up, so reserved. When you play the blues, you got to let yourself go."

"I'm not very good at letting myself go."

"No foolin'." Earl grinned, then slapped him hard on the back. "You keep workin' on it. I got stuff to take care of before the show starts." He sauntered off toward the bar, leaving Ben at the piano.

Ben ran through the number ("Since I Don't Have You") a few more times, but no matter how hard he tried to

51

remember what he had been told, no matter how hard he tried to caress it slow and easy like a woo-man, he knew he wasn't getting it. Oh, he'd get through it, if he had to, just as he got through their regular set every night. But in his heart, he knew he wasn't *feeling* it, not deep down in the core of his soul. He was just playing what he had learned, imitating, doing what he'd been told. He might be competent, but he would never be great.

"Ten more minutes, then I need you off the stage."

Ben looked up. It was Diane Weiskopf, their stage manager. She was dressed in black slacks and a black tank top. A black leather jacket hung off one shoulder. Her hair was blonde, with dark streaks, but it had all been gelled into pointed spikes that encircled her head like a halo.

"I need to get the stage ready as soon as possible. Earl wants everything just right tonight. Okay, Benji?"

Ben bit down on his lower lip. "My name is Ben. Benji is a trained dog who—"

"Yeah, I know. But you're both cute." She laughed, stroking her spikes. "So get off the stage, okay?"

Ben wouldn't have dreamed of arguing. She was the toughest person at the club, probably the toughest person he knew. When he'd first met her, he figured her for the bouncer. "Lemme see if I can get this one song down, then I'll be out of here."

"Well . . ."

"Just one more song."

"This isn't one of those endless Harry Chapin numbers, is it?"

Ben grimaced. Great to see that his abortive audition effort was already becoming legend. "No, it isn't."

"Well, all right then. But ten minutes, tops."

Ben gave it a few more run-throughs, then decided to call it quits. Even if he made a mistake, he knew Scat or Gordo would just hike up the volume and cover it. It wouldn't really matter. They were used to covering for him.

He jumped off the stage and walked toward the front

door. He wanted to get some fresh air before the crowd started rolling in. It would do him some good, he figured. Or at least he hoped.

Just before he got to the front of the club, he saw a stranger coming in. It was hard to see clearly; the lights inside were dim and the sunlight outside cast the man in silhouette. Ben couldn't make out his face, but he could see that he had bushy Afro-style hair and an equally bushy beard. He was wearing dark glasses.

"Where you want the rug?" the man barked, still several paces away from Ben.

There was something odd about the man's voice, but Ben couldn't quite place it. "The rug?"

"Got orders to deliver a rug. Wants it backstage, I hear."

"Backstage?" Ben had heard nothing about a new rug, but that didn't mean much. He knew Earl had been fretting himself sick about this anniversary show. Maybe he'd decided they needed a rug. Probably thought it might muffle some of the backstage noise.

"Go to it, then," Ben said. He dipped his head, and the workman sailed right past him.

Ben passed through the double doors and stepped out into the bright sunlight. He didn't see any of the other band members hanging around; they must have gone somewhere—maybe down to Nelson's for a quick chicken-fried steak.

Ben kicked at the gravel in the driveway. He wished he'd been invited along, wherever they went. But this was not the first time they had neglected to include him in their group. Oh, they were always cordial. Even friendly. But he never had the feeling he was one of the gang. Try as hard as he might, he knew that in their minds they were true jazz musicians, and he was some white kid who played the piano pretty well.

After a few minutes in the sun, Ben saw Earl up the street coming around the corner. He was moving at a slow trot, although after he spotted Ben he eased into a walk. Ben suspected he was trying to get some exercise and work off some anxiety at the same time. He talked a lot about trying to lose all his extra weight, although Ben had seen few signs of progress.

"Out for a jog?" Ben asked as Earl approached.

"Don't be stupid," Earl said, suddenly embarrassed. "I was just . . . lookin' around. I thought she mighta gotten lost or somethin'." He changed the subject quickly. "What you doin' out here? Shouldn't you be huddled over the piano, trying to set some new land speed record?"

"I decided to take a break. And to make room for the rug man."

"The rug man. What you talkin' about?"

A line formed across Ben's forehead. "The workman in the 'fro. Came to deliver a rug backstage."

"I never asked for no rug backstage."

"You didn't?"

"No." Earl glanced at his watch. "Damn. And the show starts in barely half an hour. I don't have time for this." He rushed past Ben and headed into the club.

Ben followed close behind. There was hardly any reason to panic. What was the worst that could happen—they could get stuck with a rug they didn't want? Still, something about the whole situation gave him a creepy feeling. Maybe it was just nerves, or stage fright, but he'd had this feeling before and it never boded well.

Tyrone Jackson strolled into Uncle Earl's Jazz Emporium feeling rich as Midas. He had changed out of those tacky overalls and put on a multicolored African jacket with a snazzy collarless shirt. He was ready to kick back and have a good time. What with all the loot he'd made at the bus station today, he could treat himself to a drink, maybe even find some young lovely and treat her as well.

Now that was something he could get into. A couple of tall cool ones, some hot jazz licks, and a beautiful babe-a-rino. That would be excellent indeed.

He saw the door guard, just now coming on duty. He was new, someone Tyrone had never seen before.

"Ten bucks a head," the man said.

"Sure thing," Tyrone replied, reaching for his wad. He started to withdraw the bill, then stopped. "Unless . . ." He glanced up at the man. "Naw. You're probably not the type."

The man frowned. "The type for what?"

"Oh, never mind." Tyrone held out the ten-spot. "You'd never go for it."

The man leaned forward, an angry expression on his face. "Why don't you let me be the judge of that?"

Tyrone held up his hands. "All right, chill. It just so happens I have some inside information on the fifth race at Remington tomorrow."

"Get out of here."

"Like I said, you're not the type." Again, Tyrone held out the bill.

"Not the type for *what*?"

"Not the type to take a chance to get ahead. No, you're the play-it-safe type. Don't take risks. That's why you're working a crummy job at a nightclub and probably always will be."

"Now listen here—"

"But what would you say if I offered you a chance to increase your investment by ten times—overnight?"

"I'd say you're full of it."

"Of course you would. Because you haven't got the imagination. That's the problem with the world today. The ones with the guts—like me—ain't got the money. The ones with the money—like you—ain't got no guts."

"What's your point?"

"It's this simple." He began talking at a rapid pace. "Momo gots a grudge against Jojo and they've both got horses in the fifth but Momo has some money riding background with the boys so he has to win but Jojo's gonna take it as a point of personal honor if he does and figures if he beats Momo he looks better with his boys and strengthens his territory maybe even expands it but Momo is determined not to let that happen so he's hired a fixer. Follow me so far?"

"Huh?"

"Momo hires a fixer but Jojo hears about it and hires his own fixer and Jojo's fixer takes out Momo's fixer and Momo don't know it so he thinks he's gonna win the race and all the easy money is on him but it gonna be Jojo's horse I'm telling you it's gonna be Jojo's and there's big money to be made at ten-to-one odds. Ten to one! And it's a sure thing."

"A sure thing, huh?"

"Absolutely. You lay down the money. I lay down the bet. And we split the profit."

"Split it? But—"

"Hey, I've got the know-how, you've got the bucks. It's a partnership."

Grumbling, the man pulled out his wallet. "I'll put down a hundred."

"Great. Just give me ninety—you can take my door admission out of the rest."

"Well—"

"Excellent." He snatched the money out of the man's hands. "The race runs about noon. I'll get in touch with you right after. Like I said, it's a sure thing. Unless, of course, Momo finds out. But I don't think that'll happen. Really. Probably."

"Hey, T-Dog!"

Tyrone whirled around. Damn! It was one of the musicians, one that recognized him and knew his street name. That was the problem with plying your craft in a place where too many people knew who you were.

"All said and done now," Tyrone said, shoving the doorman's money into his pocket. "Be seeing you."

"But . . ."

Too late. Tyrone skittered inside, ninety bucks the richer after paying his gate admission. He strolled into the heart of the club and angled for a chair at one of the tables in front of the stage, trying to avoid the musician on the other side who had recognized him. Just as he was about to sit, he saw a large man coming out the backstage door. And he did not look happy.

Tyrone didn't have to look twice to recognize that face. He remembered all his marks, especially the recent ones, and that man walking into the club was the same bozo Tyrone had scammed not two weeks ago. He'd used a wire scam, quick and painless, and made about two hundred smackers. Small change, but he still figured the man wasn't going to embrace him with open arms.

The world was getting entirely too small.

Tyrone did an about-face and moved toward the bar. He could see the man's reflection in the glass behind the bar; he knew he was heading toward the front doors. Tyrone steered himself to the opposite side.

He saw a sign pointing the way to the men's room. Perfect. He needed to take a leak anyway. He walked briskly down the corridor, then dived into the men's room.

He moved quietly toward the stalls in the back. He slipped into the nearest one and quickly took care of business. Just as he left the stall, he spotted something glistening on the grungy tile floor. Most men probably wouldn't have noticed, but Tyrone had a sixth sense. He could smell filthy lucre whenever he came near it.

He scooped the object up off the floor. He could have a ring to the pawnshop in—wait a minute. It wasn't a ring; it was long and flat. There was engraving on one side; it looked like some sort of stylized *B*.

He shrugged. Well, it was still gold—or gold-looking, anyway. Beggars can't be choosers. He slid it into his coat pocket and made a mental note to give it some further scrutiny at a later date.

As he turned, he noticed a man standing at the sink. The man raised his hands toward his big Afro . . . and removed it.

He was wearing a wig! What in the—

Tyrone looked away, suppressing a smile. A drag queen,

no doubt. He knew they hung out in some of the jazz clubs—worked in some of them, for that matter.

He grinned. Just another night in Babylon.

He started across the bathroom, then stopped. Now wait a minute. This supposed drag queen had a beard—a fake one, anyway. That would definitely make for an exotic act. As Tyrone watched, the man began peeling the facial hair off, a tiny bit at a time.

Whatever was going on here, it was more than just a drag queen getting in or out of costume. This was something strange and, in all likelihood, illegal. And he'd be a lot better off if he didn't get dragged into it. He tiptoed quietly across the bathroom . . .

But not quietly enough. The man whirled around and glared at him. Those eyes, Tyrone thought, were the darkest eyes he had ever seen. And the meanest.

Tyrone spent enough time around tough customers to know what the man was thinking. He was thinking he didn't want any witnesses to his disrobing routine. And now that he realized he had one, he would have to do something about it.

The man started across the bathroom, eyes lowered, his face still obscured by the bushy false beard. His hand was reaching for something shiny, something inside his shirt.

Good God—was that a *knife*?

Tyrone didn't know what to do. There was nowhere he could go, no way he could maneuver. He was trapped. Dead meat.

The man moved closer to him. Tyrone was pressed against the far wall with no escape route . . .

They both heard it at the same time—a loud voice from somewhere outside the bathroom. "I dunno. You try in there, I'll try over here."

The man shoved his knife back in its sheath. "Later," he whispered. Then he moved quickly toward the door. He shoved against the swinging door hard, driving it into someone on the other side who tumbled to the floor. The man with the knife lit out.

Tyrone checked himself in the mirror. His face was drawn; the panic was still visible in his eyes. He inhaled deeply, trying to calm himself, then left the men's room. He didn't know exactly what had happened in there, but he had the distinct feeling he had just narrowly escaped a particularly nasty and unpleasant end.

As he stepped into the club, he saw that a crowd was beginning to gather. The show would start soon. Well, thank God for that. He was more than ready for a little entertainment now. And more than ready for a drink. A serious drink.

He saw a pretty slip of a thing sitting at the bar and scooted onto the stool beside her. "Hey there," he said, putting on his best smile. He pulled two shot glasses and a hard-boiled egg out of his jacket pocket. "Five bucks says I can move this egg from one glass to the other—without touching it."

Within seconds, he was lost in the script for yet another con, his mind miles away from the fact that only seconds before, he had come two steps shy of being ripped to shreds by a thin, shiny serrated blade.

* 8 *

Ben and Earl scoured the backstage area, but they were unable to find any trace of the man with the rug. Earl was beginning to think Ben had hallucinated him. Ben was beginning to wonder himself.

At any rate, there was no more time for searching for unauthorized personnel. The crowd was beginning to rumble. It was five minutes past eight; they needed to get the show on the road.

Scat and Denny and Gordo and Ben took their places behind the curtain. Diane stood just offstage and gave them the one-minute sign. The musicians began tuning and warming up—except Scat. He never seemed to do anything in preparation. He just picked up his sax and slid on his glasses, and he was ready to make it happen.

"Psst, Ben! Take a look." Gordo was peering through a gap in the curtain. "Not bad, huh?"

Not bad at all. The floor was packed; they had even set up tables in the bar to accommodate more patrons. He hadn't seen such a full house in the entire six months he'd been playing here.

"Look up front. See the guy with all the hair? Isn't that Wooley?"

Ben scanned the front row. Sure enough, there he was. John Wooley, jazz critic for the *World*. Ben recognized him from his photo in the paper.

"He's the one we want to please," Gordo whispered, moving away from the curtain.

"We want to please them all," Ben corrected.

60

"Well, yeah, right." Gordo hoisted his guitar and strummed a chord. "But you know what I mean."

Ben nodded. He did. "For that matter, I saw notepads in several laps. I bet Wooley isn't the only critic in the crowd."

"There's more?" Ben immediately realized his mistake. Gordo's facial expression suggested extreme airsickness.

"On the other hand," Ben said, "they may just be waiting to get your autograph."

"Oh," Gordo said. His face relaxed a bit. "Well, that ain't so bad. Anyone got a pen?"

Scat lowered his shades a fraction. "I expect your groupies brought their own, Gordo."

"Oh. Yeah, right." He settled back on his stool and practiced the opening ten bars.

"Are you boys ready?" Uncle Earl asked from the wings.

"Ready," they shouted back—all except Ben. Ben had just noticed that, once again, the piano was bathed in darkness. He couldn't even see the set list, much less make out all his chord notations.

"Just a minute," Ben said as he climbed onto the piano bench, but it was too late. Earl had already switched on the backstage mike and begun his warmup spiel.

"Good evening, sweet ladies and gentle men," he boomed out. The crowd yipped and whistled in response. "Good evening, hustlers and hobos, rustlers with your mojos. We got a super-special spectacular for you tonight."

The crowd roared. Ben continued groping for the overhead stage light.

"We got a show like no show you've ever seen before," Earl continued. "We got living legends up here on this stage. We got the funksterators and tricknologists and true mu-jicians. We got more excitement than a D.A.'s indictment. Are you ready?"

The crowd shouted back: "Yes!"

Earl's voice swelled. "I said, are you ready?"

"Yes!"

"All right then, brothers and sisters. He-e-e-ere we go!" Earl gave the signal, and the curtains parted.

Thunderous applause erupted as the curtains split apart, revealing three musicians poised behind their instruments and one shortish white kid standing on the piano bench with his arms overhead groping for a light fixture.

The downstage lights hit Ben and he froze. Oh my God, he thought, suddenly realizing there were about a billion eyes out there—all of them staring at him. They must think I'm a total moron. He stayed right where he was, not moving, not sure what to do.

"Sit down!" Earl hissed from the side of the stage.

The other three musicians also appeared not particularly thrilled with the onstage state of affairs. Normally they would start playing as soon as the curtains parted, but Scat could hardly give the signal while their pianist was standing on the bench with his arms flung up like some perverse sun worshiper.

"Sit down!" Denny barked from behind the drum set.

"Like now!" Gordo spat out. His voice trembled a bit. Obviously, this unforeseen wrinkle was making them all nervous, Gordo worst of all.

Ben couldn't decide what to do, and his indecision was only prolonging the moment and making it worse than it already was. His heart was racing.

"Sit down!" Earl bellowed again.

Easy to say, Ben thought, but he couldn't play in the dark. He pushed up on his tippie-toes and reached for the large flat overhead light fixture.

"Leave it alone!" Earl shouted. He had gone long past stage whispers now. His voice echoed across the stage and probably well into the audience.

Diane was in the wings on the other side of the stage. "Start the show!" she said, shaking a black-gloved fist at Ben.

"I have to see!" Ben hissed back.

"The show's started!" Earl bellowed. "Leave it alone!"

Ben ignored him. He reached up even higher and grabbed

the lamp with one hand. It seemed unusually heavy; he could barely budge it. Gritting his teeth, he jerked it forward with all his might . . .

Something tumbled off the top of the stage light, something big and bulky. Ben gasped and ducked, but not in time. Screams erupted from the audience as the large burden spilled off the lamp and directly on top of Ben. It knocked him off the piano bench like a wet sandbag; both Ben and bundle fell to earth in one heavy thud.

Ben felt the air rush out of his lungs. He blinked his eyes, fighting to retain consciousness.

It was the screams that brought him back. They had intensified and diversified; he heard screams of fright, but also panic and disgust. He heard feet scuffling, people moving away as fast as possible.

He shook his head, forcing himself back into the world of the living. What the hell was going on? And why wasn't anyone coming to help him?

He pushed himself up on one elbow, and that was when, for the first time, he got a clear look at the bundle that had tumbled down on top of him.

It was unfortunate, he thought in retrospect, that he had to see the face first. There she was, ashen and cold, dark hair hanging limply on either side of her face, which was expressionless save for the ghastly red smile that had been carved upon it.

9

Ben tried to pull away, but he was pinned down by the dead weight of the body. His eyes widened like saucers; his breathing came short and fast.

Omigod, omigod, omigod . . .

He clawed the stage, desperate to escape, but he couldn't gain any ground. He was stuck like a bug in a science fair project, with that horrible face staring at him, that ghastly smile, caked blood lining the edges like lipstick.

Uncle Earl ran out on the stage. "Listen to me, cats!" he shouted at the top of his lungs. "Don't panic! That won't do no one no good!"

Nobody was listening. It was a virtual stampede. People had panicked, particularly those sitting toward the front. They were climbing on tables, clawing at the walls, knocking down whoever was in their way.

"Shut the doors!" Earl shouted.

Someone up front, probably the bouncer, obeyed. Several people collided into the doors, but they were shut and locked tight.

"There now!" Earl boomed. "There's nowhere for you to go. So sit down already, before you hurt somebody!"

The news of the futility of flight seemed to have the desired calming effect. Gradually the panic subsided and the screaming stopped. Although, Ben noted, none of the front-row patrons reclaimed their seats.

"Thank heaven for that," Earl said, wiping his brow.

"Amen," Ben echoed. "And now, Earl, if you don't

mind or anything, now that you've got the crowd under control . . . *could someone please get me out of here*?"

Earl ran to his side; Scat dropped his sax and did the same. Gordo and Denny both stayed where they were, and judging from the queasy expressions on their faces, Ben thought it was probably just as well.

The men grabbed Ben by the shoulders and pulled him free of the body. "Thank you very much," Ben muttered. He jumped to his feet and began brushing himself off. He didn't know exactly what he was brushing off, but he knew that he *desperately* wanted to brush himself off.

"First time you've ever seen a stiff, kid?" Scat asked.

"Not even close," Ben replied. "But they don't usually knock me off the piano bench."

He turned to thank Earl, but saw that Earl was looking down, staring blank-faced at the corpse.

"Oh, no," Earl whispered, barely audibly. "Oh, no."

Ben felt a hollow aching in the pit of his stomach. "Is she . . . someone you knew?"

"It's my Lily-lady. My sweet, sweet Lily."

And then, to the total stupefaction of the crowd, Earl wrapped his arms around the corpse, hugging it tightly, and began to weep.

When Lieutenant Mike Morelli arrived at the club, he took immediate control. He systematically began running through the crime scene protection checklist he kept permanently stored in his head. He cordoned off the stage with bright yellow tape and spread brown butcher paper on the floor. He deputized the bouncers and stationed them at all exits with instructions to keep potential witnesses in and, more importantly, to keep the press out. Ben could hear reporters outside the front door swarming, shouting questions; there was even a helicopter buzzing around overhead. Obviously, Mike wanted to delay the inevitable as long as possible.

Ben watched as two women in green jumpsuits hoisted the corpse onto a stretcher to take it away to the medical examiner's office. He was pleased to see they had to work at it; it would've made him look pretty wimpy otherwise.

He took this last opportunity to gaze at the mutilated face. Even with the grisly handiwork of some twisted mind's knife, Ben could see that the woman had been lovely. She was not young, but time had not masked the beauty that was her birthright. Her face shone in the low lighting. He could still see the powdery remains of makeup on her face, as well as eyeliner and mascara. A shame she thought she had to paint herself to be beautiful, he thought; she didn't. She was a born looker.

Still, Ben was not unhappy to see the body depart. The whole club was being contaminated by a heavy, musty odor. The sooner the remains were gone, the sooner they could all breathe freely again.

Ben was relieved Mike had been dispatched to handle the crime scene. Ben and Mike went way back, all the way to college days, when they had been roommates and played music gigs in local clubs and pizza parlors. Mike fell in love with Ben's sister, Julia, and ultimately married her. The marriage hadn't lasted long, and after the divorce, Ben found himself on the outs with both Mike and Julia. His friendship with Mike had never really been the same. They were still sewing it back together, one stitch at a time.

Mike was crouched over the spot where the body had dropped, scraping the wood planks for blood samples. Ben noticed Mike had managed to smear some blood on the crumpled and disgustingly dirty trench coat he always insisted on wearing to crime scenes.

"Shouldn't you be wearing coveralls?" Ben asked.

"Don't like 'em," Mike grumbled, not looking up. "They wrinkle my raincoat."

"How can you tell?" Ben nodded at Sergeant Tomlinson, Mike's protégé, who now served as a SID crime scene tech. He was fascinated, watching the players go through their motions. It was like watching an ant farm: everyone had specialized tasks, and a strictly observed caste system remained in place at all times. The detectives spoke only to each other or to Tomlinson; the uniforms spoke only when spoken to. And no one spoke to the people from the medical examiner's office.

To be fair, the detectives would confer with the medical examiner himself or his tech, if either happened to be on the scene. In the main, the conversation would be a rapid-fire series of questions, most of which the examiner either couldn't or wouldn't answer, at least not until after the autopsy had been performed and the tox tests had been processed. Of course, that didn't prevent Mike from asking "What was the time of death?" and "How was she killed?" The only inquiry that produced a useful response was: "Where was she killed?"

The tech had answered in reverse: "Not here."

"Not D.R.T.?"

"No way. She's been moved."

Maybe that wasn't all that helpful, now that Ben thought about it. Did anyone really suppose the murder had occurred on top of a stage light? But the tech's conclusion went further. She didn't think the victim had been murdered within the building. She thought the body had been transported a considerable distance.

Mike set his sergeants scurrying through the club interviewing employees and patrons, all of whom had been detained and several of whom complained audibly. Meanwhile, Mike continued his interview with Ben.

"Tell me more about this guy lugging the rug around. You say he was black?" Mike extracted a notebook from his trench coat.

"I thought so at the time. In retrospect, it could have been a disguise."

"Tell me about his face."

Ben sighed. "I didn't really look."

"Because he was a blue-collar worker, so he was beneath your notice."

"Because it was dark and he was in shadow and I was

preoccupied." Ben's lips pressed tightly together. "Don't pin the snobby-rich-boy bit on me. You know better."

Mike grinned. "I'm just trying to make you remember. It's my job."

"It's not your job. It's how you handle your job. And it sucks."

Mike's eyes fluttered. "A bit testy tonight, aren't we?"

"You would be too if the sky started raining corpses on you."

"You've seen dead bodies before."

"Yeah, but I don't normally play Twister with them!"

Mike flipped a page in his notepad. "How 'bout if I bring in a sketch artist? See if he can put together a composite."

Ben shook his head. "It'd be a waste of time. I never really saw him."

"And you're sure about the hair? Bushy Afro. Bushy beard."

"Right."

"A 'fro? In this day and age?"

Ben shrugged. "That's what I saw."

Mike grumbled. "Maybe that's what he wanted you to see."

Sergeant Tomlinson stepped up on the stage, escorting Earl. "Got a minute, Mike?"

"Yeah. What?"

"This guy owns the place."

"I know."

"And he can ID the corpse."

" 'Zat a fact." Mike's eyes narrowed. "What do you know about that."

Earl held up his hands. "Now, don't go gettin' the wrong idea. I just know her, that's all. Known her for years."

"Uh-huh. What's her name?"

"Lily." Earl said the name soft and breathlessly. "Lily Campbell. She sang as the Cajun Lily."

Mike continued scribbling. "She sang?"

"Lord, did she ever. She could put a spin on a song that would crumble your heart. She had a way with—"

Mike cut him off. "Just give me the facts, okay?"

Earl cleared his throat. "She was a hot number on the jazz circuit, back twenty odd years ago. 'Specially in this part of the country."

"And you knew her?"

"Oh, yes," he said softly.

"How well?"

His eyes darted toward the door where he had last seen Lily's remains. "Very well."

"Seen her lately?"

"No. But I got a phone call from her yesterday. Out of the blue. You can't imagine how surprised I was. I thought she'd forgotten all about me. But no, she still remembered, and she knew about my club. Said she wanted to see me; said she had somethin' to tell me."

"Did she say what?"

"Not a clue. Just said she'd meet me at the club tonight, before the show started."

"And?"

Earl looked at him helplessly. "She never showed up."

Mike arched an eyebrow. "I think she did."

"Well, I mean—" Earl became flustered. "I mean—hell."

Ben laid a comforting hand on Earl's shoulder. "Take it easy, Earl. Just tell your story." Ben knew the man was caught up in the circumstances, confused. But unfortunately, he was acting like someone with something to hide.

"I mean she didn't meet me beforehand," Earl said finally. "I never saw her. Not till she took the tumble off that goddamned light."

"I see." Mike resumed scribbling. "Any idea how she got up there?"

Earl shrugged. "No idea. It's a strong lamp and not that high off the stage. 'Spose anyone coulda propped her up there."

"Anyone taller than Ben," Mike remarked. "Unfortunately, that doesn't eliminate many suspects. In fact . . ."

He didn't have to finish his sentence. They could all see that Earl was almost a foot taller than Ben. Standing on the piano bench, he could have reached the light with ease.

"Ben tells me he fiddled with the light before rehearsal, an hour or so ago, and there was no corpse there."

Earl nodded. "Right. I remember."

"After rehearsal, Ben tells me there was only about a ten-minute break between the time he left the stage and the time he saw you outside."

"I 'spect that's right."

Mike took a step toward Earl. "Mind telling me where you went after you left the club?"

"Well, I—I—" Earl's lips went dry, and he seemed to be having trouble speaking. "I—"

"We're waiting."

"I went for a walk. Outside."

Mike's voice acquired a definite edge. "You went for a walk? Just before the show?"

Earl licked his lips. Beads of sweat were beginning to trickle down the sides of his head. "I—I was lookin' for Lily. She hadn't shown up yet and—"

"And you thought she might be walking around outside?"

"I thought she might be lost or somethin'. I don't know. I don't know what I thought. I just had to move."

Mike folded up his notepad. "And let me guess. You were all alone during this walk. No witnesses."

"Well . . ." Sweat continued to drip down his face, his chin. "I—well—"

Mike bore down on him. "Yes?"

"It's like—I mean—"

"Let me get this straight. This is your club. You had access to the place where the body was found. You're tall enough to reach the light fixture. And you're the only one who seems to know the victim."

"Well, I guess—"

Mike leaned into his face. "Are you sure there isn't

something more you'd like to tell me? Like maybe the truth!"

"I'm tellin' you I don't know what happened!"

Mike let out a disgusted snort. "Yeah, right." He motioned to his assistant. "C'mon, Tomlinson."

As they started off the stage, Mike called back, "Oh, and one more thing, *Uncle* Earl."

Earl stopped in place.

"Tonight you give some real serious thought to coming clean and telling me the truth, understand? And whether you do or you don't, I'd recommend you get a lawyer. You're gonna need one."

"A lawyer?" Earl raised his hands. "A lawyer?"

Ben squirmed uncomfortably. "It might be a good idea."

"A lawyer?" He stared at Ben helplessly. "I can't afford no lawyer. Where am I gonna get a lawyer?"

Ben looked away, not saying a word.

* 10 *

Ben stopped Mike before he left the club. "Bit hard on him, weren't you?"

Mike didn't blink. "That's my job."

"What are you, a policeman or a terrorist?"

"I'm obligated to get facts out of people who customarily start out telling lies. Or embroidering the truth. I have to break through the deception somehow. And I've found the most effective way is to instill the fear of God. Or penal sanctions, at the least."

"Seems brutal."

"But it works."

"Not tonight it won't. Earl didn't do this."

"Says you."

"It's true. I'm sure of it."

Mike looked at him wryly. "But when the man freaked 'cause I told him he needed a lawyer, I noticed you didn't jump to his rescue."

Ben's head dipped. "That's different. I don't practice anymore."

"Not even for a friend in need?"

"Look, I'm trying to put that behind me, okay?"

"Like hell. You're trying to pretend it never happened. These guys don't even know you're a lawyer, do they?"

Ben shook his head. "And I prefer it that way."

"Don't you think you're carrying this a bit far?"

"You don't know anything about it."

"You haven't told me what soured you after your last

72

big case, true. But I can guess. I may know you better than you know yourself. And this I can tell you: it's time for you to stop running and hiding and trying to be something you're not."

Ben rolled his eyes. "Not you, too."

"I don't enjoy seeing you crawl under a shell any better than anyone else. You know what G. K. Chesterton said."

"You know perfectly well I don't."

Mike held up his quoting finger. " 'Do not free a camel of the burden of his hump; you may be freeing him from being a camel.' "

"Very clever. And I gather I'm the camel?"

"Tell me something, Ben. Now that you're a musician again, is it like back in the old days? Back when we played the college clubs and pizza parlors?"

Against his better judgment, Ben decided to be honest. "Not really."

Mike nodded. "Of course not. Thomas Wolfe was right, my friend. You can't go home again. You can only go forward. Take it from me. I spent years rehashing those blissful days when I was married to your sister. Actually, they were only blissful in retrospect, but memory plays tricks. I'd sit around all day thinking, Poor me, I lost the only woman I ever loved and we never had the child we dreamed about. But living in the past doesn't do anybody any good. Took years, but I've finally put her behind me. I hardly even think about Julia anymore."

"Is that right."

"Here's to the future. That's my motto." Mike clapped Ben on the shoulder. "Sorry to hassle you, kemo sabe. I realize you've had a hell of a night."

"It's been a nightmare," Ben agreed. "They don't get much worse."

"Oh, I don't know," Mike said. "It could probably be worse."

"No way. Not possible."

"You shouldn't say that, Ben. You never know."

"Believe me," Ben said emphatically. "Nothing on earth could possibly make this night any worse."

Mike smiled. "Your mother is here."

Ben dragged himself to the backstage green room, dreading every moment. Not that he minded seeing his mother, exactly, but it seemed about par for the course that she would come the night a corpse dropped onto his face.

He found her in the green room, sitting on the piano bench beside Scat. Ben's eyes widened with amazement, and for more than one reason. For starters, he didn't know Scat played the piano. And for another—his mother was singing!

" 'It had to be you . . .' "

Could this really be his mother? Her voice was sweet and smooth, like a swan sailing across a pond. She nurtured every syllable of every word, giving each phrase a twist that was both affecting and—Ben blanched at the thought—seductive.

Ben couldn't believe it. He had never heard his mother sing, except for long-ago lullabies and car songs. He didn't even know she could sing. But she could. Boy, could she ever.

Well, he couldn't see interrupting. The cops were leaving them alone; so would he. He found a chair and sat quietly.

" 'It had to be . . . you.' " She drew out the last syllable for about a million beats, finally letting it dwindle to nothing as Scat laid his fingers down on the last rippled chord.

Ben stood and burst into applause. Scat and his mother both whirled around.

"Benjamin!" Her hand rose to her mouth. "I didn't hear you come in."

"I didn't want to interrupt. I guess you two have already met."

"Aww, Benji, Benji, Benji." Scat pushed his shades up his nose. "Your sweet mama and I go way back."

"You do?"

" 'Course we do. How come you never told me your mama is Lillian Kincaid?"

Ben's expression seemed frozen in place. "You—know my mother?"

Mrs. Kincaid raised an eyebrow. "Do you find that so shocking?"

"No. I just didn't know when . . . when . . . you would've had . . ."

She tapped her long fingernails. "We're waiting."

". . . had an opportunity to meet . . . a musician. Yes, that's it. A musician."

"Hell, Ben, don't you know nothin' about your own mama? She used to be the best singer in Oklahoma City."

"*My* mother?"

Scat looked at him as if he had just crawled out from under a rock. "Where do you think you got the beat, son?"

"Well, now, let's give Edward some credit. He was a musician, too."

Ben's expression did not change. "*My* mother?"

Mrs. Kincaid gave Scat a long look. "Did you ever have any children?"

"Cain't say that I ever had the pleasure."

"Pleasure. That would be one word for it." She directed her attention back to Ben. "Yes, Benjamin, your mother used to sing. For a living."

"You never should've left the circuit, Lillian," Scat said. "No one sings the blues like you. Before or since."

She shrugged. "Well, Edward felt that someone had to make a home. I sang part-time at first, but then Junior here"—she nodded toward Ben—"showed up in the first year. And of course, after that, everything changed."

Ben remained flabbergasted. "You gave up a career—I never knew—"

"That was a long time ago."

Ben stared, unable to utter a word.

It was Scat who broke the silence. "Well, you ain't lost the touch, Lillian. You still give me chills."

She smiled. "You're kind, Scat, but I was never that good, and I'm well past my prime now." She gave him a gentle shove. "Give me a minute to talk to my son, okay?"

"Your wish is my command, Lillian." He gave her a kiss on the cheek, then sauntered off toward the stage.

Once he was gone, Ben's mother folded her hands in her lap and smiled. "I stopped by Christina's place on my way over."

During her last visit, Ben's mother had forged a friendship with Christina, a union Ben wouldn't have bet on in a thousand years.

"She wanted to go shopping, but I insisted on attending your performance. She's a sweet girl—Christina." To Ben's surprise, she winked. "I'm surprised you haven't married her yet."

"Mother, I told you before, we're just friends. We work together. Did, anyway."

"Uh-huh."

"What, you don't agree?"

"I agree that you've told me that before. Doesn't mean I have to believe it." She patted the empty space on the piano bench. Ben awkwardly crossed the room and sat down beside her. "Christina doesn't think you'll stick with this gig much longer. She thinks you'll end up practicing law again."

"Well, she's wrong. I'm really connecting with this combo. In fact, when Earl closes down the club for his summer break, we're planning to go on tour. Hit the southwest summer jazz circuit."

His mother nodded. "Christina has a high regard for you. She thinks the law is your calling. She thinks it's your way of helping other people. She even called you an angel. Can you believe that? My Benjamin, an angel."

"Christina could put a spiritual spin on a train wreck."

"Well, what she actually said was, you're an angel on vacation. But eventually you'll get back to your true *vo*cation."

"Please, mother. I'm not giving up music."

His mother tossed her head back. "I can certainly understand the desire to perform, to make melodies. To lose yourself in the purity of music. I had that dream myself. But still . . ."

"You don't think I can cut it as a musician."

She scowled. "Don't be ridiculous. You're a Kincaid. You can cut it as anything you want to cut it as. But is this"—she looked around the green room—"who you really are?"

"You've spent too much time with Christina."

She patted his hand. "Well, you do what you have to do."

They both fell silent.

The awkwardness of the moment enveloped Ben. "I'm sorry you came tonight. I mean, considering what happened."

"I'm just sorry I didn't get to hear you play."

He fidgeted. "Anyway . . . thanks for coming down."

"It was my pleasure. I'd best be going now."

He touched her arm. "Do you have to?"

"It's late. I should get home."

"Wait." Ben tugged her gently back to the bench. "I was wondering . . ."

"Yes?"

"Well, all those years I struggled through piano lessons with Mrs. Thomas, playing stripped-down versions of bad pop tunes—how come you never came in and sang?"

She smiled. "I didn't want to crowd you, Benjamin. If I had made playing the piano seem like something *I* wanted you to do—well, you'd probably never have done it."

Ben couldn't argue with that logic. "Well then, how about now?"

A broad beatific smile spread across her face. "Why, Benjamin Kincaid. I'd be honored. What song?"

He raised his eyebrows. "*The* song." Which they both knew meant, *his* song—Ben's father's favorite song.

Ben started with a slow bluesy intro, lots of tinkling in the high registers, and his mother knew exactly where to come in. " 'A country dance . . . was being held in a garden . . .' "

Ben couldn't resist smiling as he played. It was the sweetest music he'd heard all night.

* 11 *

The instant the LED on his digital clock read 12:00, Jones logged onto the Net. An instant later, he booted up his chat software and created a private room on Channel 365.

And waited. And waited.

Where was she? he began to wonder. Was it all a mistake? Or perhaps some cruel joke?

The minutes on his digital clock continued to click past. Five minutes past, then ten. Jones stared at the blank computer screen, overwhelmed with disappointment. Half an hour past, then an hour . . .

Panic began to set in. He had never asked where she lived. He had assumed she lived in Tulsa, but it wasn't necessarily so. What if she lived in a different time zone? If she lived in California, she wouldn't expect to keep a midnight appointment for two more hours. Or—

Chills radiated down his spine. If she lived in New York, she would have logged on an hour ago, expecting to find him, but instead finding nothing. Thinking she had been stood up. Thinking he was just another jerk after all, no better than Cobblepot or PilotBob.

Or there was another possibility. Maybe she had stood him up. Maybe she had come to her senses, become frightened. Who could blame her? What did she know about him, anyway? For all she knew, he was just another semi-literate computer geek. Maybe she decided to go offline and see if she could have a real life . . .

PAULA1>Are you there?

Jones nearly jumped out of his desk chair. She was here! *She was here!*

Scrambling as fast as possible, he began to type. In his panic, he screwed his message up the first time, then had to delete and try again, then messed it up again. He inhaled deeply and slowly corrected his typos.

FINGERS>I'm here. And I'm glad you're here with me. (meaningful pause) I see you've changed your online moniker.

PAULA1>(hapless shrug)I thought it was time to come out of the closet. So to speak.

FINGERS>ROTFL!(hesitant confession)I was afraid you wouldn't come.

PAULA1>I admit I had some second thoughts. I hope you don't mind, but I took the liberty of reading your online profile.

Jones felt the air rush out of his lungs. She read his profile! But he had written that months ago, the first time he ever logged into a chat room. He was just pretending, fantasizing. He had never really expected anyone to read it, much less . . .

FINGERS>I hope nothing there put you off.

PAULA1>No! It was fascinating. Especially your detective work.

Jones's heart thudded to the bottom of his chest. What have I done?

PAULA1>I think that sounds incredibly exciting! Cruising the mean streets, being your own boss, answering to no one and nothing but your own personal sense of justice. Is it as thrilling as it sounds?

FINGERS>It has its moments.

PAULA1>Tell me about some of your most exciting cases.

Jones's mouth went dry. He'd asked for this, he supposed—pretending to be someone he wasn't. Maybe if he came clean right now before it got any worse.

FINGERS>Look . . . I don't want to mislead you in any way.

PAULA1>Oh, no. Don't tell me you lied in your profile. I hate it when men do that. :(

Jones felt his head getting light. He'd been day-dreaming about this chat all day, and now that it was finally here, it was slipping away from him. He couldn't bear to blow it now. But he knew that as soon as she learned his profile was a portfolio of lies, she'd snap off her modem in a heartbeat.

FINGERS>No, nothing like that. I just didn't mention—I don't work alone.

PAULA1>You don't?

FINGERS>Not exactly. I work with another private investigator. And with a lawyer. Sometimes we work on cases together.

PAULA1>That makes sense. I suppose they refer investigations to you. And you refer clients to them.

FINGERS>Yes, that's it. Exactly.

PAULA1>But you're still your own boss. That would be so wonderful! (swooning) Self-employment—that's my dream. I'm a librarian, and unless I come into a fortune and buy my own library, I'm always going to be working for someone else.

FINGERS>You're a librarian!

PAULA1>Very boring.

FINGERS>I love librarians. They're my favorite people.

PAULA1>Really! :)

FINGERS>Yes. Always have been. Always will be.

PAULA1>You must love books, too. I know you're very well read. That was what first caught my attention.

FINGERS>But how did you know?

PAULA1>Because you quoted both Lao-Tzu and Lord Byron when you were chatting with those morons on the Wild Side.

FINGERS>You noticed?

PAULA1>Of course I noticed. I noticed everything.

After that, there was no stopping them. They spent the next hour discussing their favorite books, poets, films. Paula favored Emily Dickinson and, after a brief childhood flirtation with Rod McKuen, W. H. Auden. Jones preferred Walt Whitman and, nowadays, W. S. Merwin. It seemed they had read all the same books, and loved or hated them in precise correspondence. They agreed on everything.

Around two A.M. Jones decided to take the plunge.

FINGERS>Paula . . . I want you to know how much I've really really enjoyed talking to you.

Almost a minute elapsed before her answer appeared. Jones felt the panic rippling up his back, felt the burning sensation under his collar. Had he pushed too hard? Gotten too forward too fast? His fingers trembled as he waited for her response.

PAULA1>I've really enjoyed talking to you too, Fingers.

He rapid-fired his response.

FINGERS>My friends call me Jones.

PAULA1>Oh! (touched and humbled) Thank you for trusting me with your true name. Thank you very much.

FINGERS>(confession)I was so worried when you didn't log on at twelve.

PAULA1>I'm sorry, Jones. I got here as soon as I could. The most amazing thing happened to me tonight. You see, I was at this jazz club on the North Side . . .

* 12 *

Ben parked his van across from his boardinghouse and stumbled across the street. It was after one in the morning and he was bushed. It had been an incredibly long night, despite the fact that the musicians had never actually played a note. But the police detained everyone in the club until well after midnight. Only after they had interrogated everyone and had secured all the names and addresses did they finally begin releasing people.

Ben had done his best to convince his mother to spend the night in Tulsa, but she declined. Places to go; people to meet. At times she could be as stubborn as—well, as *he* was, he supposed.

He tiptoed up the front porch steps and opened the screen door. Of course, the thing squeaked as if it hadn't been lubricated since Prohibition, despite the fact that he had oiled it himself barely a month before. Ever since he had moved into this house, he had been Mrs. Marmelstein's unofficial financial adviser and handyman—even though he was about the least handy person on God's green earth. But she needed someone. With her husband gone and the insistent tendrils of senility tightening around her, she needed someone to maintain the property, to pay the bills and, on more than one occasion, to make undocumented contributions to the petty cash box.

He jammed his key into the lock and crept into his room. It was dark and quiet. Lonely. But what did he expect? It wasn't as if anyone would be waiting for him. He lived alone.

Well, not totally alone. Giselle leaped off the sofa and inserted her claws firmly into his shoulder.

"Gaaah!" He tried to stifle himself, remembering that it was, after all, after one, and most sane people were in bed.

He took her firmly in his hands and air-lifted her off his shoulder. Well, what's a little blood between master and cat, he thought. He thought again. Giselle was *his* master—er, mistress.

"Why can't cats sleep at night?" he wondered aloud. Giselle wasn't around to hear. She had scampered into the kitchen and made agonized mewling noises.

"I'm coming, I'm coming." He followed her into the kitchen. He took a can of Feline's Fancy off the shelf, pried it open, and scooped the contents into her bowl.

She attacked her food ravenously. Ben grinned. Joey had been fascinated by the cat; he could watch her for hours. Maybe it was because he, at three feet, was more or less at her level. Some days, his nephew would follow Giselle all over the apartment, playing chase, sticking his hands in her water bowl . . .

Ben sighed. He wondered if Giselle missed Joey, too.

Probably not, actually. He could go only so far with this self-indulgent line of thought. Even in his most desperate hour, it would be hard to pretend that Giselle's affections ran much deeper than her food dish.

He walked back into the living room and flopped down on the sofa. And what about his own affections? Where did they run? Or where were they running from?

One thing was certain. He'd had it with virtually everyone he knew surmising that they knew better than he who he was and what he should be doing—implying that he was wasting his life, that his interest in music was occasioned only by his retreat from the law. He had always loved music, always wanted to pursue a career in it. He had the time and the money now; that was all. It didn't really have anything to do with . . . the other.

The other. What a bust that had been. Just when it appeared he was actually going to have some success, it all blew up in his face. Reality came along and gave him a bracing lesson in the true meaning of success. And the meaning of justice, too. Was it any wonder he didn't care to practice law anymore?

And yet . . .

His mind drifted back to the early days. Law school, and just after. He had always told himself that his decision to go into law had nothing to do with money, nothing to do with career, nothing to do with choosing the profession his father most despised. He wanted to make a difference. He wanted to help other people.

To help other people. Well, well, well.

He'd certainly had the opportunity tonight, hadn't he? Earl needed a lawyer—needed a lawyer even worse than he probably realized. But Ben had kept his lips shut tight. Hadn't spoken a word.

Well, it wasn't as if he was morally obligated to practice law for the rest of his life, right? Just because a man has a degree doesn't mean he has to use it every time some hard-luck story drops into his lap, right? He was entitled to pursue his dreams, too, right?

Right?

He pounded a fist into his pillow. There would be no answers tonight. It was too late and he was too tired. All he wanted was rest. All he wanted was to close his eyes and—

He felt something fuzzy tickling the underside of his nose. His eyes shot open.

It was Giselle. The feeding finished, she was now burrowing a space for herself inside his arms, pressing her furry face against his cheek.

He gave her a little squeeze and closed his eyes. Perhaps her affections ran a tiny bit deeper than the food dish, anyway.

* 13 *

Damn it all to hell!

That wasn't the way it was supposed to work! He slammed the van door shut, cursing under his breath. He had planned it all so carefully. He had worked everything out, every little detail. Only to have the whole thing fall apart at the last moment.

He opened the back of the van and pulled out the rug. Not a disaster, true. But not what he had planned. Circumstances had conspired against him. And he had almost been spotted twice. That was something he couldn't allow. If anyone had seen him who could identify him— well, that would change the whole fabric of reality as he knew it.

He scrutinized the rug carefully. Despite the fact that Lily had been dead before she hit the rug, there were bloodstains on it, and he was certain there would be other bits of trace evidence as well. The rug would have to be burned. Fortunately, there was an incinerator in the basement that would be just perfect for that chore.

He lugged the heavy wool object inside and down the hall toward the basement. He would have to keep his brain busy, try to keep his mind off all the earlier events of the night. If he continued obsessing over it, he would only become angry.

How the hell was he supposed to know Earl would come back so soon? He was supposed to be outside for half an hour at least. And that idiot piano player had of course sent Earl right backstage.

He had been forced to act fast. He had intended to plant the corpse in Earl's office, but there was no time. He had to hide it somewhere quick, and that light fixture was the first half-decent hiding place he saw. He had expected it to be days before anyone made the discovery. How was he to know that that selfsame idiot piano player would knock the damn thing down before the band had played a note?

After that, the whole scheme began falling down around him. All he could do now was stay out of the way and hope for the best. He didn't know what would happen, what the police would do. Given how stupid they usually were, they might end up trying to pin it on the piano player!

Still, there was the matter of the smile. He smiled himself, remembering that one delicious detail. He had at least had the sense to take care of that. As soon as the police ran that through their computers . . . well, that would change the whole face of the investigation. That would swing things back where he wanted them.

Yes. It might work out after all. He dragged the rug down the rickety wooden steps to the basement. The rug seemed much heavier now, even heavier than it had been with a body wrapped inside. He supposed he was just tired. It had been a hard day's night, all right. And there was still work to be done.

And one more loose end to be attended to. He felt certain the piano player hadn't looked at him closely enough to even identify his disguise, much less his actual appearance. But that kid in the men's room was another matter. He had gotten a good look at him—a good look after he had removed the wig and beard. Worse, he'd misplaced a little something that belonged to him, something he had to retrieve, because someone out there just might be smart enough to trace it back to him. And if that happened, all his plans would come tumbling down like a sorry house of cards.

He opened the heavy metal door, stoked the flames for a few moments, then shoved the rug into the incinerator.

The kid might've talked to the cops already. But for some reason he didn't think so. He didn't look like a kid who'd spent his life on the right side of the law, and people living on the wrong side tended not to be too chatty when the cops came calling.

If the kid hadn't talked yet, he had to make sure he never did. And if the kid had talked, he had to make sure he didn't have a chance to testify.

No question about it. The kid had to go the way of Lily Campbell. There was simply too much at stake to leave him breathing.

He grinned. Maybe he should've kept the rug after all.

He stared into the incinerator, watching the bright orange flames lick at the now charred rug. Well, he probably wouldn't need it—not this time around. No frame-up necessary here. Just a quick simple kill. The kind he did best.

He continued to stare, mesmerized by the flames. No rug necessary, he thought again. But the smile . . . that would be a nice touch. Yes . . . the more he thought about it, the more he liked it. There would definitely be a smile.

He gently touched the knife still strapped to his waist. After all, the world needed more smiles. Smiles make the world go 'round. Right?

TWO

* *

Remember When
the Music

* 14 *

Ben filled yet another Hefty bag full of trash, tied it off, carried it to the back alley, then started back for more. The pile of trash bags spilled out the top of the bin. And they were barely getting started.

They'd only been at it a few hours, but he was already exhausted. In the aftermath of the previous night's excitement, not to mention the forced incarceration of more than a hundred patrons, the club was a wreck. The police had taped off the stage area and posted an officer to keep everyone out and off. But the rest of the place was a disaster area.

The police had ordered Earl to keep the club closed for several days, until they finished their examination of the crime scene. Still, Earl hoped to be ready to reopen as soon as the police would allow it. Diane had enlisted every person remotely associated with the club to help her clean up the joint. Even with all hands working full-time to put the place back in shape, though, Ben knew it would take days.

He rounded a corner and found two men crouched down near the floor. One of them was Scat; the other he didn't recognize.

"Ben!" Scat pushed himself up. "I see you're hard at work."

"Well, there's a lot to be done." Ben glanced awkwardly at the other man, the one he didn't know. Scat took the hint.

"Ben, I want you to meet someone special."

Ben smiled at the stranger and extended his hand. He

was a tall man, about Scat's age and in good shape. His hair was close cropped and was just beginning to show traces of gray.

"You remember when Earl and I were talking about Professor Hoodoo?"

Ben nodded. "The greatest jazzman who ever played these parts."

"That's the man. Well, this here is the Professor's brother. Grady Armstrong."

"Really." Ben shook his hand vigorously. "Are you a musician, too?"

Armstrong shrugged. "That's what everyone asks. No, I'm just a regular guy. Got me a boring, perfectly ordinary job with an oil company. I'm afraid George got all the talent in the family."

"What brings you here today?"

"Well, I heard about poor Lily. I'd met her once—you probably know she and my brother were quite close at one time. I just wanted to pay my respects. I called up Scat and asked him to bring me out here. I had hoped to say a word of comfort to Earl—I know he loved Lily, too. But I guess I missed him. So Scat here drafts me into the cleanup brigade."

Scat chuckled, then slapped the man on the back. "The more the merrier, that's what I always say."

Armstrong smiled. "Well, I should be going. But do give Earl my regards. And, Scat—if this anniversary concert ever happens, would you give me a call? I'd—well, I'd kind of like to be here."

"It's a promise," Scat said. "If the concert does happen, it'll be a tribute. A tribute to the beautiful Cajun Lily. And of course, your brother."

"That's very kind of you."

Scat shook his head. "Wasn't meant to be kind. It's just a fact. I carry a little piece of the Professor inside of me, you know. Every time I play, I'm playing for him."

Scat escorted Armstrong to the front door, and Ben resumed his cleaning efforts. He moved to the area just below the stage, where he saw Gordo furiously working with a rag and a spray bottle of 409.

"Tell you what," Gordo said as Ben approached. "You scrub for a while and I'll collect the trash."

"What, just when I'm getting good at it?"

"C'mon, man, this spray stuff is toxic. The fumes are gettin' me high, and it ain't a good high, either."

"All right." Ben handed Gordo the trash bags. "I'm tired of bending and stooping, anyway. I'm working my way to a premature death."

"Death is a sweet maiden," Gordo replied. He bent over and scooped up the remains of some nachos.

Now that was a bizarre remark, Ben thought. Was that some sort of jazzman motto, he wondered? Or something more.

Denny came up behind Ben, feinting about with a broom. He was moving lots of dust and debris around, but Ben noticed that relatively little of it ended up in the dustpan. "How's it coming?" Ben asked.

"It's disgusting," Denny said. "All this dust and dirt and crap. Man, I need a gas mask."

Ben tried to appear sympathetic, but it took some doing.

"Coming to the poker game tomorrow night, Ben?"

Ben knew that Earl and the rest of the band played poker every Wednesday night, but he'd never joined them. "You're still going to play?"

"Yeah. You got a problem with that?"

"I don't know." Ben looked down at the floor. "It just seems . . . disrespectful, somehow."

"We asked Earl, and he said the show must go on."

"He did?"

"Yeah. But he said we should dedicate the game to that Lily babe."

"A memorial poker game?"

"Exactly." Denny propped the broom against a table. "I need a rest, man. I signed on as a musician, not a chambermaid."

Theoretically, Ben thought, since Denny was the youngest of them, he ought to have the most energy. That did not appear to be the case, however.

"I guess Earl forgot to include 'cleaning up after murders' in the job description," Ben offered.

"No kidding." Denny collapsed into a chair, then winced. "My poor little body is sore all over. Sunburn."

Ben did a double take. "Sunburn? In April?"

"And what of it? You know it's been hot out."

"I know it's been hot, yeah, but I didn't know it's been hot enough to give you a sunburn."

Denny shrugged. "Depends on what you've been wearing."

Ben decided not to pursue this undoubtedly interesting line of thought. "Anyone know where Earl is?"

"Back at the pad," Denny informed him.

Ben nodded. Earl had an apartment on the back end of the building facing the opposite street. There were no connecting doors between the club and the apartment. It was perfect for Earl; he could live close to work, pay rent to one landlord, but still feel as if he had a life apart from work.

Ben walked outside and around the building. Earl's front door was open; Ben stepped inside and closed the door. Earl was with the kid Ben had spotted at the club the night before—the one in the flashy African clothes.

The kid appeared to be distressed. "Man, I just can't get that F to happen."

Earl patted him on the back. "Don't worry, son. You'll get it. Jus' takes practice, that's all. Practice, and a little soul."

"Easy to say."

"Hey, you got an advantage on most. You already got the soul. I've seen some so-called musicians work all their lives and never get it. You were born with it. All you need now is practice."

Ben looked away, trying to act as if he hadn't been listening. He couldn't help wondering if he was one of those *so-called* musicians.

"Ben!" Earl called out. "I want you to meet Tyrone Jackson. T-Dog, to his street buddies."

Tyrone shook his head. "That was a long time ago."

Ben shook the young man's hand. "Pleasure to meet you."

"Tyrone here's been learnin' to play the sax."

"Good luck to you," Ben said. "I never managed to learn anything that required the use of the lips."

Earl and Tyrone exchanged a look. "We'll just leave that one alone, Ben." Earl chuckled heartily. "Ben's our keyboard for the combo. He's got a two-hand rhythm style that'll knock you dead."

"I know," Tyrone said. "I've seen you play. You do a mean 'Polka-Dots and Moonbeams.' "

Was this sincerity or satire? Ben couldn't be sure. "Well, thanks."

"Tyrone's got some kinda ear for the tunes. Even when he was with the gang, they called him the Music Man."

"I assume that wasn't because you were always singing 'Seventy-six Trombones.' "

Tyrone made a snorting noise. "No, man. Back then, I was strictly MTV. I knew all the words to all the tunes. So the homeboys called me the Music Man."

"Would those homeboys have been the Crips or the Bloods?"

"Matter of fact, Crips. North Side Hoover. You know the gangs?"

"I've had some contact with them."

"Tyrone don't have nothin' to do with that no more," Earl explained hastily. "He's left all that behind. He's gonna be a jazzman, right?" He beamed down at Tyrone. "You're gonna blow."

"That's what I'm hoping."

"Well, I'm glad to hear it," Ben said. "With any luck, maybe we can get you to join our combo. Keep practicing with Earl and before you—"

Ben was interrupted by a thunderous pounding on the front door. A voice on the other side boomed: "Police!"

Earl looked uneasy. "Uh ... whaddaya think they want?" With obvious trepidation, he waddled to the front door and opened it. "Can I help you?"

A plainclothes officer pushed through the opened door, with two uniforms right behind him. "Are you Earl Bonner?"

Earl took several quick steps back. "Y—yes."

"I'm Lieutenant Prescott," the plainclothes officer said, whipping out an ID. "I'd like to have a little conversation with you. If you don't mind."

Ben groaned. Why did it have to be Prescott? The man was Mike's archenemy on the force, and for a reason. He was the most incompetent kiss-up ever to work his way onto the detective squad.

"What—what do you wanna talk about?" Earl asked.

"What do you think?" Prescott snapped. "The murder of Lily Campbell."

"But why me? I didn't kill no one."

"Well now, that ain't true, is it? You did twenty-two years for the murder of one George Armstrong."

Ben's eyes flew open to the widest extreme. "What!"

Prescott laid his arm on Earl's shoulder and lowered him into a chair. "Didn't think we'd find out, did you? Wrong. And as soon as we ran the M.O. through the computer and got the files out of storage, this case was over."

"But—that was different—"

"Was it? Allow me to refresh your memory."

With a sudden flourish, Prescott whipped out a black-and-white glossy photo. Ben didn't need a detailed explanation to realize this was a picture of a murder victim. He also didn't require an explanation to tell him what aspect of this victim most interested the police.

In the photo, the black male victim was stretched out across the floor, face up. His body and face had been horribly burned and disfigured. Despite the charred exterior, however, one aspect of the victim's appearance stood out immediately.

On the victim's face, someone had carved a broad, bright red smile.

* 15 *

"All right then," Prescott said, "now that we understand each other, let's talk turkey, okay?"

"But—I didn't kill Lily!"

"Really? Well, if you didn't, you should've." Prescott sat in the chair beside Earl and leaned forward, like they were two old chums having a little chat. "But if you didn't do it, you won't mind answerin' some questions, right?"

"I don't know nothin' about it."

"I know, I know. But you gotta admit—this murder looks a lot like the one you did time for."

Earl didn't respond.

"And you knew the lady—Lily Campbell. Didn't you?"

"I—did."

"Fact is—she was your girlfriend, wasn't she?"

Earl's mouth barely seemed to move. "A long long time ago."

"Right." He leaned even closer. " 'Cause she dumped you, didn't she?"

Earl gave him a curt nod.

"Well, I appreciate you clearin' all that up for me. Look—since you didn't do it, you won't mind if me and the boys take a look around your apartment, will you?"

Ben's jaw tightened. He knew Prescott's tactics all too well. First he'd play nice-nice, and get whatever he could out of Earl that way. Then he'd play the bad guy, and see what that produced. He'd wait till the last possible moment to arrest Earl, because as soon as he did that, he'd have to read Earl his rights, and all this amiable chitchat would likely end.

"So whaddaya say, Earl? Can we have a little looksee?"

"Jeez . . . that's hard to—"

"Whaddaya know. I just happen to have some consent forms with me." He whipped some papers out of his coat pocket. "Just sign here and we'll be able to go about our business."

Earl winced. "You want me to sign somethin'?"

"Sure, why not? You don't have anything to hide, do you?"

"Well, no, but—"

"Then there's no problemo." He handed Earl a pen. "Just sign on the dotted line."

Ben watched as Earl's hand hovered over the forms. He didn't want to get involved, but he couldn't just sit still and allow this travesty of justice to take place. "Earl, don't sign."

Earl looked up. "What?"

Prescott pressed his lips together. "Butt out, kid."

Ben stepped forward. "Earl, listen to me. Don't sign the forms."

Earl rose quickly, rubbing his hands together. "Maybe Ben's right. I think I'll be going now. I got work to do."

"You don't got jack shit." Prescott pressed himself under Earl's nose. "Listen to me and listen good, chump. You're going to answer our questions. Every single one of them. And you will tell the truth. And if you don't, we'll tear this place down around your ankles."

Ben felt his teeth clench. The "bad cop" had arrived. Prescott's whole routine was loathsome. Mike might be willing to put pressure on a witness to extract the truth, but Prescott was willing to ignore the law and violate rights just to make things a little easier for himself. The man would probably still be using thumbscrews if he thought he could get away with it.

"So don't give me any lip, understand, Bonner? *Understand?*"

Earl stood staring at Prescott, trembling, sweating bullets, blubbering without managing to actually say anything.

"All right, Bonner—come clean. Where's the knife?"

"The knife? But—I don't got—I mean—I—I got a butter knife in the kitchen. For makin' sandwiches—"

"Search the kitchen," Prescott barked to his assistant.

"Please," Earl pleaded pathetically, "I ain't done anything."

"Shut up, Bonner. Just answer the questions."

Ben felt his rage boiling. This was unforgivable. And unprofessional. And unnecessary. And . . .

And exactly why people need lawyers. But—

"C'mon, punk," Prescott growled. "Talk!"

"But—but—" Earl was practically in tears. "Can't I call—or, or—"

"*No!* You're under arrest!"

Ben couldn't stand it any longer. "Excuse me," he said, addressing Prescott. "Do you have a warrant?"

Earl glared at him. "Ben! Whatta you think you're doin'?"

"Who the hell are you?" Prescott barked.

"You haven't answered my question." Ben had learned the best response to hyperbolic bluster was to remain absolutely cool. "Do you have a warrant?"

Prescott steered Earl toward the door. "I'm not going to stand here and be interrogated by some idiot."

"I gather from that nonresponse that you don't. I assumed as much, since you tried to con Earl into signing consent forms. There are no exigent circumstances present, this arrest isn't based on evidence discovered at the scene, you haven't witnessed a felony, and you've bullied your way into the suspect's place of residence. You don't have the right to make a warrantless arrest, much less to abuse the suspect or search his home."

Earl's eyes were wide and worried. "Ben, we don't wanna make the man mad. Maybe you should just stay quiet."

"Yeah, maybe you should just stay quiet," Prescott

echoed, still shoving Earl toward the door. "I don't have to answer questions from you, punk."

It was now or never. "Actually, you do." Ben pulled out his wallet and flashed his OBA membership card. "My name's Ben Kincaid. I'm a lawyer."

Earl's eyes widened. "Ben! What you talkin' about?"

"I'm a member in good standing with the state bar. My bar number is 11756. You can check it out if you like." He paused. "You may remember me—I handled the Barrett case, which I believe you had some tangential involvement with. And now I'm representing Mr. Bonner."

Prescott raised a finger. "Kincaid," he whispered, his brain abuzz. "You're Morelli's friend."

"That's right. And I'm very familiar with the Tulsa authorized arrest procedures, none of which you're currently observing. If you don't back off immediately, I'll be lodging a formal complaint. You could end up on the bad end of a lawsuit, Prescott."

"Ben," Earl whispered, "stop foolin' around. You could get us into trouble."

"The lieutenant here is the one in trouble," Ben said. "He's been trampling all over your constitutional rights, apparently for no reason other than that he thought he could get away with it."

Prescott sneered. "You don't know what you're talking about."

"I know you attempted to interrogate my client without reading him his rights. I know you attempted to take him out of his domicile by force without a warrant, although you came here with the intent of making an arrest and had plenty of time to get a warrant. I know you told the sergeant to search his kitchen, also without a warrant. Basically, I'd say you totally screwed this prosecution before it even happened."

Ben and Prescott stared at each other for a protracted moment that seemed more like hours. Their eyes burned into each other's; neither one flinched.

"You know," Ben said, giving strong emphasis to each

word, "the best thing I had going for me on the Barrett case was the fact that you had totally bungled the pretrial investigation. Are you going to make the same mistake again?"

His lips pursed, Prescott spat out his reply. "This ain't over yet, Kincaid. Don't think it is."

Ben nodded. "We will anxiously await your return."

"You know, I heard you'd retired. Quit the lawyer game for something respectable."

"I guess the reports of my death were premature." Ben glanced at Earl. "Are you all right?"

Earl was still too flustered to speak coherently. "Well . . . yeah. I mean, I guess. But—"

Ben held up his hand. "My advice is that you don't say a word in the presence of these officers. Although Lieutenant Prescott failed to mention it, you have the right to remain silent, and you should exercise it."

Earl buttoned his lip.

Prescott looked as if he'd just sucked acid. "You haven't accomplished anything here. We'll get a warrant, and we'll be back. All you've done is make us jump through some hoops."

"Those hoops are there for a reason," Ben muttered.

"Oh yeah? And what's that?"

"To protect people from assholes like you."

Prescott ground his teeth together so hard Ben thought he might pop a filling. He pressed himself back under Earl's nose. "We'll be back." He grunted to his two accomplices, then bolted out the door.

Earl turned toward Ben, his eyes wide with amazement. "But—you mean—how—"

Ben waved Earl back into the living room. "Earl, I think it's time we had a little talk."

* 16 *

Ben spent the first fifteen minutes of their meeting just establishing the essentials: that he really was a bona fide barrister, and that it hadn't all been an elaborate con to keep Earl out of jail.

Earl's face was the picture of mystification. "But if you're this hotshot lawyer and all, what're you doin' here?"

"I decided to give up my practice."

"You gave up bein' a lawyer so's you could tickle ivory in a jazz club?"

Ben tried not to squirm. "Not exactly. The point is, I am a lawyer. If you want me to help, I will. Or I'll help you find another lawyer, if you prefer. It's up to you."

"Looks like I need help bad, huh?"

Ben was inclined to agree. "Why don't you tell me what this is all about?"

"But you were here when it happened."

"I don't mean last night. I mean twenty-two years ago. That charcoaled corpse with the carved-on smile."

Earl winced. Ben could see these were extremely unpleasant memories he was dredging up, not that that was any great surprise. "It's been so long ago. I'd hoped I'd finally put all this behind me."

"I'm sorry," Ben said. "But I think it's necessary."

"All right then." Earl let himself collapse into the chair behind his desk. "You remember yesterday when I mentioned Professor Hoodoo?"

103

Ben nodded. "The greatest sax player in the Southwest. Before he died."

"That's the one." His eyes went down toward the carpet. "That was Professor Hoodoo you saw in that black-and-white glossy the cop was wavin' 'round."

"That was—" Ben stopped himself. "What happened to him?"

Earl shrugged. "I still dunno. But I did twenty-two years hard time for it."

Ben's lips parted. "For murder?"

"Right the first time."

"But you said—"

"And I meant it. I didn't kill the man. But they nailed me to the wall for it, jus' the same. Put me away for first-degree murder."

"But that picture—"

"Burned from head to toe. In his own apartment. There wasn't much left."

"Except—"

"Yeah. Except." Ben knew what they were both thinking. Except for that hideous smile. The same smile someone carved on Lily Campbell. Small wonder Prescott came after Earl. Who would ever dream that two different murderers could have the same horrible M.O.?

"How long had you known this . . . Professor Hoodoo?"

Earl almost smiled. "Oh, forever. Jus' about, anyway. George and me'd grown up on the chitlin' circuit together." He shook his head. "You know, I was good, but George was—well, he was Professor Hoodoo. He was the best."

"He played sax, just like you, right?"

"Right. 'Cept, when the Professor blew, the whole world held its breath and gaped in stupefaction. People loved him."

"Then why—?"

"Did he get killed? Don't ask me."

"Did he have any enemies?"

"In a way. You have to understand about George. He didn't have what you'd call a winnin' personality. And there was a reason. He'd had a major-league-tough child-hood. His brother was the only friend he ever had. His mom was a prostitute. His dad—one of her johns, originally—was the meanest son of a bitch who ever lived. You can't imagine what it's like, having a father who always disap-proves, always criticizes, always has something mean to say, acts like he thinks you're the worst worm who ever crawled out of the sludge."

Ben didn't bother to correct him.

"It makes a man insecure. And it makes him afraid. 'Fraid he's doin' somethin' wrong. 'Fraid he's doin' some-thin' he shouldn't. He ends up livin' his whole life tryin' to make the fear go away. But it never does." He paused, and his eyes turned inward, not seeing but remembering. "George tried to work his way into the right circles, meet the right set. And he had some success with it. Became the world-famous Professor Hoodoo. Things really started happenin' for him. He met some highbrow high-society types. And he met some lowbrow lowlifes, too. They kept the jazz world hoppin' in those days—gangsters, fixers, pushers. All the wrong sorts of friends for a man like George."

"Surely he got some satisfaction out of his music. After he became a success."

Earl shook his head slowly back and forth. "Didn't matter who George met, who he hung out with. It was never enough. Never, never enough. No matter who he was with, he always ended up alone."

"That's a shame," Ben said quietly. "Everyone should have someone."

"All George had was his music. He gave it everythin', and it gave him everythin' back. Everythin' it had, any-way. Which wasn't enough."

"Why did they accuse you of—"

"Of offin' the Professor? Wrong place at the wrong time, son. Story of my life."

"I'm sorry, but I'm going to need some details."

Earl took a deep breath. "We were makin' the rounds,

playin' a gig together. Little club not too far from here. I was havin' a great run—I was in the zone, as they say, firin' on all engines. I'd come up with a few new tunes that really worked wonders for me. I was gettin' applause like I'd never heard before."

"That sounds great."

"Great for me, yes. For the Professor, no. He was a genius, son, but like most geniuses, he was selfish and insecure. When I started gettin' popular, he saw it as a threat. And that led to trouble."

"What happened?"

"George had been in brawls before, usually for the stupidest reasons. Sometimes I thought he wanted to be hurt, maybe even wanted to die. But he'd never picked one with me before. Not till that night, anyway."

"He started a fight?"

"You got it. Right onstage. Hell, I didn't want to squabble with the man. I didn't like that scenario from the jump. But what could I do?"

"He started a fight—just because you were getting rave reviews?"

"Well . . . that wasn't the only thing."

Ben looked at him sternly. "Earl, if I'm going to represent you, you need to tell me everything."

Earl's lips thinned. "I 'spect you've guessed already. What else would we fight about? A woman."

"Lily Campbell?"

"You are a smart fellow, ain't you, Ben? Why didn't I notice that before?" He grinned, then returned to his story. "Lily was a hot number on the club circuit. Considered very high-tone. An up-and-comer. George had been tryin' to date her for years, and to everyone's surprise, he finally had some success. It was never as serious as he liked to think it was, at least not to her. She was a good-time girl, with a wild streak the size of the Grand Canyon. She liked bein' seen with the famed Professor Hoodoo, but not so much that she stopped messin' around with some of the other boys. Includin' me."

"And George didn't like that."

"No, he didn't care for that one little bit. 'Specially when he caught the two of us buck naked in the orchestra pit. He kept it pent up for a while, but for some reason, when he and I came out onstage that night, somethin' happened. I dunno—maybe it was too much better livin' through chemistry. It was like a trigger went off inside his brain. He just exploded."

"There was a fight?"

"Like you never saw before. We were like prizefighters up there, trying to smash each other's brains out. Right up where everyone could see. The other boys in the band tried to break us up, and next thing you knew, they were fightin', too. Some of the audience joined in and—well, it was a right regular brawl. Cops had to come out to break the mess up. But they did break it up, and everyone cooled off, and we all went home. It was over. Or so I thought, anyway."

"What happened next?"

"What happened was—the next morning, George Armstrong turned up burned to a crispy critter and dead as vaudeville. And about a thousand witnesses recalled seein' me onstage punchin' his lights out, shoutin' that if he didn't leave me alone I—" Earl paused.

"You'd kill him?"

Earl nodded grimly. "Those were my unfortunate words. I didn't mean it, of course—not like that, anyway. But all those witnesses didn't know that. All they knew was I threatened George, beat him up—and the next day he was dead."

"You said he had a self-destructive streak. Maybe he killed himself."

"The thought occurred. But in such a horrible way? In a fire? No, I jus' can't believe it. He may have wanted pain, maybe even needed it. But no one needs it so much they set themselves on fire. It ain't human. And besides, he couldn'ta carved that smile on his own face. It was murder, no two ways about it."

"So the police arrested you."

"Did they ever!"

"And the jury found you guilty. I'm surprised you only got twenty-two years."

"Well, you see, Ben . . ." He swallowed. "Truth is, there was no trial."

"What?"

"There was no trial . . . 'cause I copped a plea."

Ben stared at him wordlessly.

"It seemed smart at the time. The lawyer they gave me told me it was the best thing I could do for myself."

"But you said you were innocent!"

"I was. But everyone on God's green earth thought I was guilty. And what with that big fight and all—well, it just didn't look too good. I thought I'd get convicted murder one, and if that happened—"

"You'd get the death penalty."

"A black man in a white town? You know it. The jury would probably be all white. I'd be a goner." He pressed his two huge fists together. "As far as I could see, my choice was simple. Either plead innocent and die, or plead guilty, do some time, and have a life."

"After twenty-two years."

"Yeah. Twenty-two very long goddamn years. And they wouldn't let me blow my stick the whole time. Not once in all those years I was in the joint. That's why I don't play no more, see. It ain't that I don't want to. It's that I can't. I lost it. Twenty-two years was way too long to go without makin' music. Whatever I had, I lost."

Ben felt a horrible aching in the pit of his stomach. What a loss—an irreplaceable loss.

"When I got out of stir, I pulled together everything I had, called in some markers, and bought this place. Maybe I couldn't play the music anymore, but at least I could surround myself with it." He smiled slightly. "You know what they say. Those who can, do. Those who can't, buy a club."

Ben knew he ought to say something, but the words escaped him. He kept dwelling on the loss, what his life would be like if one day the music was all gone, irretrievably gone. It was beyond measure. He couldn't really conceive of it. All he could do was wallow in the horror of the thought.

He snapped himself out of it, forcing himself back into his investigator role. "Did you and Lily stay together?"

"Aw, hell, no. Soon as the cops got their grubby fingers on me, she was out of there. I never heard a thing from her till she called me up a couple days ago."

"What did she say?"

"She was in town for a few days and heard through the grapevine that I had a club. Said she'd like to see it." He paused. "Said she'd like to see me. I knew it was stupid to get my hopes up, after about a million years and all this weight I put on while I was trapped in my closet-sized cell in McAlester. But of course, I did anyway."

"You were waiting for her last night."

"I was expectin' her to turn up, yeah. But not like she did." His words became tight and bitter. "Not fallin' like a sack of potatoes off the goddamn light. Not shriveled and cold and with that sick smile cut onto her face." His head lifted, and Ben saw that his eyes were glistening. "She had such a beautiful smile when she was alive. Everyone said so. But now, I'll never be able to remember that, never be able to remember her the way she was. Now when I think of her, all I can remember is that grotesque blood-red desecration. That's all I—I—" His head fell into his hands.

Ben stared at him helplessly. Twenty-two years. And now, just when a little hope had been held out to him, someone snatched it away, replacing it with an all-new horror.

He had to figure out some way to help this poor man. He just had to.

"Well, that's probably enough for now." Ben laid his hand gently on Earl's shoulder. "If you want me to help,

Earl, I'll help. We'll fight this. I won't let them railroad you again."

"You think those cops'll be back?"

"Yeah. Given the similarity between this murder and the one you pled guilty to, and given that you were at the scene of last night's murder, and given that Lieutenant Prescott is arrogant, obnoxious, but extremely tenacious . . . I think you can count on it."

"How long do I have? Days?"

Ben shook his head. "Hours."

Earl's head bowed. "That's what I thought. You really think you can help me?"

"I can't guarantee results, but I can promise that I'll do everything possible to make sure these charges don't get you another twenty-two in McAlester."

"But that ain't all, Ben. I want to know who did this. I want the sick SOB who's torturin' me like this, who cut up my beautiful Lily."

"I'll do my best."

"You find him, Ben. You find him. And when you do . . ." Earl raised his eyes toward the ceiling. "God help the bastard."

* 17 *

Tyrone sat as quietly as the proverbial church mouse. He wanted to say something, he really did. But how could he?

He hated watching Earl squirm, hated watching that jerkoff cop play with Earl's head. Earl meant more to him than anyone. He'd been like a father to him—far more than his own father, who he'd only seen twice. He had no complaints against his mother; she'd worked like nobody's business her whole life, typing for the city during the day and cleaning houses at night. But with all that work and six kids to tend, there was little time for one-on-one with her next-to-youngest. When he dropped out of school after the eighth grade and got a job, she could hardly say no. Education was great, but they needed the money.

Small wonder he fell in with the North Side Hoover Crips, one of the hottest gangs on the Tulsa strip. Everyone he knew was doing it; it was the place to be. The organization was pretty loose; it was more like a family than the Mafia. But he needed a family. For the first time in his life, he felt a part of something, felt surrounded by people who cared about him. And it brought him some cash on the side every now and again, something else he sorely needed. It was a great deal, at least till that cop died in a shoot-out near Earl's club.

Tyrone hadn't been the one who pulled the trigger, but he was there. And he was smart enough to realize that he could be called an accomplice, that he could be nailed for felony murder, that the cops would consider it a pleasure to put away another punk gangster. When cops got killed, no holds were barred.

Tyrone pushed himself to his feet and walked outside. Gazing north from the club, he could see the site where the shoot-out had occurred, where his life had changed. It was a miracle Tyrone hadn't been arrested at the scene. He'd gotten his leg busted up during the fight. When the cops descended and everyone scattered, he could barely crawl, much less run. He thought it was all over for him when to his total amazement, Uncle Earl came out of nowhere and dragged his crippled carcass inside the club. Tyrone'd never met this man in his life. And yet here he was, sticking his neck out for him, protecting him.

"Why?" he asked Earl later. "Why did you do this for me?" But Earl just shrugged his shoulders and said he'd seen a spot of trouble in his life, too, and he didn't want a kid's life ruined over something he didn't do. Something about the way he said it told Tyrone this was important to him, something he believed, something that really mattered.

In the aftermath of the shooting, three of his gang buddies were arrested, two at the scene and another later. Two of the arrested boys got life sentences; and Hopper, the trigger man, got an appointment with a lethal injection. Tyrone knew perfectly well the same thing could have happened to him. Earl had done more than just pull him out of trouble. He'd saved Tyrone's life.

Tyrone strolled back to the club, walked up the spiral staircase to Earl's office, and picked up the saxophone that was always there. He put the stick to his lips and blew. The note came out sharp, harsh, and flat. Like usual.

He placed Earl's sax back on its stand. After the cop-killing, the Crips didn't seem like such a cozy little family anymore. That was when Tyrone first started thinking about getting out. All of a sudden, he didn't like Tyrone Jackson—T-Dog—so much; he wanted to be someone other than who he was, someone he'd never been before.

But getting out was easier to think about than to do. The Crips didn't like quitters. They didn't like people who knew too much about them leaving the fold. As soon as he announced his desire to quit, he found that his oldest and best friends weren't all that friendly anymore. And as soon as he left, he heard rumors that some of the boys might be looking for him. He'd heard that Momo wanted to have what the Crips euphemistically referred to as a "chat." He was in trouble.

And then he tumbled onto the con game. He'd been panhandling downtown one day, not having much luck, when all of a sudden, without even thinking about it, he began weaving this elaborate tale about his sister (he didn't have one) being taken captive by militant states' righters holed up near Tahlequah and trying to raise money to rescue and deprogram her. He was just spinning the tale out of nothing, spouting whatever came into his head.

But the mark had tossed him a fifty-dollar bill. Hadn't said a word. Just tossed it into Tyrone's can and that was that.

That day Tyrone realized he had found his calling. For the first time in his life, he had discovered something at which he excelled. Problem was, he felt miserable about it. After every successful sting, he was consumed with guilt. It seemed his mama and all those Baptist Sunday school classes she had dragged him to had left their mark.

It was one day when he was working the bus station that he hit on the idea of scamming the scammers. They were easy to spot—easy for him, anyway. He knew all their routines intimately. And one could hardly lose much sleep over ripping off someone who was, after all, trying to rip you off. It worked perfectly; he'd been doing it ever since.

But he didn't plan to be doing it forever, he thought, peering down at Earl's sax. To him, the sax was a symbol, a promise of better things to come. Someday he wanted to live an honest life, a life he could go home and tell his mama about. Earl had said that first day he pulled Tyrone off the battlefield that he thought he could make a musician out of him. It just took time, that was all. So this con man bit was temporary, just until he learned the sax well enough to play in the band. Once he could do that, he would leave all the scamming behind. When the day came, he knew Earl would give him a job.

If Earl could give him a job, that is. If he wasn't behind bars. Or worse.

That was what hurt most. He hated seeing Earl get the treatment, but he also knew that if Earl took the rap for this killing, it would mean no more sax access, no more free lessons, no more job prospects. Nor more chance of digging himself out.

He left the office, suddenly edgy. It was almost as if he didn't have the right to be there, didn't have the right to touch Earl's belongings. Why didn't he speak up when he'd had the chance? He'd seen that creep in the bathroom, the one with the knife. Maybe not well enough to identify him. What with the fake beard and all the excitement, the man coulda been his dear old dad for all he knew. But he knew it wasn't Earl. Earl was being set up. It didn't take a genius to figure out that okeydoke.

And yet when the police had questioned Tyrone, he hadn't said a word. And just now, when a word from him might have bailed Earl out of trouble, he stayed mum.

Why? Tyrone knew there were at least two outstanding warrants on him, one stemming from the cop killing and one stemming from a con that went bad, a mark that had the wherewithal to file a complaint. If he got involved with the police, he could count on having charges brought against him. And charges like those could lead to a long stretch behind bars.

And so he sat by silently while those creeps humiliated his only friend in the world. Good thing Kincaid was there; for a mediocre piano player, he seemed to be able to handle cops. Tyrone was glad for that.

He flopped down on a stool. He knew damn well those cops would be back, knew they'd make the arrest as soon as possible. How long was he going to let Earl dangle in the breeze without saying anything? Forever? Was he going to sit on his butt and do nothing? Let Earl spend the rest of his life in the joint, doing forever-and-one years?

Hell of a way to thank a man who had done so much for him. Who had stuck his own neck out to help a kid he didn't even know.

But no matter how long Tyrone pondered, he couldn't think of a way out. It was like a game of checkers where your last piece was covered in all four directions; no matter what he did, he was going to get jumped.

Tyrone whirled around on his stool and kicked the chair behind him, cursing silently under his breath. Why was life always such a bitch?

He sat on the back porch staring at the Tulsa skyline as the orange sun dipped below the horizon. Here, perched at the crest of Shadow Mountain, he was able to gaze down into the surrounding city and watch all the bustle. He could see everyone. And no one could see him.

He liked it that way.

He flipped on the radio, checking the news update on KWGS. No new developments on the case the whole city was talking about, the one with the very special victim. It went by various names, depending on the lurid-ness and schlock factor of the given station. One channel was calling it "The Case of the Cordial Corpse." Hell, what was next—the Sensational Smiling Stiff?

He had to laugh; who would have expected the deceased to become a media celebrity? But it was all the news folks had at the moment; it was all they could use to exploit this bit of grisliness. Because thus far there had been no arrest.

He pounded his fist down on the end table. What was wrong with the justice system these days? Here he'd gone to all this trouble, setting Earl up with a frame so strong even a blind man could see it, and they hadn't arrested him yet. Good God, what did it take these days, a live video of the murder? Cops were so stupid it was easier to get away with murder than to get convicted of it. What was the world coming to?

He shut off the radio. Perhaps he was expecting too much too soon. Still, it was troubling. When he thought of all the meticulous preparations—well, it just didn't seem fair. After all the risks he'd taken. The risk of being caught, the risk of being seen—

A risk that was realized, he reminded himself. Because he *was* seen. Because that stupid punk in the bathroom got a clear look at his face after the wig and beard were removed. If he started blabbing to the wrong people . . .

So far, miraculously, he had escaped detection. But he couldn't count on this state of grace lasting forever. The risk had to be neutralized. The discordant note had to be silenced. That kid was the fly in the ointment, the instrument out of groove.

The melody had to be sweetened, so to speak.

The kid had to be eliminated.

Problem was, he didn't know where to find the kid. And it would be hard to start making inquiries without provoking undesirable attention.

Well, something would turn up. He was sure of it. He'd made it this far, hadn't he? Even when plans went sour, when unexpected developments arose, he'd managed to deal with them. Managed to overcome them. And he would again. That was the difference between Earl and himself. He was smart, and he knew what was really important and what wasn't.

Tomorrow he would start trolling, cruise the streets of the North Side, see if he couldn't tumble onto that kid. He'd keep an eye on the club, too. And since Earl was still inexplicably on the streets, maybe when he popped the kid . . .

An ear-to-ear grin spread across his face, almost as wide as the one he had carved the day before. That would work That would be damned sweet. That would give him something worth living for.

Still smiling, he picked up his instrument and began to play. The lilting jazz riffs floated off his porch and drifted down to the city below that had no idea what was coming.

* 18 *

Ben was not exactly surprised when he heard the thunderous pounding on the front door of Uncle Earl's Jazz Emporium. He was surprised, however, when he opened the door and found a friend standing on the other side.

"Mike!" Ben said. "What are you doing here?"

"We've come to make an arrest, Ben. May we come in?"

Ben nodded and stepped aside, making way for Mike Morelli, two uniforms, and a silent, sulking Lieutenant Prescott.

"I didn't think you handled arrests yourself."

"Normally I don't," Mike said, thrusting his hands deep in the pockets of his trench coat. "But I'm still in charge of the Homicide Department. When one of my men tells me his arrest has been thwarted, I get involved."

Ben stepped between his friend and Prescott. "Look, Mike, I don't know what the good lieutenant told you, but he breezed in with no warrant, didn't read Earl his rights, and basically came on like he'd cut the man's tongue out if he didn't spill his guts."

"That's a filthy lie," Prescott barked.

"Like hell," Ben replied. "I'm surprised you didn't bring a rubber hose."

Prescott started to respond, but Mike cut him off with a gesture. "Don't even start, you two. It doesn't matter what happened before. We're starting from scratch." He withdrew a folded piece of paper from his coat pocket. "We have a warrant."

118

"Based on what? That Earl happened to be here when the body was found?"

"There's more evidence against Earl than that, Ben. And there doesn't seem to be any exculpatory evidence suggesting that he didn't commit the crime. We have more than enough to justify an arrest."

"I'll want the arraignment held as soon as possible."

"Understood."

"And the preliminary hearing. I think we can beat this rap."

"You can take that up with the judge."

"And I'll ask the court to set bail."

Prescott made a snorting noise, but Mike remained placid. "You're always free to ask. Now where is he?"

Ben leaned up the spiral staircase that led to Earl's office. "Come on out, Earl."

Earl had changed his clothes and combed his hair and generally groomed himself. It was obvious that this time he was ready to travel.

"Thank you for your cooperation," Mike said.

Earl held out his hands. "I suppose you'll want to cuff me."

"It's departmental procedure," Mike said. "Prescott, read him his rights."

"But—"

"*Do* it."

His lips pursed, Prescott pulled a card out of his shirt pocket and began to read.

While Earl was being Mirandized, Ben saw the young boy he had met earlier entering the club. He stopped several paces from the cops, then turned and ran.

Obviously not a kid who liked rubbing shoulders with police officers, Ben noted. He wondered if Tyrone Jackson's ties with the Crips had been severed as completely as he had intimated.

To his surprise, the kid stopped at the door. He hesitated, obviously deliberating. After a more than a minute had passed, he slowly made his way back to the center of the club.

"What's going on?" Tyrone asked.

"Earl's being arrested," Ben said quietly.

"For what?"

"For the murder. Yesterday. Lily Campbell."

"But—"

"I know. We're going to do everything possible for him."

"But—"

Mike cocked up one eyebrow. "But what?"

"Why him?"

Prescott sneered. "Because we think he did it, that's why."

"But—"

A deep crease lined Mike's forehead. "Kid, if you have something to say, say it. If you don't, get out of the way."

"I—but—" Whatever was on the boy's mind, he didn't seem able to spit it out.

Mike's eyes narrowed. "You know, you look familiar."

The kid turned away. "I shouldn't. I'm new in town. I don't know anybody."

"Right."

"I'm not a suspect. I don't have to answer any questions. Can I go?"

Mike frowned. "I suppose." Tyrone skittered toward the door. "C'mon, Earl, you're going downtown."

"Say goodbye to this pretty club of yours," Prescott added. "You may never see it again."

Once again, Tyrone froze. "Now why is that?"

" 'Cause once he's charged with capital murder, he ain't likely to be set free for no amount of money. And once he's been convicted, he ain't gonna see nothin' but a cell. Followed by a coffin."

Tyrone turned away. Ben had the clear impression that he wanted to say something. But whatever it was, it wasn't coming out.

He checked Mike—he was watching the kid too. Ben knew Mike was biding his time, hoping Tyrone would talk.

"C'mon," Mike growled, grabbing Earl by the shoulder. "We've got things to do."

"Look"—Tyrone squeezed his eyes shut—"you've got the wrong man."

Another snort from Prescott. "Like hell."

"It's true. He didn't do it."

Mike took a step toward Tyrone. "And how do you know that?"

"I just know, okay?"

"How?" Mike got so close to Tyrone they could swap carbon dioxide. "Is this a confession?"

"No—I—" He hung his head.

"You know, Morelli," Prescott said, "I think maybe we should bring this one in, too."

"No!" Tyrone exclaimed. "That's exactly what—" He stopped, then threw himself dejectedly into a chair.

"Look, kid," Mike said, "just tell us what you know. In the long run, it'll be for the best."

Tyrone let out a long sigh. His face reflected the conflicts and contradictions he was weighing. Finally, he spoke: "It wasn't Earl. It was the clown in the fake 'fro."

Ben stepped forward, keenly interested. Of course, he had considered the rug man a suspect. But what did this kid know?

"The rug guy?" Mike asked. "Bushy hair? Beard? So tall?"

"No," Tyrone said, his face in his hands. "That's where you've got it all wrong. You go lookin' for some chump with an Afro, you're gonna fail."

"How do you know that?"

"Because he was wearing a wig. And since no one else has worn a 'fro for the last twenty years or so, you're gonna come up empty-handed."

"Did you see the killer?"

"I think so. I mean, I didn't know he was a killer at the time. I didn't know there *was* a killer at the time."

"But you saw someone in a wig."

"Right. Watched him take off the wig. Watched him taking off the fake beard, too."

Mike made a note. "Where?"

"In the men's room." Tyrone laughed awkwardly. "Hell, I thought he was some kind of drag queen or cross-dresser. But then he saw me lookin' at him, and he got all bent out of shape. Started walking toward me like he was gonna kill me. And he was hiding something under his shirt. I think it was a knife."

"You saw—" Mike scribbled furiously in his notepad. "Why didn't you tell us this before?"

"I"—Tyrone looked away—"I didn't want to get involved."

"What's your name, kid?"

"I don't have to answer that."

"The hell you don't. You're a material witness, now. You talk to me here or I'll haul you downtown and you'll talk to me there. *Capisce?*"

He swallowed. "My name's . . . Tyrone. Tyrone Jackson."

Mike's eyes went fuzzy, as if he was trying to dredge up an association buried deep in some fold of his memory. The light slowly dawned. "You're wanted for something, aren't you? That's why you didn't want to talk."

"I don't know what you mean."

"You knew we'd want to question you, take your prints, run your name through the computer." Mike nodded. "I think I understand now. C'mon, Prescott. Let's get out of here."

"What? You mean—we aren't takin' Earl in?"

Mike shrugged. "We have a witness who places another suspect at the scene of the crime with a weapon."

"You don't believe him, do you? You should arrest 'em both!"

"I'm not going to make any half-cocked arrests that'll only blow up in my face later. Frankly, Prescott, I wasn't very impressed by your case in the first place, but at least there was no other likely suspect. Now, with this kid's tes-

timony, which Mr. Kincaid is certain to put on at the preliminary hearing, I'm not even sure we have enough to
bind the man over for trial. We need time to check this
kid's story."

"You can't just let this punk go! He killed someone!"

"If he did, we'll prove it. In the meantime, I'm not
going to bring charges that won't stick."

Prescott's fists balled up. "The Chief won't like this. He
said he wanted an arrest, pronto."

"I'm not going to waste the city's resources bringing
charges I know will be dismissed just so I can go on the
evening news and complain about how the justice system
doesn't work and judges coddle criminals. First we do our
job. Then we make an arrest."

"But—but—"

"You heard me. We're leaving." Without another word,
Mike walked briskly out of the office, followed by the two
officers.

Prescott whirled on Ben. "We'll be back, Kincaid. Don't
doubt it." On his way out, he leaned close to Tyrone. "And
next time we'll be coming for you, too." He slammed the
door behind him.

"Thank God that's over." Ben turned toward Tyrone.
"You and I have a few things to discuss."

Tyrone's eyes darted from side to side. "You think it's
true? What that blowhard said, I mean. About them comin'
back for me?"

Ben nodded. "You can count on it."

* 19 *

At eight that evening, Ben was still at the club, barely making a dent in the mess. Most of the staff had gone home some time ago; Earl and Tyrone were up in Earl's office commiserating.

"Why don't you go on home, Ben?" Diane said. "It's late."

"What, and leave you with this pit to clean up?"

"Hey, it falls in the stage manager's job description, not the piano player's." She smiled, causing her cheeks to crinkle up and spread the spikes of her hairdo. "You have to be careful. Might sprain a finger or something."

He checked his watch. "Well, I was hoping to get home by nine; NPR's broadcasting a live John Prine concert. I'll be back tomorrow to help."

Diane shrugged. "It's your funeral."

Ben was almost out the door when someone shouted at him from behind the bar. "You've got a call, Ben."

Ben scrambled to the phone. "Hello?"

"Benjamin! You gotta come! He's killing her!"

Ben's hand gripped the phone receiver tightly. "Who? What? Who is this?"

"Benjamin! He's beating her to death!"

"Who *is* this?"

"You've got to come quickly! He's killing her!"

Ben listened carefully to the voice. "Mrs. Marmelstein, is this you?"

"Of course it is! What are you going to do about Christina?"

"Christina?" His jaw tightened. "Tell me exactly what's going on. Start at the beginning."

She spoke in short broken gasps, never more than a few words at a time. "Your friend Christina called. She's in trouble."

"But why would she call you?"

"Would you listen to me? He's beating her up!"

"Who is?"

"I don't know his name. Her ex-husband."

"Ray? The dentist?"

"She was screaming, Benjamin! Crying! I could hear him hitting her!"

None of this made sense, but he was wasting valuable time trying to pry information out of her. "Where is she?"

"At her place."

"I'm going right there. Can you call the police?"

"Yes. 911."

"Right. Do it." Ben slammed down the receiver and raced out the door. He was out of the club in ten seconds, had his van started in thirty.

Fortunately, rush hour was long over, so there was not much traffic on the Broken Arrow Expressway. There was, however, construction work in progress, and it added several minutes to his trip.

As he bobbed in and around the construction cones, Ben punched in Christina's number on his car phone. He had laughed when Mike had first suggested that he get a car phone for his new van. It seemed like a frivolous nineties bit of frippery to him, but Mike had insisted it was a security issue—you don't want to be trapped on a dark, lonely road with no way to call AAA when your car breaks down. At the moment, Ben was glad he had it.

The phone rang, but no one answered. *Blast!*

Ben banged his steering wheel, as if that might make the rerouted traffic move faster. Finally he exited onto Harvard and barreled south toward Christina's apartment.

He parked his car on the street outside and ran to the front door, on which he pounded, but there was no answer.

Shades were drawn over the front windows; he couldn't see what, if anything, was going on inside.

Damn! The whole thing didn't make sense. But if Christina was in there, and she had been beaten, she might be unable to come to the door. She could be unconscious, bleeding—even dying.

He had to try something. There was a fence that divided the front of the apartments, and Ben knew Christina's place had a back screen door that faced out on the other side. He had told her a million times to keep that door locked, but she almost never did. If he could get over there . . .

Fortunately, the fence was not too high, only about six feet. He jumped up and grabbed the top with both hands, then hoisted himself over. He flopped down on the other side, landing on both feet. Not bad for an amateur, he thought. He ran around the corner and made it to the back sliding door.

Yes! It was unlocked. Good thing she never heeded his advice. He'd scold her later; today it was a godsend. He threw open the door and raced inside and saw—

Nothing.

No one was there. There were no signs of a struggle, no overturned chairs or tables. No blood on the white shag carpet. He checked the back bedroom and bath, the kitchen, even the closets. It was all the same.

There had been no brawl, no beating.

It had never made any sense. Christina might not speak all that kindly about Ray, but she'd never suggested that he'd been violent to her. And Christina could handle herself pretty well, as he'd seen in any number of situations. All things considered, she was more likely to beat Ray to a pulp than the other way around.

Ben sat down on the sofa and stared into the gilt mirror hanging on the opposite wall just above Christina's display of French memorabilia. Two possibilities shouted out to him. Either Mrs. Marmelstein was playing a cruel prank . . . or Mrs. Marmelstein was losing her mind.

Unfortunately, she had never been much of a prankster.

Ben rubbed his face. Even when the doctors had determined that she had Alzheimer's, he'd thought they could cope with it without much adjustment. But this was different. Hallucinating violent events that never happened, never even came close to happening. He had to face facts.

Her mind was slipping. Fast.

He pushed himself off the sofa and exited through the back sliding door. Poor Mrs. Marmelstein. Through it all, she had always been sweet and good-hearted. She may have periodically feigned her disapproval of Ben, but he knew that in truth she was one of his greatest supporters, someone he could always count on for a kind and caring word. And she knew he had been there when she needed someone. She knew he had taken care of her.

But Ben couldn't take care of this. He couldn't be with her all the time, preventing her from hurting herself or making panicked phone calls in the middle of the night. He had a job, a career. The band was planning to go on the road. He couldn't babysit his landlady all the time.

He jumped up, grabbed the top of the fence, and swung his legs over. He had flopped onto the other side and was just about to scramble down when he heard the staccato static of the police radio.

"Suspect is male, thin, about five foot five with brown hair, balding slightly in the back . . ."

Ben released his grip on the fence and dropped to the ground.

"*Freeze!* Hands in the air!"

Ben threw up his hands. He whirled around and saw three police cars, red sirens swirling. Officers flanked each car, their guns extended over the open car doors, ready to fire given the slightest provocation.

"I can explain," Ben said meekly.

"Of course you can," the officer in front growled as he reached for his cuffs.

Ben suspected he was not going to make it home in time for the John Prine concert.

* * *

It was almost midnight before he managed to convince the Tulsa Police Department, Central Division, that he was neither a cat burglar nor Ray, the ex-husband from hell. Mike had dropped by during the interrogation, mostly just to make fun, but he had at least put in a good word.

"Has your landlady made calls like this before?" they asked.

"No. Well, not that I know of."

"This kind of behavior could be dangerous," one of his interrogators said earnestly. "People could get hurt, including her. She needs someone watching her."

"I know."

They finally let him go with a stern warning about the dangers of breaking into apartments, even your friends', and after extracting a promise that Ben would try to keep Mrs. Marmelstein out of trouble.

He staggered home. What was this, the third night in a week, home after midnight? It was getting old.

He stopped outside Mrs. Marmelstein's door. Normally he wouldn't knock at this hour, but he saw the light was on under the door. He tapped gently.

"Come in," she said.

Ben pushed the door open and entered. She was sitting in her rocker recliner, an array of sepia-toned photographs in her lap.

"Are you all right?"

"I'm fine, thank you," she said, sniffing.

"You're up late."

"What are you talking about? I just got up."

He didn't bother to correct her. "Can we talk about that phone call you made this evening?"

"What phone call?" She picked up another photo. She seemed to be arranging them into separate piles, although what the distinctions were Ben couldn't tell.

"The one you made to me. At the club. About Christina and her ex-husband."

"I don't know what you're talking about." She continued her sorting.

"Mrs. Marmelstein, you did call me."

"Have I ever shown you this photo?" She looked up for the first time, her face bright and sunny, but still a pale reflection of the Mrs. Marmelstein that Ben had known so well. "Daniel and I were at the beach on Long Island. That was before we moved to Tulsa. Before Daniel invested in the oil industry."

Ben took the photograph from her. It was at least fifty years old. It showed the two of them, so much younger they were like different people, wearing old-fashioned bathing suits and sitting under a huge beach umbrella. Two people from another world.

"I should probably go to bed," Ben said.

"Now? But we just got up."

Ben sighed. "Mrs. Marmelstein, how would you feel if . . . well, if you went to live somewhere else?"

"Somewhere else? What do you mean?"

"You could live where people would help you, take care of things."

Mrs. Marmelstein gave him a sharp, unhappy look.

"Well, we'll talk about it in the—later." He kissed her on the forehead, then left the room and closed the door behind him.

A gloom had settled over him that he couldn't seem to shake. He thought about playing the piano a bit, or listening to a Christine Lavin CD, but somehow he wasn't in the mood. He fed Giselle, guzzled half a quart of chocolate milk straight out of the carton, and climbed into bed.

He tried to clear his head of the events of the day, the unresolved issues. He tried to forget it all so he could relax and sleep. Tomorrow was another day, he reminded himself. I'll solve everyone's problems then.

Eventually his eyelids drooped shut.

And then flew open. *Who's* balding slightly in the back?

* 20 *

First thing next morning, Ben drove south and parked beside the tree-lined sidewalks of Warren Place. He couldn't help but marvel as he stepped into the glass-enclosed elevator in the ritzy main office building. This was a first-rate office facility, far nicer than the dump he had operated out of downtown. Ben knew that Jones and Loving had taken office space, but he had no idea they might be able to get—or be able to afford—anything half as nice as this.

He stepped inside the elevator and pressed 7. How is it, he wondered, that he had practiced law in a dump for years, most of the time barely making enough to pay the rent, and now these two nonprofessionals were set up in ritzy digs on the South Side of town?

The bell rang, he stepped off the elevator . . .

. . . and into the arms of a huge barrel-chested, muscle-bound man.

"Skipper! It's you!" Loving said. He wrapped Ben into his arms and squeezed like a boa constrictor. "I can't believe it's really you!"

"It's good seeing you too, Loving," Ben said, shaking off the viselike display of affection. Ben could remember when Loving was too uptight to put his arm around another man, much less embrace one in public. Actually, he had preferred that.

"Back home again. Back to the fold. I can't get over it!" He pulled away, still clinging to Ben's arm. "So, it's gonna be like old times!"

"Well, I don't know about that."

"I can't get over it!" he repeated. "Even though Christina told us you'd be back."

Ben arched an eyebrow. "Did she now?"

"Oh, yeah." He escorted Ben down the corridor toward the outer door of their office. "She said you've run away before and you'd run away again. But you always come back."

"How insightful of her." Ben opened the door and took a step inside.

The office was magnificent. Maybe not the White House, but to Ben, it was like a professional dream come true. Plush wall-to-wall carpet. Beautiful mahogany desks. Tasteful adobe walls. And all the best office gizmos— copying machines, fax machines, computers. Even telephones with lots of little buttons.

"How did you afford all this?"

"The office space didn't cost as much as you prob'ly think. You know, since the oil biz went bust, there's been tons of empty office space around town. They're practically giving it away. Truth is, we're not paying much more than you used to pay for that dive downtown."

"You mean all the time I was sweating in that hellhole, I could've been here?"

Loving cleared his throat. "That's about the size of it, yeah."

"From now on, you're in charge of real estate. Where's Jones?"

"Over here." They rounded a corner and, to Ben's surprise, found another equally large and tastefully decorated office area. Jones was hunched over his computer, typing away.

"What's up?" Ben asked. "Hacking into the Department of Defense?"

Jones hurriedly typed another line into the computer, then shut it off, long before Ben had a chance to walk around and peer over his shoulder.

How odd, Ben thought. What's the big secret?

Jones brushed imaginary dust off his lap and rose. "It's great to see you again."

"Same here. I see you've been keeping busy in my absence."

"Oh, nothing important. Just a little typing I needed to catch up on. It's really good to see you again."

"Well, thanks."

"And surprising. I mean, I know Christina said—"

"I know what Christina said." Ben tried not to be irritated. "Where is she, anyway?"

Jones checked the clock on the wall. "Class."

"What?"

Jones looked flustered. "I mean, you know . . . Christina has *class*. Lots of class. She's . . . one classy lady."

"Uh-huh."

"And you could hardly expect a classy lady like her to be hanging around with bums like us."

"Uh-huh." Ben peered intently at his former secretary. Something weird was going on. "I talked to her earlier and told her about Earl's legal problems and that I was thinking about helping. Now that I've decided to get involved and he's formally retained me, I'd like her to get started on—"

There was a pounding on the outer office door, followed by several loud banging noises. Finally, the door opened a crack. "Could one of you bums help me?"

It was Christina. Ben ran to the door. She was carrying three heavy boxes stacked so high she couldn't see over the top. "Let me take one."

Christina didn't argue. With a grunt, she passed two of the boxes to Ben, then pushed the door open with her foot.

"Thanks," she said breathlessly, after they dumped the boxes on Jones's desk. "Like my new outfit?" She was wearing a bright lime green shirt that stopped just above her navel, a short neon orange skirt, and knee-high Day-Glo boots. "Very retro-chic, don't you think?"

"I think you look like Julie on *The Mod Squad*," Ben answered. He peered into the top box. It was filled to the brim with dusty files, photocopies, documents. "What is all this stuff?"

"Everything I could dig up in a few hours on the Professor Hoodoo murder."

"You started already?"

She shrugged. "No time like the present."

"But I didn't tell you I was taking the case. I wasn't sure myself."

She winked. "I was." She reached into one of the boxes and pulled out a stack of files. "I've been to the courthouse and the newspaper morgue. I made copies of everything they had on the first Earl Bonner murder case."

"Don't call it the Earl Bonner murder case. He didn't do it."

"Maybe not, but he sure as shootin' pled guilty to it. And that made it the Earl Bonner murder case. Now and forever."

"Unless we do something about that." He opened the top file and found the same grisly photograph Prescott had been waving around. Same blackened body. Same hideous graven smile.

"Think there's a connection between the two murders?" Christina asked.

"I'm sure someone wants us to think so. Someone wants to convince the world that both murders were committed by the same man. Earl."

"But why?"

"I can't say for sure. But if you want to throw the police off your track, this is a darn good way to do it. The police have a tendency to go after the obvious answer, and to investigate only long enough to collect evidence in support of that one, first-blush theory. Real life is often a good deal more complicated."

Christina nodded. "I didn't know how much work you would want to do now. Since they haven't actually filed charges against him yet."

"I want to do as much work as we can possibly do now. Barring a miracle, they'll bring charges against Earl. And once they do, it'll just be a matter of days before the preliminary hearing. Best to dig up as much information as we can beforehand."

"You told me they backed off after Tyrone came forward."

"They didn't change their minds about who's guilty. They just knew they had more work to do. They're tap-dancing around the speedy trial requirement."

"I don't follow."

"The right to a speedy trial was supposed to be a civil rights protection for defendants. It turned out to mostly help prosecutors. Prosecutors know that, as soon as they file charges, the speedy trial clock starts running, and they'll have only a limited amount of time to put together their case and get it to trial. Consequently, more often than not, they wait until they have everything they need, then file charges. They're ready, but the poor defendant, who may not have had a hint it was coming, has to slap everything together as quickly as possible. It gives prosecutors a big advantage."

"So you don't think Earl has heard the last of the police."

"I know he hasn't. But Mike's smart. Now that he knows about Tyrone Jackson, he won't let the D.A. file charges until they've figured out a way to break Tyrone's story. Or work around it. For once, though, thanks to Lieutenant Prescott's enormous incompetence, *we* have an advantage—we know Earl is a suspect and that charges will likely be forthcoming. So let's make the most of that advantage. That means starting work now."

"All right, you've got it. Do you have any theories?"

"Not yet. Maybe after I've sifted through all this material." He smiled in admiration. "I can't believe how quickly you put this together. I'd almost forgotten—" He looked up abruptly. "Thanks, Christina."

She did a little curtsy. "I live to please."

Ben grinned. "Next, I'd like you to see what you can find out about Tyrone."

"Okay. Anything in particular?"

Ben shrugged. "He's a former Crip. Small-time con artist. Earl tells me there are a couple of warrants out for him. He's afraid that if he testifies, the cops'll come down on him hard." Ben paused. "I'm afraid the prosecutor will wave the warrants in his face and offer him a deal if he *doesn't* testify."

"Wouldn't that be suppressing evidence? Violating the *Brady* rule?"

Ben blinked. Her command of legal jargon and procedure had certainly improved. "I believe the prosecutor's office would refer to it as impeaching controvertible evidence."

"Ah."

"So find out what you can so we can buttress Tyrone's testimony as much as possible. And stay close to the police station. If you get any hint that they're ready to move against Earl, let me know immediately."

"Got it."

"What about me?" Jones asked. He was leaning forward like a terrier hankering for a bone. "I could be using my sharply honed investigative skills—"

"Actually, I need some typing done lickety-split."

"But I could do some of the detective work—"

"I want to be ready with motions the second they decide to press charges. Motion to dismiss, motion to set bail . . ." Ben waved his hand in the air. "You know the drill."

Jones's face was set and sullen. "I certainly do."

"What about me?" Loving said. "I wanna be in on this."

Ben had to grin. There was a certain excitement in the room, almost like an electric charge. He had to admit there was something . . . invigorating about it. Something that felt very right. And he'd never seen his staff so eager to go to work. During his hiatus from the law, they'd obviously become very motivated—or very bored.

"I've got a tough one for you, Loving. I'd like you to track down the man who brought the rug to the club shortly before I, er, discovered the body."

"Got a description?"

"I didn't get a good look at him. Plus, according to Tyrone, all I saw was a disguise."

"Think he's associated with a real rug company?"

"I very much doubt it."

Loving's broad chest rose and fell. "You're not givin' me much to go on here, Skipper."

"I know it won't be easy. That's why I need you."

"You old sweet-talker you. How'd he get to the club?"

Ben snapped his fingers. "He had a van. I saw it through the window."

"What color was it?"

Ben's eyes went upward. "Well . . ."

"Do you know the make? Model?"

"You know I don't know anything about cars."

"True. I was just bein' hopeful. Could you draw me a picture?"

Ben nodded. "I can try."

"Well, that's somethin'. I'll see what I can do."

"I appreciate that."

"Anything for you, Skipper."

"Ditto," Jones said. "It's good to have you back, Boss."

Ben held up a finger. "Now you understand, this is just for the one case. After that, I'm outta here."

He saw Jones give Christina a wink. "Sure, Boss. Whatever you say."

"I'm serious. I'm not letting myself get dragged back into practicing law. I'm just helping a friend."

Loving nodded, already on his way to his desk. "Gotcha."

"*I'm serious!*"

Christina patted him on the shoulder. "We know, Ben. You're always serious." She grinned. "But that doesn't mean we have to take you seriously."

* 21 *

Although Ben had nothing but admiration for Jones and Loving's South Side digs, he was reminded of the advantages of his former low-rent downtown office as soon as he got into his van. The old place may have been seedy and cheap and surrounded by pawnshops and bail bondsmen, but it was close to the courthouses, close to the city offices, and close to the central police headquarters. Even valet parking couldn't make him overlook the twenty minutes along Riverside Drive it took to get downtown.

After he parked in the underground garage, he hopped up the stairs to the plaza level. On his way to police headquarters, he passed by the county courthouse. Once he'd been there on an almost daily basis, but this was the first he'd seen the building in six months. Walking by, he was flooded with a host of memories, some cherished, some not. This was the scene of so many professional triumphs. And disasters.

He recalled his first visit ever, pleading a hopeless adoption suit. What a wreck he'd been that day. He'd never become any kind of courtroom master, but he had at least learned when to stand up, when to sit down, when to speak, and when to shut up.

One memory sparked another. He remembered urging summary judgment for the now-defunct Apollo Consortium, remembered pleading for the life of a mentally challenged defendant. And perhaps his greatest professional triumph, defending Christina when she was charged with murder. The day he got those charges dismissed was a day

137

he was proud to be a lawyer. Even in his darkest moments, when trials degenerated, his personal life crashed, or he was forced to endure an idiotic lawyer joke for the five millionth time, he could flash back to that case and immediately know why he was doing what he was doing.

Until the Wallace Barrett case. After that wrapped up, it was as if everything he knew, or thought he knew, had been erased, invalidated. He learned he couldn't single-handedly ensure that justice was done; he learned that beyond a shadow of a doubt. Suddenly he didn't know *why* he was a lawyer. Worse, he didn't want to be a lawyer. Despite the pleading and cajoling from Christina and Jones and Loving, he just couldn't do it. He didn't know what the point was, what he was hoping to accomplish.

Except . . . here he was again, back on a case. But he still didn't have answers to the questions that had plagued him for the last six months. He had come back to work because a friend needed help and **had few** options. He couldn't let Earl down.

He rode the elevator up to the third floor of the city offices and made his way to police headquarters. The officer at the front desk recognized him. He glowered, but waved Ben through. Guess he doesn't like my tie, Ben mused.

He wound his way through the partitions until he found a closed wooden door bearing a nameplate: MICHAELANGELO J. MORELLI, HOMICIDE.

Ben cracked open the door and stuck his head through. "Is it soup yet?"

Fortunately, Mike was alone. He looked up, then glanced at the digital clock on his desk. *"Yes!"*

Ben stepped inside. "Bad time?"

"No, perfect. And with mere seconds to spare."

Ben looked at his watch. It was two minutes till noon. "I don't follow."

"I made a bet with Harry, the guy at the front desk. Twenty bucks that Kincaid would be in my office before noon."

"1...

"In ...

Ben took ... JUSTICE ... Am I so predictable?"

came to discuss Ear...

Mike stroked his chin. ...site Mike's desk. "I

I think we've had the conversation...?" ...counselor, but

work for the prosecutor and you work f... ...plain that I

Which means we don't work together." ...endant.

"I agree."

Mike's eyes widened. "You do?"

"I agree we've had the conversation before."

Mike grinned. "I think you know everything we know."

"I'd like to be sure. Can I see your files?"

"Ben—"

"You know you have an obligation to produce exculpatory evidence."

"To a defendant, yes. But your client has not been charged. Ergo, he is not a defendant."

"Don't play Speedy Trial semantics with me."

Mike folded his hands. "I repeat: you already know all we know. He committed a murder just like it over twenty-two years ago."

"He didn't commit that murder."

"He sure as hell pled guilty."

"He didn't want to play craps with the electric chair."

"Is that what he told you?" Mike shook his head. "Man, you've swallowed some pathetic hard-luck stories before, but this takes the cake. Wise up, Ben. People don't plead guilty to crimes they didn't commit. No one's that scared."

"When you're poor, black, undereducated, and probably depressed—"

"Ben, stop already. The man pled guilty!"

"He was told—"

"And I have personally spoken to the detective who handled that case. He's retired now, but he assured me he had no doubt whatsoever of Earl's guilt."

"Even if he did commit a similar crime in the past—"

"Similar in gruesome detail that more to which he had access. Plus, the wanted to. Plus, with whom he had been romantically ness, in a rest victim was linked." all circumstantial—"

...erjected. "Similar ...t duplicate even if they ...s found in his place of busi-

"...have eye- and ear witnesses, people who were at the club, who tell me Earl was acting strangely all night. Anxious, disturbed."

"That's easily explained. He was expecting Lily to show up and she never did."

"Or he had just killed her. How about that for distress?"

Ben rubbed his hands together. If he didn't do a better job of rebutting evidence at trial, Earl was sunk. "That still doesn't prove—"

"And I have several other witnesses—patrons—who will testify that, just before you moved the stage light and brought the body cascading down on top of you, Earl was shouting from the wings for you to leave it alone. True?"

Ben stopped short. He had forgotten about that until now. At the time, it hadn't meant much. But in retrospect . . . it didn't look good.

Mike leaned back. "Thought so." He folded his arms across his chest. "What d'ya think about my case now?"

"Earl just didn't want me messing with his stage light."

"Uh-huh."

"There was a big crowd. He wanted me to get on with the show."

"Right."

"All these things can be explained."

"Excuses can be contrived. But convincingly explained? Nah. Face it, Ben. He did it."

"Then why haven't you charged him?"

"Let's just say that there's the tiny matter of Tyrone Jackson to work around. But don't worry. We will."

"Are you saying his testimony isn't credible?"

Mike poked around the myriad half-tumbled stacks on

his desk till he found the file he wanted. He tossed it across his desk so Ben could see it. "This is what I've found out already about Mr. Jackson. It explains why he was so reluctant to talk to me."

Ben didn't have to look. "Two outstanding warrants."

"Right. One related to that gang shooting of Officer Torres a year and a half ago. The other was a street con."

"I've talked to him about the shooting," Ben said. "He assured me he wasn't involved."

"Which in fact, I believe," Mike said. "That's why I haven't pressed harder on that warrant. We've already convicted the main players in that tragedy. And I can't get too worked up about the scam Jackson ran on one of the most notorious pimps working Eleventh Street, either. But these matters do call into question his credibility."

"You mean you're going to use them to question his credibility."

"I'm not doing anything with them. That's for you lawyers to work out. I'm not making any underhanded deals, either, if that's what you're worried about."

"I knew you wouldn't," Ben said. "But what about the prosecutor? Bullock will do anything to get a conviction." An unkind remark to make about one's mentor, but true, just the same.

"Bullock was suspended after the Barrett case concluded. He hasn't actually tried a case for six months. I don't know if he ever will."

"Still—"

"Ben, your client has a criminal past. That's going to call into doubt the veracity of anything he says."

"I saw the rug man, too."

"I know you did. And we're reinterviewing all the potential witnesses in an attempt to track that man down. But the fact that someone else was there, even in a disguise, doesn't automatically make him a murderer. Why would someone come to the club in a disguise just to drop a body off? No, Earl Bonner is a far more likely suspect. And if it wasn't him, the second most likely suspect would be someone else who worked at the club."

That got Ben's attention. "Someone else?"

"Yeah. Someone else who would have a reason to be there. And therefore might have a reason to kill someone there or bring the corpse there. Someone who would have easy access to the stage."

Ben's brain started racing. "Like who?"

"How should I know? The crew, the guys in the band. You."

Ben thought back to the night of the abortive anniversary show. The barmaids would have no reason to go onstage where the body was found, and neither would the bouncer or the cashier. Even with the curtains closed, if any of them had moved toward the stage, someone would surely have noticed. But no one would have thought anything of seeing a member of the band up there. In fact, they could have carried large bundles without inviting the least bit of suspicion.

"Maybe I should get a lawyer myself."

"Relax, shyster. Uncle Earl did it."

Ben sighed. "Will you call me before you have Earl arrested so I can avoid some awful traumatic scene?"

Mike looked away. "Notifying defense counsel of a pending arrest would of course violate departmental policy. You might decide to do an Al Cowlings down the Cimarron Turnpike."

"So will you do it?"

"No."

Ben turned away.

"But I have been meaning to call you to see if you have any updated snaps of that nephew of yours. I like to keep tabs on that rascal. So I might do that. *Capisce?*"

Ben understood. When Mike phoned about baby photos, it was time for Earl to pack his toothbrush.

Ben rose to his feet. "I'll check by later to see if the lab reports are in."

"As you wish." Mike returned his attention to the stacks on his desk.

Ben stopped at the door. "You're a good friend, Mike."

Mike's eyes rose up from his desk. "You're a good lawyer, Ben."

* 22 *

He crushed the newspaper between his hands. Excellent! And here he'd thought this was going to be hard!

He strolled out on the patio, relishing the fresh morning air. He should have known he could count on the press to reveal every little secret. Even the ones that were likely to get someone killed.

He'd thought he was going to have to do some intense work. He'd expected to spend days trolling the North Side, watching O'Brien Park, cruising Memorial Drive or some of the other hot youth hangouts.

And now none of that was necessary. Now he had everything he needed handed to him on a silver platter.

He unwadded the paper, smoothing out the creases, anxious to read it all again.

NO ARREST IN JAZZLAND SLAYING, the banner headline shouted. He skipped the first few paragraphs, detailing the police department's "ongoing investigation" and recapping the sensational account of the corpse "plummeting to the stage in front of hundreds of spectators."

Eyewitness accounts were quoted liberally: "I was on the front row when it happened. The corpse came flying out. Blood splattered everywhere, all over me. I just started screaming, clawing to get away. I totally lost it."

None of this interested him in the least. What sustained his attention, what brought forth his beaming smile was a small paragraph toward the end: "Police are also investigating the report of one youth in attendance who claims that a workman delivering a rug may have been wearing a disguise. Although the police said they wanted to follow all possible leads, they warned that the witness in question, Tyrone Jackson, 21, a club regular and associate of the owner, had a history of criminal activity and may not be reliable."

He closed the paper again and hugged it close to his breast. He couldn't ask for much better than that. Talk about sweet music! This was a Coltrane original, a Gershwin rhapsody, and a B. B. King solo all set out in newsprint.

He fell into the patio chair. This certainly simplified things, didn't it? All he had to do was keep an eye on the club and wait for the brat to show his ugly black face.

His hands skittered across the glass-topped patio table and began stroking the shiny silver serrated blade. He didn't like loose ends, but when he had one, he knew what to do about it. He turned to his polished silver, his treasured weapon. The razor-sharp knife he liked to call Mr. Entertainment.

And why Mr. Entertainment, you might ask?

A glow settled over his contented face. Because it could bring smiles to the faces of so many people.

* 23 *

Ben enjoyed the smooth scenic ride of the glass elevator as he soared up to Jones and Loving's office. He still couldn't get over what plush digs the two of them had come up with. They had the right idea, he realized. When you're starting over, you should make everything fresh, new, exciting. With a place like this, he could almost imagine . . .

But no. One more case and he was out of here. He still had plenty of money in the bank, and his music career was just getting started. Maybe he'd start work on another book. He wasn't going to let himself get derailed again.

Loving was just locking up when Ben approached the outer office door.

"Skipper! I wasn't 'spectin' you back tonight. Need somethin'?"

"Well, actually, I was looking for you. I wanted to consult with you about something. I hate to take up your time when you're off duty, but . . ."

"No problem, Skipper." He beamed, clearly flattered. He reopened the door and stepped into the office. "What's up?"

Ben leaned against his desk. "You used to play poker, didn't you, Loving?"

He shrugged. "Some nickel-and-dime stuff. Me and the boys down at Orpha's Lounge. They had a little place in the back . . ." He looked up. "That was before I met you, of course. 'Fore I got myself straightened out. Why d'you ask?"

"Well, I'm playing poker tonight myself."

Loving looked at him with large round eyes. "You?"

"Right."

"Playing poker?"

"You think I can't do it."

"No, Skipper. It ain't—I mean, I'm sure you could learn the rules—"

"But you think I'll get creamed."

Loving craned his neck awkwardly. "You gotta understand, Skipper. Poker requires a certain . . . subterfuge, you know? Deviousness."

Ben tapped his foot. "And?"

"Well, Skipper, you're about the most totally transparent person I've ever known."

Ben frowned. "Is that good?"

"Not when you're playing poker."

"Look, all my life I've heard this macho male bonding hype about what a deep, strategic game poker is. Personally, I think it's about as deep and strategic as Old Maid."

"As far as the rules go, yeah. But if you want to win, you've gotta be able to bluff."

"Which is a nice word for lying."

"Bluffing isn't lying, Skipper. Bluffing is not telling. See, your problem is, you're so blasted honest, you always come straight out with whatever you know. But sometimes it's best to hold somethin' back. Sometimes it's best to make the other guy guess, maybe let him imagine somethin' that ain't necessarily so. That's half of what poker's all about."

"And the other half?"

"Taking risks. And frankly, Skipper, that's not your strong suit, either." His face scrunched up. "Why on earth would you want to play poker? Ain't you still got lots of dough from the Barrett case?"

"Yes. But Earl and all the other guys in the band are playing poker tonight."

"So?"

"Mike has the idea that the most likely suspects in the

Campbell murder are the people who had access to the stage."

"I see. This is part of your investigation."

Ben nodded. "I remember something Harry Truman said once. If you really want to get to know a man, you should play poker with him. And I really need to know these people. I want to see how they react when I bring up the murder. When the cops drag them in, they're guarded, prepared. I want to see what I can find out when their guard is down."

"You're going to need help." Loving wrapped his muscled arm around Ben's shoulder. "Lemme give you some tips. Three rules to live by."

"That would be appreciated."

"If your hand sucks right off the bat, fold."

Ben grimaced. "Why do I not think this is the secret of champions?"

"Look, maybe you can bluff, maybe you can't. But no one can do it every time, and no one is going to succeed every time. It's just like cross-ex—you gotta pick your battles. And there's no point riskin' a tub of money on somethin' that's prob'ly hopeless from the get-go."

"Okay, fine. I'll fold. What else can you recommend?"

"Watch the other players' faces. Most everyone in the world has some facial tic, gesture, or automatic response to a certain kind of hand. If it's good, they lean back in their chair. If it stinks, they draw themselves up and pretend it's a royal flush. Whatever. Almost everyone does somethin' without thinkin' about it—and most important, without knowin' it. If you watch 'em, you can learn the signals."

"That sounds like good advice. What's the third rule?"

Loving grinned. "Set aside your cab fare home."

"Well, well, well. Our esteemed piano player. Now this is a special occasion. Come in."

Gordo escorted Ben inside his spacious South Tulsa apartment. The poker game floated; tonight it was at Gordo's. His apartment was much nicer than Ben would have expected for a marginally employed guitar player. Fancy furniture, plus an ample outside porch with an impressive view of the city.

Gordo escorted Ben to the living room, where the other players were huddled around a green table. Cash was flying; chips were being distributed. In addition to Earl and the three musicians, Diane was present; she was wearing a black cap that read TOP GUN and smoking a long skinny cigar. Earl was shuffling, looking none the worse for wear despite all the stress of the past few days. Scat was wearing his trademark dark shades despite the fact that, if anything, it seemed a bit dark in the room. Denny was wearing a blue floral fishing cap, something like a tourist might wear in Hawaii.

"Have a seat, Benji," Gordo said, pulling out a chair.

Ben slid into position and pulled out his wallet.

"So, Ben, this is a surprise." Diane spoke through the teeth clenching her cigar. "I didn't think you played."

"Normally I don't," Ben said. "But since this is a memorial game . . ."

She nodded toward the spinner rack holding the chips. Apparently she served as banker, which didn't particularly surprise him. "So, did you bring any money?"

"Oh, right. What's traditional?"

"Each of us puts in fifty bucks," Diane explains. "And that's all you get. You can't bring in new money. Once you're out, you're out. We play until someone has all the chips."

Ben gulped. "How long does that take?"

"Sometimes all night."

Scat laughed. "Ten bucks says Kincaid doesn't last till sandwiches."

Gordo laughed. "I'll go fifteen."

Ben tried to smile jovially. "Hey, I might surprise you."

Scat and Gordo did not respond, but Ben had the distinct impression they thought this an unlikely possibility.

Gordo sniffed the air. "I think I smell a fish."

Denny did the same. "Yeah. Tuna. Major quantities."

They both laughed. Ben knew he was missing something.

"A fish is a sure loser, in poker parlance," Diane explained. "A tuna is a big fish."

"Watch out for Diane," Gordo advised. "She used to be a professional."

"A—wha—you mean—"

"Not that kind of professional." Gordo laughed. "Well, only in my dreams."

Diane blew smoke in his face. "Grow up, Gordo."

Scat explained. "She used to play poker professionally."

Diane nodded. "Back when I lived in Vegas. Came in second at the World Series of Poker freeze-out at Binion's in 1992. 'Course, I had a little more money to work with back then."

"I had no idea you guys were so . . . serious about this." Swallowing hard, Ben pulled fifty dollars out of his wallet and plopped it down on the table.

"Easy come, easy go, right, Ben?" Diane said, snatching the money up.

"Nice of you to come out tonight, Ben," Earl said quietly. Against all odds, it appeared he was taking this memorial game stuff seriously. "You honor Lily's memory."

Ben collected his chips. "Well, it was the least I could do."

"Ever been to a memorial game like this?"

"Can't say that I have. Have you?"

"We had one for George—Professor Hoodoo—after he was gone. Very next night, in fact. Good thing, too. After that, I woulda been . . . unavailable."

As in *incarcerated*, Ben surmised.

"Now that was a night," Earl continued. "You boys can't imagine what it was like back then. George Armstrong was the best of us and we all knew it. He knew everythin' there was to know about music. That's why we called him the Professor. We loved that man. Most of the time, anyway. There must've been thirty, forty people showed up to play that night. Everyone wanted to pay their last respects to the Professor."

"So they came to a poker game?"

"Why not? Beats gettin' drunk and wailin' at some wake, or standin' like cake decorations around a new-dug grave."

Ben nodded. He supposed it did at that.

"I'm glad to see you here tonight, too, Scat," Earl continued. "I didn't 'spect that. 'S good of ya."

Scat nodded, but made no reply.

What did that mean? Ben wondered. "You knew Lily, didn't you?" Ben asked Scat.

"Yeah," he said, eyes still hidden behind the shades. "I knew Lily."

Earl cut in. "Hell, son, Scat here knew Lily and Professor Hoodoo and everyone else on the circuit. He used to hang with Huey Smith. Played sax with Red Tyler. Traded licks in OKC with Bob Gilkeson. Went to Paris with Lightnin' Hopkins and T-Bone Walker."

Scat dipped his head slightly.

"Oh, old Scat's known most everybody in the biz at one time or 'nother. He's been around almost as long as I have!" Earl laughed, then slapped Scat heartily on the back.

"Did any of the rest of you know Lily?" Ben asked casually.

No one indicated that they did, although Ben knew that probably didn't mean much.

"I think it's really bizarre, this mysterious man with the rug showing up just before the corpse does. You guys were all around then, too. Did any of you see him?"

"What about you, Scat?" Gordo said. "I remember you said you had to run an errand before the show started. Did you bump into this creep?"

Scat turned his shaded eyes away. "I didn't see a damn thing."

"So, like, are we going to play cards here or what?" Diane interjected.

"Straighten up, boys," Denny said. "Diane's gettin' serious."

Gordo grinned. "Diane, honey, you can get serious with me anytime."

Diane ignored him. "All right, you peckerwoods, listen up. The game is Texas Hold 'Em. Two cards down, five in the middle of the table we all share, the first three at the same time, then the fourth, then the fifth. Got it?"

Ben nodded, since he assumed the detailed game description was mostly for his benefit.

"All right. Here we go." Diane dealt out two cards face down to each player.

Ben checked his draw. Two of clubs and six of hearts. Remembering Loving's first rule, he folded.

After everyone else made their bets, Diane dealt three cards to the center of the table. An eight and two jacks. Obviously, if anyone held a jack as a hole card, they were in clover.

Another round of betting was followed by another card to the middle, this time a nine. By the time the betting was finished, only Diane and Gordo remained.

"So," Diane said, chomping down on her cigar. "Now it's just you and me."

Gordo snickered. "I've dreamt of this moment."

"I'll try to make it something you'll remember for a good long time." She reached for her chips. "Five bucks says you don't have a jack under there."

Gordo matched the wager. "Five bucks says I do." He reached back for another chip and raised her another five. "Or maybe even two."

"I doubt it." She called. "Let's see what's coming." She flipped a fifth card onto the table. It was another jack.

Eyes widened around the table. Following Loving's second rule to live by, Ben watched the faces. Diane didn't appear too delighted with this development.

All eyes were glued to their hands, still face down on the table. Ben suddenly realized his heart was beating faster—and he wasn't even playing. Maybe there was more to this game than he realized.

Gordo pushed at least ten dollars' worth of chips into the center. "Lily must've been some lady," he clucked. "Tonight is my night."

A somber expression cloaked Diane's face. She was obviously thinking, calculating. Ben didn't see how she had any choice. Sure, she had a lot of chips on the table, but Gordo obviously had a jack. She couldn't possibly beat him.

Diane's hands dipped back into her chips. "I'll call," she said.

Gordo's eyes flew open. "Are you crazy, woman?"

"I called," Diane said calmly. "Let's see your cards."

All the elation drained out of Gordo's face. With lips tightly pursed, he reached down and flipped over his cards.

A four and a seven. Barely better than the hand Ben had folded. Gordo didn't have the jack at all. He'd been bluffing!

Diane turned over her own cards: a pair of tens.

Gordo was flabbergasted. "How did you know I didn't have the goods?"

"Call it a hunch." Diane scraped the chips into her pile. "Was this special time we had together all you dreamed it would be, Gordo?"

Gordo grinned—awfully gracious, Ben thought, for someone who'd just had his clock cleaned. "It was. But now I have nothing to live for."

"Well, don't kill yourself. It's only a game."

"Life is a game," Gordo replied. "And death is the sweet reward."

That was the second time in as many days that Ben had heard Gordo make a weird remark about death. Note to self, he thought: pay Gordo a private visit to follow up on this.

Diane shuffled the cards a few times, then leaned across the table like a piranha closing in on its prey. "All right," she said. "Who wants to be devoured next?"

* * *

It was almost two A.M. when they played the final hand. The match was down to two players: Diane, as everyone expected, and Ben, as no one expected—including Ben. Ben had in fact lasted well past sandwiches, to the surprise of all, and the disgust of some, like Scat and Gordo, who had to make good on their side bets.

Basically, he had just followed Loving's suggestions. He had folded more than anyone else in the game, but as a result, he had conserved his resources. He hadn't dared a bluff, but by sitting out the bad hands and playing the sure winners, he had slowly put together some winnings. Plus, he'd had the good fortune to take out two players, inheriting all their remaining chips. He'd taken Gordo with a pair of queens, then managed to do the same to Earl only two hands later with two sevens and two fives.

And now it was just him and Diane. Diane, unfortunately, had just won several high-dollar hands in a row. Ben could see the handwriting on the wall. She'd keep whittling away at him until he was gone. If he was to have any hope of winning, he had to try a different approach. And fast.

"Would you guys hurry up already?" Denny said. "I've been wearing these clothes for days. They're getting uncomfortable."

Ben glanced up. "Why? Are they scratchy?"

Gordo laughed. "Denny thinks all clothes are uncomfortable."

"He does?"

"All right, let's do it," Diane said. The antes were laid and she dealt out the cards.

Ben lifted up the corners and peered at his cards.

Two tens! Hardly invincible, but a start. His heartbeat accelerated. Maybe this was the time to go for broke. It made sense, but . . .

He couldn't bring himself to take the risk. He made a modest bet: one dollar.

"I'll call," Diane replied.

After the bets were in, she flopped three cards into the center of the table: the ace of diamonds, the nine of clubs, and the seven of clubs. No help for Ben.

Diane, however, had a more positive reaction. "I'm betting it all," she said.

"What?" Ben looked up at his companions. "Can she do that?"

"She certainly can. Are you in?"

Ben glanced at his cards. It was a good hand. But she must have a good hand, too. Probably a pair. If it was a pair of nines, fine, he could beat her. But if it was a pair of aces . . .

"All right," he said, pushing out all his chips. "I'm in."

"The betting is over," Gordo announced. "Let's play out the cards."

Since it didn't matter at this point who knew, Diane complied. She flipped over her hand. She had an ace and a nine in the hole. And now, with the cards in the center, she had both a pair of nines and a pair of aces. Two pair! More than enough to trounce Ben's puny tens.

"And you?"

Ben exposed his hand to the world.

Diane smiled, pleased and, Ben thought, a bit relieved. Her go-for-broke paid off. Still, there were two more cards to be dealt.

"Play the table," Gordo said, grinning. He seemed to be enjoying himself a good deal more now than he had when he was still in the game.

Diane turned the next card: a three. No help to anyone.

Everyone in the room huddled around the table— Gordo and Denny and Scat and Earl. They were like vultures, anxious to see what happened next.

Ben held his breath. What was it about this game anyway? It wasn't as if his life depended on winning. So why were his hands shaking and beads of sweat dripping down his forehead? C'mon, he thought, I need a ten. Luck be a lady tonight . . .

She turned over another card. Ben's heart sunk.

It was an ace. As if she needed more help.

Diane leaned back in her chair, blowing smoke rings into the air. She had a full house, a killer hand in this game. And much better than Ben's now very stupid-looking pair of tens.

She treated herself to a new cigar. "It's been a pleasure, Kincaid."

Ben threw down his cards in disgust.

"And so," Gordo said, "once again, Diane proves that she is, in fact, mistress of the universe."

Earl patted Ben on the back. "Tough break, kid. You played well. You just didn't get the cards."

Nice sentiment, but Ben knew it wasn't true. If he had been the one to put all his chips on the table, or even a big chunk of them, back when he got the pair of tens, she probably would've backed off. She would've folded, or at any rate wouldn't have bet everything, and Ben would've survived the hand and lived to play another.

It was a matter of strategy, and he had blown it. He lost because he couldn't bluff, because he wasn't willing to take a risk.

"Congratulations," Ben told Diane. "You deserved to win."

"Darn tootin'," Diane replied.

"So," Earl asked, "what you gonna do with all the loot?"

"Gee," Diane said, glancing at Ben, "maybe I'll make a donation to the Society for the Prevention of Cruelty to Animals."

Gordo made a snorting noise.

"Or we could all just get drunk."

That brought a raucous round of cheers.

Diane stepped out of her chair and began pulling on her leather jacket. "See you next time, Kincaid."

Ben shuffled away from the table. "Yeah."

Gordo gave Ben a nudge. "Hey, don't take it so hard, Benji. At least you still have your health."

Yes, that's true, Ben thought, pressing his lips tightly together. But if you call me Benji one more time, yours may be in serious danger.

* 24 *

Tyrone crossed the gravel parking lot of Uncle Earl's Jazz Emporium, admiring the vivid sunrise. The iridescent rays were just beginning to seep over the skyline, illuminating the Bank of Oklahoma Tower and other downtown skyscrapers, the refineries on the far side of the river, and the miles and miles of woodland beyond. Someday, he thought, once he'd mastered that sax, he was going to come out here and write a song about a sunrise like this.

That was his ultimate goal—not just to play but to write. He wanted to take everything he saw and did and knew and to transform it into music. Think of all he could bring to the music table—life in the gangs, life on the streets, life on the con. Sure, he was young, but he had experiences like no one else in the world. Think what Gershwin did—and what did he know about the blues anyway? Tyrone had lived it. He knew he could compose something special, something that would live forever—if he could just learn how to play.

He heard a scraping noise, a crunching of gravel. He turned, but didn't see anything.

That was odd. He turned back toward the sunrise. Probably nothing. Still . . .

He heard the crunching sound again.

"T-Dog!"

A wave of relief swept over him. Earl was standing near the entrance to the club, waving. He waited patiently as Earl waddled out to the parking lot.

"You gonna be around for a while?" Earl asked.

"Nah. Sorry to blow and run, but I got work to do."

Earl jammed his big fleshy hands into his pockets. "Look, we need to talk."

" 'Bout what?"

Earl eyed him carefully. "I think you know."

Tyrone suspected he did. And it was a conversation he didn't care to have. "Look, Earl, I have things to do. Places to be."

"Like what?"

Like the Okarche bus came in at 9:02, but he wasn't going to tell Earl that. "Just takin' care of business."

"Then when will we talk?"

"I don't know, Earl." Tyrone started toward his car and opened the door. "Maybe at the next lesson."

"That's too long."

"Well, I can't do it now." He slid into the seat.

Earl clamped a solid hand down on the steering wheel. "You're not goin' anywhere till you tell me when we're gonna talk."

"Earl—"

"How 'bout tonight?"

Tyrone shook his head. "Can't. Got major plans."

"You ain't puttin' me off, Tyrone."

"I got plans—"

Earl laid his hand firmly on Tyrone's chest. "Tomorrow night then. No later."

"Fine. Tomorrow night. Ten P.M. Right here."

Earl eased off. Tyrone gave him a tiny push, then closed the car door. He shoved the stick into reverse and backed out.

Tomorrow night, he thought, as he zoomed onto Brady. Great. That gave him about forty hours to figure out what the hell he was going to say.

He waited until Earl had disappeared inside the club, then slid the knife back into its sheath.

That had been a close one. He'd been lurking behind the

club next to the Dumpsters when the kid came out. He'd started to make his move, but his foot slipped on the gravel and the kid whirled around. He'd have gone for it anyway, but who should stumble by but good ol' Uncle Earl himself.

He'd had to take cover. Earl could've made him, even with the new disguise. He would've had to kill them both, and he didn't want that. The kid, yes—that was necessary. But he was much happier letting Earl boil in the brine. He wanted Earl to suffer. Earl deserved to suffer.

Just as he had suffered.

Well, there would be another time, and sooner than he had expected. Tomorrow night, ten o'clock. That's what the kid had said. He didn't know what Earl was so anxious to talk about, and frankly he didn't care. What they planned to discuss was irrelevant.

Death would be the main topic for conversation.

* 25 *

Ben caught Gordo at his apartment. From the looks of him, he had just awakened, although it was almost noon. Come to think of it, Ben recalled, Gordo had been drinking pretty heavily during the poker game; he was probably suffering the aftereffects. His hair was a mess, his chin was stubbly, and he was wearing boxer shorts and a Metallica T-shirt.

"Benji, what're you doing here?" he said, showing Ben through the door. Whether he'd been asleep or merely comatose, he didn't seem particularly disturbed by Ben's arrival. "Come to return to the scene of your poker Waterloo?"

"Actually, I was hoping I could ask you a few questions." Ben ambled around the apartment, again admiring the quality furnishings and tasteful decorations. Under an end table, he spotted a stack of books he hadn't seen the night before. They were all Elisabeth Kübler-Ross titles: *On Death and Dying*, *Living with Death and Dying*, *Death: The Final Stage of Growth*, *The Wheel of Life: A Memoir of Living and Dying*. All had bookmarks jammed in them. "Mind if I sit?"

" 'Course not. What's up?"

Ben cleared a place for himself on the sofa. "I wanted to talk to you about the murder."

Gordo sprawled out in a big overstuffed chair and propped his feet up on the hassock. "Why me in particular?"

"I'm talking to everyone who had access to the stage the

161

night of the murder. And that means every member of the band."

"Not just the band," Gordo corrected. "Don't forget the lovely Ms. Weiskopf, our stage manager. She was there, too."

A good point, Ben thought. He ought to have a little chat with Diane, too.

"What's your interest in this, anyway, Kincaid?"

"I'm trying to prevent Earl from being arrested, and then convicted, for this murder."

Gordo slapped his hands together. "Damn! That's right. Scat was spreading the rumor that you're a lawyer. Say it ain't so, Joe."

"It's so," Ben said dryly.

"No shittin'? Damn!" He slapped his hands again. "And here we all thought you were just some white piano player who didn't know what to do with himself. And it turns out you were just slummin'!"

"I was not slumming," Ben said emphatically. "I quit practicing law because I wanted to concentrate on music. But Earl needs help."

"I guess that's right. I heard the cops just about hauled his carcass to the pokey yesterday."

"Twice. And they'll be back for a third try. So your help would be appreciated. Did you see the man with the rug?"

"No way. I would've said something if I had."

Ben watched his eyes carefully. This wasn't a poker game, but he still thought he might learn something. Especially since he was not at all sure he was getting the straight scoop. "Did you see anyone?"

"No one who wasn't supposed to be there. Earl, Scat, Diane. And you, of course." His eyes narrowed comically. "You know, you've always seemed like a suspicious character, Benji."

"Ha-ha."

"Not tellin' anyone what you really are and all. What're you tryin' to hide?"

Ben ignored him. "Did you see the body? Or anything that in retrospect might have been a body?"

Gordo thought for a moment. "Can't say that I did." He peered toward the kitchen. "Say, would you like some cereal? I've got some Froot Loops."

"Thanks, I already ate." He plowed ahead: "It seems to me whoever killed that woman went to a lot of trouble to frame Earl. You know any reason why anyone would want Earl put away for a long time? Maybe forever?"

Gordo thought for a moment. "You know, any man lives long enough, he's likely to pick up some enemies."

"I need more to go on than that."

"You know much about him and Scat?"

"No."

"Well, neither do I. But I know they go a long ways back. Twenty, thirty years. And sometimes when they're talking, I get the definite impression that there's some history there."

Ben knew what Gordo meant, but it still wasn't very helpful. "If there was some serious bad blood between them, why would Earl hire Scat to play in his club?"

Gordo shook his head. "I don't know, man. People do strange things."

Gordo the philosopher. "Well, I'll talk to Denny, too. Maybe he knows something you don't. Do you know where he lives?"

A goofy grin spread across Gordo's face. "I know where he lives, man, but I don't think you wanna go there."

"What's that supposed to mean?"

Gordo scribbled an address on a scrap of paper. "I'll let you find out for yourself."

Ben took the paper and shoved it into his pocket. "I don't suppose you know of any grudge Denny might have against Earl."

"Well, he doesn't pay us what we're worth."

"No one does. I doubt if that qualifies as a motive."

"Hard for me to imagine, man. Denny is a gentle guy. Very into harmony. Peace. Staying in tune with nature."

Again the grin. "I get the impression you think one of your band buddies is behind this killing."

"I don't think anything," Ben answered. "I'm just checking out everyone who had access to that stage, including you. You weren't by any chance involved with this death, were you?"

"I'm involved with death on an intimate, daily basis," Gordo said, settling back into his chair. "But not this one in particular."

Ben glanced again at the pile of death and dying materials. "Mind telling me what this is all about?"

"I'm part of the movement, man."

"Which one?"

"The death-awareness movement."

"I didn't realize there was any lack of awareness of death."

"Not just that it exists. We're tryin' to help people understand what it really is. Do you know much about what happens to us after we die, Ben?"

"I have a friend who believes in angels."

Gordo shook his head. "Not religious fantasies. The real thing. We're tryin' to help people understand what death truly is. To break people away from their childish cliché notions—death as a horror to be dreaded. We want people to understand that death is a natural part of life. That it's not an ending, but a transition."

"Like graduating from college?"

"Well, in a way. Problem is, people are all wrapped up in these antiquated ideas they've gotten from the media or the medical community. The cure-oriented, interventionalist, life-prolonging regime."

"You're against cures and life prolongation?"

"After a point, yes. We're defying the natural order. Putting off what was meant to be." He gave Ben a long look. "I gather you find these ideas revolutionary? That's because you've been brainwashed by the establishment. These ideas are not new, and they didn't originate with me. You've heard of Elisabeth Kübler-Ross, haven't you?"

"Right. Five stages of dying."

"That was the start. In subsequent works, she went well beyond those early ideas. In the movement, she's considered the Queen of Death."

"Lucky her."

"She's written volumes on this subject. Slowly but surely she's transforming the world. There are over a hundred thousand death and dying college courses taught every year. These ideas have gained broad acceptance among thanatologists and other death professionals."

"Death professionals?"

"Hospice workers, clergymen, psychiatrists, doctors, nurses." He paused. "I gather from your attitude you've never done any serious thinking about death."

"It's not my idea of a fun Saturday night, no."

"You should. Take some of these books. You'll be astounded at how widespread the movement is. Millions of people all over the world have joined." He pulled a few volumes off a shelf. "Kübler-Ross established a nationwide chain of death and dying centers—they're called Shanti Nilaya. There's also the Exit Society, which distributes home suicide guides. There's the Conscious Dying movement, which motivates people to devote their lives to death awareness. They open Death Centers to help bring people to the movement. And there's another group that's trying to initiate two-way traffic with the afterlife."

"Two-way traffic?"

"Kind of a courier service. They recruit people who are dying to carry messages to those who have already passed on. And of course there are various reincarnation and past-life groups, although that's really a different cup of tea." He pulled a brochure out of a drawer. "Here's a group promoting near-death experiences. You know what they are?"

"Well, my mother gave me *Saved by the Light* for Christmas."

Gordo snorted. "This is nothing like that. This is the real thing. You don't go back in time to your childhood or meet Jesus or any of that rot. What would be the point of going backwards? Near death gives you a peek at the world to come. You must've seen some of the critical articles that have been written on the subject."

"Well, I've seen a few *National Enquirer* headlines."

He handed Ben the brochure. "I haven't done it, but they say it'll turn your head forever. Make you understand death as an altered state of consciousness. Kind of like the ultimate acid trip."

Ben thumbed through the brochure. "Tune in, turn on, drop dead."

Gordo laughed. "Something like that."

"So your theory is sort of, *do* go gentle into that good night. And be quick about it."

"Hey, that's pretty good. Did you think of that yourself?"

"Me and Dylan Thomas." Ben frowned. "Gordo, you're even younger than I am. How did you ever get wrapped up in this death movement?"

Gordo slowly brought his hands together and steepled his fingers. "I would expect you to keep this to yourself."

"If it relates to this case, I can't promise I won't use it in court. If it doesn't relate, I'll keep my mouth shut."

Gordo bobbed his head from side to side, as if mentally weighing whether those assurances were good enough. Evidently he decided they were. "I have Addison's disease," he said finally. "Do you know what that is?"

"I'm afraid I don't."

"It's what JFK had. Causes a drying up of the joints. It can be treated with cortisone but . . ." He paused. "It's painful at times. There are treatments now, but—my doctors say it's gonna kill me, eventually."

"I'm sorry to hear that," Ben said softly.

"I was diagnosed when I was seventeen. So you see, death and I have been constant companions for a good long while."

Ben shifted awkwardly in his chair. This was the last direction on earth he would have expected this interview to take. "I can see how you might be . . . interested in the subject."

"More than interested. I was looking for hope. Assurances."

"People have always looked for hope," Ben said. "The promise of an afterlife. That's what faith is all about. But this death movement you're describing . . ." He paused, casting his eyes across the piles of materials. "This goes beyond the promise and anticipation of an afterlife. This is more like a . . . sentimentalization of death. A worship of death, even."

Gordo pulled a well-worn magazine off his shelf. "This is an interview Kübler-Ross did some years ago." He thumbed rapidly through the slick pages. "Listen to this. According to the Queen, 'People after death become complete again. The blind can see, the deaf can hear, cripples are no longer crippled after all their vital signs have ceased to exist.' " He grabbed a nearby book. "Here's what she says in her latest work. 'Death is a wonderful and positive experience. . . . When the time is right, we can let go of our bodies and we will be free of pain, free of fears and worries—free as a very beautiful butterfly, returning home to God.' "

"So death becomes the ultimate panacea."

Gordo's eyelids fluttered as he settled back into his chair. "It's a beautiful thought, isn't it?"

"Well, actually, no." Ben knew he shouldn't argue; this wouldn't advance his investigation. But he couldn't help himself. "Don't you see that sentiments like hers in effect encourage people to kill themselves? No wonder suicide rates are at an all-time high, and euthanasia is becoming downright trendy. People should be encouraged to make the most of this life, no matter what hand they're dealt, rather than just anticipating some supposed miracle to come after they're dead and buried."

"The truth is, Ben, you've been brainwashed by conventionality."

"The truth is, Gordo, no one really knows what, if anything, happens to us after we die. This death and dying stuff doesn't have any more scientific basis than astrology or spoon-bending." Ben bit down on his lower lip. He knew he wasn't handling this very well. "Gordo, I'm sorry to hear you have a serious disease. But a lot of people who learned that they might not have a full-length life have used that knowledge to drive themselves to work harder and accomplish more. Kennedy, for example. But this death and dying crap pushes people in just the opposite direction. Instead of urging them to accomplish more, it urges them to accomplish less. Don't make the most of your days. End it now. Make the transition."

Gordo shook his head. "You just don't understand, Ben. But you will in time. Everyone will, in time. Either before the transition, or after. Death claims us all."

True enough, Ben thought as he rose from the sofa and prepared to leave. Death had certainly claimed a victim here. The only problem was, the victim wasn't dead.

* 26 *

Ben turned off Cherry Street and maneuvered to an alleyway behind the first row of street-front buildings. He found an area where the tallgrass had been plowed under; it was being used as a makeshift parking lot.

He parked his van, then headed back toward the stores and offices. It took him only a few moments to find the sign directing him to Theatre Tulsa. He found a backstage door and entered.

There was a woman standing near the door. The costume designer, Ben guessed, judging from the disorganized array of thimbles and colored threads and needles. She directed him to the back of the stage. Ben wove his way through the hubbub of actors and stagehands and crewpersons, all darting in different directions at the same time. Soon he saw a familiar crown of yellow spikes poking over the top of a stage flat.

She was hammering away, utterly oblivious to the chaos surrounding her.

"So this is where you unwind," Ben said.

Diane glanced up, then returned her attention to her hammering. "This is where I make a living," she replied. "You don't think I can live off what Earl pays me, do you?"

"Probably not," Ben agreed. He crouched down. She was nailing the base of a vertical beam—part of an office set, he guessed—to the flat. "But I wouldn't have guessed you were involved in stagecraft. A poker professional, a stage manager, and a carpenter. I'm impressed."

169

"Don't be." She propped herself up on an elbow. "It's all just hammer and nails, basically. And the occasional splash of paint. My dad had a workshop in the garage. He loved carpentry—loved it far more than selling insurance, which was how he spent most of his life. Till he died. Anyway, he showed me how to do all this stuff. It's easy, really, once you know how. Nothing to get excited about."

"You must do it well. The woman on the phone told me you've been here for six seasons."

"It's a great group. Everything about their productions is excellent, except the budget. They need someone who can get the job done without spending a lot of money." She smiled. "I can fill that bill. I don't do anything brilliant. They just need someone to make decisions. That's me."

"You don't give yourself enough credit."

She laid down her hammer. "Such flattery. Ben, if I didn't know better, I'd swear you were trying to get in my pants."

Ben's face suddenly turned crimson.

She grinned. "But since I do know better, you must want something else."

"Well, it isn't that I want something—"

She cocked an eyebrow. "Oh?"

"I wanted to talk to you. That's all. In private."

"So you *are* trying to get in my pants."

"No! I just—"

She laid her hand on his arm. "Ben, you are so fun to play with." She straightened up and sat on the stage with crossed legs. "So what is it you're so anxious to discuss?"

"Well, the murder. That night. Earl."

"Right. I heard you were representing him." She placed a finger against a cheek. "Personally, I wasn't that surprised when I heard you were a lawyer. I'd always figured you had an ugly secret buried in your past. I just didn't realize how ugly it was."

"You were at the club the night the body was found," Ben said, moving briskly along. "And I remember you asked me to clear the stage while I was practicing. That was just a few minutes before the man with the rug showed up. Did you see him?"

She shook her head. "If I did, I didn't notice. But I tend to think I would've noticed, because I get pretty protective about that stage when we're close to showtime. So I probably didn't see him."

"It was barely half an hour before the club opened. I'm surprised someone other than me didn't see him."

"I'm not. That was the ideal time to come. Earlier, the club would be closed, or the band would be rehearsing. Later, the crowd would have started to gather. But he caught us after rehearsal, after the front doors were unlocked, but before any patrons had arrived. Perfect."

It was perfect, Ben agreed. Almost too perfect. It was one more reason to believe the most likely suspect was someone who worked at the club. Someone who knew. Or someone working with someone who knew.

"I don't suppose you saw that corpse up on the stage light."

"Not before you did."

"Or any evidence that it was up there?"

"Ben, I'm the stage manager. Do you think that if I knew there was a corpse dangling over my pianist I would have just ignored it?"

"Sorry, stupid question."

"No kidding."

"Did you see anyone or anything else of a suspicious nature? Either at the time or after the fact?"

She shook her head. "I'll tell you what I told the cops. I didn't see anything out of the ordinary. Until you started snuggling with the stiff, that is." She snapped her fingers. "Although, now that you mention it, Denny was acting bizarre. Even more than usual."

Ben's head snapped to attention. "How so?"

"It's hard to explain. It was more . . . a feeling I had, a feeling I got when I was around him. Didn't you notice anything?"

Ben shook his head no.

"Just after rehearsal, he was wandering around with his head bowed, muttering to himself." She whipped back her dangling blonde spikes. "If I were you, I'd talk to Denny."

"I saved him for tomorrow. He lives out of town, you know."

"Oh, yes, I know. Do you?"

Ben blinked. "Do—what?"

She grinned. "You'll find out."

A tall man approached Diane, with shimmering diaphanous costumes draped over each arm. "Diane, honey, I need a decision."

"That's why I'm here."

"Which do you prefer, the pink or the chartreuse?"

"Mmm . . . the pink."

"Good, I thought so." He whirled around and headed back toward the wings.

Diane smiled at Ben. "See? They love me."

"Do you know anything about costumes?"

She laughed. "I'm not even sure those were costumes. For all I know, Scott's picking out drapes for his living room."

Ben tried to steer the conversation back to the murder. "What about Earl? How much do you know about him?"

"Not much. He's the boss, that's all. And a pretty mediocre poker player."

"Know anyone who dislikes him?"

"I've seen him toss out a drunken patron or three."

"I need something more than that. Something that would create a strong motive."

"But Earl wasn't killed. It was that Lily woman."

"Yes, but someone went to a lot of trouble to implicate Earl. Know of anyone who would have a motive for that?"

She thought for several moments. "Sorry. I really don't."

"And you probably didn't know Lily Campbell."

"No, I didn't. But Scat did. Her death really hit him hard."

"Why do you say that?"

"It was something I heard just after the corpse tumbled

to the ground. I was in the wings at the time, closest to
Scat. As soon as the corpse rolled forward, and we both
got a clear look at her face, he murmured, 'The lily's been
clipped.' It was under his breath, just barely audible. I'm
sure I'm the only one who heard it. I didn't understand
what it meant at the time; I thought he was being poetic.
But then, after I heard what the woman's name was . . .
well, I knew better."

"Hmm. That's something, anyway. Thanks, Diane."

"Anytime."

"Thanks. Maybe I'll drop by later and let you make a
decision for me."

It couldn't hurt, he thought, as he ambled across the
stage toward the back door. After all, he had several
pending at the moment. And he didn't seem to be making
any progress on his own.

* 27 *

Christina showed up at Ben's apartment around eight, not long after he himself arrived.

"I got everything you asked for," she said, reaching into a paper sack. "Two platters of cashew chicken double delight, egg rolls, lumpia dogs, dessert, coffee"—she paused—"and this." She withdrew a small handheld mirror. "So what's shaking, Ben? Don't you already have a mirror in your bathroom?"

"Um, yeah," he hedged. "A wall mirror. But I wanted . . . another one."

"You did? Why?"

"No reason."

A tentative smile crept across her face. "You're going to look at the back of your head, aren't you?"

His chin rose. "I don't see that it's any concern of yours."

"That's the only time guys need a second mirror." She spread the food across the kitchen table. "May I ask what's brought on this sudden concern about the back of your head?"

He thought carefully before answering. "When those cops surrounded me at your place yesterday, I heard one of them describing me on his car radio. He said I was a white male, five five—and I'm actually five six—"

"In shoes."

"Slim—and get this—brown hair, 'slightly balding in the back.' Can you believe that?"

Christina looked away. "Well . . ."

174

He grabbed her by the shoulders. "Give it to me straight, Christina. Is my hair falling out?"

She shrugged. "Just a little." She touched a place on the back of his head. "Just a teeny-weeny little bald spot."

"A bald spot? He didn't say there was a bald *spot*!"

"Ben, it's tiny."

"I can't believe this! I'm too young!"

"Apparently not."

"My father lived to be fifty-nine and he never balded at all."

"Your father's hairline is irrelevant. It's your mother's genes that matter."

"My mother isn't bald!"

"Yes, but are any of the men on her side of the family?" He hesitated. "Well . . ."

"See?" She gave him a friendly jab. "Don't worry about it. It's perfectly natural. Who cares?"

"Who cares? I care!"

"Well, I don't. Let's eat."

Somewhat reluctantly, Ben followed her lead. A few moments later, they were both digging in.

"I got everything I could down at City Hall," Christina explained between bites. "Of course, since they haven't charged Earl, they don't think they have any obligation to share evidence, exculpatory or not."

"That's how it usually works," Ben replied. He grabbed a lumpia dog and dipped it in the yellow sauce. "They want to get all their ducks in a row before they give us anything."

"I did start processing motions and pleadings. When the time comes, all we'll have to do is fill in the blanks. Still, we'll be at a disadvantage." She frowned. "It doesn't seem like this is how the law should work. If they've already made the decision to charge Earl, it's just semantics. He is in fact a defendant. The *Brady* rule should require them to produce any exculpatory evidence."

"You'll get no argument from me. But the Supreme Court said otherwise. *Boren v. Oklahoma*."

"No, that was about gender discrimination in drinking laws. You're thinking about *Conners v. Wisconsin*."

Ben set down his fork. "Since when did my legal assistant have a better command of case law than I do?"

She hesitated a moment. "I've been hanging around you lawyers for over ten years. I was bound to pick up something."

"Yes, but—"

She changed the subject. "So you don't think Gordo was hiding anything?"

"I didn't see any evidence. But who knows? All that death worship stuff was so weird. Who knows what might be buzzing around in his brain? Who knows what someone might do, especially after they've decided that death is no big deal." He shook his head. "For that matter, Diane seemed perfectly open to me. But you know what a lousy judge of character I am."

"I certainly do." She scooped some more white rice onto her plate. "Do you intend to see Denny?"

"Tomorrow."

"Good. How's Mrs. Marmelstein doing?"

"I'm going down there after I eat. I really don't think she should be left alone."

"That's fine for tonight. But what about tomorrow? And the next day?"

"Christina, I can't watch her day and night for the rest of her life."

"So what are you going to do? Send her off to some home filled with people she doesn't know?"

"She needs to have people caring for her. Full-time."

"She would hate that."

"True. When I suggested it, she became hostile."

"I'm sure she's very scared. She knows what's happening to her. At least some of the time she knows." Christina paused a moment. "You know, Ben—she depends on you."

Ben's eyes narrowed. "And what is that supposed to mean?"

"She doesn't have any living family. No one she's ever mentioned, anyway. She's come to depend on you."

"What are you saying—that I should become her private nurse?"

"Not that exactly, but—"

"Do you have any idea how difficult it would be caring for an elderly woman with Alzheimer's?"

"As a matter of fact, I do. But I still think—"

"I have things to do! I'm going on tour with the band this summer."

Christina didn't respond, but she gave him a look he didn't like a bit. "Oh, I almost forgot. I brought up your mail." She tossed a few envelopes his way. "Looks like you got something from New York."

Ben rapidly thumbed through the letters till he found the one in question. He ripped it open with his thumb and began to read. His eyes darted quickly down the page.

"Well?" Christina asked.

Ben sighed. "Same old same old." He affected an impersonal baritone. "We're sorry, but we regret to inform you that your manuscript does not meet any of our current needs. Thank you for considering us." He wadded it up and lobbed it into the trash can in the corner. "I wish I'd never written the damn thing."

"You have to be patient. Getting published is tough. Some of the greatest writers who ever lived spent years trying to get published."

"Well, I'm not one of the greatest writers who ever lived. Maybe I should just hang it up."

"C'mon, Ben. You're not a quitter. Just ride this out."

"Right, right."

"If you don't sell this book, maybe you'll sell the next one."

"I don't have time to write another book."

"Grueling life of a part-time pianist weighing you down?"

He gave her a sharp look. "No, but there's the minor matter of this murder case. And I'd like to check on Joey.

Even if he is with his mother, I feel responsible. I'm his guardian, after all. Or was, anyway."

Christina nodded. "I'm not surprised. You've always taken that *parens patriae* stuff very seriously."

Ben set down his fork. "Christina, when did you trade in your French?"

"Huh?"

"Ever since I've known you, you've driven me nuts with the pidgin French you picked up in that extension course at TCC. But lately, you've gone Latin."

She laughed unconvincingly. "How odd."

"Yes, very. And you're dropping case names like they were common knowledge and arguing legal issues like—" He stopped. His eyes widened. "You're going to law school, aren't you?"

Christina remained perfectly still, a frozen smile on her face. "Why would you say that?"

"Because it's true." He tossed down his napkin. "That's what all this mystery has been about. Those classes you've been going to—it's not some past lives nonsense. You've been taking classes at TU law school!"

Christina's eyes lowered. "I suppose there's no point in denying it."

"Why didn't you tell me?"

"Well, I wasn't sure how you'd take it."

"What do you mean?"

"Sometimes lawyers aren't all that pleased when their legal assistants try to . . . join them."

"Ben Kincaid—the insecure sexist pig?"

"I'm not saying that. I just thought it might be . . . awkward."

"Awkward? Awkward?"

"Yeah. Like now." She pushed away her plate. "Me and my big mouth."

"I don't know why you're acting this way." He folded his arms across his chest. "Why should I care that you're going to law school?"

"See! I knew it would be like this!"

"Christina, I could care less if you go to law school. I just can't believe you thought you couldn't confide in me."

"I thought it might make you uncomfortable. You know. Someone who used to work for you, on her way to becoming . . ."

"An equal?"

She shrugged. "Whatever."

"What is this, nineteenth-century England? You can damn well go to law school if you want, damn it! I can't stop you."

She put her hands to her face. "I knew you'd be upset!"

"I can't believe you thought I'd be upset!"

"But you *are* upset!"

"Yes, but not because you're going to law school!" He stopped himself, realizing he was almost shouting. "I just didn't think we kept secrets from each other. I tell you everything."

"You do not."

"Do too."

"Really! Did you tell me you were writing a book?"

"Well . . . no. But I was going to."

"Did you tell me about your father? Why he wrote you out of his will? Why he disowned you and said you weren't his son anymore?"

"Well, that's different."

"Did you tell me your favorite TV show is *Xena: Warrior Princess*?"

"What?" He sat bolt upright. "It is not."

"I found a tape full of *Xena* in the VCR in your living room."

"That . . . isn't mine."

"Yeah, well, I put it in the drawer with all the other *Xena* tapes that aren't yours."

"Christina!"

"The point is, no one tells anyone everything."

"No, the point is, you should have trusted me. The

point is, we shouldn't keep secrets from each other. We shouldn't—"

He stopped suddenly. What was going on here? They were starting to sound like—

He blinked. Now *that* was a disturbing thought.

He took a deep breath and tried to calm down. "Look, Christina, I *don't* mind. I'm just surprised, that's all."

"Uh-huh."

"I didn't even know you were interested in law school."

"I didn't know myself until about six months ago. After you decided you'd just up and stop practicing. Where did that leave me—a legal assistant with no lawyer? Then suddenly it dawned on me. Why should I be at the mercy of some lawyer all my life? Why should I be out of work every time he decides he wants to move or join a corporation or sing depressing folk songs in nightclubs? Why shouldn't I be a lawyer myself? I'm smart."

"You *are* smart."

"So I took the LSAT, just to see how it went. Turned out I did pretty well. So I applied at TU. And lo and behold—I got in. Cleaned out my savings, but I got in."

"So you're in your first year. Miserable, isn't it?"

"Yeah. This Socratic method bit really sucks."

"It's a rotten way to educate students," Ben said, "but a great head trip for professors."

"Yeah. That's it exactly." She slowly lifted her eyes. "So you're not mad at me?"

"Christina, you're being ridiculous. Of course I'm not mad at you. I'm proud of you." He winked. "And as soon as you get out of school, I'll give you a job."

"Who are you kidding? When I get out, I'll give *you* a job. And the paychecks will be a lot more regular, believe me."

"Christina, I'm wounded to the quick."

"Yeah, well, that's what we lawyers do, isn't it?"

* 28 *

The next morning, Christina drove the van while Ben navigated. They took the Cherokee Turnpike south out of Tulsa, turned near the Port of Catoosa, and headed toward Claremore.

"This place is somewhere along the side of the road," Ben said as he studiously pored over a map. "Before you get to Claremore, according to Gordo."

"I'll keep my eyes peeled," Christina answered. "What's the name again?"

"The Christian Purity Bible Camp."

"Right. How could I forget?" She pulled into the left-hand lane. "And Denny is staying here?"

"So I've been told. Some people live there all year round."

"They must be very pure."

"Apparently."

A few miles later, Ben pointed out the turnoff on the side of the road. Christina swerved over and drove down a dirt driveway barred by an iron gate. There was a speaker box beside the gate, with a big blue button beneath.

"Looks like they don't let just anyone in here," Christina commented.

"They wouldn't stay pure long if they did."

"Is anyone expecting us?"

"No. I was hoping we could just slip in and chat with Denny for a bit, then slip out again. Before we got contaminated with too much purity."

"Right." Christina reached out and pushed the blue

button. A few moments later, the speaker box crackled alive.

"I hope you're enjoying this beautiful day God has given us," said the tinny female voice emerging from the box. "Welcome to the Christian Purity Bible Camp. How can we serve you?"

"We're here to talk to one of your . . . er . . . campers."

The box crackled. "I'm afraid we have to maintain the privacy of our members. Admittance is only granted to members and prospective members. Are you interested in joining us?"

Christina hesitated barely a second. "Yes, that's right. We are."

"Very well," the voice in the box said. "I'll open the gate. Please drive straight to the administration cabin at the end of the main road. I'll meet you there. And of course, please refrain from taking any photographs along the way."

Ben's forehead creased. Did photography have a depurifying effect?

Christina pulled the van to the end of the road and parked. Ben opened the passenger-side door, hopped out, and found himself face-to-face with the woman behind the voice.

He froze, lips parted. "Buh—wha—I—"

She was an older woman, hair brown but flecked with gray. There were a few pronounced wrinkles in her face, but she was still healthy and attractive. She seemed friendly and relaxed, and yet her face bore a suggestion of sophistication. In fact, in many ways, she reminded Ben of his mother. Except for one minor detail.

She wasn't wearing any clothing.

"Welcome to the Christian Purity Bible Camp," she said, extending her hand. "I'm Rona Harris."

Wordlessly, Ben took her hand and shook it.

"Thank you for joining us. May I show you around?"

Ben tried to keep his eyes glued to her face, which was a considerable challenge under the circumstances.

"I'd be happy to give you the grand tour. Or if you'd like, you can talk to some of our happy campers." She paused, waiting for a response that didn't come. "Would that be acceptable?"

"Buh—" Ben replied.

"Is there something wrong?" Rona raised a hand to her face. "Oh my. You didn't know, did you?"

"Buh—wuh—" Ben sputtered.

Christina walked around from her side of the van, her eyes widening slightly as she took in the view. "We knew you were pure," Christina said. "We just didn't realize how pure."

Rona laughed. "I thought everyone knew by now. Everyone who knew enough about us to visit, anyway. How did you find out about us?"

Christina stepped in front of Ben. "Denny Bachalo is a friend of ours. He recommended it."

"Good for him." She turned back to Ben. "Perhaps Denny should be your tour guide."

"That's a great idea," Christina supplied. "Do you know where he is?"

"I don't, but Kerrie will. She's in charge of daily activities. Sort of like our cruise director." She laughed. "Why don't we head toward her cabin? We can talk along the way." She took Ben's arm and wrapped it around hers, drawing him close. "Shall we?"

"Buh-wuh—*wuh*—" Ben said compliantly.

Ben walked side by side with Rona, with Christina just a few steps behind. Somewhere along the way, he managed to find his voice.

"Would you feel more comfortable if I put something on?" Rona asked.

"In a word, yes."

"All right." She reached into her small purse, withdrew

a chiffon scarf, and wrapped it artfully around her head. "There. Is that better?"

She and Christina giggled.

"Much," Ben said quietly. "Thanks."

As they strolled through the grounds, they passed several people sitting under shade trees, reading, meditating. Male and female. And every one of them naked as the day they were born.

"Somehow," Ben said, "despite all the strange things I've encountered these past few years, I never expected to stumble into a Christian nudist camp."

Rona tittered. "Well, a few years ago, I would've laughed if someone had told me I would be superintending one. But here I am."

"I didn't think Christians liked nudity."

"That's the impression we're trying to correct. Christian discomfort with nudity goes back to Adam and Eve. You know, in Eden we were naked, but after we sinned, we were clothed. Hence nudity is associated with sin. And of course, most fundamentalist groups encourage modesty in dress so as not to provoke . . . passionate responses."

"Some of Christina's outfits have provoked passionate responses," Ben said, "but probably not in the way you mean."

"Here at the Christian Purity Bible Camp," Rona continued, "we believe these views have distorted the proper focus, have obscured the true meaning of the parable. Why go on obsessing over Eve's mistake? After all, when we become Christians, our sins are forgiven. We hope we can recapture some of the purity of spirit that must have been present at the beginning. Some of that original goodness."

Ben looked at her blank-faced. "By shedding your clothing."

"How better? If clothes are simply a reminder of our fall, why shouldn't we cast them aside? Here at the Christian Purity Camp we say, let's put away the reminders of what we failed to do, and seek instead to discover what we can do."

"The Bible does say God created man in His own image," Christina offered.

"Exactly." Rona was getting excited, catching fire on her favorite subject. "And if that's so, what right have we to hide God's own image? His image reflects one aspect of His divinity. It's a gift—not something to be buried under T-shirts and stonewashed jeans."

"So you founded the Christian Purity Bible Camp."

"Oh my, no. I didn't start it. I'm simply a local facilitator. And a believer, of course. The first camp was established in North Carolina. This is the seventh in the nation, and we have plans to start three more next year."

"Wow."

"We even have a national newsletter—*The Fig Tree Forum*. Ah, here we are." She stopped in front of a tiny cabin. "Let me step inside for just a moment." She knocked gently on the door, then entered.

As soon as she was gone, Christina whirled to face Ben. "Ben, you've gotten me into some pretty bizarre situations over the years. But a Christian nudist colony? This takes the cake."

"Look, it's not as if I knew—"

"Well, you should have. From now on, before you take me anywhere, I want you to thoroughly investigate one major question: do they wear clothing?"

He patted her on the shoulder. "Christina, just say a little prayer. I'm sure your angel will get you through this."

"Get me through? My angel is telling me to get the hell out of here!"

Before they had a chance to continue the discussion, Rona emerged with another woman. Kerrie was much younger than Rona—probably mid-twenties, Ben guessed, and he had every reason to be able to make a good guess, because all the available evidence was on display.

"Hi, I'm Kerrie," she said, with a buoyant bounce in her

voice and, Ben noted, the rest of her as well. "I'm glad you could come."

Ben struggled ruthlessly to maintain strict eye contact. "This is Christina McCall," he said, pointing. "And I'm Ben Kincaid."

Kerrie drew back suddenly. "Not *the* Ben Kincaid."

Christina's lips parted. "*The* Ben Kincaid?"

"I mean—" Her hand rose to her mouth. "The lawyer. The one who represented Mayor Barrett."

Ben tilted his head to one side. "That was me."

"I can't believe it! I used to watch you every day on television during the trial."

"You must've been terribly bored," Ben said.

"Oh, no. You were fabulous! Before I joined this camp, I considered becoming a lawyer myself. Especially after I saw what you did in the courtroom."

"Believe me, it was nothing great."

"You're too modest. I'm surprised they haven't put you on Court TV or something. You've got it all. You're young, smart, cute—"

Christina rolled her eyes. "Maybe I should wait in the car."

Kerrie flew toward Ben, practically overflowing with enthusiasm. He tried to step away, but she clasped his hand and held him fast. "If I can help you in any way, Mr. Kincaid, I would be so honored. Really I would."

Ben cleared his throat. "We want to talk to Denny Bachalo. If you know where he is . . ."

"He'll be down at the prayer meeting right now. I'd be honored if you'd let me show you the way."

Ben glanced up. "Well, okay. Christina—"

Kerrie didn't quite frown. "She's welcome too, of course."

Christina smiled wryly. "Like I said, maybe I should wait in the car."

"That'll be fine. Of course"—Kerrie turned back toward Ben—"if you're attending the prayer meeting, you'll have to . . . change your attire."

"You mean . . . put on something a little less—"

"Yes, exactly."

"I don't think—"

"If you're not ready to go completely nude yet, we have some little towels you can wear around your waist."

Christina pressed her hand against her mouth. "I'm definitely waiting in the car." She turned back the way they'd come, a waved hand in the air. "See you later, Ben. I'll expect a full report."

"But, Christina!"

Kerrie whispered into his ear, "I'd let her go."

Ben felt her hot and very present flesh pressing close to him. "Why?"

Kerrie sniffed. "I only have one towel."

"Are you sure this is absolutely necessary?"

"I'm afraid so, Mr. Kincaid."

Ben stared at himself in the mirror hanging on the wall of the changing room. It was him all right—skinny, white as a ghost, and wearing nothing but a ridiculous white terry-cloth cover-up around his waist. He looked like an extra from *The Ten Commandments*. Without the Man Tan.

"Couldn't you just explain that I'm not a member?"

Kerrie shouted back at him through the curtain. "I'm afraid it would be considered very offensive. Just imagine. How would you feel if you were attending your church service and someone walked in—"

"Naked?"

"Yes. Well, this is the same thing. Except exactly the opposite. If you know what I mean."

He continued staring into the mirror. "I can't believe anyone would be comfortable in a getup like this."

"Most people aren't. That's why they go nude. The towels are just for the newcomers and people with . . . special problems."

Ben's eyes widened. "Special problems?"

She nodded. "Susceptibility to sunburn. In the least desirable places."

"Oh." As a delaying tactic, Ben decided to read the RULES OF CONDUCT posted on a sign in the changing room:

PLEASE REMEMBER THAT THIS IS A CHRISTIAN FAMILY PARK. WE EXPECT YOUR CONDUCT TO CONFORM WITH THE MORAL STANDARDS OF A FAMILY ENVIRONMENT AT ALL TIMES. CAMERAS AND CAMCORDERS ARE NOT PERMITTED EXCEPT BY SPECIAL PERMISSION OF THE MANAGEMENT AND THE PHOTO SUBJECT. NO PETS ARE ALLOWED IN THE COMMON AREAS. PLEASE SHOWER— WITH SOAP—BEFORE ENTERING THE POOL OR HOT TUB. REMEMBER, YOU MUST BE NUDE. NO CLOTHING, BATHING SUITS, OR INTIMATE BODY JEWELRY WILL BE PERMITTED.

Ben winced. Intimate body jewelry?

He made a few more minute adjustments to the tiny towel. It seemed there was no turning back, so he took a deep breath and pushed himself through the curtain. "Ta-da."

Kerrie giggled. "You look divine, Mr. Kincaid."

"Right." He walked brusquely toward the door. "And by the way, call me Ben."

"Oh, wow. I can't believe it. This is like a dream come true."

"For me, too. Now where's this prayer meeting?"

They left the cabin and strolled down a hilly expanse, threading their way through unclothed acolytes and meditators. Kerrie chattered virtually nonstop. She had apparently tuned in for every day of the gavel-to-gavel coverage of the Barrett case. Consequently, she was abundantly knowledgeable about Ben's cases and career.

"I think it's just wonderful the way you've been able to help people," she chimed.

"It would be more wonderful if they paid regularly."

"I'm sure helping people isn't the way to get rich, but you had to do what was in your heart. You know what being a lawyer is supposed to be about, even if the rest of the world seems to have forgotten." She touched his exposed shoulder. "What cases are you working on now?"

"To tell you the truth, Kerrie—" He stopped. He couldn't bring himself to dash her enthusiasm with the revelation that he wasn't practicing anymore.

A few moments later, they arrived at an open-faced clamshell-style arena with rows and rows of stone-bench seating. The arena was about half occupied.

The attendees were on their feet singing "Amazing Grace." Up front, a video screen was flashing the words in a follow-the-bouncing-ball style.

"Christian karaoke," Ben noted. "I love it."

He scanned the rows of benches as the multitudes finished the song: " 'We've no-o le-ess days, to si-ing God's praise, than when we-ee first began.' "

A man with an impressive hairdo—and nary a stitch of clothing—walked to center stage and began preaching.

"At least you know he has nothing to hide," Ben said.

Kerrie nudged him. "I see Denny. He's in the back." She pointed.

"Okay. Thanks."

"Ben?"

He stopped. "Yes?"

She stood awkwardly beside him. Ben realized that one of the problems with wearing no clothing—one of many—was that you had nowhere to put your hands. "After you've had a chance to talk, do you think maybe . . ."

He waited anxiously for the end of the sentence. "Yes?"

She twirled her fingers. "I know it's presumptuous of me, but I just thought maybe we could get together. You know—to talk. I'd love to hear more about your work." She took a step closer to him. "And then we'd just see what developed . . ."

He took a step back. "Unfortunately, I'm very busy right now."

"Oh. Of course." Her eager smile faded.

"I've got this new investigation going. And time is of the essence."

Her eyes met the floor. "Sure. I understand."

He peered down at her crestfallen face. "But look. Can I call you here at the camp? Maybe we can set something up. After the crunch has passed."

Her chin lifted. "Would you? Would you really?"

"If I can. And for that matter, my number's in the book."

"I can't believe it!" She wrapped her arms tightly around him. "This is so exciting! I can't believe this!"

Ben sidled out of her embrace. "I'd probably better talk to Denny now."

"Right. I don't want to slow you down, 'cause I know how important your work is." She turned away, then turned back. "But if there's anything I can do—"

"You'll be the first one I call."

She wrapped her arms around herself. "I can't believe this! I just can't believe this!"

Neither can I, Ben thought. Neither can I.

He carved a path through the thick of the congregation. He did his best to wind his way through the pews without letting his eyes drop below chin level. It was a challenging exercise in mental concentration.

Finally he made it to Denny's row. He slid into the pew beside him.

"Ben!" It was the same old Denny he had known and admired behind the drum set, except that he was now naked as a jaybird. "What are you doing here?"

"I wanted to see you." Although, he thought, I didn't want to see as much of you as I'm seeing.

"Hey, you look good in a towel. Nice pecs."

"Gee, thanks. Look, can we talk?"

"Well, I don't know." He gestured toward the front. "We're having Bible study."

"I'll keep my voice down." Ben slid in close. "I wanted to ask if you saw anything the other night. You know, before I found the body."

"Man, I've already answered these questions for the cops. Who are you, Junior G-man?"

"No, I'm a lawyer."

"Oh, man, right. Like, I heard that, but I didn't believe it."

"Believe it. The cops are on Earl's tail, and he's asked me to help. Find out what really happened."

"Just like *Matlock* on TV."

"Something like that. Did you see anything out of the ordinary? Anything maybe you didn't remember at first, but did later?"

Denny shook his head. "I don't think so, man. The whole evening seemed perfectly same-old same-old to me. Till that corpse flopped down in your face." He leaned closer. "Hey, what did that feel like, anyway?"

"Like a sack of cold slimy Spam giving you a full-front tackle," Ben answered. "Except it turns out not to be Spam."

Denny shook all over. "Brrrrrrr. Glad it wasn't me. Worse than fingernails on the chalkboard."

"Much." Ben tried to get back on track. "Did you hear anyone say anything unusual?"

"Not that I recall. Well, just Earl. Muttering about something—I didn't know what. Man, he was really uptight that night."

Ben nodded. "Diane told me she thought you seemed rather uptight yourself."

"Me? Hell, I'm always uptight before a show. Stage jitters, that's all."

"You've probably heard that I saw some guy who said he was delivering a rug. I don't suppose you saw him, by any chance?"

" 'Fraid not. After we finished rehearsing, I went out to have a smoke and pray. I like to get in a worshipful mood before we perform. So I walked out toward the woods till I found a place I could be alone."

"So you could . . . pray?"

"Right."

Ben's lips parted. "But you didn't—"

Denny laughed. "No, Ben, I didn't strip off my clothes. That isn't a requisite, you know. We do it here, where we have some privacy, because we think it brings us closer to God. But I don't do it, like, in the middle of the workday. What do you think I am, some kind of nut?"

"Perish the thought." Ben decided to try another tack. "How long have you known Earl?"

" 'Bout a year. Since he opened the club."

"Not before?"

He shook his head. "I'd heard his name, mind you. I was playing some clubs down in Dallas and Oklahoma City. Of course, whenever people started talking jazz sax, someone would mention Earl Bonner. Earl Bonner and the great Professor Hoodoo. They'd tell the whole story. You know, how they were the best of friends and played together like magic, but then they fell in love with the same woman, and Earl blew the Professor away. It's almost a legend now. Like Frankie and Johnny."

"So you knew Earl had done time for that murder."

"Oh, sure."

"And you assumed he was guilty."

"I think everyone assumed he was guilty, Ben. It, like, went without saying, you know?"

"And that didn't bother you?"

Denny grinned. "What, like, he might come after me next?" He chuckled softly. "I don't think so. I wouldn't cross the man. Covet not another dude's squeeze. That's my motto."

Words to live by, Ben thought. "Still, if he lost his temper once . . ."

"Hey, everyone's got a temper, okay?" For the first time Denny was showing a trace of his. "You just have to learn to keep it under control. And Earl's had twenty-two long years to practice, okay? Next question."

Ben squinted. What had he triggered? "Did you ever hear Earl talk about . . . what happened before?"

"Of course not, man. That's not somethin' a man drops into casual conversation."

"Can you think of anything else you know about the murder?"

"Which one? You seem to be investigating both."

Ben paused. He supposed he was at that. But that grisly smile told him that the two killings were connected. Or that someone wanted it believed they were, at any rate. "Either one."

"Well, the expert on Professor Hoodoo would be Scat. Scat goes back further than Earl or the Professor combined. He's been playin' forever, man. Word is he taught Gabriel how to blow."

"And he was with them at the time of the first murder?"

"I think so. They were thick as thieves. Played together, worked together. Inseparable. Till they were separated by the law, that is. And the grim reaper." He smiled. "But Scat's the expert on Professor Hoodoo. I'd talk to him if you're really interested in this whole big back-story thing."

Given the circumstances, Ben thought, that seemed like pretty good advice.

"For that matter, didn't Hoodoo have a brother?"

Ben snapped his fingers. "That's right—Grady Armstrong. I met him at the club."

"He might have some light to shed on the situation."

Ben made a mental note. Maybe he would at that.

He glanced up at the front of the arena. The preacher was still bellowing away, raising his fist, giving the call to action—without a single reference to the fact that he wasn't wearing any clothing.

"How long have you been a member of this group?" Ben asked.

Denny shrugged. " 'Bout three years now."

"Mind if I ask how you got into it?"

Denny hesitated a moment. "A few years back . . . I was pretty messed up. You know, drugs and all. I was taking uppers before I played, downers to sleep. Coke for a good time. Almost all the musicians I knew did it. Difference was, they could handle it. I couldn't. Pretty soon, I was so screwed up, I didn't know night from day. Didn't know when I was on and when I was off. Used to be the music was all I needed to get me through, you know? But after a while, that wasn't enough. I needed the junk. I needed the bright lights. Truth is, I was about one short step from a pine box. And I knew it." He inhaled slowly. "I knew it, but there wasn't a damn thing I could do about it."

He paused before looking up again. "And then Rona Harris introduced me to this place. Now, it's not like everything changed all at once. I was a junkie; I had to dry out. But they helped me, you know? They got me through it. I felt for the first time like someone really cared."

"I know how important that is," Ben said.

"Once I had my head clear, I took to this place like a duck to water. I believed what the preachers had to say. And this whole business of taking your clothes off—it may sound like nothing to you, but I found it liberating. Like I didn't have to hide anymore. Like the real me was set free." He smiled. "I still play the music, as well you know. But I don't feel like I have to. It's something I do, but it doesn't own me. It doesn't control me. It's part of my life, but it's not my life. Am I making any sense?"

Ben nodded. "I'm glad it worked out for you."

"Hey, it's not just me. It could work out for you, too."

"Well . . ."

"If you don't mind me saying so, Ben, you seem a little tight, you know? All locked away. If you started coming out here, you could feel a little . . . freer."

"I don't think I want to be that free."

"What's the big deal? People make such a fuss about nudity—it's not like we're having some big orgy out here. It seems strange, but it's almost a totally asexual experience."

"Asexual," Ben echoed.

"Right. We're all so used to it, we hardly even notice."

"I would notice," Ben said emphatically.

"Maybe at first, but that would pass. You'd forget about the need to hide and start to just—well, be who you really are."

Good grief, Ben thought, are we back to that again? "I'll keep that in mind."

"You should." He glanced over Ben's shoulder and saw Kerrie waiting in the background. "Like I said, it could be a meaningful spiritual experience."

"That's what you said."

"And, if it turns out I'm wrong, hey—that Kerrie is a hot chick."

Ben tried not to smile. "In a totally asexual way."

Denny winked. "My thoughts exactly."

* 29 *

Tyrone threaded his way through the mazelike alley-ways of the condemned Rockwood section of North Tulsa. It was already dark, and the streetlights had all been broken out a long time ago. No one bothered to replace them. After all, no one lived out here anymore, right? No one was supposed to, anyway.

He tried to remember the path that took him where he needed to go. All of these buildings were crumbling, barely enough remained to be called ruins. They were just worthless piles of rubble waiting for someone to care enough to bring in a wrecking ball and lay it all flat. He felt like Theseus trailing his way through the Minotaur's labyrinth, something he'd read about in one of Earl's books. 'Cept he didn't have any string with him at the moment; he would have to rely on memory. And make sure he didn't bump into the Minotaur.

He hadn't warned anyone he was coming. It seemed safer that way. Most boys who left the gang moved to parts far away and unknown. But not Tyrone. He'd stayed right here in town. That must've really bugged Momo, and bugging Momo was something you definitely didn't want to do.

He crisscrossed through a street corner and brought him-self to the north edge of the Rockwood area. You could see the Broken Arrow Expressway from here. You could also see a huge crater in the middle of the alley. What had happened—lightning? A bomb? Tyrone tended to favor unnatural causes, given where he was.

He leaped into the air, grabbed a rusted fire escape ladder that was hanging off the side of the nearest building, and swung himself over the crater. He dropped onto the other side, slapping his hands together. Nothing like a little physical activity to get the adrenaline pumping. He needed that, needed to be at the top of his form. If he was gonna survive this next bit of business.

He rounded the corner, took a few steps into the dark alley, then froze.

Someone else was here. He wasn't sure how he knew, but he knew. Maybe he heard something too soft to register except with his subconscious. Maybe he saw something—a shadow, a reflection. Maybe he could just feel another set of eyes on him.

He laughed nervously, then took a step across the gravel ground. The echo came just a beat late.

Right the first time. He was not alone.

"So who is it?" he said, using his loudest and boldest voice. "I'm coming your way, anyway. There's no need for bein' so goddamned mysterious."

Brave words, he thought to himself. But he didn't feel that brave. He didn't feel brave at all.

"C'mon already," Tyrone repeated. Damn—there was just the slightest tremble in his voice. Slight, but plenty enough to be heard. He cranked up the volume a notch. "Show yourself or I'm gonna start shootin' into the shadows!"

"You never carried a gun before," the voice behind him said.

Tyrone whirled around. It was pitch black; he couldn't see a thing.

"And I seriously doubt you've started now. Too risky in your line of work. If you get picked up carryin', your sentence is gonna double, maybe triple." The voice laughed. " 'Sides, I don't think you've got the cojones."

"Bulldog," Tyrone murmured. "What the hell do you want?"

The man at the end of the alley stepped out of the shadows. It was Bulldog, all right, and one look at his face reminded Tyrone how he came by his colorful nickname. He was wearing a long overcoat and had both hands tucked into his pockets. And Tyrone felt certain that Bulldog, unlike him, really did have a gun firmly clenched in each hand.

"The question," Bulldog said smoothly, "is what do you want?"

"I want to be left alone."

"Evidently not." He stepped closer—closer, to be sure, than Tyrone would have preferred. "Nobody what wants to be left alone comes strollin' in our territory."

"I need to see Momo," Tyrone said. He tried to keep his knees from knocking. Never let them know you're afraid.

"The only thing you need is to get out of here before I have to take an extreme sanction."

"Shouldn't you ask Momo about that? Word on the street is that he wants to see me."

"He does. But that doesn't mean you want to see him." A thin smile curled up on Bulldog's face. "Momo says you owe him."

"Momo's delusional. I don't owe nothin' to nobody. I paid all my debts before I got out."

"Momo says different."

"Momo is wrong."

"Momo is our leader. Ergo, Momo is never wrong." He paused, moving even closer to Tyrone. "Momo was displeased when you left us."

"Yeah? Well, tell Momo I wanted to live to see my twenty-second birthday, and the way things were going, I didn't think my prospects were very good."

"Momo says he put years into your training and development. He says he didn't get an adequate return on his investment."

"That doesn't entitle him to put a price on my head."

"He thinks it does."

"Well, he's wrong. I got enough problems with two warrants hanging over me. I might become fairly high profile pretty soon, and I can't do that thinkin' some asshole punk gangster might take the opportunity to blow my face off. If Momo doesn't call off the heat, I'm not gonna be able to help a friend of mine."

Bulldog pressed his lips together. "You're talkin' about Earl Bonner."

"Maybe."

"We know Earl. We respect him. Momo was not happy when that shoot-out happened so close to Earl's place. He figures we owe Earl one."

"Then Momo needs to call off the dogs."

Bulldog stood so close to Tyrone he could feel the man's breath on his face, and it wasn't a pleasant experience. Tyrone's knees were trembling; his teeth wouldn't stay still.

"You set a bad example for the troops, T-Dog. You cut out without so much as a word to no one. You don't even have the good grace to leave town. What would happen if all the boys did that?"

"The world would be a better place," Tyrone said, immediately regretting it. That was stupid—but it was too late to will the words back. "Look, Bulldog, help me out here. We're homeboys. We grew up together."

"That was before you cut out. Now we're nothin'."

"There must be something you can do. Talk to Momo for me."

"Momo will not discuss this matter with me. He says he'll only talk to you."

So that was how it was. Momo wanted a meeting on his turf—a meeting Tyrone might never walk away from. But if he didn't take the chance, he'd never be free.

"When does he want to meet?"

Bulldog pressed his hands against the sides of his coat from inside the pockets. "No time like the present."

"I've got another meeting tonight. Shouldn't take long, though. How about in half an hour?"

Bulldog shrugged. "I'll propose it to Momo. I can't promise he'll be here."

"You can make it happen, Bulldog."

He shook his head. "You overestimate me."

"Please, Bulldog. Do it for me. Or do it for Earl. Whatever. Just do it, okay?"

"I'll do what I can." He took a few short steps back and disappeared into the shadows.

Tyrone raised a hand and wiped his forehead. He was dripping with sweat. He leaned against the brick wall, using it for the support he could no longer give himself.

He'd forgotten how hard all this gang crap could be, how terrifying. How badly he'd wanted out. Momo had to give him his walking papers, once and for all. He had to do this for him.

Tyrone pressed his hand against his temple, trying to slow his breathing, to calm himself. When he finally felt certain he had himself back together again, he started retracing his steps back through the labyrinth. He had another meeting to make now, with Earl. To plan out the future. And after that—

After that, he would return here and find out if he had a future.

* 30 *

Ben met Earl at Nelson's Buffeteria, Tulsa's most famous downtown eatery. This restaurant was such an established landmark it had been written up in *National Geographic*. Nelson's had been around for a million and one years, and it still retained its Depression-era ambience. Most of the menu was carbo heaven—chicken-fried steak and mashed potatoes, everything smothered in gravy. It was Earl's favorite dining experience.

Ben told Earl what he had learned during the course of his interviews. "I still need to talk to Scat. He's the only member of the band I haven't spoken to individually."

"Scat don't have nothin' to do with no murder," Earl said as he terminated his apple pie. "I can tell you that right now."

"Maybe not. But he might still come in handy. Maybe he saw something; maybe he heard something."

"Don't you think he would've said so by now?"

"Sometimes people don't realize the significance of what they know. Sometimes they forget. I've seen people totally forget important pieces of information till they're on the witness stand. You never know."

"Well, I'll set somethin' up, but I don't want you givin' Scat no bad time. He's been around a while, you know?"

"I know."

"Man's old as Moses, and about as good. He's done a lot for me. Me and the Professor both. So I don't want you treatin' him like no criminal."

"You have my word, Earl."

201

"All right then." He wiped his face with a napkin. "What else?"

"I've spoken with Lieutenant Morelli at police head-quarters," Ben explained. "He's says they're still not pre-pared to make an arrest. But he also told me Police Chief Blackwell is under pressure, both from the press and from the city council, to make an arrest. So you figure it out."

Earl grunted. "It's gonna happen. They're jus' bidin' their time."

"Yeah, but their time's gonna come quickly. We have to be ready. That includes Tyrone. He's all that's kept you out of the hoosegow this long."

Earl coughed into his hand. "About Tyrone. I wanted to talk to you about that."

"Is there a problem? Is he threatening to recant?"

"No, no. I jus' don't want the boy involved."

"Earl, we don't have any choice. He's critical to our case."

"If he testifies for me, he puts himself on the line."

"He's already on the line. Those warrants bearing his name will exist whether he testifies for you or not."

"But he could get out. He could deal. Right?"

Ben didn't say anything.

"If he becomes the witness that puts a dent in their nice neat case against me, they're gonna go up against him with everything they have. Hell, they'll probably call in both warrants and charge him jus' so they can say he's a criminal when he takes the stand." He leaned forward. "Right?"

Ben pursed his lips. "It's possible."

"But it's a sure thing they'll go against Tyrone, right? Don't lie to me, Ben."

"Lieutenant Morelli doesn't think either charge amounts to much. But if your case goes to trial"—Ben drew in his breath—"you're right. The prosecutor is certain to go after Tyrone."

"Well, I don't want that to happen. Tyrone's a good boy. He's tryin' to straighten himself out. He deserves a chance."

"But if he knows something, he has an obligation to come forward."

"You're not listenin' to me, Ben. They'll crucify him."

"You can't be sure of that. You don't even know he's guilty."

"I know the cops have a way of makin' a man guilty if they want him to be."

Ben didn't argue; Earl was the expert on that subject. "Look, let me talk to Tyrone. See what really happened. If this fraud warrant is a bum rap, I'll do everything in my power to get him off."

"And if it isn't?"

"We'll find out how strong the prosecution case is. We'll see what they've got, then take it from there."

"Meaning what?"

"Meaning we'll talk about the possibility of not using Tyrone as a witness. Just let me talk to him."

"I'm supposed to be meetin' Tyrone tonight." Earl checked his watch. "In fact, I'm late."

"It's a little late in the day for a sax lesson, isn't it?"

"This wasn't no sax lesson. This was for me to give him a wad of cash and tell him to get the hell out of Dodge. Before he gets dragged into this mess."

"Please don't do that, Earl. Please." Ben leaned across the table. "Look, let me keep your meeting. I'll see Tyrone, try to get this thing worked out. There must be some solution that doesn't send anyone to prison. Or worse."

"I don't know. I—"

"Please, Earl, trust me on this one. Give me a chance."

Earl stared at Ben. "All right," he said finally. "You keep the meetin'. But I want to hear about it, and if you can't get him off the hook—"

Ben nodded. "We'll discuss that when we get there."

He checked his watch once more before leaving. Good, just enough time to make the appointment.

He was pleased to see it was a dark night. He had completely repainted the van; still, it was best not to take any risks. The whole purpose of this venture was to terminate the risks, not to create new ones.

He made sure he had everything—keys, wallet, and most important, the shiny silver blade. That would come in handy tonight.

He'd had trouble sleeping lately. He was plagued by nightmares. Fears that the stupid-ass kid in the bathroom might finally realize who and what he had seen.

He couldn't let that happen. He would get no rest until that threat was eliminated.

Which was what tonight was all about.

He fingered the handle of the long serrated blade tucked in the holster of his belt. This was the night he put his fears to rest. This was the night the nightmares stopped, the long darkness ended.

He stopped on his way out the door, touching that shiny gold Supertone sax for luck. There had to be some luck coming off that, didn't there? Had to be something special about it.

He left the house and started toward the garage. He was feeling lucky already. This would be the last night for his problems. The last night he would have to worry.

And the last night—period!—for one Tyrone Jackson.

He smiled, his hand gripping the knife. Tyrone Jackson—and anyone else who got in his way.

* 31 *

When Tyrone arrived at Uncle Earl's, no one was there. The lights were out and the door was locked. He waited ten minutes, but no one showed. He peered through the club window, but he didn't see anything untoward. Maybe Earl had forgotten. Maybe he'd gotten tired and gone home.

Long enough, Tyrone decided. It was dark out here, and he was alone, and for some reason, the whole situation gave him the creeps. He'd better start heading back if he expected to make his other appointment. He definitely did not want to be late. He was in deep enough with Momo already. He'd come back tomorrow and find out what had happened with Earl.

He returned to his car. Why did he have this overwhelming *creepy* feeling? Shivers raced down his body. He checked the backseat, making sure he was alone. Then he slid into the driver's seat, locked the doors from the inside, and started the car. It was stupid, but he couldn't shake the feeling that someone was watching him.

He backed the car down the gravel driveway and pulled onto Brady, heading north. He could be in Rockwood in ten minutes, and the sooner the better, as far as he was concerned. He was ready to finish this. There was too much uncertainty in his life. Too much risk. Too much of this nauseating feeling that at any moment he might go tumbling over the brink.

He had left the gang for a reason—so he wouldn't have to go through his entire life feeling this way. He didn't like it. He wanted to spend his time blowing the sax, not worrying about whether—

His eyes darted to the rearview mirror. A pair of headlights gleamed in the distance, maybe a hundred feet behind him. High off the ground, too—probably a pickup or a van. Not that close; actually, he'd be happier if it was closer. Then he wouldn't have this uncomfortable feeling that whoever was driving the thing didn't want to be spotted.

Those headlights had been with him since he'd left the club. And he didn't like that at all.

He leaned forward, squinting slightly, trying to see the car behind the headlights. He couldn't make out any details, couldn't get the color or the make. But it wasn't long enough to be a pickup. It had a different shape, a wider, roomier look.

It was a van. Had to be.

He pressed his foot down on the accelerator, creeping steadily over the speed limit. The van fell back at first, as if taken by surprise, but soon accelerated to keep pace. No closer, no farther. It just maintained the same distance behind.

The driver couldn't really do anything to him while he was driving, Tyrone reasoned. But as soon as he stopped somewhere . . .

Tyrone made an abrupt right turn, careening off the main road and tearing down a residential street at a speed much too fast for the narrow, pothole-pocked road. He bumped and rattled, scraping his muffler on the concrete.

The turn had been quick, but not quick enough. The headlights followed.

As his pursuer rounded the corner, Tyrone got a good broadside view.

It was a van, all right. Definitely a van. And who did he know that drove a van?

Well, Kincaid, for one.

And the man in the disguise who delivered the rug. The man who probably killed Lily Campbell.

Tyrone made another sudden right turn, then another at his first opportunity. He didn't have any illusions that he was going to lose this van, but he suddenly had a desperate desire to get back to the main road. If something did happen, he didn't want it to happen here in the shadows, off the beaten track. Most of these houses were empty, and of the few that weren't, there was no chance the residents would be opening their doors this late at night.

On a sudden hunch, Tyrone slowed his car outside the last house on the block, stopped, and laid on the horn. In his rearview, he saw the van slow and stop just before it made the last turn. It was waiting for him to move, not getting too close, just in case someone responded to the horn.

He honked again, several times rapidly, as if trying to get someone's attention. With luck, the driver of the van would get the mistaken impression that he was waiting for someone, expecting to pick someone up. Or to put it another way, that he had made this detour through the residential section for a reason other than losing his tail. Tyrone thought it best that the driver not realize he had been spotted, or at the least, that he not be sure.

After a few more honks, Tyrone made a big show of shrugging his shoulders, then put the car back into drive. He returned to the main road and started cruising, just a few notches beneath the speed limit. Sure enough, the van followed him onto the road and assumed its former near-invisible position about a hundred feet behind.

Who the hell was it? Tyrone pounded on the steering column. He could feel sweat trickling down the side of his face—for the second time tonight—and he didn't like it. Damn. He thought he'd left all this crap behind, all this cloak-and-dagger, macho, crimes-and-misdemeanors BS. He didn't want this in his life!

Especially when he didn't know who was after him. That was what bothered him most. It wasn't Momo back there. It wasn't Bulldog and it wasn't the cops. It was some unknown asshole in a van. Tyrone didn't know who he was. And he had a distinct feeling he didn't want to find out. Or that if he did, it would be the last thing he ever did.

He was getting close to Rockwood now. In a few minutes, he would return to where he had left his car earlier that evening. Then he would have to get out and thread his way through the back alleys to Momo's hideout. And he didn't particularly want to be doing it with Mr. Rug Delivery breathing down his neck. If that guy got his hands on him, Tyrone felt certain he'd never make it to his meeting.

He eased off the gas pedal, slowing the car. Nothing sudden, nothing that would raise immediate suspicion. Forty-five, forty, thirty. As before, the car behind him was initially surprised, then adjusted its speed to compensate. As soon as the van was back in its respectfully distant place, Tyrone slowed the car even more. Thirty, twenty-five, twenty.

Just as he reached the point where he would've parked anyway, he brought the car to a sudden stop. He was going slow enough that he could do it quickly, without tipping off the van driver until it was too late for him to do anything about it. The van passed Tyrone, still cruising, then rounded the curve in the road ahead, brakes squealing.

Tyrone knew he didn't have much time. He scrambled out of his car and made a beeline for the safety of Rockwood. If he could immerse himself in that labyrinth of ruins and rubble, the van driver would never be able to find him. And he could still get to Momo before Momo was even madder at him than he already was.

Doing his best impression of an Olympic sprinter, Tyrone bolted across the highway and made for the nearest building. The ABC Cab Company—at least that's what it used to be. It was nothing now, rusted old cab frames hoisted onto cinder blocks and forgotten.

He plunged into the dark alleyway and pressed up against the side of a building to listen. He didn't hear anything, thank God. The Rug Man was not in pursuit. Tyrone actually managed to give him the slip.

Tyrone found a fire escape ladder on the north side and scaled it till he found a safe perch on the roof. He stepped cautiously; he knew this roof was probably far from safe. Crouching on all fours, he crawled across till he got a view of the street below.

He could see his car, even in the darkness of these unlit streets. And from his high perch, he could see the van, around the bend and perhaps four or five hundred feet ahead. He had expected the driver to turn around and double back. That would be the logical thing to do.

Unless the driver was smarter than that.

He peered down at the van, dark and motionless. There were no lights on. Although he couldn't be certain, he saw no indication that anyone was sitting inside.

The driver had abandoned his car, just as Tyrone had abandoned his. Neither of them could use them, or would need them, on this particular battlefield.

The driver was on foot.

He could be anywhere now. Anywhere at all.

Ben checked his watch, checked his speedometer, then pressed the pedal all the harder. He'd been late for Earl's appointment with Tyrone even before he knew there was an appointment, and he knew Tyrone wouldn't hang around forever. If he didn't get to talk to him now, there was no telling when or if he would. Tyrone might do a bolt, might decide to forget what he saw. Anything could happen, none of it good. He needed to talk to the kid.

He crossed over Archer and headed into North Tulsa. He was coming up on what was left of the old Rockwood development. He hated this part of town; it reminded him of the profound disparity that still existed, too often along racial lines, between the haves and the have-nots in this city. Worse, it reminded him of a harrowing chase he and Mike had made through this part of town after a little boy who had been abducted. Just driving down the road gave him the shivers.

A few minutes before he would have reached the club,

he noticed a car on the side of the road; he was traveling so fast he passed it before his eyes registered what it was. Some old van, probably broken down and abandoned. A second or two later, he came upon yet another car, a beat-up red Firebird.

What was the deal? Too lazy to take them to the dump? Or did they think Rockwood was close enough to being a dump? As he passed the second car, something caught in the corner of his eye. He saw the distinctive racing stripes ornamenting the hood and the sides—double bolts of jagged yellow lightning. Wait a minute . . .

He slowed down and pulled over to the shoulder so he could get a closer look at the car through his rearview. He was almost certain he had seen that car before—in the parking lot at Earl's.

Of course. That was Tyrone's car. But what was it doing on the side of the road?

Maybe Tyrone'd gotten tired of waiting for Ben. Understandable, but why would he come here? Why would he ever want to leave his car in this neighborhood?

Something screwy was going on. After making a quick check for traffic and cops, Ben made a U-turn. Slowing, he pulled up behind Tyrone's car. There didn't appear to be anyone inside.

Ben understood what people meant when they talked about their blood running cold. He felt as if ice floes were coursing just below his skin. He was getting goose bumps from head to toe. If he was smart, he realized, he'd start his car and get the hell out of there.

But Tyrone might be in trouble. And if they lost Tyrone, the D.A. would run over Earl with a steamroller.

Slowly, trying to stay alert for any sign of anything, Ben popped open his car door and stepped outside.

He hadn't noticed until just that second how dark it was out here. He could see street lamps, but none of them were functioning. He heard a noise and his hand clenched down on the side of his car. It was a bird—a crow, he thought, though he was no expert on birds.

He walked up to Tyrone's car and peered through the windows. Lots of cassette tapes, trash, and wadded wrappers from a variety of fast-food palaces. But there was no sign of Tyrone. Or anyone else, for that matter.

He tried the door; it opened. There didn't seem to be anything wrong with the car; the door light came on and an annoying buzzing noise told him the keys were still in the ignition.

The keys? Did he want it to be stolen? Abandoning his car was incredible enough, but leaving it here, in the worst part of town, with the keys still in it? That was beyond incredible. That was something Tyrone simply wouldn't have done. Unless he had no choice.

Ben didn't know why exactly, but he knew he didn't want to be here anymore. His knees were trembling; his palms were getting clammy and wet. He wanted out.

He returned to his own car. Just as he arrived at the driver's-side door, he heard a sound he couldn't possibly write off as a bird.

"Excuse me. Is that your car?"

Ben froze. His hands clutched the door handle. "Who are you?" He whirled around in the darkness. "Where are you?"

"I'm over here," the voice replied.

Ben tried to keep his voice steady. "I can't see you."

"It's dark." Ben heard a crunching of gravel that told him that whoever and wherever the voice was, it was coming closer. "I repeat, is that your car?"

"No." Ben squinted, scanning the darkness. "Are you a police officer?"

There was a soft chuckle. "Not hardly." Ben heard a brief intake of air. "So why did you stop?"

Ben's brain was racing. "I—I thought I recognized the car."

"And did you?"

"No, it was a mistake. It just looked like my friend's car."

Ben heard more footsteps. A few feet in front of his van, he saw a dark silhouette emerge.

"A very distinctive automobile. Hard to mistake."

"Yeah, well, I did." Ben inched closer to his van. Had he locked the door? He couldn't remember. He fumbled for the keys.

"Don't run off," the voice in the blackness urged.

Ben tried to grip the keys with his sweat-soaked fingers. "I have an appointment." He slid the correct key into the lock and turned. There was no resistance; the door had not been locked.

He popped open the door. A seeming flood of light burst out of the cracked door, illuminating Ben's face.

The other man's voice cut through the darkness like a knife slicing through butter. "It's you."

Ben froze. He knew what that meant.

It was the man with the rug, the man at the club, the man Tyrone saw in the bathroom.

The man with the knife.

Ben jumped into the driver's seat of the car and shoved his keys toward the ignition. He heard the crunching footsteps outside, closing fast. Ben switched on his headlights, bathing the area in front of the car with white light. The instant the lights came on, he saw a dark shadow just leaving the illuminated area. He was only a few feet away.

Ben grabbed the van door and pulled it to him, but not in time. The other man shoved his arm inside, preventing the door from closing. Ben continued to pull tightly on the door, clamping the man's arm like a vise, holding him fast.

"Let go!" the man shouted. His voice was livid with rage.

"Think I'll pass," Ben muttered. Cautiously, holding the door tight with one hand, he used the other to fumble with his keys, trying to find the one that started the car.

"I said let go!" the man bellowed. An instant later, his loose fist came barreling toward the window. It crashed through the glass, shattering it, sending safety glass flying in all directions.

Ben turned his head and closed his eyes. He felt the glass rain down on his face, his hands, his body.

With the hand through the window, the other man clamped down on Ben's throat and squeezed. His fingers were like steel, tightening by the second.

Ben felt the air rush out of his lungs. The man was choking him, crushing his windpipe. What could he do? He held one of the keys in his hand like a dagger and jabbed it down onto the man's arm.

The man cried out. He released Ben's throat, but an instant later, his fingers balled into a fist and jackhammered forward.

Ben's head slammed back against the headrest with a thud. He felt blood trickling out of his nose.

His lids fluttered; the combination of having his air cut off followed by a sharp blow to the face had dazed him. Still grappling with the keys, he struggled to push them toward the ignition.

The man brought his fist around again and knocked the keys out of Ben's hand. They tumbled onto the floor, disappearing into the black interior. "I have you now," the man outside muttered. "Release my arm!"

"Whatever you say," Ben gasped. He eased off the pressure, but a nanosecond after he did—and before the man had a chance to move—he pulled it back with all his might, crunching the man's arm.

The man howled. He cried out even louder than before. "Son of a bitch!" he bellowed. "You are one dead fucking piano player."

Ben tried to make him out, but all he could see were the arms, one trapped, the other grappling for his throat. The fist came at him again, this time banging into the side of his face.

The blow knocked Ben backward, pulling his arm off the door for an instant. It was enough. The man outside pulled his trapped arm free, then used both hands to yank the door wide open.

The hands Ben had struggled with so long shot into the van, one of them holding a long shimmering blade. "Your time has come," the man growled, raising the knife into the air. "Put on a happy face."

* 32 *

Ben saw the blade coming toward him, but there was nowhere he could go, nothing he could do. His eyes darted around the van's interior, searching for a weapon. He was trapped like a fox with the hounds circling, absolutely powerless to stop the inevitable.

"If you don't struggle," the man said, "I can end this quickly. If you fight me, I might draw it out for days. I might carve your smile several times, over and over again. While you're still breathing."

Ben tried to scramble out of the seat, but the man's free hand clamped down hard on his shoulder.

"Either way, you're going to die. Why not make it easy on yourself?"

Ben grabbed the hand and pulled it toward his mouth. He opened wide and bit down hard.

"Eeeeeeah!" The man drew his hand back, his blood spilling. Barely a second later, though, the fist returned. It slammed into Ben's face, once more pummeling his nose. He felt a crack and in that moment realized that the man must have broken his nose. Blood was jetting downward onto his lips. The world was whirling; he could barely see, much less focus. He couldn't possibly resist any longer.

"You've played your swan song," the man said, and Ben watched helplessly as the silvery serrated knife inched closer to his throat . . .

The man with the knife suddenly lurched sideways, his head striking the steering wheel.

"What the—"

Ben stared, not comprehending. He'd thought his time was up, but someone appeared to have struck the killer from behind.

"Who—"

Before Ben could spit out another word, the man lurched forward again.

"Here's a little something to remember me by," Ben heard another voice say.

"Gaaak!"

All of a sudden, the man with the knife tumbled into the van. At first Ben thought he was lunging to make the kill; then he realized the man's legs had gone out from under him. He fell forward; his chin thudded down on the steering wheel.

Ben had no idea what had happened, but he knew he wouldn't get a second chance. Summoning all his might, he grabbed the man's head and bashed it against the steering column. The man cried out again, and his head and body slid out the door.

Ben made his move. He scrambled up on all fours and crawled into the passenger seat, then crawled out the other side of the van.

He sped away, heading at top speed toward the safety of the opposite side of the street.

"Kincaid!" It was Tyrone Jackson, standing behind the crumpled assailant. "Are you all right?" Tyrone cried.

"I'll live," Ben shouted. "Get out of here. Go to—"

He never had a chance to finish. Like some crazed monster out of hell, the man brandishing the knife suddenly reared up, blood dripping from his chin. He lunged toward Tyrone.

Tyrone jumped back, lost his balance, tumbled onto the gravel. The man just kept coming, knife extended. Tyrone scrambled to his feet, turned and ran, never looking back. He passed the road and headed toward Rockwood.

The man with the knife seemed to have forgotten all

about Ben. He was following Tyrone now, matching his speed.

"Damn!" Ben swore to himself. All he wanted now was to get the hell out of here. But he couldn't abandon Tyrone to that maniac. He ran across the street after them, running as fast as he could, but he'd lost sight of them before he even made it to the ruins. His first instinct was to plunge on in, to try to pick up their trail. But he knew that wasn't the smartest option. He wasn't likely to find them by himself, running around in the dark. He needed help.

"Damn!" Ben raced back toward the van. He could call 911 on his car phone. That had to be smarter than wandering around dark unfamiliar ruins by himself. He just hoped it wasn't too late already.

As he punched the beeping buttons, Ben cursed himself for not being faster. "Damn, damn, damn!" he repeated, as if it might do some good. "Damn, damn, *damn!*"

Stupid, stupid, stupid, Tyrone kept telling himself, as he raced through the mazelike alley he'd once called home. What did he think he was doing? Who did he think he was, some superhero or something?

He had been perfectly safe up on the roof. He could see everything that happened, and no one could see him. No one could get to him. No one could even imagine he was there.

But then he had seen that fool Kincaid drive up, and a few moments later, the killer had emerged from the darkness. He'd been lurking in the trees on the other side of the street—waiting for Tyrone to return to his car, no doubt. When Kincaid showed up, he decided to take him instead.

So Tyrone ran down and tried to help Kincaid out. Looked like he would've been a goner if Tyrone hadn't come up from behind and given the man a swift kick where he knew he'd feel it. Problem was, now the killer was after him.

He saw the fire escape approaching on the right. It

would be great to be able to retreat to the roof, but he knew he'd never make it. He could hear the footsteps of the man chasing him; he wasn't far behind. If Tyrone tried to climb that ladder, the maniac would cut his legs out from under him. He just didn't have time for that. He had to keep running.

He had to keep running, sure, but unless he thought he could run forever, he had to lose the man, and the sooner the better. Even though he knew that creep had to be hurting from the beating he'd taken, he was having no trouble keeping up.

He seemed to be inexhaustible. He would never give up. He would hunt Tyrone till he killed him.

He whipped around the next corner, ducking into an alleyway. It was littered with debris, bottles, crushed cans, human waste. He leapt from side to side, trying to avoid anything that might slow him down. He couldn't see anything until he was almost on top of it.

He made it to the end of the alley, weaving and dodging, then leaned against the wall. He had to take a breather.

He pricked up his ears. Maybe he'd lost the creep, he thought and prayed. Maybe, just maybe.

But no. An instant later, he heard footsteps entering the alley. There was a loud metallic clanging; the man had crashed into something, probably an overturned trash can. He was bare seconds behind.

Tyrone forced himself to run. His throat ached with dryness and he had a stitch in his side that wouldn't go away, but he had to keep running. If he stopped he was history. But for how long? he asked himself. How long could he keep this up?

As long as that maniac with the knife?

Probably not.

If he was going to survive, he had to figure out a way to end this chase—before it ended him.

He did have one advantage, he reminded himself as he raced down the next dark corridor. He knew Rockwood. He'd grown up around here. He'd played in these ruins. As a teen gang member, he'd practically lived here. He knew the terrain, and that knife-wielding crazy behind him almost certainly didn't. There had to be some way he could use that particular piece of information. There had to be some way he could use it to turn this hopeless situation into a fighting chance to live.

There had to be a way, he kept repeating to himself. And then he thought of it.

Tyrone took a sharp right and detoured into a darkened alley, circling back toward the side from which they had entered. Two alleyways later, still running at top speed, he was beside the old cab company building, coming at it from the opposite side. He couldn't possibly see in this pitch blackness, but he knew the crater was still there.

He ran toward it with all the strength he could muster, all the wind he could kick out of his lungs. Coming down at top speed he hit the midpoint and jumped. He flew through the air; probably setting some new long-jump record, he thought, but no one would ever know it but him.

He tumbled down onto the concrete on the other side, hands and feet first. It was an inelegant landing, but that didn't matter. What mattered was that he'd made it across.

Gasping for breath, he hobbled over to the side of the wall, pressed himself against it, and listened. Barely a second later, he heard the all-too-familiar crunch of footsteps barreling down the alley, coming closer, closer still . . .

And then suddenly—nothing. Feet touching down on air. He heard a short gasp—all the man could get out before he tumbled into the crevice. Tyrone heard the crunch of flesh on rock as the man tumbled into the deep crater.

Tyrone didn't wait any longer. Pressing one hand against the wall, he started moving down the alley, heading away. He had no way of knowing how long his pursuer would be incapacitated; it was best not to take any chances. He had to use this opportunity to put as much distance between them as possible.

After he had crossed a few alleyways, he broke into a

light jog. It felt good—the rhythm of his arms and feet, the feeling that he was going somewhere. That he had finally left that walking, talking nightmare behind. That he might live to scam again.

Finally, more than half a mile from the pit, he stopped. He ran into a one-way alley and crouched down in a corner—crouched like a baby. It was a dead end; there was no way out but the way he'd come in. But that didn't matter now. He was safe. He'd left that bogeyman far behind.

He wrapped his arms around his knees, hugging himself tightly. He had been so scared, so so scared. Running through those dark corridors, he'd thought he'd finally gotten himself into a situation he couldn't talk his way out of. That he was finally going to have to face up to his own life, his own bullshit. That he was going to end up dead in some dark alley, just like his father had said he would.

What a relief. He smiled, stretching his legs out, massaging the aching joints. That had been pretty clever, remembering the pit, luring that sorry sack of shit over there. He couldn't help patting himself on the back. He might not be the toughest dude in town, but he was definitely one of the smartest. That's what had saved him before. That's what had saved him again.

He was still sitting there congratulating himself when he heard the soft crunch of gravel at the end of the alley that told him that he was not alone.

As the icy grip of panic clamped down on his spine, he realized that this time, there was absolutely nowhere he could run, nowhere he could hide.

THREE

* *

Murder and All that Jazz

* 33 *

Ben awoke hearing voices.

He sat bolt upright. He'd been deep inside a nightmare, and not the usual one about showing up for court in his underwear, either. He was running through a seemingly endless maze, except the more he ran, the more it became clear that the maze was actually Rockwood, and no matter how fast he ran, he couldn't get away, couldn't escape, and he knew that at any moment the man in the shadows would reach out and clench his steely fingers around Ben's throat—

He shook his head back and forth, trying to clear the cobwebs. Cool off, he told himself. It was just a dream. This time, anyway.

But he still heard voices. They were coming from outside his bedroom.

He pulled himself out of bed, every inch of his body aching, not to mention his nose. The folks at the emergency room had determined that it wasn't actually broken, but it was ripped and battered just the same. They'd put a thick bandage over it, which, Ben noted, did nothing to prevent it from hurting.

Tiptoeing quietly across the creaky wood-paneled floor, he cracked open the bedroom door and poked his head out.

Mike and Christina were sitting on the sofa in his living room having a particularly animated discussion.

"Anything I can do for you two?"

They both stopped for a moment, then turned to face him.

"Oops," Christina said. "Were we talking too loud?"

"Depends." He ran his fingers through his matted hair. "Were you trying to wake me up?"

"Well, we hoped you'd get up eventually."

"Then you weren't too loud. Care to explain what you two are doing in my living room jabbering away at this hour of the morning?"

Mike leaned forward. "Ben, have you looked at a clock yet?"

"No. Should I?" Ben craned his neck till he could see the small digital job over his oven.

It was three-fifteen. In the P.M.

"Have I slept that long?" Ben asked.

"Hardly surprising," Mike said, "after what you've been through."

"Even so, I've got things to do today. Give me five." Ben ducked back down the hallway and veered into the bathroom. He jumped in the shower, washed his hair, then went through the essential morning ablutions necessary to make himself halfway presentable. He had to dry gently; there was a visible red ring, sore and irritated, around his neck—the mark left by his near strangulation the night before. And he didn't dare touch his nose.

He threw on some clothes and returned to the living room. Mike and Christina were still in deep conversation. Their voices had crept up several decibels. He had known Mike and Christina to disagree before, and since both of them were strong-willed individuals who went into every situation assuming they were always right, these disagreements could go on for days.

"Hey, guys, calm down," he said, planting himself between them. "What's the topic?"

"How to keep you from ending up dead and buried before you turn thirty-four," Christina replied.

"Oh."

Christina continued. "Mike here favors locking you up in the county jail on a charge of stupidity in the first degree. I myself think we should wrap you in a straightjacket and put you in an asylum—*where you belong*!"

"Oh, come on now." Ben held up his hands. "Let's not make too much of this."

"Make too much of this!" Her face was red and flushed. "What did you think you were doing out there, playing peekaboo with a killer!"

Ben cleared his throat. "I guess Mike filled you in."

"Damn right he did, you imbecile! Why do you think I'm here?"

Ben could feel the heat emanating from her. "I'm fine now. You two didn't need to come."

"Oh, right." Mike leaned back, rolling his eyes. "You leave a message on my answering machine describing this elaborate attempted murder, followed by a hair-raising chase through the worst part of Tulsa, followed by calling 911 and joining the plainclothes officers on an all-night, utterly fruitless search of Rockwood. And I guess you thought after I heard your message I'd just erase it and go about my daily business."

"I wanted you to know what happened. This proves that Earl isn't the murderer."

"Like hell."

"It does! I saw the man."

"Uh-huh. So who was it?"

"Well . . . I don't know. But it wasn't Earl."

"Did you see his face?"

Ben bit down on his lower lip. "Not clearly, no."

"So it could've been anyone."

"But I heard his voice. And it wasn't Earl's. I don't think it was anyone I know."

"Unless it was someone disguising his voice. Some people are pretty good at that, you know."

Ben knew, all right. Jones, for one. "True . . . but—"

"And if the killer was disguising his voice, it could've been anyone. Hell, it might have been a woman!"

"Are you saying you think Earl was trying to kill me last night?"

"I'm saying the fact that someone else was trying to kill you, when you were stupid enough to drop by Rockwood and get out of your car in the middle of the night, doesn't prove Earl didn't kill Lily Campbell."

"I'll testify."

"Oh. So Chief Blackwell is supposed to announce that Earl Bonner is no longer the lead suspect, based on testimony from Earl Bonner's lawyer. That'll play well on the six o'clock news."

"Mike—"

"Face it, Ben. Blackwell's had a grudge against you since that Kindergarten Killer mess. He doesn't trust you. He thinks you probably invented the whole story just to throw us off your client."

Ben fell silent. There was no point in arguing. And he had something more pressing on his mind. "Any word on Tyrone?"

Mike glanced toward Christina, then glanced back. "No. We haven't been able to find the slightest trace of him. We've checked the club, his apartment, all his known hangouts. And I've still got men crawling over Rockwood. But we haven't found him."

"He must be there somewhere."

"I don't know, Ben. But even if he is, so what? We're talking about testimony from an accused, if not convicted, felon. How much is that going to get you? Are Chief Blackwell or the D.A. going to change their minds based on that? I don't think so."

"Tyrone saved my life," Ben said flatly. "And put his own life in danger to do it. We have to find him."

"I'm doing everything I know to find him, Ben. It just isn't working."

"Do you—do you think—"

"I don't know what to think, Ben. The whole thing is an ugly blood-stained mess. All I know for sure"—his voice grew bolder—"is that you had no business running out by yourself to play cops and robbers with a murderer!"

"Amen to that," Christina echoed.

"I wasn't looking for the murderer," Ben insisted. "I was looking for Tyrone. The murderer just sort of happened."

"How many times has this just sort of happened to you, Ben? You can't keep thrusting yourself in the path of danger. Especially when you're so ill equipped to deal with it."

"I don't think—"

"You've been lucky so far." Mike looked at him sternly. "But that won't last forever."

"I have a duty to represent my client zealously, Mike."

Mike waved his hands in the air. "Spare me the lecture. I've heard it all before. Every time some criminal attorney does something odious and irresponsible, he hauls out the Rules of Professional Conduct to show that he had an obligation to do it. As if common sense and conscience had been supplanted by a half-baked set of rules."

"Mike, that's not fair—"

"Never mind," Christina said. "We didn't come here to get into a philosophical debate. I have something for you." She reached over Ben's shoulders and wrapped a silver chain with a small silver medallion around his neck.

"What's this? Are we going steady now?"

"It's my Saint Christopher's medal."

"What? But—"

"I know what you're going to say. You don't believe in this hocus-pocus. Saint Christopher never really existed. Listen, I don't know anything about that stuff. All I know is this: I've always worn that medal, and it's always brought me luck. So now I want you to have it, 'cause I figure you need it more than I do at the moment. All right?"

Ben knew better than to argue. "Whatever you say. But I don't see what good it will do."

"It's a beacon, you ninny."

"Beg your pardon?"

"A beacon. To help your angel find you. I don't expect you're likely to make the call yourself, so I'm hoping the medal will do it for you."

Mike pushed to his feet. "I also brought something for you."

"What now—crystals?"

"I brought a somewhat more practical form of protection." He picked up a wooden box resting on the coffee table. He turned it toward Ben and slowly lifted the lid.

Inside the box, wrapped in a velvet form-fitting compartment, was a brand-new bright and shiny handgun.

Christina gasped.

"This is for you," Mike announced, pushing it toward Ben. "It's a Sig Sauer .38, probably the best, most lightweight, most accurate small pistol in existence. I want you to take it."

Ben pushed it away. "No way."

"Take it!" Mike insisted. He shoved the box forcefully into Ben's lap. "And if the situation arises, use it."

"But I can't—"

"I've already taken care of the license and registration. As you know, thanks to the NRA and its gun-fondling friends, carrying a concealed weapon is legal in Oklahoma now. So you should have no problems."

"But, Mike," Christina said, "Ben's clueless about guns. He doesn't know how to use it. He'll shoot his foot off. Or worse."

"Thank you very much," Ben replied.

"I intend to teach him how to use it," Mike answered. "I've reserved time for us at the firing range down at Eastern Division headquarters." He handed Ben a piece of paper. "Here are the times. Be there."

"I won't come," Ben said firmly.

"Then I'll arrest you, put the cuffs on you, and drag you there!" His whole body shook as he spoke. "Your choice!"

Ben gingerly touched the weapon resting in the purple velvet. It gave him the willies just being near it. "I don't think I can—"

"You can and you will," Mike said firmly. "Pick it up."

Hesitantly, his hand trembling, Ben lifted the weapon out of the box. He folded it into his palm the way he imagined you were supposed to, at least as far as he could tell from TV cop shows. He squeezed the weapon, feeling it in his hand. All at once, he felt sick to his stomach.

He dropped it back into the box like a hot potato. "I'm telling you, Mike: I can't do this."

"You can and you will. Now take this schedule. I expect to see you at the firing range."

"Mike—"

"Listen to me!" His voice exploded with frustration and anger. "I'm not asking you to become Charles Bronson. I just don't want to have to explain to your sister why your carcass is lying on a slab at the county morgue!"

Ben realized resistance was futile. In his own way, Mike was just showing that he cared. He took the paper and tucked it into his pocket. "Well, I suppose it wouldn't hurt to learn a little something about firearms."

"Thank God for small favors." Mike pushed himself off the couch. "And I was thinking a little self-defense training might not be such a bad idea, either. Maybe a little kung fu."

"Now wait a minute—"

"I'll send you that schedule as soon as I get it worked out."

Ben turned toward Christina. "Christina, would you tell him he's overreacting? Tell him he's being ridiculous."

She shook her head. "Sorry, Ben. I'm just dying to see you in one of those cute belted pajama outfits."

"Oh, ha-ha."

"Relax. You can't look any sillier than you did in that teeny little terry-cloth towel."

"Wait a minute. You went back to the car before I changed."

"I sure did." A grin crept across her face. "But it's amazing what you can do with a pair of high-powered binoculars."

* 34 *

He picked up another plate and tossed it across the room, watching it shatter into a thousand pieces as it crashed against the opposite wall.

Goddamn it all to hell!

What was happening to him, anyway? Why couldn't he finish a simple matter like this without creating so many complications?

He hurled another plate across the room. The sound of the impact, the sight of the destruction, had a soothing effect on his soul—but not nearly soothing enough. Why was this so hard? When he had done it before, it had gone without a hitch. And now it seemed everything he did led to one more screw-up, one more loose end needing to be tied, one more person who had to be killed.

And Earl Bonner *still* wasn't behind bars!

He grabbed the entire stack of plates and flung them across the room. They didn't make it all the way. They went down in the middle of the living room, crashing down on a glass tabletop, shattering everything, sending porcelain and glass shards flying in all directions. It made a terrible, soul-satisfying noise, one he was sure all the neighbors could hear as well.

Screw the neighbors. He needed this. He *needed* it.

He ran through the entire chain of errors in his mind. He'd managed to kill Lily and plant her in such a way as to make Earl Suspect Number One, but not without being spotted by that pipsqueak Tyrone Jackson, and not without losing something that could lead them all to his doorstep.

He'd had to take care of the kid, but that had led to being spotted—again—by that piano player out on the highway. He wasn't sure, but it was just possible the asshole could identify him.

The piano man had to be dealt with.

His hands clenched down on the kitchen cabinets. He wanted Jackson, wanted him so bad he could barely stop thinking about it. It was what he lived for now. It was the only music that soothed his savage breast.

And the final triumphant coda would come when he found that punk—the one he should've strangled to death last night in his own van. When he found that punk again, he would play the fucker's farewell fugue.

* 35 *

PAULA1>I don't know why you're acting this way. Was it something I typed?

FINGERS>Of course not. Our chats have been the most wonderful thing to happen to me for I don't know how long.

PAULA1>Then why are you saying no?

FINGERS>I don't want to rush things, that's all.

PAULA1>I'm sorry. I don't understand. :(

Jones pushed himself away from his keyboard. Truth was, he didn't understand himself. He wasn't just feeding her a line. These online chats were what he looked forward to more than anything else in his life. He couldn't get enough of them. They chatted for hours every night, till he could barely keep his eyes open any longer. Now they were chatting during the day, during the lunch hour or her coffee breaks at the library. No matter how much they chatted, he always wanted more. So why was he withdrawing?

PAULA1>I just don't think our relationship can go any further on the keyboard.

FINGERS>You mean (gasp)—

PAULA1>You know what I want. Face time. No more cyber-snuggles. The real thing.

FINGERS>Is that wise?

PAULA1>I don't know if it's wise. But IMHO, it has to happen. It's the next step on the evolutionary ladder of our relationship.

FINGERS>Relationship?

PAULA1>Does that word scare you?

FINGERS>I didn't expect it, that's all.

Jones wiped his brow. What was happening here? He wanted to meet her just as much as she seemed to want to meet him. Didn't he? So why was he holding back?

Of course he knew the answer to the question almost before he asked it. He was holding back because he was afraid. Afraid that once he left the security of the CPU and actually met her face-to-face—she wouldn't like him.

After all, what was there to like? Honestly, he was a skinny geek with a big nose and eyeglasses with lenses as thick as the bottoms of Coke bottles. No one could fall in love with that.

And there was the tiny matter of his profession. He hadn't meant to mislead her, but she thought he was a private investigator. She thought he lived some glamorous life solving mysteries and tracking down archfiends. But he didn't; he couldn't even get Ben to let him help with the investigation. When Paula found out he was a secretary, and a currently unemployed one at that, she was bound to be disappointed. She would never want to see him, much less chat with him.

When all was said and done, as much as he desired to meet her, he couldn't bear the thought of losing her, even in the limited capacity he had her now. He couldn't take the risk.

PAULA1>I'm disappointed, Jones. And I don't understand. There's no reason why we shouldn't meet. It
doesn't have to be a big deal. We both live in the same
city. We'll just arrange to be somewhere at the same
time. If it's awkward, you can leave.

FINGERS>I don't know . . .

PAULA1>What about Uncle Earl's Jazz Emporium?
They're reopening Friday night. I know you like music.

FINGERS>(despondent) I don't know. I just don't know.

For a long time, the screen before Jones remained
blank. Apparently, Paula had exhausted her stock of ways
to persuade him. Or perhaps she had decided it wasn't
worth the effort.
Finally, the talk line on his screen came back to life.

PAULA1>It's because you don't think I'm sexy, isn't it?

FINGERS>No! (forcefully) That's ridiculous.

PAULA1>It's because I'm a librarian. Everyone knows librarians are timid, mousy creatures with their hair all
pulled up in a bun who run around shushing people all
day, right?

FINGERS>That's absurd.

PAULA1>No it isn't. It's what people think. Librarians
are frigid virgins.

FINGERS>You're being ridiculous.

PAULA1>Don't humor me. That's the stereotype and
I know it. (Pause) But the stereotype is wrong. I can
be sexy.

FINGERS>I don't know what you're babbling about.

PAULA1>Close your eyes.

FINGERS>Paula, I'm at my office.

PAULA1>Just humor me for a minute. Concentrate—block out everything—everything but me. Narrow your vision till you can't see anything but the computer monitor.

Jones couldn't say no to her now. He closed his eyes and breathed deeply, blocking out all thoughts of the office and the case and Loving hovering much too nearby. Once he had shuffled all that debris out of his brain, he slowly opened his eyes, just letting in enough light that he could see the screen.

FINGERS>Okay, done.

PAULA1>Good. Now, imagine that it's Friday night. We've been to the club, and we loved it. Jazz is the sexiest music, you know. The tinkling of the ivories. The doleful wail of a solo saxophone. It speaks to something inside all of us. Makes the blood pump faster. It hurts just a little, but it's a good hurt. It makes us remember. It makes us desire.

FINGERS>Paula . . .

PAULA1>Just listen. The show is over, and we've gone back to my apartment.

FINGERS>We have?

PAULA1>I go to the bedroom to change into something more comfortable. You sit on the sofa in the living room. When I return, I turn out all the lights. You sit motionless, just watching, waiting, as I slowly light a candle. First one, then another, until the room is bathed in candlelight.

FINGERS>I like candles.

PAULA1>In the golden glow of the candles you see that I'm wearing something white and diaphanous. It has a shimmering quality—or is that just the light? You can see through it, but just barely—all you get are impressions, shadows.

FINGERS>You're wearing a toga?

PAULA1>I'm wearing a negligee. A sheer silk one from Victoria's Secret.

FINGERS>Oh. Wow.

PAULA1>I approach you. You start to speak, but the words catch in your throat. All you can think about is us, here, now. Your heart is pounding in your chest. Your palms are sweating. You're about to explode.

FINGERS>(heart pounding, palms sweaty) What's going to happen next?

PAULA1>I lean across you on the sofa and without so much as saying a word press my lips against yours. Hard. I mean to hold back, but I can't. My desire is too strong; my need is too great. I'm kissing you now, just as hard as I possibly can. Can you feel it?

FINGERS>Oh, yes.

PAULA1>We're still kissing, but now I'm running my hands up and down your back, just lightly brushing against you, tickling your spine.

FINGERS>My goodness.

PAULA1>You begin to reciprocate. You put your arms around me and pull me close. I can feel your strong arms drawing me near, pressing me against your chest. I can feel your strength, your hardness. Then I pull away—

FINGERS>Don't!

PAULA1>—and begin unbuttoning your shirt, one button at a time, slowly, carefully, kissing each patch of newly revealed skin as it is uncovered. I remove your shirt and run my hands all over your manly chest.

FINGERS>I love it when you do that.

PAULA1>I feel your fingers on my back, rising to the occasion, searching for my buttons. They find them, and a moment later I feel my negligee flutter to the floor. I stand before you naked, vulnerable, *wanting*—

FINGERS>You and me both.

PAULA1>You pull me to you in that strong manly way that tells me that we were meant to be joined, that now that we're together you will never let me go. That I'm your personal love slave, now and for all time, and that whatever you want me to do, I will do without question. Come to me, Jones.

FINGERS>I'm coming, I'm coming.

PAULA1>You take control. I groan with ecstasy. We've gone too far to turn back. Your hands find my sweet spot, the button that turns me into a mindless ball of uncontrolled desire. I part my lips, searching for a target. And then—

There was nothing more. Jones lurched forward, typing frantically into the keyboard.

FINGERS>*Yes?* What happens next?

PAULA1>(licking her fingers) I don't know. Want to meet me Friday night and find out?

FINGERS>*Yessssssssssssss!*

PAULA1>The club opens at seven. I'll meet you there about seven-thirty. Bring your candles. :)

The line disconnected. The scroll bar on the right told Jones he was now alone in the chat room.

He took a personal inventory. He felt as if he had just finished running the Boston Marathon. He was drenched in sweat; dark patches showed through his shirt. His hands were equally sweaty and trembling slightly.

He pushed himself to his feet and stumbled toward the bathroom, thinking he would strip off his shirt and splash cold water all over himself. If they didn't have cold showers here, he would have to improvise one.

Ben stepped out of the elevator and headed toward Jones and Loving's office on the seventh floor. To his surprise, he met Jones in the hallway. He seemed a bit shaky on his feet and his face was devoid of color.

"You feeling all right?" Ben asked.

Jones looked up, startled. "Oh—I'm . . . fine. Must've been something I ate."

Something he ate? It was only ten in the morning. And he knew Jones never had breakfast.

He opened the door and they walked into the office. "What about you?" Jones asked. "What's with the big bandage on your nose? Christina said you ran into some trouble."

Loving leaped out of his chair. "Are you okay, Skipper? Should you be on your feet? Here, take my chair."

Ben waved him away. "I'm fine. Promise. I just wanted to see how your investigation is going. From what I hear from Mike, the police are likely to file charges against Earl at any moment."

"Didn't have any luck tracking down the Rug Man," Loving grunted. He was obviously disgusted with himself. "I can tell you this—he ain't workin' for any of the honest-to-God carpet companies or rug dealers in town."

"What about the van?"

"None of the rug companies reported a missing van. I also checked the rental agencies, but I came up with nada. I think it must be a privately owned van that our man just dressed up for the occasion. And probably repainted as soon as he was done. Even if we could peer into every garage in town, we wouldn't find it."

"What about paint companies? There can't be that many places around that sell auto paint."

Loving snapped his fingers. "You're right, Skipper. There ain't."

"Good. Check 'em out. Maybe you can work up a sketch based on the disguise he wore to Earl's club. Maybe he wore the same disguise when he bought the paint."

"But even if I find the place where he bought the paint—what good will it do us?"

"Who knows? Maybe he said something to the sales-person that might help us track him down. Maybe they took down his address for the receipt or their computer records. Maybe he paid with a credit card."

"All right." Loving grabbed his coat. "It's a long shot, but I'll give it a go." He hustled out the front door.

Ben turned back toward Jones. "As for you—"

"I could help out on the investigating," Jones said quickly. "Let me do a little fieldwork. I might turn up something."

"Actually," Ben said, "I have some more pleadings I need you to type. And I have a list of cases I'd like you to pull off Lexis."

"Ooh, how exciting."

Ben frowned. "Is something going on I don't know about?"

"No, nothing." Jones folded his arms unhappily. "It's just—well, sometimes I get tired of the same old drudgery. I'm underutilized."

"No doubt. Have you finished your report on the first smile-murder?"

"Natch. On my desk."

Ben picked up the computer printout and skimmed through the first few pages. He began to read aloud: " 'I can feel your strong arms drawing me near . . . I can feel your strength, your hardness . . .' " He looked up. "What on earth is this?"

Jones's jaw dropped. "Give me that."

Ben moved it out of his reach. " 'I'm your personal love slave . . . whatever you want me to do, I will do with-out question.' " He flipped through the next few pages, grinning. "This came out of one of those chat rooms, didn't it?"

Jones snatched the printout from Ben. "That is absolutely none of your business."

"Jones, you old dog. Have you been swapping fantasies with some cybertramp?"

"Paula is not a cybertramp."

"Paula?" Ben's eyebrows rose. "On a first-name basis, are you?"

"And what of it?"

"Oh nothing, nothing." Ben continued to grin. "Have you actually met this Paula?"

"Not yet. But we have a date for Friday night."

"You're going out with her?" Ben grabbed Jones by the shoulders. "Have you lost your senses?"

"It seemed harmless enough."

"If she were harmless, she wouldn't be spending her time in chat rooms! Why do you think people do that? She'll probably turn out to be a transvestite. Or a psychopath. Or both."

"Paula is not a transvestite or a psychopath."

"How do you know? She could be an axe murderer, for all you know."

"She's not an axe murderer. She's a librarian."

"Oh, well then." Ben shook his head. "I'd give this a second thought if I were you, Jones."

"It's none of your business."

"Maybe not, but I consider you my friend, and I don't want to see you get hurt."

Jones frowned. "Maybe you're right. But I promised her—"

"Unpromise her."

"I can't do that." He paused. "But nothing says I have to go alone."

"It would be safer if you didn't."

Jones grabbed Ben's arm. "You could come with me."

"Now wait a minute!"

"C'mon. We're meeting at that club where you play.

You'll be there anyway. You can just step down from the stage and hang with me for a bit."

"Absolutely not."

"You said you considered me a friend. You said you cared about me!"

"Well, true, but—"

"You meant it, didn't you?"

Ben drew in his breath. "Yes, I meant it. But—"

"Good." He held tight to Ben's arm. "So I'll show up a little early. You can come down from the stage during your first break. And we'll see what happens. Good enough?"

Ben sighed. "I can't wait."

* 36 *

As soon as Ben got out of the office, he headed for the west end of town, across the Arkansas, toward the Buxley Oil refinery. Once you were on the west side of town, it was impossible to miss it; like any other blight on the horizon, it stood out for miles around.

Tulsa didn't have much urban sprawl, didn't have many ugly skyscrapers, didn't have a high crime rate. But it did have refineries. Big sprawling monstrosities with metal catwalks and huge storage tanks and tall smokestacks that spewed smoke and fire into the air. The rotten-egg smell of refinery was so intense people had been forced to move, unable to bear the odor, especially when the Oklahoma winds were sweeping down the plain. The constant output of smoke didn't create that much smog, but it did help create an ozone problem so severe that radio DJs tracked it all summer long. The refineries were the dark side of the economic boom that had brought in people from all over the world and made Tulsa the cosmopolitan city it was.

A small Buxley office building was adjacent to the refinery. The parking lot was not full and Ben was easily able to find a parking place for his van. He held his breath and dashed toward the front door.

Inside, the air-conditioning was running at high power, presumably to ensure that none of the eye-watering smell outside got inside. Ben opened his mouth and sucked in air in one greedy gulp.

The receptionist at the front desk smiled. "You made it. Congratulations."

Ben looked embarrassed.

"I'm serious. Sometimes they don't make it, and I have to call for men with stretchers after they pass out on the steps. That smell is atrocious."

"Well, I managed to get in without exposing myself to much of it."

"In your lungs, you mean," the receptionist replied. "Wait till you get home and smell your clothes." She smiled. "How can I help you?"

"I'm here to see Grady Armstrong. He's expecting me." Resourceful as ever, Jones had tracked the man down and made an appointment.

The receptionist checked her list, then pointed Ben toward the elevators. "Second floor," she said.

Ben rode up. He didn't have to search long. Just outside the elevator doors, he saw a wall sign with Grady Armstrong's name on it.

Ben leaned into the office. "Mr. Armstrong? Ben Kincaid."

The man behind the desk rose to his feet and gestured for Ben to come in.

Armstrong's office could only be described as entirely ordinary. It looked like every other oil and gas office Ben had ever seen, and thanks to his brief stint as legal counsel for the now-defunct Apollo Corporation, he'd seen a few. There were tall stacks of paper piled up on the man's desk and plat maps on the walls—the whole state divided into drilling and spacing units. Photos of recent oil wells hung crookedly on the far wall.

Grady Armstrong was wearing a white shirt with the sleeves rolled up to the elbow.

"Good to see you again," Ben said. "I'm sorry to interrupt your work. I think my secretary explained that I'm representing Earl Bonner, who's a suspect in the recent murder of Lily Campbell. Unfortunately, that murder seems to dovetail with the murder of your brother twenty-two years ago."

Armstrong nodded. "Right. Just makes me sick to my stomach."

"I can imagine."

"I don't know anything about this new murder."

"I understand. But since there seems to be a connection between the murders—or someone is trying to suggest a connection—I hoped you could tell me what you know about the first murder. Maybe that will give me some insight on the new one."

"All I know is what the police told me." His head fell; there was a slight catch in his throat.

"Were you with your brother when it happened?"

"Oh, no," Armstrong explained. "We've always gone our separate ways, ever since we were old enough to leave home. Earlier, really. You may have heard that we ... well, we didn't have the best home life. Neither of us stayed any longer than we had to."

"Your brother George escaped to the New Orleans jazz world."

"That's right," Armstrong said. He laughed abruptly. "George was the one who had all the talent. I was the boring one. Man, I couldn't play the kazoo. George tried to train me to beat drums so I could travel with him, but it was hopeless. Just couldn't keep the beat. So we drifted apart. He went into the glamorous world of entertainment, and I started working my way up in the world of oil and gas."

"I see you're now a Buxley senior vice president."

"Right, right. Me and forty other guys. Believe me, I'm not that big a deal. If I were, I'd have an office in the St. Louis world headquarters, not next door to the smelliest refinery in the Southwest. Oh, I'm not complaining. For a boy who started out as a field hand, this is a pretty cushy situation. For my first four years, I was a roughneck for Esso. I worked the wells, traveled from town to town, working all day every day in the oil and muck. Those four years probably put ten on my face. And look what they did to my hands. Still, I didn't mind. Kind of enjoyed it, to tell you the truth."

He leaned back expansively. "I always knew I wasn't cut out for the kind of life George had. I couldn't do the things he could do; I couldn't make people feel the way he could make them feel." He smiled gently, then shrugged. "But who's to say which is better, right? He may have had a higher profile, for a while, but I had a lot more steady paychecks." He paused. "And of course, I lived a good deal longer."

"Yes," Ben said, nodding. "Do you have any insight on your brother's death? Why it happened?"

"Like I said, I wasn't around. I was on the road most of the time. I was a land man by then, always scouting for new oil or gas properties. Even my bosses didn't see me often. I got word about what had happened eventually, but not in time to do much about it. Didn't even come back for the funeral. Made the arrangements over the phone. Always felt bad about that, but I was in the process of changing jobs and moving to another state and—well, we were living separate lives by then."

"Did you ever hear anyone talk about who killed your brother?"

"Only the police. They were convinced it was your client."

"I don't mean to upset you, sir, but I believe the police were wrong. Did you ever hear anyone express any other theories?"

"No, I didn't. Frankly, given what I knew about my brother, it made perfect sense."

"It did?"

"Sure. I hadn't seen George for years, but he was my brother, and I knew him. Specifically, I knew what a temper he had. He was just one of those guys, you know? Calm as an angel, most of the time. But when he got set off—man, he was a terror. Absolutely uncontrollable."

"Are you saying he might've provoked Earl?"

Armstrong shrugged. "I wasn't there. I'm just saying

it's possible. I know there was more than one time when he made me so mad I could've killed him on the spot."

"Would you mind telling me about it?"

"Which time? I was on the wrong side of his temper more than once. I pity anyone who had the same experience." He shook his head. "In fact, the last time I saw George, we had a fight that probably registered on the Richter scale. Our father had just died. Turned out, to everyone's surprise, the SOB had accumulated some money. I don't know how he got it; some way the IRS wouldn't approve of, I suspect. Anyway, the point is, he left it all to me. You may have heard—George and our father never got along too well. It shouldn't have been a surprise but—well, I guess it was. George just went mad, I mean totally crazy mad. Lost all control, all sense of perspective. He ranted and raved—even took a punch at me. It seems silly now, but at the time, I thought the man might kill me if he had half a chance. So I left." He sighed heavily. "And I never saw George again."

"Do you know anything about the dispute that supposedly led to his murder?"

"George could be a raving lunatic when it came to women. Absolutely caveman territorial."

"Earl says that both he and George were . . . interested in Lily."

Armstrong spread wide his hands. "Well, there you go. Nothing set George off faster than the thought that someone else was moving in on a woman he considered to be rightly his. Unfortunately, he considered all women to be rightly his."

Ben made a few notes in his pocket pad. Some of this was new information, and it was sparking a few ideas he hadn't considered before.

"Anything else that's relevant? To either murder?"

Armstrong shook his head. "Not to my knowledge. If I do think of anything, I'll let you know."

"I'd appreciate it."

"I want to help if I can. I just heard from your secretary

yesterday afternoon—this all comes as a surprise. Let me think on it for a while and see if I remember anything more."

"Thanks." Ben pushed himself out of the chair. "Oh. There's one other thing I wanted to ask. I almost hate to, but"—he swallowed—"you know, both corpses were . . . disturbed. After they were killed."

"Yes, I know. The smiles."

"Do you have any idea what that means? Where it comes from?"

Armstrong lowered his head. "No. How could I?"

"I just wanted to—"

"There is one story, though. I don't know that it relates, but—" He stopped, started again. "I mentioned my father. He was a drunk, he beat us till we bled. And he used to make us smile."

Ben took a step closer. "Excuse me?"

"He was a petty tyrant. He didn't have anybody else to push around, so he took it out on us. He ordered us to smile. I don't know why. Maybe it was his way of pretending we were all one big happy family. You know, by forcing these fake Ozzie and Harriet smiles on our faces. All the time. Like when we'd sit down to dinner. 'Smile!' he'd bellow. Or when he came to kiss us good night, long past midnight, with that disgusting smell of whiskey on his breath. Even after he beat us. He'd hit us so hard we were barely conscious, then he'd order us to smile. 'You *will* smile!' he'd shout. 'You *will*!' "

Armstrong's hand pressed against his forehead. "I could always manage to plaster that fake smile on my face, no matter how much it hurt. But George couldn't. Or more accurately, wouldn't. He wouldn't give our father that satisfaction. He could beat George till he bled, but he couldn't make him smile. So Father would beat him some more. Beat him till he was senseless. But he never made George smile."

Armstrong's head rose, and Ben could see traces of tears in the corners of his eyes. "Poor George. Is it any wonder he ran away from home? Any wonder he got hooked on drugs, the only thing that could make him forget?" He brushed the moisture from his face. "I like to think that, for a while anyway, George found a little bit of peace. A little bit of happy." His eyes clenched shut. "Until someone took all that away from him. Until George had the misfortune to run into someone who truly could make him smile."

* 37 *

Ben met Christina back at the office and provided her with an update on his day. Afterward, they stopped by Ri Le's for takeout and headed back to Ben's place.

As they stepped inside the main corridor of the rooming house, Ben saw the light on in Mrs. Marmelstein's apartment.

"Looks like she's still up," Ben said quietly. "I'd better check on her."

"Couldn't we eat first?" Christina implored. "My tummy is crying out for Szechwan noodles."

"In a minute." He knocked quietly on the door. "Mrs. Marmelstein? It's Ben."

"Come on in."

He entered the small apartment, Christina close behind. Mrs. Marmelstein wasn't in the living area. His nose told him to turn the corner, pass the Reader's Digest Condensed Books and the twenty-four volumes of the Warren Commission Report and enter the kitchen.

"Fixing a late-night snack?" Ben asked.

She looked up, her face a mixture of dismay and despair. She was wearing a blue print dress, but the dress was overlaid with her underwear, all balled up and backwards. She was wearing socks with sandals. Her lipstick was a thick red smear across one side of her face.

"I just wanted a little breakfast. But I can't get these fool eggs to scramble. I put in the milk and I stirred and stirred. I don't understand it."

Breakfast? It was practically bedtime. Ben took a few

steps forward and looked into the frying pan. He saw the mixed and stirred residue of three eggs, shells included. Small wonder the eggs wouldn't scramble.

"Mrs. Marmelstein," he said gently, "I'm no cook, but I think you're supposed to throw away the shells."

"The shells," she echoed. Her voice was a wispy nothing, caught in the air then quickly swept away. "I—" She stopped, either unable or unwilling to complete the sentence. As Ben peered into her eyes, he saw the dawning of the realization of her mistake. And the utter humiliation that followed.

"You know," Ben said quickly, "I hate it when that happens." He lifted the frying pan off the stove and turned down the heat. "I must've done this a thousand times. Anymore, I just stick to Cap'n Crunch." He opened the cabinet under the sink and poured the sticky remains into the trash.

"Those were the last eggs I have," Mrs. Marmelstein whispered.

"Tell you what, Mrs. Marmelstein. Christina and I picked up some Vietnamese on the way home. There's more than enough for you, too."

She shook her head sadly. "I couldn't—"

"Please."

"No, I mean it. I couldn't. Too spicy for me."

"Oh. Well, I think I have some eggs in my refrigerator. Why don't you let me get you some, then I'll come back and—"

"No," she said, wandering out of the kitchen. "That's kind, but all of a sudden I feel very tired."

Ben nodded. She was sundowning, he realized. At times she could still be perfectly rational. But after the Alzheimer's kicked in, she had no idea what she was doing. "Why don't you let me help you get ready for bed, then?"

"No, no, that wouldn't be right."

"Or Christina could do it. She knows all those girl-things, don't you, Christina?"

Christina forced a smile.

Mrs. Marmelstein drew a hand to her bosom. "Thank you, no."

"I hate to leave you here alone. Did you call that number I gave you?"

She looked at him sternly. "Benjamin, I'm an adult, not a child. I do not need anyone to take care of me. Do you understand?"

"Yes, but I still wish—"

"Benjamin, if you don't mind, I'd like to get ready for bed."

It was evident to Ben that his clumsy charity had served only to embarrass her. "If you need anything, call me, okay? You have my number. Or just let out a yell. I'll hear you, I promise."

"Good night, Benjamin."

"Good night, Mrs. Marmelstein." He escorted Christina to the door and left the apartment.

Ben noticed that Christina ate with great vigor, as usual, but didn't speak a word to him, which was most unusual.

"Is something bothering you?"

She eyed him with great irritation. "What do you think?"

"I don't know. Tell me."

"Don't play dumb."

"I'm serious. I don't know what your problem is."

"I'm worried about Mrs. Marmelstein."

"So am I. So why are you being hostile to me?"

"She needs help."

"I know that! I'm trying to find a home—"

"You know that isn't what she wants."

"She needs someone to look after her."

"She wants you."

The room fell silent.

"You don't know what you're asking," Ben said finally.

"I do. It would be difficult. Incredibly difficult."

"Impossible."

"Pardon my French—"

"I always do."

"—but that's bullshit! Ben, she needs you! She wants you to help her."

"I *have* helped her—ever since I moved into this place. I'm the only thing that's kept her out of bankruptcy court."

"I know that, Ben. But people's needs change. Now she needs more."

"What are you saying? That I should just give up my life so I can babysit my landlady?"

"You wouldn't have to do it alone. Joni and Jami would help. Hell, even I would help."

"I can't do that. I have an obligation to the band. We're going on tour in five weeks."

"Well, I guess that settles it." She jumped out of her chair with such force that it fell to the floor with a clatter.

Ben also rose. "This is ridiculous, Christina."

"It is not ridiculous!" Her voice suddenly caught, startling Ben. "And if you weren't so busy running away from yourself, you'd see that."

"Christina . . ."

She turned away. "I wish you believed in angels," she said quietly. "I wish just once you could close your eyes and ask someone to help you find the way. Because I know you're a good person, Ben. I know you are. And I can't stand watching you screw up like this!" She raced out of the kitchen.

"Christina—"

He had just started to follow her when they were both startled by a crash outside Ben's door.

"That was on the stairs," Ben whispered. Without another word, he raced out of the kitchen, crossed the living room, and threw open the door.

Lying at the bottom of the stairs was the broken body of Sheshona Marmelstein, socks in sandals, underwear on the outside.

* 38 *

Ben felt a nudge on his shoulder.

"Ben. The doctor's coming back."

He batted his eyes and brought himself back around. As soon as they found Mrs. Marmelstein's prostrate body at the foot of the stairs, Christina doubled back to dial 911 while Ben ran down to help her. There was not much he could do; she was unconscious, and given the awkward jumble of limbs he found in a heap on the floor, he knew better than to move her. All he could do was check her pulse, make sure she was breathing, and hold her hand till EMSA arrived.

The ambulance did arrive, in record time. Less than ten minutes later, she was wheeled into St. John's, and the emergency treatment staff went into action.

That had been over six hours ago. He and Christina had been in the waiting room the entire time.

The doctor crossed the emergency room and held out his hand. "Are you the people waiting for Sheshona Marmelstein?"

"Yes," Ben said, finding his feet and shaking the man's hand. "How is she?"

"She's stable," he said. "In no immediate danger."

"No immediate danger," Ben repeated. "What does that mean?"

"It means that for the moment, you can relax. But some time in the next week or so, she's going to need hip replacement surgery."

"Is that necessary?" Christina asked.

"I'm afraid so. You have to understand—when a woman her age injures her hip, it's extremely serious. Frankly, in most cases, it's either fatal or the beginning of the end. In this case, I think we can bring her back around. But she'll require surgery if she ever hopes to move on her own again. Even with surgery, it may be awkward and uncomfortable."

"My God," Ben said, covering his face with his hand. "Poor Mrs. Marmelstein."

"What's the prognosis?" Christina asked. "Assuming she has this surgery."

"Above average, I'd say," the doctor replied. "Of course, she'll need a lot of help. She won't be able to move at all for probably a month after the surgery, even if it's successful. Someone else will have to be with her at all times."

"How is she now?" Christina asked.

"She's sleeping," the doctor replied. "And probably will be for another twelve hours or so, thanks to the sedatives. She'll come around this evening."

"And then?"

He smiled. "Then I'll talk to her about the surgery. See what she wants to do."

"I'd like to be here for that conversation," Christina said. She glanced at Ben. "We both would."

"That's fine," the doctor said. "She'll want to be with friends when she hears the news."

Christina nodded. "We'll be there. Is there anything else we can do?"

"No. You look like you've been up all night. Go home. Get some rest. I'll see you again this evening." He shook Christina's hand, then left the waiting room.

Christina slumped down in a chair. "Did you hear what he said?"

"Yes. Including the part about getting some rest. Which I intend to do."

She placed her hand on his arm. "Have you forgotten?

We have an appointment with Mike this morning. Seven A.M. sharp."

"Let's call and cancel."

"You promised him."

"But I didn't know I'd be up all night at the hospital!"

"Like it or not, it's morning. We have work to do. And besides"—she hoisted him forcibly to his feet—"I want you to keep this appointment. It's for your own good."

He went out grumbling. "That's what my mother said when she made me take tap dancing lessons."

It took Ben thirty minutes to track down the South Side address Mike had given him. Sleep deprivation had undoubtedly reduced his mental agility. Eventually, he pulled his van into the parking lot outside the Culver Corners strip mall.

"So why did Mike bring us here?" Ben asked. "I don't need one-hour Martinizing, and the video store doesn't open for two hours."

"Keep looking," Christina advised. "End of the strip."

Ben strained his eyes and read a sign decked out with Asian pictographs, dragons, and samurai warriors: CHINESE BOXING INSTITUTE.

"Now wait just a minute." Ben took a step back.

"C'mon," Christina said, grabbing his arm and dragging him toward the door. "Mike's expecting us."

Inside, the school was more like an empty warehouse, with no notable decoration or furniture other than the wall-to-wall padded mats on the floor and mirrors on the walls. Mike was indeed waiting; he was chatting with a small, portly man Ben didn't recognize.

Mike waved. "Ben! Good to see you." He turned to make introductions. "Jim, this is Ben Kincaid. Ben, this is Sensai Papadopoulos."

Sensai Papadopoulos? Ben stepped forward nodding; Sensai Papadopoulos bowed. He had deep-set eyes with heavy shadows, all masked behind a pair of aviator-style glasses. Tight pants, a shirt open to the navel, gold neck jewelry, and lifts. He sported a handlebar mustache and a Fu Manchu beard.

Turned out he even spoke with a clipped, no-*r*'s faux-Chinese accent. "Very pleased to meet you, Ben-san," he said.

"Likewise, I'm sure," Ben replied. He glanced at Mike. "What's this all about?"

"I told you already. If you're going to continue throwing yourself in the hands of thugs and serial killers, you need to learn to defend yourself."

Ben grabbed Mike by the arm and pulled him aside. "You're telling me you dragged me down here at seven in the morning so I could play Hi Karate?"

"Actually, Jim's discipline is kung fu."

"I don't care what it is. I'm not doing anything with this clown."

"Jim? What have you got against Jim?"

"Something my mother once told me," Ben said, grimacing. "Beware of Greeks wearing lifts."

Mike rolled his eyes and dragged Ben back to Sensai Papadopoulos. "Shall we begin?"

"No, we shall not." Ben turned away. Christina caught one arm, Mike caught the other. "Both of you: leave me alone!"

"Perhaps the young grasshopper is not prepared to make the journey," Sensai Papadopoulos suggested.

"He is, he is," Mike insisted, yanking on Ben's arm. "He just doesn't know it yet."

The Sensai nodded. "Sometimes the young duckling does not realize that the rushing waterfall is actually the stream leading home."

"Yeah, exactly." Mike pulled Ben close and spoke clipped terse words into his ear. "Ben, I want you to do this!"

"I don't."

"It could save your life!"

"My life is not going to be saved by this reject from *Kung Fu: The Legend Continues*."

"Will you give him a chance? Jim used to be a cop, okay?"

Ben blinked. "He did?"

"One of the best, till he took early retirement and went into business for himself. Three-time intermural martial arts champ. Believe me, he knows his stuff."

"Well . . ."

"See that sash across his waist?" Ben checked it out—a black sash with five white bands. "That's not just a pajama tie he picked up at Sears. That's a fifth-degree black belt."

"Well . . ."

"See the embroidery on the back of his shirt?"

Ben made out the intertwined letters. AKMF. "American Kung Fu Masters Federation?"

"As it turns out, yes," Mike answered. "But when he was on the force, we all thought it stood for Ass-Kicking Motherfucker." His eyes darted toward Christina. "Pardon my language."

She fluttered her eyelids. "Pretend I'm not here."

"You get the drift? He's good."

"All right, all right," Ben pushed himself free. "Relax with the strong-arm tactics. Just let me breathe for a minute."

Mike nodded toward Sensai Papadopoulos. "Okay. I think we're ready to begin."

"Is the young grasshopper ready to seek the path to enlightenment and self-discovery?"

"Yeah, yeah," Mike said. "Just teach him how to deck somebody, okay?"

The Sensai bowed obediently. "Perhaps we should begin with some historical background."

"I don't—"

"Kung fu dates back to the fifth century B.C. It is a discipline of defense, not offense. It is a way of harmonizing with the universe, not conquering it. It was Lao-tzu, the great Taoist philosopher, who said, 'The world is ruled by letting things take their course.' "

Mike interrupted. "That's great, Jim. But let's get on to the—"

"Lao-tzu also said, 'When nothing is done, nothing is left undone. In the pursuit of Truth, every day something is dropped.' "

"Right, right, right. But our time is limited. Cut to the chase."

Sensai Papadopoulos sighed. "That is the problem with the world today. No one wants philosophy; they just want to get on with the head-bashing."

"Too true. But I'm only going to be able to sit on my man here so long."

"Very well. Perhaps we should begin with the forms."

The forms were a series of traditional postures and positions adopted by the Buddhist monks who first devised kung fu. Some forms were designed to thwart an attack; some were simply used for meditation purposes. Ben never obtained a clear sense of which was which, but it didn't much matter, because he couldn't do any of them.

Sensai Papadapoulos started by trying to show him the panther's crouch.

"You must bend the knees," he repeated, kicking Ben's knees in the most vulnerable spots.

"They're bent already," Ben snapped.

"They should be bent like you are about to pounce, not like you are about to pass out. Lean back. Raise your arms."

"What do the arms have to do with it?"

"It's part of the form."

"You don't pounce with your arms."

"I'm aware of that. But it's part of the form."

"I don't see any reason—"

"It's been done that way for twenty-five hundred years."

"But it's pointless. Why should I do it if it serves no purpose?"

"What are you, a lawyer or something?" The Sensai whipped his head back in time to see Mike wearily nod his head. "That explains a great deal," he growled. "Now bend your legs."

Ben managed to complete the form, but he looked more like a man experiencing gastrointestinal difficulties than a crouching panther. Nonetheless, Sensai Papadopoulos decided to move on.

He tried introducing some kicks, but that was even more fruitless. Ben's kicks wouldn't have tickled a butterfly, much less crippled an assailant. Every time Sensai Papadopoulos said "Harder," Ben made a louder grunting noise, but the kick was no more forceful than the one before.

Two hours later, the Sensai had taken Ben through the first ten forms, and none had come out looking half like they were supposed to. Mike called the Sensai over for a brief moment of meditation.

"He's going to walk soon," Mike whispered. "What do you think?"

"What do I think? What do you think? He's hardly ready for the Circle of Fighting."

"Look, I know you're supposed to start with the forms and all that, but he's probably never going to practice what you've taught him, and he's probably never going to come back. Couldn't you teach him some little flip or something that might help him get out of a scrape?"

"Sure. Why not? I'm sure this is exactly what the Buddhist monks had in mind when they invented kung fu. Helping lawyers out of scrapes!"

Papadopoulos walked over to Ben, who was panting heavily and dripping with sweat. "When you enter the discipline of kung fu," the Sensai explained, "you must forget your former judgmental concepts of good and bad. You must seek out a higher Truth. Whatever you do is an expression of your inner nature, the Original Face you wore before you were born."

"That would be kind of a scrunched-up wrinkled face, right?"

Papadopoulos clenched his teeth. "No. But never mind.

When you see danger coming toward you, you must forget good and bad, forget true and false. Act, don't think. Uncover the Original Face."

"And kick the hell out of 'em?"

Papadopoulos threw up his hands. "Something like that. Here, let me show you a flip." He turned around and took Ben's right wrist.

"A flip? What, like in the movies?"

The Sensai ignored him. "The advantage of a flip is that you can use your opponent's greater strength to your advantage."

"How do you know my opponent will have greater strength?"

"Just a hunch. Now look. It's this simple. Your opponent rushes toward you. At the last sparrow's breath before he arrives, you whirl around, grab his extended arm and, using his own velocity for momentum, flip him over your shoulder."

"Sounds easy enough."

"It is, if you time it properly. Timing is everything. Timed properly, an insect could flip an elephant. Timed wrong, the opponent will fall on top of you and crush you like a bug."

"Wonderful."

"Let's give it a try." Papadopoulos walked to the opposite end of the studio, then began moving toward Ben in exaggerated slow-motion. "I am approaching you," he shouted.

"I know that," Ben replied.

"What will you do about it?" Too late—the Sensai was nose to nose with Ben.

"No, no, no!" he shouted. "You were supposed to whirl!"

"I knew I forgot something."

"We'll do it again. And this time, whirl!"

Sensai Papadopoulos came at him again, this time even slower than before. A few moments before he arrived, Ben whirled around. Papadopoulos thrust his arm over Ben's shoulder and waited. And waited. And waited.

"Take my arm!" he shouted at last.

"Oh. Right." Ben took the arm.

"And pull!"

Ben pulled, but nothing happened. "Nothing's happening."

"You're not pulling hard enough."

Ben pulled harder.

"Aaarghh!" The Sensai leaped away. "Are you trying to kill me?"

"You told me to pull harder!"

"You're supposed to use the opponent's velocity for impetus."

"You were standing still."

"I know that!" He waved his hands in the air. "It's useless. I cannot teach this man!"

Mike stepped forward. "But it's very important, Jim. He could be killed—"

"Let him be killed then! Survival of the fittest!"

"Now, Jim, calm down."

"I will not calm down. And I will not continue this waste of my life."

"I was hoping you could give Ben some serious training."

"You can't train cannon fodder!" Papadopoulos marched to the back of the studio and disappeared into a private office, slamming the door behind him.

Ben stood in the center of the studio. "So," he said, "how do you think I did?"

Neither Mike nor Christina felt moved to respond.

* 39 *

As soon as Ben escaped from the Chinese Boxing Institute, he headed south toward the Memorial Heights Condos. His eyes widened as he drove his van through the restricted entry gate. Perhaps he shouldn't be surprised—what was he expecting, after all? He wasn't sure. But it wasn't this.

He pulled into the parking lot and slowed, checking the doors until he saw number 22. It was a two-story condo with a wood and white plaster, faux-Tudor exterior. Ivy crept up the walls surrounded by assorted greenery Ben couldn't begin to identify. They were very attractive condos—well-kept, exclusive and expensive.

Which was what was bothering him, Ben realized, as he climbed out of the van and ambled toward the weathered steps that led to the front door. He hadn't expected Scat to be living anyplace half so nice. He had expected something, well, grungier. Scat was, after all, a jazz musician—one who had been making the rounds for a long time. Where was the two-bit rooming house with the grumpy alcoholic matron, the buzzing blinking red light, the rummies draped across the stairs? This place looked like it catered more to suit-and-tie types than musicians.

Well, he was probably being ridiculous. The influence of too much bad TV. If Scat had been a professional musician for thirty or forty years, there was no reason he couldn't have saved enough money to afford a decent place to live.

He rang the doorbell. The response was a nine-note chime.

Ben smiled. He recognized the familiar opening riff from Gershwin's *Rhapsody in Blue*. This must be the right place.

He heard some shuffling on the other side of the door. He knew someone was there, but it was taking him an eternity to answer.

A few moments later, Scat opened the door. "Ah, Ben, my man. You're early."

Ben nodded. "I found your place sooner than I expected. Following directions normally isn't my strong suit. Is this all right?"

"Sure, sure." He was trying to seem relaxed and at ease—trying a bit too hard, Ben thought. "Come on in."

Ben entered the condo. The interior did not disappoint; it was every bit as impressive as the exterior had suggested. The furniture was all top quality, if ordinary. Two plush sofas flanked the living room. There was no coffee table, though Ben saw small round indentations in the carpet that suggested there had been one in the past. The kitchen was modern, lots of open spaces and white, and equipped with many snazzy appliances, including a cappuccino maker.

And there was a porch with a panoramic view of the city. "Do you mind?" Ben asked.

Scat shook his head. "Please do."

Ben opened the sliding door and stepped out. He hadn't noticed coming in, but the condos were constructed on the edge of Shadow Mountain. From this perspective, the whole city seemed to be at his fingertips.

"That's spectacular," Ben said.

"You should see it at sunset," Scat replied. "It'll stop your heart."

"I'll bet."

"Some of the best music I've ever played came out right here on this porch, drinking in the sweet sights and sounds and smells of the city." He turned toward Ben. "Would you like to stay out here?"

"Sure."

Scat pulled over two deck chairs and gestured for Ben to sit.

"Now," Scat said, "what's so important it couldn't wait till we all get back together in the club tonight?"

"It's about the murder," Ben said. "Murders, actually."

"Murders? There's been another one?"

"A long time ago. Twenty-two years to be exact."

"Oh." Scat's face became grave. "You're talking about Professor Hoodoo."

"I'm told you knew Earl and the Professor—George Armstrong."

" 'Course I did. I played with both those boys. We were considered the best blowers in the business. Some said the best on all of God's green earth. They even compared us to Charlie Parker."

"And you were still around when the Professor was killed."

Scat lowered his head. "That's true. I was there."

"And you knew Lily Campbell?"

"Oh, yes." A soft smile played on his lips. "Everyone knew the Cajun Lily. And everyone loved her. She could do things to a song no one else ever even thought about doin'. Ever dreamed about doin'." He looked up. "We were all four in Oklahoma City, as I recall, playing the Double-Deuce Festival, when the trouble came down."

"I've been told Lily and the Professor were . . . dating?"

"I probably wouldn'ta used that word, son, but you've got the right idea. They were definitely together."

"But Earl also had a thing for Lily."

"Like I said, everyone loved Lily."

"I heard there was some . . . unpleasantness between them."

"There was always unpleasantness between Earl and the Professor. That was just the way it was. They were both so good, so strong. Music lived and breathed in their souls. There were bound to be complications. Hell, they never hammered out a number together but what they didn't end up screamin' and shoutin' at each other. And if it wasn't the music, it was women. And if it wasn't women, it was booze." He paused, drew in his breath. "And if it wasn't booze, it was junk."

Ben listened intently. This was quite a different account of the two men's relationship than the one he'd gotten from Earl. "Junk?"

"Drugs, son. Sweet white snow."

"Apparently the Professor had a drug problem."

"I suppose that's what you'd call it today. Nobody saw it like that back then, though. We just thought it was a way for the Professor to escape. Maybe the only one he had."

"Escape what?"

Scat drew in his breath. "You gotta understand what it was like, hearing the Professor play. It's like you've lived your whole life thinkin' you're just an ordinary mortal, and suddenly, you hear the Professor work his axe and you think—my God! There must be something more! I must be some kinda angel or somethin', 'cause this is absolutely for goddamn certain the music of the gods I'm hearin'! That's what the Professor could do for you."

"I wish I could've heard him," Ben replied. "Earl said he never made any recordings."

"That's right. Never even had his picture taken, that anyone knows of. Once he was gone, he was all the way gone."

"That's a tragedy."

"More than that, son." Scat sank lower into his chair. "It was the end of an era. Thanks to the Professor, we all had a chance to glimpse somethin' better than ourselves." He paused thoughtfully. "But after he was gone, well, so were all those dreams, those possibilities. Without him, we were mere mortals again. Absolutely ordinary, workaday mortals."

The porch fell silent. "It must've been tough on you," Ben finally ventured. "When the Professor died."

"It was. But that's not what I was talkin' about. The Professor was gone a long time before he died."

"I don't understand."

"It was the junk, boy. When he started with it, he thought it would squelch the pain. Let him focus on his music. But it didn't work that way. All those stories about people creatin' great art or havin' brilliant ideas when they're high—it's just crap. Ain't possible. May seem brilliant at the time, but when you're cold sober, you realize it's crap. And meanwhile the junk is killin' your body. Eatin' away at your soul."

"Is that what happened to the Professor?"

Scat nodded. " 'Stead of helpin' him, it hurt him bad. He was losin' the music 'cause he couldn't shake the habit. That's what he and Earl fought about most of the time. It wasn't Lily, least not till the bitter end. It was the music. Earl tried everythin'. He dried the man out, learned his songs and played them so they wouldn't be lost. He tried to save the man before he lost his music to the smack. But he couldn't do it."

"They did fight about Lily, though, right? In the end."

"They did," Scat said, nodding gravely. "And that's where I still hold myself accountable. That's why I still wake up some nights in a cold sweat."

"Why?"

" 'Cause I coulda stopped it."

"How?"

"Least I think I coulda. I knew what was happenin'. I knew her better than any of them. Nothin' good ever come from a woman like that."

"You're talking about Lily? But I thought—"

"Lily was a beautiful songbird, all right, with a set of cords Ella herself might've coveted. But when it came to men, she was bad news with a capital B."

"How so?"

Scat shrugged. "Oh, she was all the time flirtin', comin' on to the boys. Leadin' 'em on. Makin' 'em think there was some hope. She did it to everyone."

"Even you?"

Scat grinned, but Ben thought there was something awkward and forced about it.

"I shoulda told Earl to hang it up, told him she was just a flirt and a tease and not to make anything of it. But I didn't. And as a result, we had a tragedy."

"Then you believe Earl killed Professor Hoodoo."

"Hell, yes, son. Weren't no doubt about it then; ain't no doubt about it now."

"Earl says he didn't do it."

"What do you expect him to say? He must have some terrible guilt about it. Earl ain't a violent man. Never was. He just lost his head, that's all."

"It would take more than just losing your head to drive a man to murder."

"Don't be so sure of that, son. A man with a temper is a dangerous thing. Those calm, cool collected types like Earl are sometimes the worst. It may take a lot to push them over the edge, but once they go, they go all the way."

"Temporary insanity?"

"I guess that would be a lawyer's way of puttin' it. All I know is that Earl did somethin' he ordinarily wouldn't do."

Ben wondered if Scat was right. If Earl had been temporarily insane, he might've gotten off—if he hadn't pled guilty. "You're sure it was Earl?"

"Ain't no doubt. I heard them fightin'. I heard Earl threaten him. I saw Earl go to the man's apartment. And not an hour later, the joint's on fire, with George inside. I hate to think of it—that poor messed-up man, maybe still alive, burnin' to death. Now that's the stuff nightmares are made of."

Ben had to agree. He still had nightmares about the time he and Christina had been trapped in a burning church. Burning had to be a horrible way to go—and burning alive! That was simply too gruesome to imagine.

"Did you know Lily was meeting Earl at the club last week?"

"No clue. I could see somethin' was up, with Earl actin' like a father whose daughter's out on her first date. But I never woulda guessed it was Lily. Hadn't heard nothin' about Lily for years."

"Do you have any idea who might've killed her?"

Scat tilted his head to one side. "You mean besides the obvious?"

"You don't think Earl killed her, too!"

Scat shrugged. "He had good reason, didn't he? In many ways, it was that woman who ruined his life, ruined his career. Drove him to murder—and still never was his girl."

Ben frowned. This interview wasn't helping a bit. Worst of all, it was raising some very disturbing possibilities in his mind. "Well, if you can think of anyone else who might possibly have a reason to kill her, let me know, okay?"

"I will," Scat replied. "But I don't think that's likely."

"I wish I could've heard the Professor play. It's a shame he died so young."

"I don't know," Scat said softly. "Sometimes I think that. Other times I think—maybe it's just as well."

"What?"

"The Professor was a brilliant musician—head and shoulders above the rest of us miserable day players. If he had lived—really, what did he have to look forward to? The Sonny and Cher show? *Lollapalooza?* Let's face it, the music industry today is controlled by teenagers and morons who think music is what you see on MTV in three-minute videos. There ain't no place for a musician like Professor Hoodoo in this world."

The man was probably right at that. "You know, there's just one thing that's bothering me. If you're so sure Earl is a murderer, maybe twice over, why do you work for him?"

Scat spread his arms wide. "Hey, kid—I'm a musician. I go where the music is."

"But—I always thought you liked Earl."

"Me? Hell, no."

"But you play in his club. You play poker—"

"So what? I don't like Earl. I didn't like him twenty-odd years ago. I think he stole the magic from the greatest jazz musician who ever lived in these parts." His eyes darkened. "Stole a woman he didn't deserve."

"You loved Lily, too," Ben said quietly.

Scat shifted uncomfortably in his chair. " 'Course I did. Everyone did."

"There's something more." Ben inched forward. "Something you're not telling me."

"Maybe it's none of your goddamned business."

Ben didn't let up. "Did you want Lily for yourself?"

"I didn't have to want nothin'."

"Were you sleeping with her?"

Scat's teeth ground together. " 'Course I was sleepin' with her, you little twerp. I was married to her!"

Ben fell back in his chair, stunned.

"How do you think she happened to be at that club? Who do you think introduced her to our little group? She came on my arm, pal. She was my lady." He wiped a hand across his brow. "I was always loyal to her, too. Always. But she strayed. When she started in with the Professor, that was one thing. They could make music together in a way I could never hope to, could never dream of. The Professor was beyond human rules." His eyes narrowed. "But Earl was just a gross disgusting pig. A thief, that's all he was. He stole things that weren't his. Music. Women. Whatever he could get his hands on."

"But if you hate Earl so badly—"

"A man's gotta eat, you know what I'm saying? Earl has a nice place, and he's one of the few around who still knows what a club should be, what music should be. Just between you and me, he's one of the few in this town who really understands the meaning of jazz."

"Earl quizzed me on that subject. I flunked. I don't suppose you'd like to clue me in?"

Scat grinned, then spread his arms wide. "It's like the great Satchmo himself said—"

Ben nodded. They finished the sentence together. " 'If you gots to ask, you'll never know.' "

"Is he gone?"

As soon as Ben left the condo, the other man stepped out of the shadows of the rear bedroom. He paused just outside the living room, waiting for his answer.

"I said, Is he gone?"

Scat plopped himself wearily into a chair. "He's gone."

The other man entered the room and fingered the back of a linen chair. "What took you so long?"

"What did you want me to do?" Scat asked. "Push him over the railing?"

"Wouldn't be a bad idea," the man growled. "I've had about as much of that little turd as I can take."

"Well, you do what you want. But not in my digs. I don't want anythin' to do with it. And I don't want anythin' to do with you."

The man's eyes lowered. "Bit late for that now, isn't it?"

"No, it ain't. I didn't know what you were plannin'. I didn't know you were gonna kill anybody!"

The man displayed a thin smile. "Be honest, Scat. Weren't you just a little bit happy when you saw Lily's dead body on that stage? After all she'd done to you— didn't that give you just the tiniest bit of pleasure?"

"No, you sick sucker, it didn't. Just get the hell out of here and leave me alone."

An eerie smile crept across the man's face. "You know what they say, Scat, old man. In for a penny, in for a pound."

"Yeah, well, now I'm out for a ton, you got it?"

"It's not that simple." He lowered himself into the chair opposite Scat, so close their knees brushed together. Much too close for Scat's liking. "My business isn't finished."

"Is that my fault? Are you blamin' me because you keep—" He stopped himself just short of the punch, but not so soon his companion couldn't tell what had been coming.

"You're not going to chicken out on me, are you, Scat?"

"I don't know what you mean."

"I'd hate to see you go chicken. I'd hate to see you become a problem." He leaned oppressively forward. "Because you see, I've got enough problems right now. I don't need any new ones. I don't want to have to deal with them." His eyes hardened. "But if I have to, I will."

Scat leaned away, pressing himself against the back of his chair. "Wha—what're you saying?"

The other man did not break eye contact. "I think you know, Scat. I think you do."

Scat laughed, a nervous, high-pitched titter. "Whoa, now, let's back off, man. We're buds, remember? We're in this together."

"Oh, I remember, Scat. I just wanted to make sure you did."

"You don't have to worry about me." He stood suddenly, walking away, an unnatural twitch in his step.

"Good." The man eased back into the chair, steepling his fingers, peering through the apertures. "The end is near, you know. The fat lady is about to sing." He allowed himself a small chuckle. "For ol' Uncle Earl. And his piano-playing pissant friend."

* 40 *

Ben was almost shaved and ready to leave for the club when he heard a furious pounding at his front door. He wrapped his untied tie around his neck, dried his face, and headed for the living room.

"Jones! What are you doing here?"

Jones rushed in before Ben had a chance to suggest anything different. He was in a bad way. Although he was decked out in his Sunday duds, he was walking hunched, hands clasped and brow furrowed, more like a man on death row than a man about to go out on a date.

"I can't do it," Jones said. His voice was hoarse and broken.

"Can't do what?"

"This." He paced around the room in an aimless circle. "This . . . date thing. With Paula."

"Paula? Oh, right. The cybertramp."

"She is *not* a tramp!"

" 'I can feel your strong arms drawing me near. I can feel your strength, your hardness.' Give me a break."

"She's not a tramp!" Jones's face was tight as a drum. "She was just trying to . . . inspire me to agree to a face-to-face."

"Well, I think she accomplished that."

"I thought so, too. But I was wrong. I can't do it." He threw himself down on Ben's ratty sofa, in a would-be fetal position. "I want to meet her. I've been thinking about this date all week. But I can't do it!"

"Just as a point of interest," Ben said, "how can you meet her when you don't know what she looks like?"

"She's going to be at the club tonight at seven-thirty wearing a red carnation." He shook his head. "But it doesn't matter. I can't do it."

Ben smothered his smile. It was obvious Jones was truly upset and sick about this. He tried to be sympathetic. "I'm sorry, Jones. I can see this is tearing you apart. What's causing all this worry? I thought you had no doubts about her. I thought you knew everything about her."

"Oh, don't patronize me," Jones said, twisting away. "You said it yourself. No one normal meets in a chat room. She's probably an axe murderer."

"Well . . . perhaps I was exaggerating."

"Maybe you didn't exaggerate enough. Maybe she's a stalker who uses chat lines to lure men to their deaths. Maybe she's really a *he*!"

"Jones, come on." He looked Jones straight in the eyes. "I've already agreed to keep an eye on you. This isn't what's really bothering you, is it?"

Jones turned away. "No. I suppose it isn't."

"What then?"

Jones spoke with the tiniest of voices. "What if she doesn't like me?"

Now they were getting to the heart of the matter. "Come on, Jones, buck up. You don't have any reason to think she won't like you."

"I don't have any reason to think she will like me, either."

"Nonsense. What about all those online chats? You said she was desperate to meet you."

"Only because she *hasn't* met me. Once she has, that'll all be over."

"You're being ridiculous. You're a very likeable person."

"I'm a secretary, Boss. Let's face it. Her heart won't go pitty-pat over a thirty-two-year-old secretary."

"There's nothing wrong with being a secretary. And besides," he added, "you're an executive office assistant."

"Semantic games aren't going to help me here." He stared down at the carpet. His voice dropped to a whisper. "She thinks I'm a private investigator."

"What?"

"I know, I know. Don't start—"

"Why on earth would you lie to her?"

"I didn't mean to. It was in my online profile. I didn't know she was going to read it."

"Why did you lie in your profile?"

Jones shrugged. "I just—I started writing about some of your cases. Just to make myself a bit more interesting. It was a game, you know? Pretending to be someone I wasn't. Then she read it and started asking questions. She kept pressing to know what I did and what role I played and—what was I going to say? 'Well, I typed the pleadings.' "

Ben shook his head. "This is bad, Jones. Really bad."

"I know, I know."

"You have to tell her the truth. First thing."

"I can't."

"The longer you let the lie fester, the worse it'll become. If you tell her straight away, perhaps she'll forgive you."

Jones swallowed. "There's more."

Ben covered his face. "More?"

"I kinda sorta exaggerated my physical description."

"You've got to be kidding."

"Well, what was I going to tell her? That I'm skinny, puny, poorly dressed—"

"Jones, you've really gotten yourself in deep now."

"I don't know what to do. But I can't show up looking . . . like I do."

"You have to. You made a date. You can't stand her up."

"I know. But I can't go, either. I thought . . . maybe I could get someone to take my place."

"Oh, right. You're going to hit the streets till you find

someone who matches this imaginary physical profile you invented."

Jones coughed. "Actually, Boss . . . I based the physical description on you."

Ben froze, then began slowly moving away. "Now, wait a minute."

"It wouldn't be hard. You're going to be at the club anyway."

"Forget it, Jones. It isn't going to happen."

"You could just meet her. Check her out, make sure she's on the level."

"I'm telling you, Jones, I'm not going to do it. This is not going to happen!"

"Please, Boss! It would mean so much to me!"

"Absolutely not!"

"But, Boss—"

"*No!*"

Ben stood in the lobby of Uncle Earl's Jazz Emporium watching for a woman wearing a red carnation. At least he hoped it would be a woman.

Why do I let myself be talked into these things? he asked himself for about the millionth time. But there was no point. It was done, he had relented, and here he was— wearing a tan jacket with a red rose and pretending to be someone named Jones. He hoped she didn't ask what his first name was, because he didn't know. He'd asked; Jones wouldn't tell. Even the paychecks Ben signed had been made out to "O. Jones."

Jones tried to brief Ben on his online conversations, but he and Paula had done a lot of talking and it was only a ten-minute drive. Plus, Ben had the distinct impression that Jones was doing a lot of mental editing. Still, even the expurgated version had a lot of seriously hot and heavy content.

"This is insane," he had told Jones during the drive. "I have serious misgivings about anyone who would seek out conversation of this nature."

"Relax, Boss. You can handle her. For Pete's sake—she's a librarian."

"Yeah. Like you're a private detective."

Watching the front door, Ben saw a petite young woman wearing an elegant black dress . . . with a red carnation near the neck.

He stepped forward, already relieved. If nothing else, she was clearly a real live woman. Moreover, she was not at all unattractive. She was small and thin, with a pleasant face and auburn hair cut just above her shoulders. She had obviously gone all out to make herself look nice tonight, and with considerable success.

He stepped in front of her. "Are you Paula?" he asked.

"And you must be Fingers." She giggled. "Jones."

Ben smiled, but didn't say anything. Just to preserve what little conscience he might have left, he was going to avoid out-and-out lies whenever possible. "I've got a table waiting. Let me show you." He took her arm and escorted her to a quiet nook in the back by the spiral staircase that led to Earl's office.

"Would you like something to drink?"

"Yes, please." She was obviously nervous—who wouldn't be?—but she was doing a good job of containing it.

Ben signaled the waiter, who came straight to their table. "What'll it be, Ben?"

Paula looked up. "Ben?"

Ben winced. "Uh—"

"Oh, of course. Is that your first name?"

"Um, well, no . . . I mean—"

Earl came bounding down the spiral staircase. He brushed against Ben as he hit the landing. "Hey, Ben, how's it hanging?"

Ben smiled awkwardly. "Everything's fine, Earl. Just peachy."

Paula tilted her head. "But I thought you said—"

"Scat's up in my office," Earl continued. "Try to see that he ain't disturbed, okay? Got some big important announcement planned."

"You got it."

Earl scurried away.

Paula picked up where she left off. "Ben? I thought you said that wasn't your name."

Ben glanced up at the waiter, who was still standing by. "Well . . . it's not that it isn't . . . I mean, it isn't, but . . ." He wiped his brow. "I only use it here."

"You use a different name when you're at the club?"

"Yeah. That's it. You know, like you use a different name when you're online. Can't be too careful."

"Oh." She nodded her head slowly. "I see. I guess."

"What would you like?"

"Scotch and soda, please."

The waiter nodded. "And for you, Ben? The usual?"

Ben glanced at Paula. "Yes, the usual." The waiter scurried away.

"He seems to know you," Paula said.

"I come here often."

"Really? You know, now that you mention it, you do look familiar . . ."

Ben blanched. "I just have that kind of face. Everyone says that."

"Oh." She glanced up at the waiter, already on his way back to their table. "So what's the regular? I bet it's a margarita. I remember you waxed quite poetic about the sour and salty ecstasy of margaritas."

"Uh . . . right." The waiter plunked the glasses down on the table, the clear one before Paula, the brown one before Ben.

Paula stared at his glass. "Chocolate milk? Your usual is chocolate milk?"

"Funny, huh?" He swallowed. "I don't like to start on the margaritas before . . . uh . . . midnight."

"You said you like to take a thermos full on picnics."

"I did? Oh, right. But only on midnight picnics."

"Midnight picnics?"

"Right. Under the moonlight. Very romantic."

Paula stared at him for a moment, then downed about half of her Scotch. "I never would have guessed."

Ben decided it was best to change the subject. "Would you like something to eat? An appetizer, perhaps?"

She grinned. "I already ordered something special. Just for you!" She waved, and a different waiter appeared out of nowhere with a tray.

Paula beamed. "Oysters!"

Ben stared at the contents of the tray, the blood draining from his face. "Oysters?"

"And all for you!"

"Actually, seafood makes me break out in—"

"Ecstasy! I remember you told me that Tuesday night."

The word Ben had been planning to pronounce was *hives*, but he could hardly say that now. "To tell you the truth, I'm not terribly hungry."

"You don't—I mean—You won't—Well, of course, you don't have to."

"All right," Ben said, closing his eyes. "Maybe I could try just one."

"That's more like it."

Ben reached out, careful to stifle the trembling, and took one of the oysters from the tray. "So how exactly do you eat this?"

"Well, you have to open the shell."

Thank goodness for that. He pried open the shell and stared at the goopy contents. "And . . . you eat this?"

"I thought you loved oysters."

"It's just been a while, that's all." He took a deep breath and poured the oyster down the hatch. The instant the slimy contents touched his tongue, he made a gagging noise and reached for his chocolate milk.

"Now that's disgusting," Paula remarked as he guzzled the drink.

Out of the blue, Denny came stomping down the aisle, shaking his fist. "Damn! Damn him to hell!" He spotted Ben. "Do you know what he just did?"

Ben squinted. After their previous encounter, it almost

seemed strange to see Denny wearing . . . well, anything. "Who?"

"Earl. Our Uncle Earl." Sarcasm dripped from his voice. "He took away my solo. I've been practicing that for months. And he took it away."

Ben could feel Paula's eyes bearing down on him. "Did he say why?"

"Yeah. He's giving it to Scat. Can you believe that? Giving my solo to Scat. Those two sons of bitches are conspiring against me!" He stomped away.

Paula peered across at Ben, obviously waiting for an explanation. "People here seem to have no trouble confiding in you."

Ben laughed nervously. "Isn't that strange? I guess I just have one of those faces people trust. I'm sure it won't happen again."

He had barely finished his sentence when Diane came racing up to their table. Her lipstick was smeared and her hair was even more of a mess than usual. "Earl's changed the schedule, Ben," she said, almost out of breath. "We're on in twenty minutes."

"Uh, okay."

"Don't be late. We're gonna try the 'Sweet Georgia Brown' set again. Hope we get further than we did last time." She skittered away. "Gotta tell the rest of the guys."

Ben turned back to find Paula gaping at him. "You're a musician?"

Ben cleared his throat and laughed awkwardly. "I guess there's no point in denying it, is there?"

"I never pictured you as a musician. You never mentioned it."

"Well . . ."

"Why didn't you tell me? You know I love music."

"I guess it never came up."

"Never came up? We've spent hours talking about—" She snapped her fingers. "That's where I've seen you. You play the piano!"

"Well . . . yes."

"You're the one who found the corpse the other night!"

"You were here?"

"Of course I was. Remember? That's why I was late for our first private chat date. The police held us for questioning. But—if you were here too, you must've also been late."

"Uh . . . yeah. I guess I was."

"But you said you'd been waiting for me for more than an hour."

"Did I?" Ben could feel red splotches starting up his neck. "I have a tendency to exaggerate."

"Exaggerate is not the word I would have used." She lifted her glass and finished the Scotch in a single gulp. "Never mind. Doesn't matter." She leaned forward, a mischievous smile illuminating her face. "All right, Jones. Ben. Whatever. Tell me your fantasy again."

Ben felt his throat go dry. "My . . . fantasy?"

"Your guilty pleasure fantasy." She leered. "You remember. The one with the cucumbers. And the grapes."

"Cucumbers and grapes? Is this a fantasy or a recipe?"

She jabbed him in the side. "You remember. The cucumbers and the grapes. And the vestal virgins."

Dizziness began to set in. Ben gripped the edge of the table. "Vestal virgins?"

"Right. And then I come in riding the unicorn." She giggled. "Stark naked."

"Oh, *that* fantasy." He signaled for the waiter, who appeared almost instantly. "I'm going to need something a little stronger."

Ten minutes later, Ben was still trying to reconstruct Jones's guilty pleasure fantasy. "So then, after I rescue you from the fire-breathing dragon, I sweep you off your feet and carry you into the cave. Without saying a word, you remove that tall pointed hat, unfasten a single button, and your gown drops to the ground, revealing you wearing nothing but a sheer diaphanous teddy." He wiped his brow. Although the air conditioner was pumping away, he seemed to be sweating profusely. "You look me in the eyes and pull me toward you, and I'm powerless to resist—"

He realized she was pouting. "What's the matter? Did I say something wrong?"

"You're leaving out all the best parts."

"The best parts? I worked in the vestal virgins."

"But you left out the body paint."

"Did I? How careless of me."

"And Merlin's medieval petroleum jelly."

Ben cleared his throat. "That too?"

"And the edible underwear."

"The—" Ben rose to his feet, his knees trembling. *"Jones!"*

Paula stared at him as if he were a few fries short of a Happy Meal. "Have you totally taken leave of—"

"Jones!" Ben's face was flushed red. "I'm not doing this anymore!"

A moment later, Jones slithered out of the crowd. "You called, Boss?"

Paula looked more confused by the second. "Jones? Boss? What in the hell—"

Ben grabbed Jones by the shoulders. "Paula, this is Jones. Fingers. Whatever you want to call him. This is the man with whom you've been spinning fantasies on the Net."

"But you—"

"You heard me correctly. It was him. Not me, him. I had nothing to do with it. Ben is my name, not his. I'm a musician, he's not. He was the executive office manager at my former law office. A fine human being. But he had some crazy idea you might not like him, so he asked me—"

"You mean it wasn't you?" She slowly rose out of her chair. "The man I chatted with online. It was him."

"That's what I'm saying."

Paula looked at Jones. "Is that true?"

Jones averted his eyes. "Mm-mmm."

"Oh, thank God." Paula fell forward and clutched Jones's shoulders. "Oh, thank you, God."

"I don't understand."

"I was just so distraught." Relief washed across her face. "I was so looking forward to this meeting. And then to find that the words I had fallen for"—she held her hand limply out toward Ben—"came from this . . . this . . ."

"I beg your pardon?" Ben said.

"Well, I mean, really." She grabbed Jones's hand and pulled him down to the table. "I can't tell you how happy this makes me."

Jones peered up at her. "It does?"

"I knew something was wrong the second I saw him."

"You did?"

"I'm sure he's a fine person and all that, but when I heard he was a musician—brrrr!" She did a mock shiver from head to toe. "Musicians are so self-absorbed, you know? Always looking for the limelight. Never giving a moment's thought to other people's needs."

"I'm not like that at all," Ben said, but he had the distinct impression no one was listening.

"I like men who are down-to-earth. Men who are doing things that really matter."

Jones swallowed hard and closed his eyes. "I'm—" He took a deep breath. "I'm not really a private investigator."

She waved her hand dismissively. "Of course you're not. We were just playing around. Sharing fantasies."

"We were?"

"Sure. But you don't have to pretend anymore with me. I just want you to be who you really are. So you're an office manager?"

Another deep breath. "I'm a secretary."

"Really!" She squeezed his hand. "So you work with words, too. I should have known—you're so literate." She scooted her chair closer to his. "You know, Jones, I have a very good feeling about this."

"Well," Ben said, "I guess if I'm no longer needed . . ."

Paula didn't look up. "Don't you have some piano-playing to do?"

Couldn't be much less subtle than that, Ben thought. "Right. I'll go . . . tune my piano."

Ben started toward the stage. He met Gordo on his way up. "How's it hanging?"

"Not well. This is craziness, man."

"Could you be more specific?"

"This place is nuts. Nuts. No one's promise is worth anything. No one can be trusted. Death is in the air."

"Ah. But from your standpoint, that's a good thing, right?"

They stepped onto the stage, behind the curtain. Denny was already there, but Scat's sax was unattended. Ben was halfway to the piano when, out of nowhere, he heard a bloodcurdling scream.

"What in the name of—" He whirled around.

"It's blood! *Blood!*"

Ben raced offstage and blitzed through the tables, pushing gawkers back into their seats.

It was Paula. She was right where he had left her, but she was screaming, near hysterical. Her face was contorted by panic and fear.

And there was blood splattered all over the table, all over her hands, all over her face.

Another thick dollop of blood appeared out of nowhere and splattered down on her chest. She totally lost it. Her scream sliced through the club, sending the crowd leaping to its feet and rushing toward the door.

"Not again!" he heard someone scream as the stampede started. "Not again!"

Jones wrapped his arms around Paula, trying to calm her, getting fresh wet blood smeared all over himself.

What was going on? Ben wondered, trying to keep his head about him. He had left only moments ago and everything had been fine. Now the table looked as if it had been the site of some sick ritual sacrifice.

The screaming was infectious. Some saw Paula, saw the

blood-spattered table, and began to panic. Some screamed just because others were screaming. Tables and glasses crashed to the floor. People rushed onto the stage, into the wings, trying to escape they knew not what. In less than a minute, the club had descended into chaos.

Ben knew the blood had to be coming from somewhere. But where? No one appeared to be wounded.

He looked up. Sure enough, there was a huge red spot on the ceiling; something red and unmistakable was seeping through the plaster.

Blood. Lots of it.

Ben hit the spiral staircase running. He raced up, taking the stairs two at a time, till he reached the door to Earl's office. He threw the door open and ran inside.

Scat's remains lay in a crumpled heap, blood forming a huge puddle on the floor beneath him. He had been stabbed in more places than Ben cared to count. But that wasn't the worst of it.

The worst of it was, he was smiling.

FOUR

* *

Freeing the Camels

* 41 *

"Mike, you're making a mistake!"

"I've already made the mistake," Mike said, snapping the cuffs over Earl's wrists. "What I'm doing now is making sure I don't repeat it." He pinned Earl's arms behind his back and began reading him his rights.

Ben followed close behind as Mike pushed Earl toward the door. "Mike, listen to me. Just because the corpse was found in Earl's club doesn't mean he committed the murder."

Mike kept marching. "What about the fact that the body was found in his private office? What about the fact that Earl specifically told you not to go looking for Scat? What about the fact that about a dozen people saw Earl hurrying out of that same office minutes before the blood started dripping through the plaster? Including you."

"That doesn't mean anything." Ben turned sideways, cutting a path through the crowd, trying to keep up. "There are other ways out of the office. There's a window. And a back door leading to the stage."

"Which no one saw anyone suspicious pass through. Ben, give it a rest."

"But what about Tyrone Jackson? If he testifies—"

"Last I heard, you didn't know if Jackson was dead or alive. Even if he's alive, he's not here tonight, so he's not going to be able to alibi your client out of this one."

"But, Mike—"

287

"And frankly, I don't think the testimony of some career hood is going to change anyone's mind at this point. After one circumstantial murder, maybe. After two, no way."

"Just let me find him. We'll see what—"

"Sorry, Ben. It won't wash anymore."

"But what about the rug man? What about the man who attacked me in my car?"

"I don't know who that was, Ben, or what he has to do with these crimes. But I do know that every scrap of evidence we have points to Earl Bonner as the murderer of Lily Campbell and Scat Morris. I should have arrested this man a long time ago." He pushed the front door open, Earl in tow. "I'll be back to supervise after I make sure this suspect is in custody. Tomlinson?"

Mike's right-hand man appeared at his side. "Yes, sir?"

"Secure the crime scene and make sure no one contaminates it. Send in the video crew and tell the other evidence teams to get ready. Start some of the uniforms circulating through the crowd. Find out what if anything anyone knows."

Ben wedged himself in between them. "Mike, you're making a big mistake."

Mike pushed Ben out of the way. "And if Kincaid here gives you any trouble, sit on him."

Tomlinson suppressed his reaction. "Got it, sir."

They both watched as Mike and Earl left the club.

"Wanna watch the video team work?" Tomlinson asked after they were gone.

"No, thanks. I'm going downtown." As soon as they finished processing Earl, Ben would be waiting for him. He would guide Earl through the ropes, try to put him at ease. And he would bully all concerned to get an arraignment set as soon as possible. And there was the matter of setting bail. Bail was always a long shot in capital murder cases, but he had to try.

"Mike told me not to let anyone leave until they've been identified and questioned."

"Mike can question me all night if he wants. I expect I'll be spending it in his jailhouse." Ben walked outside into the parking lot. Damn! They needed Tyrone—even more desperately than before. Even if Tyrone couldn't help Earl on the new murder, he could go a long way toward stopping the chain of circumstantial evidence that was piling up.

Ben slid into his van and started the engine. He was assuming, of course, that Tyrone was still alive. No one had seen any trace of him. Loving had been checking the underside of every rock in Tulsa, but he hadn't turned up a lead. Ben hated to admit it, but in all likelihood, Tyrone was dead.

And if Tyrone was dead, poor Earl already had one foot in the grave.

Tyrone switched off the radio. It had happened, just as he'd feared it might. The maniac had struck again. He'd killed Scat—poor helpless Scat!—and framed Earl in the process. Now Earl was in custody, certain to be charged. Hell, certain to be convicted.

Unless Tyrone came forward. Unless he told what he knew—and showed what he'd found.

Not that that was any guarantee Earl would walk. But at least he'd have a chance. Which was more than he had at the moment.

Tyrone closed his eyes, trying to shut out all the noise, the confusion, the conflict. He'd been holed up here for days, here with the homeboys in the gang headquarters that used to be his ace hang spot, back before he liberated himself. He'd almost gotten to spend the rest of his life here—as a corpse. When he'd been running from that crazy, and he heard that sound behind him—well, he'd been certain that was the last sound he would ever hear. Turned out it wasn't the crazy at all, it was Momo, coming to keep their appointment, which Tyrone had somehow managed to forget all about after being hunted by the knife-wielding maniac. Momo guided him through the maze of Rockwood till he was safely ensconced in the gang's hideout.

And that was where Tyrone had remained ever since. No reason to go out there and risk getting cut by some smile-carving sicko, right? No reason to walk the streets till the cops pick you up on some bogus charges and beat you over the head with them. Better to stay safe right here at . . . home?

The home he'd sworn off, sworn he'd never return to. But here he was, first time he needed help. First time he needed a friend, a place to hole up. Something.

Here he was. Safe.

Except in his nightmares. He kept replaying the chase through the ruins, a psychopath at his heels. Except in Tyrone's nightmares, the psycho always caught him. He held him down while the knife came closer and closer, trying to carve him like a jack-o'-lantern, trying to give him a smile that was not his own.

And then Tyrone would wake up screaming.

When had the nightmares started? Probably two days ago. He'd thought he was safe until then, when one of the boys spotted someone searching through the ruins. The description had sucked; he was probably wearing another one of those stupid disguises. It didn't matter. Tyrone knew who he was. And what he was looking for.

Correction: *who* he was looking for.

The first few days after the murder, he'd forgotten all about the shiny bauble he'd found on the men's room floor—a penknife, as it turned out. Momo had been the one who suggested that it might have been dropped by the same man who'd been removing his disguise, the same man who was in all likelihood the killer. And if so, then maybe it could tell them who the man was. Tyrone didn't know what to make of it, but Kincaid was just smart enough that he might. So Tyrone mailed it to him.

Momo was being kind letting Tyrone stay here. He hadn't complained, and he hadn't made demands—not in so many words, anyway. But Tyrone knew Momo, and he knew Momo did nothing for free. Eventually it would be payback time. Tyrone would be back in the gang once more.

Right back where he started.

They say you never quit the gangs, not really. Tyrone had tried to prove them wrong. But now it looked like he was going to fall right back into the trap.

He couldn't let that happen to him. Not again.

Comfortable as it was here, safe as he was in the cocoon, he had to get out. He couldn't put it off any longer. If he did, Earl would go up the river. The psycho would keep killing.

He opened his eyes and pushed himself out of his chair. Like it or not, it was time to leave home.

Tyrone already knew about Ben's new office at Warren Place; he'd had to get the address so he could mail him the package. Sending mail was one thing. Driving there was another. He had hoped to keep a low profile, and now it looked like he was going to be driving clear across town. Twenty minutes in the car he'd borrowed, never knowing who might pull up and see him.

He parked the car on the curb and quietly eased out onto the sidewalk. Someone must be paying the gardeners here a tidy sum, he thought; these lawns looked like they'd been manicured. The trees were all perfectly spaced and cared for. It was a class A location—not, frankly, the type of place where he expected to find Kincaid.

As late as it was, Tyrone could see lights blazing on the seventh floor. With any luck, Kincaid was still there. It made sense; with Earl being arrested, he probably had a ton of work to do.

Well, if nothing else, he could make Kincaid's load a little lighter. He could tell Kincaid his chief witness was still alive. True, it was risky, but he couldn't play it safe. Not while psychopaths roamed the streets and the only man who ever really gave a damn about you was being charged with murders he didn't commit.

Tyrone had almost made it across the street when he heard a rustle in the bushes behind him. He whirled around, staring into the darkness.

He didn't see anything. Had he imagined it? Or had he been so busy congratulating himself that he missed something?

Or someone.

He turned back toward the building, this time moving a good deal faster than before. He felt exposed, and rightly so—he was. Out in the open, unprotected. No one even knew where he was.

He tried not to panic. Once he got inside, Kincaid would know what to do. Where to go. How to be safe.

Tyrone's feet moved even faster. He was running, racing toward the glass revolving doors that led to the main lobby. And he was almost there when a black shadow leaped out from behind one of those perfectly spaced trees and wrapped its arms around his neck.

Tyrone's speed worked against him; he hit the ground before he even knew what had happened. He tried to struggle, but the shadow had him pinned down and was using all its weight against him.

The shadow pressed a damp cloth over his mouth and nose, and before Tyrone could stop himself, he inhaled something with a sharp and pungent odor. Sort of sweet, like peppermint, but Tyrone knew that wasn't what it was. Almost immediately, his vision went blurry and his brain began to reel. He was losing consciousness. He was helpless, absolutely helpless.

The shadow pressed closer, and in the very last instant before everything went black, Tyrone saw the face emerging from the darkness, the same face he had seen that night in Rockwood—the same face he had seen in his nightmares, which, as it turned out, were nothing compared with the real nightmare that was yet to come.

* 42 *

When Ben saw Rick Anglin at the opposite end of the county courthouse corridor, he knew it wasn't just a coincidence. There weren't many people at the courthouse this time of night—and especially no senior members of the prosecutor's staff.

They met outside Judge Sarah L. Hart's courtroom. "Evening, Rick. Hope I didn't get you out of bed." Ben stretched out his hand.

Anglin didn't take it. "As a matter of fact, you did."

"Oh. No wonder you seem grumpy. I hate being awakened when I'm sleeping."

"For your information, I wasn't sleeping. Which is why I'm particularly pissed off!"

Ben decided not to pursue that tidbit of information. "Haven't seen you in a while. Not since that prairie dog case. Where you been hiding?"

"In Jack Bullock's shadow. Till you and Judge Hart got him suspended."

"Hey, I didn't have anything—"

Anglin held up his hands. "Don't waste it on me, Kincaid. I couldn't stand the man." He popped open his briefcase and took out a file. "Look, we both know your client is guilty, so why don't you make it easy for everyone and cop a plea now. I promise I'll do everything possible to keep him away from the Big Needle."

"No chance, Rick. Earl didn't do it."

"Yeah, yeah, I'm sure. Still, he'd be better off taking a plea."

"That's what his last lawyer told him, and he did twenty-two years for a crime he didn't commit."

Anglin blew air through his lips. "Man, it's true what they say about you, isn't it? You'll swallow any sob story."

"It's not a story. It's the truth."

"And the cow jumped over the moon."

"Rick, Earl Bonner is innocent."

"Bullshit."

"He didn't kill Lily Campbell or Scat Morris."

"Bullshit."

"He's being framed."

"Bullshit."

Ben pressed his finger against Anglin's chest. "You need a thesaurus!"

They passed through the swinging doors and entered the courtroom. Judge Hart was sitting at the bench awaiting their arrival. Moreover, Ben was surprised to see his entire former office staff waiting for him. Christina and Jones and Loving were all lined up in the front row of the gallery.

"Who told you guys about—" He stopped. Anglin was tugging at his sleeve.

"Look, why don't we work a few things out before we get to the judge? Surely you don't have any fantasies about getting the charges dropped. Or about getting your man out on bail."

"Actually, I do."

They were interrupted by the sound of Judge Hart's gavel rapping the bench. "I don't want to interrupt you boys, but it is late and my collie gets very lonely if I'm not home by midnight. Could I possibly have a few minutes of your time?"

Ben and Anglin straightened up and approached the bench. "Yes, your honor."

Judge Hart peered through her half-glasses and examined a sheaf of papers. "I've read the early report. We'll have a formal arraignment day after tomorrow, but I must say, this arrest appears to be entirely in order."

"I'll take that up at the preliminary hearing," Ben said. "Right now, I'd just like to make a motion."

She nodded. "Very well. Give it to me."

Ben coughed. "I was planning to make the motion orally."

A silence covered the courtroom like a blanket.

What? Ben wondered. Do I have food in my teeth or something? He heard a low chuckle emerging from Anglin. Which he didn't care for in the least.

"I guess you didn't read Judge Hart's amended court rules last month," Anglin said at last.

A furrow crossed Ben's brow. "Uh . . . no. Actually I've been out of touch with the legal world for a bit—"

"Judge Hart no longer accepts oral motions. Everything has to be in writing."

Ben peered up at the bench.

"It's the computers," Judge Hart said, sighing. "They can't track oral motions. That's why I need everything typed up in the correct form."

"Oh." Ben swallowed hard. "What an interesting rule. I didn't—"

Jones suddenly sprang to his feet. "Here's your motion, Boss. Typed just the way you wanted it."

"I—" Ben took the file folder and removed the motion within. It was perfectly prepared; Jones had even thought to make copies.

He handed a copy to the judge and to Anglin. "Here it is, your honor."

Judge Hart took the motion and scanned it. "Yes, this will do nicely."

Anglin stepped forward. "Your honor, I must object to this absurd attempt to have his client released on bail. The defendant is a convicted murderer!"

"Earl Bonner has served his time," Ben rebutted. "He has a clean slate."

"I agree," Judge Hart said. "The man has paid his debt to society. We can't hold that against him."

"What about his behavior since he's been released?"

Anglin offered. "My sources tell me he's been living on the edge since the day he left McAlester. He's been linked to organized crime, drugs, prostitution—you name it."

"That isn't true!" Ben insisted. "He's stayed out of trouble."

Anglin leaned forward. "Yeah? Prove it."

Ben stammered. "Well, I didn't know—"

Loving rose to his feet. "Skipper? Here's that probation report you asked for."

"Probation—? Right—the probation report!" He snatched the folder from Loving's hands. "See for yourself, your honor."

Judge Hart took the proffered report and flipped through the pages. "According to this, Mr. Prosecutor, the defendant has been a model of good conduct. Never missed a probation meeting. Established his own business. Employs several people, including some inner-city youth who need jobs badly. There's not a word about any criminal activity. Do you have a conflicting report?"

Anglin coughed into his hand. "Not at the moment."

Judge Hart closed the folder. "That's what I thought. Well then, with regard to this motion—"

Anglin cut her off. "Your honor, this is a capital offense. The death penalty is a real possibility here. Courts never consider bail in capital cases. Even for an honest man, the temptation to give flight is too great. And if the man bolts, we may never find him again."

"There's a way around that." Somehow Ben wasn't all that surprised when Christina leaped to her feet and passed through the swinging gates. She handed Ben a file and winked. "Like you suggested earlier, Ben, I think this is the perfect case for this."

Ben began rapidly scanning the file. "Right. Perfect case."

Judge Hart peered down from the bench. "Excuse me, Mr. Kincaid. Is this a member of your staff?"

"Yes, she—" He looked up abruptly. "She's my legal assistant—and partner."

Christina's eyes expanded.

"She's a law student, you know," Ben added.

The judge nodded. "Indeed."

"Oh, yeah," Ben said. "Very promising. Top of her class."

"Is that a fact? Well, congratulations, young lady. We need more female faces in this profession."

Christina dipped her head. "Thank you, ma'am." She nudged Ben in the side. "Thanks for the kind words— *partner*."

Anglin cut in. "Look, I hate to interrupt this Hallmark moment, but there's a motion pending. Setting Earl Bonner free would constitute a gross injustice, not to mention a threat to public safety."

"Earl Bonner will not bolt," Ben said firmly. "But it doesn't matter because I have a suggestion that will eliminate the risk in any case." He placed the file on Judge Hart's bench. "Thanks to my staff."

* 43 *

As Ben walked across the plaza to the county jail, he couldn't help but reflect on how well the hearing had gone. That had been great—the whole staff pitching in, working together like a well-oiled machine. And of course he had been successful, which put a rosy glow on any hearing.

He had almost forgotten how satisfying practicing law could be. How rewarding. It was almost enough to make him consider . . . just consider . . .

As he stepped into the front office, he was relieved that the guard on duty at the county jailhouse didn't ask for any identification or to inspect the traditional Tulsa County bar card, especially since he didn't have it on him and wasn't entirely sure he had paid his dues.

"Haven't seen you in a while," the guard said, easing out of his chair.

Ben searched through the cobwebs of his memory, trying to come up with the man's name. It was something short and traditional. Bob? Tom? Best not to risk it. "I've been on an extended vacation."

The guard unlocked the outer door to the cell block. "You picked a hell of a time to return. He's back here."

Ben followed the man down the metallic corridor, ignoring the gauntlet of drunks and wife-beaters and other assorted lowlifes on either side. Earl was at the end of the corridor, lying on the bottom bunk of a no-frills bed with a barely discernible mattress.

Earl sat up as soon as he heard the two men coming down the corridor. "Ben!" He leaned forward eagerly.

The guard gave Ben a nod. "You need anything, I'm right behind that door."

"Thanks. I'll be all right." The guard locked the cell door behind them and left them alone.

"Are you okay?" Ben asked Earl. He cleared a space on the other end of the bunk.

Earl grunted. "If your idea of okay is having someone take all your stuff, strip-search you, spray you with delousing powder, and throw you in this hellhole, then yeah, I'm having a great time."

"Everyone treating you all right?"

"Hell, no. What'd'ya expect? These people all think I killed three people, 'cludin' a woman. And mutilated their bodies. I didn't expect no Tom Cruise treatment." He shrugged. "You know that guard?"

Ben gave it a try. "Bob?"

"Tom. He drops by every twenty minutes or so jus' to tell me about how I'm gonna"—he held his hands up like a monster—"*frrryyy!*"

"Oh, geez."

"He's been givin' me the lowdown on the lethal injection table, how it works, how they shoot the poison into your body. He says I got lucky once, but not twice. He says the cops've got secret ways of remixing the poison so it hurts, but a man's paralyzed so he can't say or do nothing about it." Earl's voice began to tremble. "He says I'll be dyin' in agony, but no one will know it. He says they got ways of makin' it happen over and over again. He says they'll make me die three times over, once for each person I killed."

Ben put his arm on Earl's shoulder, trying to calm him. "That's all a load of crap, Earl. Typical jailhouse rot. He's just trying to scare you. Put it out of your mind."

"Hard to put somethin' like that out of your mind, Ben. Man says I'm gonna pay the price. Three times over!"

"You didn't commit those crimes, Earl. And besides,

you already paid the price for the murder of George Armstrong. You were convicted and you served your time. To try you again would be double jeopardy. They can't touch you."

"If you say so," he said without much conviction. "It's just so damn . . . hard." He pressed his fists against his face. "Hard to sit here and listen to that bull. Hard to listen and know how much they hate you. And it ain't right. I didn't do it!"

"I know you didn't, Earl. You have to understand—law enforcement officials have a terrific responsibility. They do a tough job, usually without half the support or appreciation they deserve. It's understandable that sometimes they become overzealous. You can't let it get to you."

"It will get to me. It will!" He grabbed Ben by the lapels. "Can't you get me out of here?"

Ben paused. "Maybe."

"What's that supposed to mean?"

"I just had a hearing before Judge Hart. The prosecutor's against bail, of course, and Judge Hart normally doesn't even consider it in capital cases. But fortunately, Judge Hart trusts me. I've been before her on several occasions, and she knows I wouldn't ask for bail if I thought there was any danger you'd disappear. I told her you were an honest man, that you wouldn't flee, that you had a business to run, and that the prosecution's case was unconvincing and entirely circumstantial."

"So she's going to let me out?"

"Well, conditionally. You have to agree to wear one of these." Ben pulled out of his pocket something that resembled a plastic dog collar. "It goes around your ankle. As soon as it's activated, it gives off an electronic homing signal. Allows them to track you wherever you go."

"So they can hunt me down like a dog!"

"If you try to run, yes. And if you try to remove it, they'll know instantly."

"I ain't gonna be treated like some kind of animal!"

"Believe me, Earl, you don't want to be in jail a second

longer than you have to be." He laid the collar down on the bed. "I had to argue my guts out to get you this. These collars are still relatively new; a lot of people don't trust them. But you have to realize—it will be weeks, maybe months, before your case comes to trial. You don't want to spend all that time in this crappy jail cell."

Earl ground his teeth together. "Can I wear the damn thing under my pants?"

"Of course. No one will even know you've got it on."

"Wrong. I'll know." He scooped it off the bunk. "But you're right. It's better than spendin' another minute behind bars. Let's get outta here."

When at last he opened his eyes, he couldn't see anything. And his eyes hurt.

Tyrone tried to survey his surroundings, but all he saw was pitch-black darkness. He tried to stretch, but his limbs wouldn't move. He was curled in a narrow space; his hands were tied tightly behind his back, and his shoulders were wedged in a painful, contorted position.

And there was something wrong with his face. The pain was agonizing. When the air rushed up against him, Tyrone could feel open sores, wounds to his flesh. And he could taste blood at the corner of his lips.

He had been beaten, even while he was unconscious. Beaten savagely.

And the worst of it was, he had no way to check the damage, no way to see himself. All he knew was that he ached—and that the damage was probably worse than he imagined. Maybe even permanent.

He cursed himself under his breath. How could he have been so stupid? Back with the gang, he had been safe. But no, he had come out of hiding. The killer already knew he and Kincaid were connected—were working together, even. It didn't take a rocket scientist to figure out that eventually Tyrone would show up at Kincaid's office. He'd been a fool, a shrimp swimming with a piranha. He deserved what he got.

What he got, and what he would get. Because Tyrone knew that, whatever had happened to him before, it was only a prelude to what was to come.

He heard a whirring noise somewhere in the background. The sound of an engine, he thought. A steady droning noise.

Suddenly his entire world lurched to the right. He would have been thrown sideways, except there was nowhere for him to go. He was pressed against—well, whatever it was. It was hard and metallic, just like the cold sharp something that was beneath his face.

There was a bump, and Tyrone bounced into the air. He didn't bounce far; there was a low ceiling, and he smashed right up against it.

That's when it came to him—he was in a car! The car was going somewhere, going fast, and he was tied up in the trunk. That explained the engine noise, the darkness. That explained the cramped space and the low ceiling. That explained everything.

Everything except where they were going. And what was going to happen to him when they arrived.

The car did not seem to be moving as fast as it had been before. There was a good side to this: it meant fewer bumps, fewer bruises to his already battered body. But there was something disturbing about it, too. No one who was trying to get anywhere drove like this. No, this was more like the way someone drove . . . when he had almost arrived.

Fear began to take over, replacing pain as Tyrone's dominant sensation. It was making his blood race, making his heart skitter-skat. His mouth went dry, and his brain was filled with horrible thoughts of what might lie ahead. He tried to distance himself from it, tried to remove himself from his own body. This isn't happening to me, he told himself. I'm just a spectator, a watcher. I will observe, but I will not feel . . .

Knowing he was in a car helped explain the smell—the nauseating odor he had been aware of since he first came to. It was turning his stomach, literally making him sick. It was petroleum, the smell of the gas tank, motor oil, and perhaps the tools in the trunk. Whatever. It was hot in here, he was sweating, and the heat made the smell all the worse.

The car hit another huge bump—a pothole probably, knowing Tulsa's roads as he did. He bounced violently up against the trunk lid, then his cheekbone smashed down on the sharp metallic something. Was it the jack? Or maybe that metal frame the spare fits into? Whatever it was, it hurt—hurt so much he cried out. Stupid. Why let his captor know he was in pain? Why let him know how scared he was? Why let him know he was conscious? That could only lead to . . . unfortunate consequences.

He felt blood trickling down his cheek. The bump hadn't been that bad—he must have reopened something, some wound from the beating before. He wished he had stayed quiet.

But it was too late. He felt the car pulling over to the right, then slowly coming to a stop. Tyrone panicked. His pulse was racing; he felt a surge of fear-drenched blood rushing through his veins. He could barely breathe. His face was wet and sticky, drenched with blood and sweat.

A crunch of gravel. Tyrone lifted his head slightly, turning toward the sound. The steps were coming closer; they circled around the back of the car. He heard a jingling of keys.

His heart skipped a beat. His breath was suspended, frozen. He felt as if a thousand days passed during the second it took his captor to poke the key into the trunk lock and turn it till it clicked.

The trunk lid popped open. A bright light shone in Tyrone's face, so blinding he had to clench his eyes shut.

"You're up early," the man hovering over him said. He reached beside Tyrone and pulled a long iron object out from under him. Tyrone slowly opened his eyes, let the light seep slowly in . . .

It was a tire iron. Poised just above his face.

"Sleepy-bye time," the man said. There was a burst of whiteness, an explosion of pain.

And then Tyrone drifted back into merciful unconsciousness and was left with only his dreams, his haunted tortured dreams of the pain still to come.

* 44 *

Ben spent the next day pursuing every lead imaginable. He bullied Mike into letting him see the reports taken from the patrons at the club the previous night; the ones who seemed promising he tracked down and interviewed himself. He sent Christina to the courthouse and Jones to the computer to pore through any records that might bear on Scat, his background, his history—anything that might suggest why he was killed or who would have a motive to do it. And he sent Loving out to investigate Scat's neighbors, people who knew him.

And at the end of the day, Ben knew not a whit more than he had known when the day began. Which was next to nothing.

What was he missing? Somehow, he couldn't make it add up. He had all the necessary information; he just wasn't putting it together right. It was like he had all the pieces to a jigsaw puzzle, but they were turned face down so all that showed was the brown cardboard backing.

And he hadn't found Tyrone Jackson, either. Not so much as a trace of him.

At sundown he returned to the office, where he was greeted by Jones—and Paula. What was she doing here? Ben wondered. Were they holding hands under the desk?

"Jones," he said in a businesslike tone, "did you have a chance to run those Internet searches?"

"I spent most of the day on it. I ran all your searches and several others besides."

"Masterfully," Paula added.

"I used all the major search engines—Alta Vista, Yahoo! Excite. To increase my search capacity, I reprogrammed my web browser."

"Ingeniously," Paula added.

"Finally, with Paula's help"—he looked lovingly in her direction—"I went to the library and did some research the old-fashioned way."

"You mean—you used books?"

Jones gave Paula a knowing look. "You see? I used to put up with this every day." He turned back toward Ben. "I used their electronic card catalog to search the collections of other libraries, including newspapers and periodicals, for information that might be of use.

"Brilliantly," Paula sighed.

"No doubt," Ben said. "Did you find anything?"

"A lot. About Scat. And about this Professor Hoodoo he and Earl used to play with. But probably nothing you don't already know. Certainly nothing that suggests a motive for murder."

"Oh."

"I printed it all out," Jones said, pointing to a stack of computer paper on the edge of his desk. "But I don't think there's anything in there that's going to solve your case."

Ben laid his hands on the information. He'd been hoping for a miracle. But all he got was a tower of feed-form paper.

"There's some mail for you as well," Jones added.

Ben saw a small package wrapped in brown paper. He picked it up and ripped it open.

Inside he found a golden bauble, a small thin sparkly—and beneath that a note in a handwritten scrawl: *Found this in the men's room the night of the murder. Probably Rug Man's. Don't know what it is—but thought you might. T.*

Tyrone! He was alive!

Ben held the golden object in his hands. It was a penknife—a fancy one, from the looks of it. And on the side, in an overwrought, stylized lettering, he saw a mono-grammed *B*.

B, he thought to himself. *B*. Who could that—

"Is it something important?" Jones asked, interrupting his thoughts.

"Huh? Oh, I don't know. I need to talk to Tyrone." He pushed the penknife into his pocket. "I don't suppose you saw anything in your computer research that might help us figure out what happened to him?"

" 'Fraid not," Jones said.

"Who's Tyrone?" Paula asked.

"Kid who saw a man at the club wearing a disguise," Ben explained.

"A disguise?"

"Right. Which led me to believe he might've been the killer. Why else would a man go out in a fake Afro?"

Paula's head tilted slightly. "Ben, he was wearing a fake Afro?"

"False beard, too. Shades."

Paula slowly rose out of her chair. "Sunglasses with silver lenses? The kind that look like mirrors from the outside?"

"Yes, exactly. Why?"

Paula looked from Ben to Jones, then back to Ben. "I saw him, too."

Ben gripped her by the arms. "You saw him? You were there the night Lily Campbell was killed?"

"Sure. I told you that last night. Heck, I told Jones the night it happened. In the chat room."

Ben whirled around toward Jones. "You knew?"

"Well, I didn't know she saw the Rug Man!"

"The Rug Man?" Paula frowned. "What are you talking about?"

"The man we believe killed Lily Campbell was car-rying a rug. We think he may have used the rug to get the body into the club. Did you see it?"

"No. When I saw him, he was moving away from the stage. Maybe he'd already deposited the body."

Ben lowered her back into her chair. "Paula, tell me everything you saw. Everything."

"There isn't much. The club had barely opened. This guy was moving out; I was moving in. We brushed shoulders; I gave him a bit of a knock. And I saw the way his hair bounced on impact. I mean, independent from his head. I used to wear a wig myself when I was younger, so I knew what that meant."

"Did you tell anyone?"

"No. Why would I? I just thought the man was losing his hair and didn't want to settle for a toupee. You never know. Men are weird about hair loss."

"Is that a fact?" Ben said evenly.

"Even after the murder, when I was talking to the police, I didn't think anything about it. I didn't make the connection. A woman was murdered onstage; I had no reason to link that to some guy wearing a wig."

"Paula, this is very important." Ben gazed steadily into her eyes. "I want you to cast your mind back to that night. Concentrate. Try to remember what you saw. Tell me everything you can remember."

Paula took a deep breath and closed her eyes. "Okay. I'm taking myself back to that night. I'm remembering. He was wearing—well, I've already told you about the shades."

"Right. What else do you see?"

"That's about all. Silver mirror glasses. He's about my height. Maybe a bit taller. He's black, or looks black, anyway. His hands are disgusting; fingers are stained an ugly blackish-yellow. He's strong-looking, well-muscled."

"What else do you see? Go through the whole scene. You're walking through the club . . ."

"I'm walking down the floor, picking a table. I see this guy coming, but he's moving quite fast and I don't have time to get out of the way. We bump shoulders, his wig bounces. I say I'm sorry; he makes a grunting noise. He moves on toward the bathrooms."

"Was there anything else, Paula?"

"I'm trying, but that's all I can remember." She opened her eyes. "I'm sorry I can't be of more—Ben?"

Ben wasn't looking at her. He had turned away, was staring off into space. "Can it be?" he muttered. He took the penknife out of his pocket and stared at it.

"What are you talking about?"

Ben still didn't look at her. "But if—" His face suddenly blanched. "Oh, my God," he whispered. "Oh, my God."

"Ben, what is it?" Jones stood beside him. "What's going on? Do you—do you know who the killer is?"

Ben slowly turned his head till his eyes met Jones's. "Oh, my God," he repeated, even more softly than before. "I think I do. I think I do."

When Tyrone awoke, he was blind, chained, naked, and cold.

He didn't know where he was or what had happened to him. His mind was all a blur at first; he was barely able to pull his thoughts together long enough to remember who he was. Slowly and painfully it began to come back to him.

His arms were chained above his head. Handcuffed, he thought. He didn't know how long they had been locked up there. It felt like forever. He couldn't sit down; the cuffs held him too high, too tight. The best he could do was lean against the wall beside him, and he could only barely do that. His legs were so tired; his knees ached and throbbed. He was so weak he wouldn't have been able to stand— except that he had no choice. He was chained into position; no matter how badly he wanted to move, to sit, to lie down—he couldn't.

And he was naked. He was certain of that. He didn't know when he had lost his clothes or who had taken them, but he was absolutely certain they were gone. He was exposed, vulnerable.

And he was blind. Not permanently, he hoped. There was something draped over his head, something that extended down past his neck. He wasn't sure what it was. It felt hot and scratchy. It let no light through, none whatsoever. It was hot and stifling; it made it hard to breathe.

He had no idea where he was. He seemed to be standing on a tile floor. He thought the wall on his right side was tile also, but he couldn't be certain. He could only touch the wall with his shoulder, which made it hard to reach a certain conclusion. He felt nothing on his left side. Nothing but open air.

He didn't know how long he had been here, how long he had been chained up like a slab of beef in a meat factory. It felt like days, weeks even, but he knew it had probably not been that long. He had had no company, no interaction, no food or water, since he had come to his senses. Nothing to help him measure the passage of time. Nothing to connect him to the world of the living.

It seemed his captor wanted it that way.

That was his best guess anyway. And all he could do was guess. Why hadn't the man killed him already? What was it he wanted? Was it the penknife?

"Come and get me, you bastard!" Tyrone shouted suddenly. He didn't know what had come over him. It had bubbled forth all at once, an uncontrollable rage, like a cyclone. "Talk to me!" he screamed. "Talk to me!"

Was it his imagination, or did he hear the soft impress of footsteps somewhere in the distance? It wasn't much, barely more than the beating of his heart. But it was something, wasn't it? Or was it just that he so desperately, desperately wanted it to be something . . .

A door pushed open. He heard the turning of the knob, the brush of wood against carpet. It was something. No, someone. Someone was coming.

Someone was coming!

His elation faded almost instantaneously as the sound of the footsteps told him the approaching figure was off the carpet, walking on tile. Very close.

"Get me out of here!" Tyrone shouted. "Now!"

There was no response.

"I know you're there, you son of a bitch! Don't pretend

you're not!" He was breathing hard and fast, causing the bag over his head to cling to his lips. "You don't have the right to chain me up like a dog!"

He paused, sucking in air, trying to calm his trembling. But there was still no response. Not a word.

"Unchain me, you sick bastard!" Tyrone was shouting at the top of his lungs, giving it everything he had. "Do you hear me? Take these goddamn—"

He never got to finish the sentence. Tyrone heard the swift rush of air followed by an explosion in his groin. He tried to cry out, but there was no air left in his lungs. His knees crumbled, but the cuffs held his wrists up fast, giving him no release.

Second and third shock waves of pain coursed through his body. It had been a direct kick to his exposed and vulnerable genitalia, and it hurt like nothing he had ever before experienced in his entire life.

"Wh-why?" he whispered. His body was like a dead weight, threatening to pull his arms out of their sockets. The pain would not stop, and there was nothing he could do.

He heard a squeaking noise and suddenly it was raining. Raining hot water.

It was a shower! That's where he was; that's why the wall and the floors were tile. His wrists must be cuffed to the showerhead.

The elation of discovery soon faded to the threat of imminent danger. The water was pouring down on him. Hot water. And getting hotter . . .

Much hotter. Tyrone screamed. The water was scalding him, sizzling his skin. He pushed back onto his feet and danced around, trying to escape the fiery rain, but there was nowhere he could go. The water burned down on his exposed skin, on every part of his body. He felt as if his flesh was melting, then slowly peeling away.

"Stop!" Tyrone cried. "Please—stop!" He flung himself against the wall, but the showerhead held him tight. Maybe if I bash my brains out, he thought to himself, maybe if I just kill myself now. I have to end this. I have to escape the pain somehow—

"You're killing me!" he screamed, but then he realized that that might well be the point of the exercise.

The water continued to burn down. It had to be boiling temperature now. His body felt cooked, ruined, like it had been dipped into the sun. He felt weak and destroyed, and he knew he couldn't last much longer.

And then, as suddenly as it had begun, the rain ended.

"Oh, thank God," he said, breathless, pressed against the wall. "Oh, thank God."

And then he heard the squeaking noise again.

"No! Please, no!"

This time the water was cold. Ice cold. At first, it was almost comforting, soothing—but that didn't last long. The frigid water seemed to paralyze him, to send him into shock. He was trembling out of control, losing consciousness. His body couldn't adapt to these drastically changing temperatures. He could feel his heart doing flip-flops, breaking down under the pressure.

He wanted to scream, but he didn't have the strength. He just hung there, motionless, and the cruel water pounded down on him, freezing his veins and the flow of blood and everything else that made his body work. This was the end, he knew. The absolute bitter end. He couldn't possibly survive this. No one could. No one—

And then the water shut off again.

Tyrone was hyperventilating, gasping for air. "Puh—puh—" He tried to stop stuttering, but he was so cold. He never felt so cold before. "Wh—what do you want? Why are you doing this?"

But there was no reply. Until—

Tyrone heard the swish of air just seconds before the blow landed. It smashed into the soft part of his stomach, pummeling him back against the tile wall. His body had been stretched to its limits when the blow landed, making it hurt all the worse. Tyrone instinctively tried to clutch his middle, but his wrists were still cuffed.

His stomach ached. He felt as if something had been severed, some tendon or muscle. He wondered if he wasn't bleeding internally. For that matter, he might be bleeding externally, for all he knew. He could see nothing.

The next blow came mere seconds after the first. It hit near the same soft place as the first and was even harder. His cuffed arms were twisted to one side, wrenching his left arm almost out of its socket.

He couldn't scream anymore, just couldn't do it. Everything that had been in him, every bit of fight, of resistance, had been sucked away. Instead, he cried. He wept. He was embarrassed, but he couldn't stop. Once he started, the tears tumbled out of his eyes in an unending stream. He felt pathetic, humiliated. But he couldn't stop.

"Please," he said, barely above a whisper. It was all he had left. "Please stop."

But the attack did not stop. The next blow came to his head. The sharp sudden impact of a fist drove like a hammer into his face. His sore, aching, scarred, soft putty face. Tyrone felt his nose split open and explode, cartilage and blood flying, and not a second later, he felt the back of his head slam back against the tile wall.

All at once, his legs disappeared. He hung limp, like a dead turkey, forcing the showerhead to hold him dangling in midair. And the blows didn't stop.

Another fist smashed into his face, so hard he felt as if the knuckles touched his skull. And then again. And again. And then he felt the man's foot in his stomach, pounding and pounding, followed by another incapacitating kick to the groin. He hurt so badly he couldn't separate one pain from another. He was bleeding in every place he could possibly bleed, aching with every neuron of his body.

More blows rained down on his gut, his kneecaps, and worst of all, his poor pitiful face. He couldn't speak; he thought some of his teeth were broken. He couldn't run, he couldn't hide. He couldn't even kill himself, which he would gladly have done at that point. But he couldn't. All he could do was cry and whimper. Cry and whimper and wish he was dead.

And then, without warning, the man decided to speak. His voice cracked down like thunder. "When I return, you will tell me where the penknife is," he said in precise, measured tones.

The man didn't wait for an answer. He didn't need it. Tyrone heard the footsteps recede; he listened until he was alone again. Alone with his guilt and his shame and the certain knowledge that when the man returned, he would tell him anything. Anything he wanted to know. Anything at all.

* 45 *

"Then tell us!" Jones implored. "Who's the murderer?"

"I can't be sure," Ben replied. "But given what Paula said, and this little bauble I received in the mail . . ."

"Would you please not do that mysterious trailing off thing again? You're making me insane!" Jones shook him by the shoulders. "If you know something, tell me!"

"Or tell *me*!"

They all whirled around to see Earl ambling through the office door.

"I see you've been released as scheduled," Jones remarked.

"Yeah. With a goddamn dog collar!"

Jones nodded sympathetically. "Maybe it will keep away fleas."

The phone rang. Jones left Ben and walked to his desk to take the call. A few moments later, Ben heard Jones calling to him. "Boss?"

Jones was covering the mouthpiece with his hand. "Yeah?" Ben said.

"A call for you."

"Tell him I'm busy."

"He says he wants to talk to you right now."

Jones was acting strangely, stuttering and hesitating. He was acting almost . . . scared. "Who is it?"

"I don't know. He won't say." He leaned forward, hissing, "Ben, I think it's *him*!"

Earl ran beside Jones and pressed his head next to the receiver. Ben picked up the other phone. "I'm here."

316

"I think you know who this is," the voice growled, "so let's not screw around with the preliminaries." The voice was strange and muffled; Ben guessed he was holding something over the receiver to mask his voice. "Is it safe?"

Ben's lips parted. What was he talking about? "Is *what* safe?"

"If you have illusions of killing time so this call can be traced, forget it. Two minutes and I hang up. So let me try again. Have you still got it?"

Ben hesitated, trying to think fast. "But I don't know—"

"Don't screw around with me!" the man bellowed. "I've got Jackson. What's left of him, anyway. And if you ever hope to see him alive, you'd better cooperate."

"Okay," Ben said. "I've still got it."

"Have you told the police?"

"No."

"Have you told anyone?"

"No."

"Good. I want you to come and see me. Bring it to me immediately, no stops in between. And come alone."

"But—"

"No buts. You'll come now."

"But—alone? I'd have to be crazy."

"If you don't, the kid dies!"

"But how do I know—"

"You don't believe me? Just listen." Ben heard a heavy thumping sound on the other end of the line, followed by a scraping, a pounding. And the unmistakable sound of human pain.

"Say a few words to your buddy," the man growled. "You can still talk, can't you?"

The line was silent for what seemed an eternity. Finally Ben heard a broken, raspy voice. "Puh—puhlease. Help . . . me . . ."

The phone was ripped away, and Ben heard the sound of another blow landing on something soft, followed by a huge agonized cry. "He ain't got much time left, Kincaid.

He's bleeding to death, among other things. If you don't come, he's gonna die. And soon. Understand?"

Ben bit down on his lower lip. "I understand."

"You know where I am?"

"Where we met before?"

"Right. I'll give you fifteen minutes to get here before I start cuttin' your friend into pieces. I'll meet you outside. Don't call the cops or anyone else. If you do, I'll kill Jackson and disappear."

"You have to give me a chance—"

"I don't have to do anything. Listen to me. There's only one road up here, so I'll see you a long time before you see me. If you're not alone, this kid's a dead man. That's a promise."

Ben heard a click, then a long droning tone that told him the line was dead. He dropped the receiver into its cradle.

Jones was still holding his phone in his hands; he and Earl had heard the whole thing. "What are you going to do?"

Ben glanced down at his watch. Fifteen minutes. He barely had enough time, even if he left immediately.

Jones's eyes widened. "You're not thinking about— you're not going to—"

Ben turned away. "I have to get my keys."

Earl jumped in front of him. "Take me with you."

Ben shook his head. "You heard what he said. I have to come alone."

"I'll hide in the backseat."

"It's too risky. To you and to Tyrone."

Jones jumped in. "C'mon, Boss. Do you dream for a minute that he's going to let Tyrone go?"

"Maybe not. But I have an idea—"

"That's crazy. He'll kill you."

"There's one thing we know for certain. If I don't come, he'll kill Tyrone. Do you want that?"

Earl's jaw clenched together. "No, man. 'Course I don't. But this is suicide."

Ben tried to get past him. "I have to try."

"Then take me with you. I'm the one who started this. I'm the one he really wants."

"And if he knew you were out of prison, he probably would've asked for you. But he doesn't. You're safe for now. Let's keep it that way."

"Ben, I insist—"

"No." Ben went into the side office where he'd left his coat. He rustled through the pockets till he found his keys, then emerged.

Jones was blocking his way this time. "Boss, you can't do this!"

"Don't call Mike," Ben said. "You know him. He'll march in with a SWAT team."

"Boss, this is crazy. This is nuts."

"It isn't nuts. He's got Tyrone. He's hurting him. Probably torturing him."

"But you're risking your life!"

"Tyrone risked his life to save mine. If it hadn't been for him, I'd just be a name on a tombstone right now." Ben marched toward the door. "I don't have any choice."

* 46 *

Ben jogged across the parking lot to his car, climbed in, and started the engine. He was so lost in thought as he drove crosstown that he was startled when his car phone rang.

He pushed the Send button, then set it to Hands-free so he could listen through the speaker.

"Hello."

"What the hell do you think you're doing?"

No introductions necessary. "Just having a pleasant moonlight drive, Mike."

"Stow it, Ben. I just talked to Jones."

"I told him—"

"Fortunately, he had the good sense not to listen. Unfortunately, he doesn't know where you're going, which makes it kind of hard for me to meet you."

"Mike . . . this maniac's got Tyrone. He's . . . hurting him. He says he'll kill him."

"That's what they all say. It's a trap!"

"Mike, I have to go."

"Fine. Pick me up. I'll come with you."

"I can't do that, Mike. He'll see us coming."

"I'll hide in the back."

"I'm sorry, I can't take the risk."

"Ben, you're being a damned fool!"

"Maybe so. But I'm going, just the same."

"Ben!"

"The discussion is over, Mike." He reached for the End button.

"Wait! Goddamn it, if you have to do this, at least take the gun I gave you. Do you have it?"

Ben hesitated. "It's in the glove compartment."

"Then use it."

Ben frowned. "I don't know how to shoot it. I don't even know how to load it."

"*He* doesn't know that."

"Well . . . I'll give it some thought."

"Ben! You can't just walk in there blindly without a plan!"

"I have a plan. I'm not sure it'll work. But I have a plan."

"Ben! Damn you—!"

Too late. Ben pushed the button, disconnecting the line. He exited Highway 75 and headed west. Another couple of minutes and he'd be there. He might already be in sight of the killer, especially if he was using high-powered binoculars. Ben's heart was beating so hard he could feel it; his hands were so sweat-drenched they kept slipping off the steering wheel.

There was no turning back now. This particular fugue had begun.

Ben stared straight ahead, letting his eyes drift toward the twinkling stars—particularly visible now that he was beyond the bright lights of the city. He couldn't help remembering a few weeks before when he and Christina had been gazing at some of the same stars, and wishing he were back there now. This would be a wonderful time to be able to believe in angels, he thought. This would be a hell of a lot easier if he could believe there was someone, somewhere, watching over him.

"All right," he said, just over his breath, "if Christina's right, if I really do have some guardian angel up there, I could use some help, okay? I mean, I would really appreciate it. I have to do this, but I don't want to, you know? Most likely, I'm—I'm not going to come out of this." His voice caught in his throat. "I could just use some help, okay?"

"Then take the gun."

Ben blinked. "That's not a very angelic response."

"I ain't no goddamn angel."

Ben's head jerked back. "Earl!"

"Right the first time. And I'm tellin' you to take the damn gun."

Ben slammed down on the brakes, swerving wildly onto the shoulder. He twisted around toward the back of the van. "What are you doing here?"

Ben saw the silhouette of a head rise up between the two back bench seats. "I'm tryin' to help."

"Keep your head down!" Ben whirled around, faced the front, and eased back onto the road. If the killer was as good as his threats, he might already be watching them.

Ben hissed between his teeth. "I told you—"

"Hey, is it my fault you ain't got the sense to lock your car?" He paused. "Ben, you can't face this creep alone."

"Earl, if he sees you, Tyrone's dead. And you and me, too, probably."

"I couldn't let you come out here alone."

"Do you want Tyrone to die? Do you?" Ben left the main highway and turned onto the service road leading to his destination. "Answer me! Do you?"

"Of course I don't."

"Then listen up. Stay on the floor and stay out of sight. Okay?"

There was no response.

"Do you understand me? Tyrone's life is at stake, Earl." He waited through the silence, his hands clenching the steering wheel. "Answer me!"

Earl's voice dropped to a whisper. "I understand."

"Will you promise to stay in the car? Out of sight?"

There was another long pause, but he finally answered. "I promise."

Ben exhaled. He continued down the winding service road. He was dripping with sweat; he could almost feel the adrenaline surging through his body.

And he wasn't even there yet.

He emerged from the service road and guided the van into the parking lot. There were a lot of empty places this time of night—all of them, in fact. He parked in the nearest row, then shut down the van. Without saying a word, without even thinking, he stepped out and closed the door.

It was all right ahead of him. The Buxley Oil refinery. And the killer.

* 47 *

Mike ran all the way from his office to the sheriff's, his unbuttoned trench coat flapping all the way. By the time he arrived, he was panting and out of breath. Maybe not as bad as he would've been back when he smoked, but bad, just the same.

The sheriff wasn't there this time of night, of course. There was only one deputy on duty, a young brunette female, and Mike didn't know her. She was standing on the far side of a transparent acrylic barrier.

"You had a prisoner in here today," Mike said, gasping for air. "You let him go with a collar."

The deputy looked at him cautiously. "May I ask who wants to know?"

"I'm Lieutenant Morelli. Homicide." He flashed his badge.

The deputy snapped to attention. "Right." She glanced at a clipboard. "That would be Earl Bonner."

"Exactly." Mike paused, trying to catch his breath. Thank heavens Jones had the sense to tell him Earl had smuggled himself away in Ben's van. "Is the collar active?"

"Of course. Why? Has he violated the terms of his bail agreement?"

"No. But I need to know where he is."

The deputy took a step back. "I'm sorry, but if he hasn't violated bail we're not permitted to—"

"Listen to me. Someone's life is in danger. Maybe several people's."

"I'm sorry, but the procedures are—"

324

"I don't give a damn about the procedures. Show me where the tracer unit is."

"But you need a warrant."

"I don't have time to get a warrant!" Mike pressed himself against the acrylic; but for the barrier, he and the deputy would be standing toe-to-toe. "I'm giving you an order."

"You can't give me an order. I work for the sheriff's office, not the police depart—"

Mike pounded against the wall between them. "Look, after this is over, you can file any complaint you want. You can go after me for violating procedure, due process, civil rights—whatever makes you happy. You can say I overpowered you and forced you to cooperate. I don't care. But my idiot friend is walking into trouble and if I don't get there fast, he's probably going to die. And I will not stand by and let him die just because of some stupid procedure! Do you understand me? *I will not let that happen!*"

The two officers stared at each other, neither of them blinking. Finally, after several long seconds, the deputy set down her clipboard and buzzed him inside.

Ben started toward the office building, but he heard a loud booming voice drifting down toward him as if from the heavens. "Not in there! The refinery!"

Great. It seemed he wouldn't even have the comfort of being inside while this drama unfolded. He would remain outside, exposed.

He veered left and headed toward the refinery. If anything, in the dead of night it was even more ominous than during the day. There was no overhead light save for the moon. No streetlights, no lights in the office windows. The thick clouds of smoke curling out and around the refinery seemed like moving shadows, taunting him, daring him to come closer.

He stepped off the sidewalk onto the gravel-covered refinery grounds. In a matter of minutes, the metal monster was all around him, surrounding him with its catwalks and ladders, bloated silos and petroleum tanks. All the tubes and pipes and conduits seemed to connect and intersect like some science fiction monster. Particularly in the darkness, it looked more like a living entity than he could have imagined. The smell did not disappoint: it was putrid, just as he had anticipated. And there was the noise, the steady, rhythmic pumping sound that was always in the background. Like a heart beating to keep the beast alive.

"Up here," Ben heard the voice shout again. There was a metallic ladder just before him leading to a raised platform above. Apparently that was where the killer wanted him.

So that's where he went. He mounted the ladder and began to climb.

The ladder went a good deal higher than it appeared from the ground, at least twenty-five, thirty feet. Ben looked down, checking the distance.

Big mistake. He closed his eyes and brought his head back up. There was a time when he had been afraid of heights. He liked to think he was over that now—no, he *was* over that now. Even so, he kept his eyes focused upward.

One of the smokestacks nearby flared. Ben jumped, almost losing his footing on the narrow ladder. His feet slipped; he banged his chin against a rung while scrambling to get his feet back on something solid. It hurt, but he gritted his teeth and didn't make a sound.

He continued climbing the ladder. There was a layer of thick smoke rising off the metal surfaces above him. He pushed through it, like a mountain climber rising through the clouds. He might not be quite that high at the moment, but it sure as hell seemed like it.

Finally Ben reached the top of the ladder. He climbed onto a narrow catwalk and followed it a short distance to a wider, more expansive platform, probably the roof of some office or storage tank.

"Took you long enough."

Ben squinted. A figure was emerging from the smoke on

the opposite side of the platform—a broad, strong figure, blocking out the stars.

"I wasn't sure if you'd come," the dark figure said.

"You didn't leave me much choice. Where's Tyrone?" The acoustics up here were strange; his voice seemed to ripple out in waves, then dissolve. "Where is he?"

"Where's the knife?" the man replied.

"I'm not giving you anything until I see Tyrone," Ben said emphatically.

A soft titter came from the other end. "Do you really think you're in a position to negotiate?"

"I'm not giving you anything until I see Tyrone."

"Have it your way." The husky shadow crossed the platform to an alcove jutting up from the surface. Door to the roof, Ben thought. Probably how he came up. And how he probably plans to return.

A few seconds later, the man emerged dragging something large and limp and heavy. "Here he is. For all the good it will do you."

He threw his load forward as if it were nothing more than the sack of potatoes it seemed. It fell with a sickening thud.

"Tyrone?" Ben took a cautious step forward.

Tyrone did not respond with words, but Ben could detect a low moan, more like a motor left on idle than any sound you would expect from a living creature. It was a sound of hopelessness, a sound of constant pain.

"Tyrone. It's Ben Kincaid. How are you?"

Ben moved even closer, then gasped.

Tyrone had been, for all intents and purposes, destroyed. His naked body was broken, folded, and crippled in more places than Ben could imagine. He was bruised, battered, and bleeding. His face had been pummeled to such an extent it was barely recognizable; his nose was almost entirely gone. His eyes were open but still, lifeless.

"Tyrone!" Ben ripped off his windbreaker and wrapped it around one of the worst gashes on Tyrone's abdomen, trying to stop the bleeding. Even as he did it, he knew how futile it was; Tyrone bled from more places than Ben had clothes to cover. If he didn't receive medical treatment, and soon, Ben knew he would die.

"I have to call an ambulance," Ben said, rising to his feet.

"No."

"Why not? Why does he have to die? Is that what you want? Is that what your brother would have wanted?"

"Frankly, my dear, I don't give a damn." The man stepped forward, crossing the gap between them, emerging from the shadows. When they were perhaps ten feet apart, Ben had his first clear glimpse of the man's face.

Grady Armstrong. Professor Hoodoo's brother. And his fists were caked with blood.

"When did you first realize it was me?" he asked.

"When I heard the description from one of the witnesses at the club the night you delivered Lily Campbell's body. She said the Rug Man she saw, the man wearing the wig, had fingers stained a blackish-yellow color. When I first met you, you showed me your fingers. You told me how they had been permanently stained from working as an oil field roughneck. That's when I realized the B on the penknife didn't stand for a person's name. It stood for Buxley Oil."

"It's the company logo," Armstrong explained. "They're nice knives. All us vice presidents got one at the last annual meeting. Unfortunately, there are only forty or so of us, which is an uncomfortably small suspect pool." The smile faded from his face. "I want the knife."

"I have to call an ambulance," Ben insisted.

"Not a chance." Armstrong's hand emerged from his pocket. The gun rose until it was pointed directly at Ben's chest. "Give me the knife. Now."

The thing that most amazed Ben, as his brain raced through a thousand thoughts, a thousand possibilities, was that he almost answered, almost did what the man said. As soon as he had the knife, however, Ben knew Armstrong would kill him and Tyrone both.

If he was to have any hope of surviving this mess, he would finally have to learn to bluff.

Ben forced himself to look the man straight in the eye. "I have the knife. But you don't get it until I get Tyrone to a doctor."

"You don't seem to understand." Armstrong made a great show of cocking the gun. "You will give me the knife now, or I will put a bullet in that punk's heart, and the doctor will be irrelevant. And you'll be next."

"How do I know you won't kill us as soon as I give it to you?"

"You *don't*!" Armstrong cried. He rushed forward, shaking the gun like a madman. "Now give it to me. Now!"

"All right, all right." Ben held up his hands. "Stay calm. Let's not get excited here, all right?" He reached into his pocket and felt the penknife—and two dimes.

It was very dark up here. Was it possible . . .

He pulled out one of the dimes. "Here it is."

"Give it to me!" Armstrong barked, still waving the gun about.

"It's all yours," Ben said, extending his arm. He tossed it out onto the ground between them, where it made a satisfying clinking noise.

"You goddamn son of a—" Armstrong pressed the gun forward. "I ought to plug you right now."

"I thought you wanted the penknife," Ben said, trying to stay cool.

"If I have to pick it up, I can at least have the pleasure of shooting you dead."

"You're assuming I really threw you the knife." Ben's brain was racing, synapses firing more quickly than he could track. "But what if I didn't? What if I bluffed you? What if you kill me and you still don't have the knife? What if I sent it to a friend? Like maybe a friend at the *Tulsa World*? Or the police department?"

Armstrong's entire face seemed to contort. His teeth were locked together in red-hot rage. "You little—"

"I want to make a deal."

"A deal?"

"A trade. Him for me." Ben took a deep breath. "You have no reason to kill Tyrone. He doesn't know who you are. Sure, he found the penknife, but he didn't know what it meant. That's why he sent it to me. I'm the only one who poses a threat to you."

"I want the knife!"

"Let me call an ambulance and get Tyrone to the hospital. Then you can have the knife."

"And you?" Armstrong bellowed.

Ben nodded quietly. "And me."

He laughed suddenly, frighteningly. "Did you really think you could do a deal with me? Did you think you have what it takes to go toe-to-toe with me?" Ben could see veins throbbing and pulsing in the man's neck, the tightening of his entire body. He was livid with rage, ready to strike out at anything. "You fucking weasel. I'll bet you've got the penknife on you right now."

Ben stopped his hand just a second after it involuntarily moved toward his pants pocket. Damn!

Armstrong's smile was an eerie white gash in the darkness. "I'm going to enjoy killing you," he said as he moved toward Ben.

As Armstrong crossed the platform, he passed Tyrone's broken body lying in a crumpled heap between them. Ben watched as the man approached, trying to figure out his next move. He'd bluffed his way this far, but what had it gotten him? Where was he going next?

He was still holding his breath, still watching the footsteps, when he saw Tyrone's hand twitch. Ben caught his breath, tried not to show any reaction. But he kept watching.

It was more than a twitch. The hand was moving. Slowly, so Armstrong wouldn't notice. But it was moving.

As Armstrong passed beside him, Tyrone suddenly rolled around with a force Ben would not have thought possible. Both arms swung about as Tyrone grabbed the man's leg and pulled with all his might.

"Son of a bitch!" Tyrone grunted, as Armstrong's foot slipped out from under him. The gun fired. Ben felt the bullet whiz by somewhere overhead. A second after, Armstrong crashed to the floor. The gun fell out of his hand and slid behind him.

Ben had to think quickly. His first impulse was to go after the gun, but he couldn't get to it before Armstrong did. If he tried, he'd only be giving Armstrong an easy shot. This was one time when discretion was the better part of valor.

He turned back toward the catwalk and ran.

"I'll be back for you, Tyrone," Ben shouted as he raced across the narrow catwalk. It gleamed silver in the moonlight, catching the glow of what little illumination penetrated the dense clouds of smoke and brimstone all around them.

Just as he reached the ladder, Ben heard the first shot peal out. He didn't have to look back to know what was happening. Armstrong was back on his feet with the gun in his hands. He was mad as hell and ready to kill.

Ben hit the ladder moving as fast as he could. He placed his hands and feet on the outside of the ladder and slid down into the darkness like a firefighter descending a fire-pole. It was a lot faster than he normally cared to travel, especially when he was high up in the air, but he had no choice. He had to move fast.

He heard another shot ring out, this time much closer. He dared a look up. Armstrong was hovering overhead, gun in hand, firing to kill.

Ben was still looking up when he hit the ground hard. It took him by surprise, knocking him off his feet. He rolled around, scrambling for cover. He pushed back to his feet, then let out a yelp. He'd hurt his ankle in the fall. A sharp burst of pain radiated up his leg; he wouldn't be moving anywhere very fast.

He limped and lurched to the side of a nearby storage tank, rounding a corner and pressing himself up against the wall.

The shots had stopped. Ben looked all around him, trying to remember which way led to his car. It was impossible; in the darkness, it was a gigantic smoke-filled maze with no landmarks or clearly marked exits. Ben's sense of direction wasn't great in the best of circumstances, and these were far from the best of circumstances. All he could do was plunge ahead, hoping for the best, well aware that the killer was hot on his heels. He was the hunted and the maniac upstairs was the hunter. And if he caught Ben, that would be the last note in the concerto.

* 48 *

Earl heard the shots, first one, then another, close after the first. He raised himself cautiously out of the back of the van, careful to avoid any sudden movement, keeping his head low.

What the hell was going on out there? He'd like to think Ben had the upper hand, but he knew damn well the fool had refused to take the gun with him. Whoever was firing, it wasn't Ben. And if Ben wasn't the shooter, chances were, he was the shootee.

Damn it all to hell. He'd promised the boy he'd remain in the van. But this was just too much. First Tyrone, now Ben—how many people were going to die because of him? How many friends were going to fall because this sick bastard kept missing the target?

The hard truth was he was responsible for this mess. It was time he started acting like it.

He quietly cracked the door open. He crawled out quickly, not wanting the light inside the van on any longer than necessary. He didn't know where Ben was; he couldn't tell where the shot had come from. Somewhere in the refinery, maybe, or the office building. He couldn't be sure.

He stopped in his tracks. Wait a minute! He was being just as stupid as Kincaid. Maybe stupider. He knew the killer was armed; he'd heard the shots.

He turned back toward the van, opened the passenger-side door, and popped open the glove compartment. He took the shiny new Sig Sauer out as quickly as possible and closed the door.

Still no sign that anyone had seen him. The man with the gun evidently had other things to do at the moment than watch the parking lot.

Earl gazed at the treasure he had extracted from the glove compartment. It was a nice piece—first class, and if he wasn't mistaken, pretty expensive, too.

He shoved it inside his belt and lumbered across the lot. There were no lights on inside the building; still, it seemed more likely that they would be in there than running around the refinery. He decided to try that first.

He pushed on the front doors—unlocked, even at this hour. He stepped inside, looking and listening for any sign of Kincaid or Tyrone or the man with the gun. Damn, but this gave him the creeps. The man had already taken Lily, Scat—he couldn't bear the thought of losing Tyrone and Ben as well.

He gritted his teeth and plunged down a darkened corridor. He just hoped he got there in time.

Ben raced through the dark passages of the refinery favoring his right leg, trying to keep moving. It was like an open-air haunted house, full of dead ends and dark secrets. He plunged down a pitch-black opening only to find his way blocked by a huge storage tank. He whirled around, desperate to find some exit before Grady Armstrong found him.

Ben had no idea where he was going. He was stumbling blind, lurching through the smoky darkness without a plan or a clue.

But Armstrong knew this place, probably knew it well. He had chosen this location for their meeting. He was comfortable here.

That gave him a huge edge—a killing edge, in all likelihood.

If Ben could just get to his van, he could drive out of

here. Even if he just got to his car phone, he could call for help, get an ambulance for Tyrone.

Problem was, he didn't know where it was.

Everyplace in the refinery looked like everyplace else, at least in the dark. There were no landmarks he could use to find his way. Perhaps, he thought, if he just raced ahead in one direction, eventually he would find an exit. Unfortunately, no path ever followed a straight line for long. He'd hit a storage tank, be forced to make a turn, and then be totally disoriented all over again.

After several minutes of this aimless stumbling and groping, Ben spotted a huge metallic coiled structure in front of him, something that fed into one of the larger storage tanks. He was almost certain he had seen it before, on his way in. He followed the gravel path beside that thing, hoping it would lead him out of the dark maze and into the parking lot.

He heard another shot and froze, then let out his breath slowly. Where the hell was it? Was it ahead of him? Behind him? To the side?

The answer to all those questions was no. He concentrated, replaying the sound in his head.

The sound had come from *above* him.

Ben broke out in a full-out run. He darted across the gravel, limping and slipping, kicking up clouds of white dust. His ankle couldn't take this kind of stress. He'd made a ton of noise. Worse, he'd kicked up a big cloud of white dust—a marker in the darkness. Here I am, it was saying. Come and get me.

Ben moved out of the open area as quickly as possible. He pressed himself against a tall silo, trying to disappear into the darkness. It was then he saw it—a flicker of light or a reflection? He wasn't sure. But it was definitely something.

He squinted his eyes, trying to capture what little ambient light there was and focus straight ahead.

It was the parking lot. He was almost sure of it. And

there was a glimmer of light there, just barely visible. A reflection off the headlight.

Ben pushed away from the tank and lurched forward as fast as his injured foot could take him. He could see it more clearly now. It *was* the parking lot, and there was his van, front and center. If he could just get inside, get it started, get the hell out of here . . .

He heard a crunching sound and looked up. Armstrong was hovering overhead on a catwalk almost directly above him. There must be a network of them, perhaps covering the entire refinery. Access platforms for workmen. Armstrong would know that. Ben didn't.

The next bullet came so close Ben felt a gust of air on the side of his face. He threw himself down, rolling back toward the safety of the tall storage tanks. He scrambled to his feet, trying to stay out of sight.

He couldn't possibly get to the van without being shot. His only hope was to bury himself deep inside—to hide and stay hidden. Armstrong couldn't shoot through metal. If he wanted Ben, he would have to come down and get him.

And if he did that, Ben might have a chance. Not much of a chance, but a chance.

Ben kept running until he was deep inside the refinery, deep in the bowels of the maze. He pressed himself into a dark corridor and stopped to catch his breath. The shooting had stopped. Armstrong knew it was futile; he wouldn't waste the ammunition. Not yet.

Ben imagined he could hear footsteps, hear the clang of shoe leather on metal rungs, although he probably couldn't. Whether he heard it or not, he knew what was happening.

Armstrong was descending.

The killer was coming to get him.

* 49 *

Cursing under his breath, Mike tore off his trench coat and threw it down on the leaf-covered ground.

He hated to do it. He loved that old coat, but it was slowing him down, and he had to make time. He had been hurrying before, but after he heard the shots, he pulled out all the stops.

Mike had managed to trace Earl to the Buxley offices and refinery. He did not appear to be moving much; that made Mike's task about a hundred times less complicated. What the hell anyone would be doing out here at this time of night was beyond him, but if Earl was here, that meant Ben probably was too.

And the killer.

Mike remembered what Ben had said, what the killer had threatened to do if Ben didn't come alone. That wasn't going to keep Mike from coming, but it did make him approach cautiously. He left his car outside the service road entrance, before anyone could possibly see him, and jogged the remaining couple of miles toward the refinery. He'd been trying not to stir up any attention. After he heard the first round of shots, however, he cast caution to the wind. He had to be there, and he had to be there now. Because Ben was up there and someone was shooting. And he knew Ben well enough to know it wasn't Ben.

Mike reached the top of the hill and plowed into the parking lot. It wasn't tough to find Ben's van; it was the only vehicle in sight. He ran up to it and peered inside the windows.

No one was there.

Mike turned toward the Buxley complex. Where the hell was he?

He heard another shot, then another. They were definitely outside, coming from the refinery. And they were not far away.

Mike raced into the refinery, pulling his own weapon out of his holster. For once, he was glad he had traded his old Bren Ten for a more modest Sig Sauer, like the one he gave Ben. The Bren Ten was more dramatic in appearance, but harder to haul around and less useful in a tight situation. The Sig Sauer was just as flashy, just as overpriced, and just as deadly. And hell of a lot easier to carry.

It was pitch-dark in here. Mike could see how someone could easily become disoriented. Smoke billowed out from the low-burning smokestacks and steam rose off the storage tanks, obscuring his vision. He was cut off from any source of light, isolated. The silver walls seemed to close in on him, wrapping him in their jet-black shadows.

Mike shook himself. Get a grip, he muttered under his breath. Find Ben. Find him and that kid and get out of here. And don't get shot in the process.

He had to assume Ben was still alive, and if so, he was in trouble. The killer was armed and Ben wasn't. He needed help.

Mike decided to risk a yell. It might tip off the killer, but it also might let Ben know he was here. If Ben was nearby, he would run to him. Even if he wasn't, he would know he was no longer alone.

"Ben!" he shouted at the top of his lungs. He waited for a response, but nothing came. To the contrary, if anything, it seemed to become more still, more quiet.

"Ben!" he tried again. There was a small echo somewhere behind him, on the left side. An echo—no: the crunching of gravel. A footstep. Someone . . .

"Ben!" Still no response. Maybe he didn't want to give his position away. But if Ben were this close to him, surely he would whisper back. So Mike had to assume it wasn't Ben. And if it wasn't Ben . . .

Mike ran for cover, ducking behind a nearby ladder. He still couldn't see anything down the corridor where he had heard the noise. Had he just imagined it? Was the dark, the quiet, getting to him?

Christ, he told himself. You're supposed to be the professional. You're supposed to be the tough cop. That means you don't get scared. Even when it's dark and you can't see a damn thing and some maniac is running wild with a pistol. You don't get scared!

But he was scared. And with reason.

Mike backed into the passageway behind him. There was a large bowl-like tank about three or four feet off the ground. He crouched under it, watching all the time in as many directions as possible.

He was in a different part of the refinery now, a different corridor, something. It was a small enclosed space, but there was an opening on one side.

Damn this darkness. How could he do anything when he couldn't see!

Well, he couldn't do anything trapped in this crawl space. He pulled out slowly and rounded the corner . . .

The fire extinguisher came at his head so quickly he couldn't even register what was happening, much less do anything about it. It smashed into his face, sending him reeling. Mike staggered backward, found himself pressed against a metal latticework. His head was throbbing and he couldn't maneuver—

The fire extinguisher came crashing down again, this time on the top of his head. He fell forward, the only way to go, collapsing on his hands and knees.

Fight it, he told himself. You're no good to Ben unconscious. *Fight it.*

But there was no fighting it. When the fire extinguisher came for the third time, it smashed down with such intensity that it knocked Mike flat onto the gravel. The darkness of the refinery was replaced by a darkness born of his own brain.

"Ben," he whispered, barely audibly. And then he was gone.

* 50 *

"I got your friend!"

Ben froze, his body pressed against a silvery tank.

"Do you hear me? I got your friend. I'm *killing* him! Slowly."

Ben swore under his breath. He scooted out from under the tank, cautiously looking in all directions. How could this happen? He told Earl to stay in the car.

"What do you know?" Armstrong bellowed. "A police officer."

Ben's head jerked up. What—?

"Lieutenant M. Morelli, Tulsa Police Department."

Mike? How did he get here? How did he find him?

"A policeman. Well, well, well." Ben heard a heavy thumping sound, as if something large had fallen to the ground. "Take that, Lieutenant."

Ben's blood chilled as he heard the report of a gun. It was above him, to the left. It seemed Armstrong had returned to the same high perch where this elaborate cat-and-mouse game had begun.

"I told you if you didn't come alone everyone would die, Kincaid, and I'm a man of my word."

Ice cold shivers ran down Ben's spine.

"Don't worry. He's not dead yet, though I banged him up pretty good dragging him up those stairs. I like to take my time. You could still help him."

Ben crawled out into the open. "What do you want?" he shouted.

341

"You know what I want," Armstrong answered. "Come to me. Come to me, or I empty my gun in this stupid policeman's head!"

Ben walked to the bottom of the ladder. He didn't know what to do. His brain was racing through all the options and potential outcomes. He couldn't just sit in hiding and let this madman execute Mike, or let Tyrone bleed to death. At the same time, if he did show himself, Armstrong was certain to kill him. And in all likelihood, everyone else. This man had killed so many times, so wantonly—Ben knew he would only keep the others alive as long as he needed them to get the penknife.

It was a no-win situation, however it played out. But he couldn't run away, couldn't just leave Mike and Tyrone in this man's clutches.

Slowly, grimly, he placed his hands on the ladder and began to climb.

A few moments later, he arrived at the top. He crossed the catwalk deliberately, trying to remain alert, ready for anything. He was barely halfway across when he saw Armstrong waiting for him, gun posed directly at Ben's head.

"Keep walking," Armstrong growled. His voice was hoarse and his gun hand wavered. Ben sensed that he was dealing with a man who was dangerously close to the end of his rope. The chase had gone on too long and he was tired of it.

But, he also thought, it was possible he could use that to his advantage.

"Step off the catwalk." Ben did as he was bidden, stopping when he was barely a foot away. The instant he arrived, Armstrong reached forward with his gun hand and clubbed Ben on the side of the face.

Ben tried to roll with it, but it still stung. The hard metal of the gun cut his cheekbone; he could feel blood trickling forth.

"You've given me about all the trouble I can stand," Armstrong growled. "I'm going to enjoy seeing you die."

Ben scanned the surroundings. He saw Mike lying prone beside them. He appeared to be unconscious, but as far as Ben could tell he wasn't bleeding or wounded. That gunshot must have been into the air. Just for drama's sake.

He saw Tyrone, too, still lying in a hideous heap a few feet behind. He looked even worse than before.

"I'll take the penknife now," Armstrong said, spitting as he talked. "And no more small change, please."

Ben cleared his throat and swallowed. "I . . . don't have it," he said.

Armstrong's eyes narrowed to tiny glowing slits. "You didn't bring it?"

"Right. And only I know where it is."

"But you said—"

Ben pursed his lips together. "I bluffed."

Armstrong's entire body shook. "But you—you—" He swung his gun hand around again, this time even harder than before. It hit Ben's face with a crack. Ben cried out; he couldn't help himself.

Armstrong glanced back at Tyrone, then at Ben. His eyes glowed with rage. "Goddamn you!" The arm swung around again. Ben tried to duck, but he was too late. The metal fist hit him in the jaw, knocking him back onto the catwalk.

"I want the penknife!" Armstrong was spitting, screaming. He seemed to have lost all semblance of sanity. "Do you *hear* me? I want the fucking penknife!"

"I don't have it," Ben whispered.

Armstrong began moving wildly about, flinging his arms around. He fired a shot into the air. He grabbed Ben by his shirt, shaking him brutally.

Ben cast a wary eye on either side of him. Here, beneath the railing, it would be a simple thing to fall off the catwalk. And it was a long way to the ground.

"Don't think this helps you. Don't think you'll get away with this. I'm going to kill you and all your friends. And I'm going to enjoy it. And then I'm going to go to your office, tear the place apart, find the knife, and kill everyone there. And anyone else who gets in my way."

Ben bit down on his lower lip. The gun was in Armstrong's hand, pressed against Ben's forehead. He couldn't allow this to happen, couldn't let this maniac slaughter all his friends, his coworkers.

Armstrong's eyes burned down into Ben's. "And I'm going to start with you!" Before Ben could react, Armstrong lifted him into the air by his shirt collar and tossed him backwards. Ben skittered across the catwalk, coming dangerously close to the edge. He clutched at the guardrail, trying to keep himself from falling.

"What's the matter, Kincaid? Scared of heights?" Ben saw the shadow before he knew what was happening, then saw the swift boot impact on his stomach. He bent over, spitting blood, clutching his stomach.

"Move your hands," Armstrong grunted. "Move 'em or lose 'em." The boot thudded down into Ben's gut. All of a sudden, the world around Ben seemed to turn a brilliant white. He felt something crack inside—a rib? He couldn't be sure, but whatever it was, it burned like fire inside him.

Ben tried to scramble away. It was a mistake; he was woozy on his feet, could barely keep any sense of equilibrium. He saw the ground beneath him wobbling, rushing up to him . . .

"Sayonara, Kincaid."

In the nanosecond that he saw Armstrong rushing toward him, his brain flashed on a thousand images, a million memories. He saw his father, his mother, his sister. And Ellen. He saw Christina and Mike, telling him he needed to learn to defend himself. He saw Sensai Papadopoulos, trying to teach him the simplest manuever. Trying to teach him . . .

Armstrong came at him at full speed, arms extended. Just before impact, Ben ducked and spun around, showing Armstrong his back. Armstrong's arms flew over his head; Ben grabbed them and flipped with all his might.

And it worked. For once, it actually worked. Armstrong flew over Ben, thrust forward by the speed of his own momentum. He skittered down the catwalk, careening dangerously toward the precipice. He almost spilled over the edge; at the last minute, he dropped his gun and used that hand to grab the guardrail. The gun fell silently down, down, to the ground far below.

Ben saw his opportunity and bolted. He lurched toward the other end of the catwalk, back toward Mike and Tyrone. Every step hurt; now both of his ankles were complaining. He ignored them. He had to keep going. He had to move forward.

He had almost made it to the end of the catwalk when he felt strong hands clamp down on his shoulders. "I don't need a gun to take care of you."

Armstrong grabbed Ben by the collar and slung him back against the guardrail. Ben came down hard on his sore ankle and screamed out as the pain rippled through his aching body. He felt himself wobbling, losing his footing.

Armstrong brought his fist around and smacked Ben hard in the face—right on the nose still damaged from their last encounter. Ben knew he was losing consciousness. He knew he was about to pass out, and that as soon as he did, he couldn't possibly keep himself from tumbling off the catwalk.

Ben saw the fist coming around again. He tried to push away, but he was trapped, pinned against the guardrail with nowhere to go but down. He closed his eyes.

The fist thudded into his face. His head exploded, leaving him all but senseless. He could feel unconsciousness creeping up on him like a dark shroud. He knew the next blow would knock his feet right out from under him. After that, it would only take a gentle push.

"Rest in hell, Kincaid," Armstrong growled. Ben felt more than saw the fist rearing back, getting into position for the final death blow . . .

"Freeze, you bastard!"

Armstrong's arm stopped in midflight.

Ben recognized the voice, even if he couldn't make out the speaker. It was Earl. *Earl!*

"I got a gun, sucker!"

Ben felt the impact of heavy footsteps crossing the catwalk. He pried his eyelids open.

Earl crossed the catwalk, a gun aimed directly at Armstrong's head. "I'll blow you to kingdom come if you so much as move. Get your hands up! Move away from Ben!"

Armstrong took a step back, obeying.

"Now get off the goddamn catwalk!"

Armstrong walked away, slowly, eyes to the front.

Earl caught up to Ben. "How you doin', Ben?"

Ben gripped the guardrail. "Tryin' to hold together," he gasped. "Tyrone and Mike need help."

"Looks to me like you could use some yourself. Let's—"

His voice disappeared. When it returned, it was barely a whisper. "Oh, my God. Oh, Jesus in heaven!"

"What?" Ben saw Earl moving off the catwalk, gun aimed ahead, moving toward Armstrong. "What is it?"

"I just now saw this son of a bitch's face. Do you know who this is?" He grabbed the man and shook him by the lapel of his coat. *"Do you know who this is?"*

"It's . . . Grady Armstrong. Professor Hoodoo's brother."

"Brother, my ass. This *is* Professor Hoodoo!" Earl shoved him down to the ground; his head banged against the metallic surface. "He's *alive!*"

"What?" Ben tried to stay conscious long enough to understand.

Earl cocked the gun and pressed it flat against the man's temple. "Talk, sucker. And you'd better make it good."

Armstrong smiled bitterly. "I believe I'll decline."

"I said talk!"

"Go fuck yourself."

"I said, *talk!*" Earl pounded his face, once, twice, then

again for good measure. "If you want anything to be left of
your face come morning, *talk!* Who died in your apartment? Who burned in the fire?"

The man on the receiving end of the gun licked his
swollen, bleeding lips. "That was my brother. The real
Grady. We always resembled one another. Certainly enough
to fool people after the body was burned. So I fixed things
up so it looked like I died and you did it. Added a grisly
little touch with my knife, just to make sure you got
the maximum sentence, and as a tribute to my goddamn
good-for-nothing daddy. And then I went to Grady's
lonely outpost in Montana and became him. It was easy;
he went years without seeing anyone. Then I switched
jobs, joined Buxley—as Grady Armstrong—and no one
was the wiser."

Earl stared at him, gaping. "But why?"

He shrugged. "Grady and I had a disagreement. The
tiny matter of our daddy's money. Grady got it. I didn't.
Even killing him wouldn't get me what I wanted. But
becoming him would. So that's what I did." He paused.
"And once I'd decided to become Grady, Professor Hoodoo
had to disappear."

"I don't care about that." Earl lifted the man up and
shook him, slamming his head back. "Why'd you do this
to me? Why'd you do it to *me*?"

A sneer crossed Armstrong's face. "You were never
anything but trash, Earl. Bad gumbo scum-of-the-earth
trash. You stole my woman. And worse, you stole my
music. Said you were tryin' to preserve it. Bastardize it
was more like it. After Lily, my music was the only thing I
had, the only thing that mattered. And you stole it, just like
you stole Lily. So I took care of you. I fixed you up even
worse than killing you would."

"Twenty-two years," Earl whispered. "I did twenty-two
years. And you weren't even dead!"

"During those twenty-two years, I forgot music, hid
myself in Grady's humdrum life. Quit the clubs, the drink,

the junk. Tried to become someone I wasn't, someone I'd never been before. I finally found some peace. I thought I was over hating you—till I heard you'd gotten out, started over, and opened a club—trading on your puny stolen reputation. The hate started boilin' up inside me all over again. I couldn't stand the thought of you on the outside, enjoying life. So I began making arrangements to put you back behind bars. Back where you belonged, in a life worse than death."

"Twenty-two years," Earl murmured. "Twenty-two years of my life gone—forever. I lost everything—my friends, my career—and my music. *My* music!" His hands shook with rage. "You deserve to die."

"Earl, don't!" Ben cried, gathering all the strength he could muster. "Don't become the murderer he's tried to make people think you are."

"He deserves to die," Earl repeated.

"Don't do it!" Ben shouted. "You'll spend the rest of your life in prison!"

"I don't think so," Earl said. His voice had a chilling quality. "You explained it to me yourself, Ben. A man can't be tried twice for the same crime. I've already been convicted for the murder of George Armstrong. I've done my time. Double jeopardy has . . . what's the word?— attached! There ain't a damn thing they can do to me now." He cocked the gun.

"Don't do it!" Ben shouted, but it was too late. The gun fired at point-blank range, and Professor Hoodoo's head exploded right before Ben's eyes.

"No!" Ben shouted. He tried to push himself to his feet, but the moment he tried, all the pain and dizziness rushed back to the surface. The world began to swim around him, floating in elastic ripples, like a movie shot with a trick focus. He planted his feet, but his weight came down on the sore ankle and suddenly there was nothing between him and the ground. He was a bird, except this bird only flew in one direction: down. He sensed his body leaving the catwalk, tumbling under the guardrail, almost as if he

wasn't inside it anymore. He saw the ground rushing toward him.

It was the last thing he saw before, mercifully, the dark shroud wrapped him in its cold cold embrace.

FIVE

*   *

The Meaning of Jazz

* 51 *

He heard someone singing:

> Quand il me prend dans ses bras,
> Il me parle tout bas
> Je vois la vie en rose . . .

It was French, so it must be Christina. He might have known.

"Ben, can you hear me? It's Mike."

Ben sensed the discomfort in the voice, the tension.

"I don't know if you're getting this, Ben, but the doctors said we should talk to you, so here goes. Hoodoo's dead. George Armstrong. Whatever you want to call him. He's history. Dust in the wind."

He heard the shuffling of hands, the scraping of a chair.

"Your buddy Earl told us everything that happened, everything Armstrong said. Turns out it was true. He killed his brother, took his place, and framed Earl. He'd been off in Montana with his brother's name and his brother's money for twenty-two years when he got wind of the fact that Earl had been released. He couldn't stand that. So he got himself transferred to Tulsa, then looked up his old jazz buddy Scat—Lily's former husband—the one man on earth he knew didn't like Earl any better than he did."

He heard Mike take a deep breath, then continue. "The

same hatred George had for Earl extended to Lily Campbell, since she was the one who dumped him to be with Earl. So he killed her and used her as a tool to frame Earl. He delivered the corpse in disguise, just in case he bumped into Earl. I think he was planning to plant it in Earl's office, but when Earl came back to the club sooner than he expected—thanks to you—he had to ditch the stiff in a hurry. The stage light wasn't the perfect place, but it was all he could get to without being seen. I don't know why he took his disguise off in the men's room; my guess is, once Earl was safely tucked away backstage, he planned to stay for the show. Probably wanted the pleasure of seeing Earl get hauled away by the cops with his own two eyes. After he was spotted by Tyrone Jackson, however, he changed his plans. Worse, he dropped his Buxley penknife.

"Armstrong came to the club the next day as Grady—at a time when Scat told him Earl wouldn't be around—to recover it. I understand you caught them in the act of searching, so they acted like they'd been helping clean up, and introduced George to you as Grady. But they were too late—Tyrone had already found the penknife. Those little treasures were only given to the forty Buxley vice presidents. Once Tyrone figured out what it was, George knew it wouldn't be hard to figure out who the man in the men's room had been. So he had to kill Tyrone before he put two and two together."

Ben heard the sound of knuckles cracking. "You're probably wondering why Armstrong turned on Scat. Best I've been able to figure is that Scat was happy to help George along—till things started getting too hot. He probably didn't know Grady planned to kill Lily, his ex-wife. And I think you put the fear of God into him when you went over to his place. He probably started talking about getting out or telling what he knew, so George killed him. He needed a second corpse anyway, since the first murder hadn't put Earl behind bars.

"After Earl offed the Professor, he used your car phone to call 911 and get an ambulance for Tyrone and me and you. Tyrone was beat up something awful, but the doctor says he'll recover—in time. And I'm fine." He paused. "You're the one we're worried about."

The room fell silent, but Ben sensed that Mike had not left the room.

"The D.A.'s office is going nuts trying to think of some way to charge your buddy Earl, but so far they haven't thought of a thing. We can't try the man for committing the same crime to the same person he's already done time for. We can't charge him with attempted murder or any other lesser included offense; as you know, double jeopardy bars the main offense and all the lesser includeds. They can't stand the thought of letting him get away with murder. But even if they did think of a charge to bring against Earl—what jury would convict him when he's already served twenty-two years for a crime he didn't commit? They're inclined to call it self-defense and let it go. In short—I think he's gonna walk."

Another silence permeated the air around them, longer and more awkward than before.

"I . . . uh . . . wanted to say something else. Something about . . . well, back at the refinery. Sure, I took some bad bumps on the head, but I came around a few minutes later. You—well . . . you didn't."

He realized that the strange tone in Mike's voice was not so much discomfort as . . . guilt.

"Damn it, I never should have let this happen. How could I let that old creep get the drop on me? It was just so damn dark. I yelled at you for running in there by yourself, and then what did I do? The same idiot thing. I took the threats seriously enough that I didn't call for backup before I ran in. An incredibly stupid mistake. And now you're paying the price for it."

Ben heard the chair scrape the linoleum a few more times; he heard the heavy intake and outflow of breath.

"Let's face it, Ben. You pulled my fat out of the fire and it cost you. I know I make fun of you sometimes, and I know I've been bitter about your sister dumping me and the whole thing with your family, but . . . Jesus."

Ben heard the chair scrape again, this time coming closer. "It's not easy for me to say this kind of stuff. You know that. But I just wanted you to know that whatever the hell I might have said, and however I might have acted, I think you're pretty damn all right, okay? Even though we do things differently, you've got a lot of guts. I consider you a friend, a good one. And I'm not just saying that because you're . . . you're . . ." His voice faded. "I'm saying it because it's true."

The voice moved away, circling at the outer edges of the room. "Jesus, I feel like I've been talking forever. Can't we get some music in here or something? Maybe some of that folk crap he likes. Christ, some of those songs go on forever."

His eyes were so swollen they felt as if they'd been glued shut. Was it the beating or the fall? He couldn't be sure, and frankly, what did it matter? He wasn't going any-where; he didn't seem to be able to move at all. So why worry about it?

For the brief moments that he knew anything, he knew he was completely nauseated. Movement would only make it worse. There was a tube taped to his mouth, and he could hear the balloon beside his cheek inflating and de-flating with each breath. Another tube was strapped to his wrist, feeding him something cold and sweet. It hurt a little, but at the moment, what didn't? Frankly, conscious-ness was not all it was cracked up to be. He decided not to force it, to relax, to let himself go. One moment he was in a Tulsa hospital bed, and then he was somewhere else. But mostly he was nowhere at all.

"Are you the wife?" There was a stiff impersonal tone. He did not recognize the voice.

"No. Just a good friend." That voice was a different matter. Definitely Christina.

"Does he have any living family?"

"A mother and a sister. But the mother is out of the country and the sister . . . well, we don't know where she is. His mother is rushing here, but she probably won't arrive today. I'm his emergency contact person."

"Very well. I need to discuss his situation with you. I'm afraid there's been little change. When Mr. Kincaid was brought to St. John's several days ago, he was in critical condition, and he's remained there ever since. He is completely comatose. We believe he is entirely unaware of himself and his environment. He does not respond to external stimuli. There is no evidence of language comprehension. A ventilator has been helping him breathe. If the respirator were removed . . . well, we just don't know."

"There must be something you can do."

"If so, I'm afraid no one here knows what it would be."

"So what do we do?"

"Well, we wait. We hope he comes around. But eventually . . ."

"Yes?" There was an urgency in her voice, a pressing quality that told him she knew what was coming.

"Well, at some point we'll have to make a decision about the desirability of perpetuating life support."

"It's too soon for that."

"I agree. But . . . you might be thinking about it, just the same."

The silence seemed interminable. He had almost moved on when he heard: "Thank you, Doctor. Now, if you don't mind . . ."

"Of course. If there's anything I can do . . ."

"Actually, there is. Do you know of a place nearby where I could get a harmonica?"

"A harmonica? May I ask why?"

"I'm going to play Bobby Darin songs. You know—like 'Mack the Knife.' I know it seems crazy. But he likes them."

* * *

He had expected everything to be white, all white, but was pleased to find instead that it was a vivid Kodachrome green. It was a forest, deep and impenetrable and alive, just like the one he had played in as a boy behind his grandmother's house in Arkansas. In fact, it *was* the one he had played in as a boy behind his grandmother's house in Arkansas.

Never mind that his grandmother was long since dead, that the property had been sold, and that the forest had been clear-cut by a major lumber company. It was here, and he was in it.

"Be-en! Are you ready?"

He turned and saw her running toward him, weaving expertly between the trees, pigtails flying. It was his sister, Julia, except she was only nine years old. Come to notice, he was only eleven himself.

He remembered this summer. His parents had gone abroad for some Mediterranean cruise, and he and Julia had stayed with their grandmother, playing, drinking lemonade, basking in the sun. This was before puberty, before adolescence, before college and husbands and broken promises. This was back when the world was about lightning bugs and comic books and blindman's bluff, and he and Julia had been the two best friends in the entire world.

"Are you ready?" she asked breathlessly.

"I am," he said. He wondered what they were going to do this afternoon.

"Where's the first clue?"

Ah, a treasure hunt. Ben had prepared dozens of elaborate treasure hunts for his younger sister, with clues sending her far and wide across the property until at last she reached the Snickers bar buried at the final destination.

He handed her a scrap of paper. She unfolded it eagerly and read: " 'Not C, nor D, nor E, F, G, H, I. To the home of the traveler you must now fly.' "

She peered up at him, confused, thinking it over. The

sunlight made her freckles appear golden. "Traveler? You mean Mom and Dad. But they're—"

All at once she beamed. "No, you mean the bird's nest." Yesterday, during their exploration of the forest, they had discovered a blue jay's nest on a high branch of an old oak tree. They had watched it for almost an hour. They didn't disturb anything. They just watched, watched the mother care for her hatchlings, watched her bring them grubs and bugs to eat.

"I get it." The pride of solution made her face glow. "Not C, D, E, F, G, H, or I because they're blue *jays*."

She raced toward the old oak tree with Ben close behind. At the base, she stopped unexpectedly, pushed up on her tiptoes, and kissed Ben on the cheek. "You make the very best ever treasure hunts, Ben." Her eyes were wide with excitement and admiration. "I hope this goes on forever."

Ben watched as she shimmied up the tree, his eyes brimming with tears. I hope it does, too, he thought.

"Ben?"

What? What? Why was she interrupting?

"Ben, this is Nurse Tucker. You can call me Angela. I'm here to take care of you. Whatever you need, I'm here to provide."

Go away, he thought. I don't want to be bothered.

" 'Course, it's going to be hard for you to tell me what you want, since you're not talking. Tell you what. You just think about whatever it is you want, and I'll see if I can't figure it out."

He heard footsteps moving around the bed, surveying the situation.

"Sheets all appear to be properly tucked and folded. Your IV bag is filled. Ventilator seems to be working normally. All outward appearances are A-OK." There was a pause, and the voice drew closer. "What I'm more concerned about is what's going on inside."

He sensed her presence more than felt it. Was it the

shadow, the warmth? Somehow, he knew she was drawing near.

"Ben, listen to me. I know it may be very . . . peaceful where you are right now. Very tranquil. It must be tempting to just stay there. But, Ben, you're needed here. By your friends, your loved ones. All the people you've helped. And the however many more you could help in the future. If you come back."

Yes, yes, no doubt. May I go now?

At the end of the summer, Ben's parents arrived to collect their children. Julia met them both at the door, wrapped her arms around them, and smothered them with hugs and kisses. Young Ben stood by himself in the corner of the room.

His father noticed. He pulled a small package out of his coat pocket. "Hey, Ben. I have a present for you."

Ben glanced up, then looked back down at the floor. He didn't budge.

His mother, peering over Julia's shoulder, frowned. "Benjamin?" She exchanged a glance with her husband. "What's wrong with him?"

"I don't know." He walked over to Ben and laid his hand on Ben's back. "Perhaps we should have a private talk."

He escorted Ben into one of the back bedrooms and shut the door. "All right, son. Let's have it."

Ben twitched uncomfortably but didn't say anything.

"Come on, now. I've seen that guilt-ridden expression before. Tell me what you've done."

Ben's mouth was so dry he could barely speak. "You remember . . . before you left you lent me your pocket knife."

"Of course. My top-of-the-line Swiss Army knife. Bought that thing in Zurich when I was just a college kid."

"You said I could use it if"—he coughed, sputtered— ". . . if I promised to take care of it."

His father looked down at him sternly. "Ye-es . . ."

hurt, so broken. "—I just thought that if I could find something new or exciting, something that would give you a *reason*, well, then I could make you come back."

He heard the rustling of the envelope, the unfolding of the paper.

"Are you listening, Ben? They want to publish your book. Did you hear that? I'll say it again. They want to publish your book! I'm not kidding."

My book? *My* book?

"They think it has real commercial possibilities. Of course they want to make some changes."

Changes? What—

"They say your use of language is a bit awkward in places, but they think their editorial committee can fix it."

Fix it? *Fix it?*

"The art department wants you to add more vivid descriptions of the murder victims so they'll have something to use for cover art. And the publicity department wants you to pump up the action. Maybe add a car chase."

Now wait a minute . . .

"And of course, they want to change the title."

Change the title? Change it to *what*?

Scales seemed to fall from his eyes. The gummy blackness faded away. He was aware of his arms, his legs . . .

"Change . . . the . . . title?"

He opened his eyes.

"Ben!" Christina exclaimed. "You're back!" S[he] lurched forward and threw her arms around him, hugg[ing] him tightly. "I asked you to come back and you did! [You] came back!"

A trembling hand removed the tube taped to his n[ose.] The muscles of his jaw were like rusted gate hinges [as he] made them move. "Have . . . I . . . ever . . . denied [you] . . . anything?"

* 52 *

Three weeks after he was discharged from the hospital, Ben made his way back to Jones and Loving's offices. He still didn't move with quite the bounce he once had; a broken rib was knitting and his head hurt whenever he moved too much or too fast. But all things considered, he was recovering quite well. Of course, all things considered, it was a miracle he was alive.

He rode the elevator to the seventh floor. He had left many of his belongings there while he was working on Earl's case, and he didn't want to abuse his friends' generosity by trashing up their office space.

He crossed the corridor and headed for their office. He pushed himself through the double doors and . . .

"Surprise!"

The place was decorated in a cross between Mardi Gras and a nine-year-old's birthday party. The lobby was festooned with crepe paper and brightly colored balloons. Streamers trailed down from the ceiling and across the walls. Christina and Jones and Loving and Paula all stood in a row blowing noisemakers and those party favors that stick out their tongue when you blow into them.

"Welcome home!" they shouted.

Ben stared at them, stunned. "Well . . . thank you, but actually, I just came to—"

"Let me show you your office." Christina wrapped her arm around his and escorted him down the hallway. The others trailed behind.

"We gave you the largest office in the suite," Christina explained. They swerved into the dark room and she flipped on the light. A fully furnished, fully equipped office sprang to life.

"See? It's just like your old office. Well, except that the furniture is nicer. And the carpet is nicer. And the phone is nicer. Actually, everything is nicer. But other than that, it's just the same."

Ben's eyes floated across the room, drinking it all in. It did have a pleasant look to it. A good feel. He could be comfortable here. Of course, Christina would know that. She would know how to decorate to his taste, just as she somehow knew he was coming to the office this morning.

"There's more," she said, shoving him back into the corridor.

"Right," Jones said. He dropped Paula's hand and skittered back to his desk, returning seconds later. "This is for you."

What he held out to Ben was a snazzy brown leather briefcase with a bright red ribbon tied around the handles.

Ben took the gift from him, lightly brushing his hands over the smooth brown surface. "You shouldn't have," he said quietly.

" 'Course we should, Skipper," Loving said, piping in. "You can't be a lawyer without a briefcase. I think that's in the code of ethics or somethin', ain't it?"

Ben held the briefcase close to him and smiled.

Paula cut in. "Have you people forgotten this man was injured? Get him a chair." Jones and Loving raced to be the one to do it. "How do you feel, anyway?"

As he took the proffered chair, Ben let his eyes wander all around, to the spanking new office, the new briefcase, and best of all, the beaming faces of his coworkers. His friends.

"I feel . . ." He paused, drawing in his breath. "I feel like I've come home."

* * *

That evening, when Ben returned to his apartment, he found Christina sitting on the sofa and writing on a scrap of newspaper.

"There you are," she said. "What took you?"

"I've been downstairs. What are you doing here?"

"I'm taking over your apartment by adverse possession *ab initio*."

Ben sighed. More legal Latin. "Christina—"

"I thought now that I know all this Latin, you'd think I was more sophisticated."

"Christina, you don't have to switch from French to Latin for me. You don't have to change anything for me. I like you just fine the way you are."

Christina sat bolt upright. "You do?"

Ben turned away from the penetrating gaze. "Uh . . . what are you doing?"

"Well, I saw that you were stuck on your crossword, so I finished it for you."

"I was not stuck," he said, bristling. "I was pacing myself."

"Ben, this puzzle is a week old."

"Is there a rush?"

Christina set down the paper. "So . . . did you see Mrs. Marmelstein?"

Ben nodded.

"I suppose you told her about the nursing home."

"I've worked out a schedule," he said. He plopped a sheet of paper down on the coffee table. "Joni and Jami and their mother all said they would help. With four of us, and you pitching in for emergencies, we can manage to have someone looking after Mrs. Marmelstein all the time."

"You mean—"

"That way, she can stay right here, where she wants to be."

"But your tour—"

"There'll be other tours. Besides, I need to focus on my

law practice. Now that I have a spiffy office, it'd be nice to have a few clients to go with it."

Christina raised a hand to her mouth. "Mrs. Marmelstein must've been . . . very happy when you told her."

"Well . . . yeah. I think she was, actually." He grinned. "Surprised?"

"That you did the right thing? No. I knew you would."

"And how, may I ask, did you know?"

She pressed forward on her tiptoes and kissed him on the cheek. "Because that's who you are."

About a week later, after Ben finished up at work, he hopped into his van and drove toward St. John's. It had been a great day at the office—new clients, new cases, new challenges. Somehow it all seemed fresh again; he was recapturing the pleasure of practicing law.

Why had he ever quit? he wondered. What was it about life that made people want to be something other than what they were? Sure, some changes were improvements: Tyrone leaving the gang, Christina going to law school. But some changes weren't; some were just people hiding from themselves. Professor Hoodoo, trying to bury himself in his brother's life. Jones trying to create a false cyber-persona that almost chased Paula away. And Ben—running away from the thing he did best.

He was just lucky he'd managed to get himself straightened out. Lucky he had people who cared.

Which was why he was making this little trip. He passed through the electric doors outside St. John's with a jumbo box of chocolates and a bouquet of roses tucked under his arm.

The nurse on duty recognized him as he approached the receiving station. "Mr. Kincaid. Good to see you again. How are you feeling?"

"Fit as a fiddle, thank you."

"I can't tell you how nice that is to hear. When they first brought you in here, well, I didn't hold out much hope. But look at you now!"

"Well, I've been very lucky."

The nurse nodded. Her eyes diverted to his goodies. "Got a girlfriend here?"

Ben laughed. "No, no. Actually, these are for a nurse. When I was here before—when I was in the coma— well—" He swallowed, started again. "There was one nurse who was very special to me. Some of the things she said—really helped. Meant a lot to me. So I just wanted to give her a little something."

"That's very kind of you. Who was it?"

"Well, I was hoping you could help me find out. Her name was Nurse Tucker. She told me to call her Angela."

The nurse blinked. "Angela?"

"Right. She had a soft voice, very soothing."

"Angela Tucker? There's no one by that name on this floor."

Ben's lips parted. "Perhaps—perhaps she came from another floor."

The nurse shook her head. "Not without my knowing about it. What did she look like?"

"Well, I never actually saw her." He frowned. "Perhaps she used a different name—"

"What, a nurse with a pseudonym?"

"Perhaps it was a nickname. Perhaps—"

"Mr. Kincaid, I've been working here for eighteen years. I've seen the personnel records on every nurse in this hospital. Believe me—there's no Angela and no Nurse Tucker, much less an Angela Tucker."

"But—" Without even thinking about it, Ben's hand went to Christina's Saint Christopher's medal, still dangling from his neck. The beacon.

"Then—I—" He stumbled, not knowing what to say. "Th-thank you," he said finally. He dropped the candy and flowers on the counter. "Here. Give these to . . . I don't know. Someone who needs them."

He turned and shuffled back down the corridor, a million questions racing through his mind. How? and who? and most of all why? He continued his contemplation on the drive home, for the shank of the evening, and into the dark of the night until finally, by the time he lay his head on his pillow and surrendered to sleep, he thought that, at last, perhaps, he understood the meaning of jazz.

* ACKNOWLEDGMENTS *

Once again, it's thank-you time.

I want to thank everyone who read this book before publication: my wife, Kirsten, who talked me out of the "telltale vibrator" scene; Arlene Joplin, at the OKC U.S. Attorney's Office, who gave me a refresher course on the Fourth Amendment; Kim Kakish, who provided much needed background information on Oklahoma street gangs; and my editor, Joe Blades, who always manages to deliver a better book to his Out box than the one that came to his In box. I also want to thank Gail Benedict for typing my virtually illegible handwritten revisions, and Vicky Hildebrandt, whose life I continue to plunder for most of my best plot twists.

Since this book is about music, it might be an appropriate time to thank my piano teacher, Julia Thomas, for a gift I'll cherish all my life. I must also thank my friend and fellow novelist Teresa Miller, the best friend Oklahoma writers ever had.

Special thanks to our family angel, Angel Taylor, for her constant assistance and support.

I want to thank John Wooley for his incisive coverage of

the Tulsa jazz scene, which I cribbed from repeatedly, and all my friends who invited me to their favorite jazz nightspots. I want to thank Gwen Gilkeson, daughter of Oklahoma jazz great Bob Gilkeson, for all her help and insight. I should also mention Dr. John's remarkable memoir, *Under a Hoodoo Moon* (St. Martin's Press), which helped me learn the lingo and formulate the backgrounds for many of the old-time jazz musicians in this book.

My e-mail address is: willbern@mindspring.com (no period). I love to hear from readers. Thanks also to Michelle Sala who, on her own initiative, created the William Bernhardt Home Page at http://www.mindspring.com/~willbern/ (no period). Great job, Michelle.

This book is dedicated to my boyhood hero, Harry Chapin (1941–1981), who not only wrote some incredibly moving folk music, but also managed to donate fifty percent of his concert profits to charity, to counsel young people and speak at hundreds of schools, to financially support a Long Island theater, to raise millions of dollars for organizations dedicated to preventing hunger and malnutrition, and to lobby into existence a Presidential Commission to study the causes of world hunger—all before dying in a car accident at age thirty-nine. I leave you with some of Harry's words, the ones chosen for his epitaph:

If a man tried to take his time on earth
And prove before he died what one man's life
could be worth,
I wonder what would happen to this world.

A Conversation with William Bernhardt

Q. *Bill, how did your first novel—*Primary Justice*—come about? Did you know from the beginning that* Primary *was the start of an eight-book (to date) series?*

A. I've always wanted to write, since I was in grade school. I used to go the library, gaze at the pictures of authors on the dust jackets, and think that being a writer must be the coolest possible occupation in the world. I got my first rejection letter when I was eleven (still have it). And many more afterwards. By the time I got out of law school, I had published a few short stories, but nothing more. I decided it was time to try a novel. But what to write about? People always say—"write what you know." But what did I know? I couldn't think of anything I knew that could possibly be of interest to others. Except . . . it occurred to me that I had just been through this whole law school/law firm experience, sometimes bizarre, sometimes disillusioning. Maybe I could write about that. This was the genesis of Ben Kincaid, who in the first novel has graduated from law school, moved to Tulsa, and joined a big firm—just like me.

Happily, it worked. I enjoyed writing Ben Kincaid from the first day he crawled into my brain. Of course, it had occurred to me that Ben could be a series character, but at this stage in my non-career, that seemed like too much to hope for. I just wanted to be published. As luck would have it, when the first book was acquired at Ballantine, my editor, Joe Blades, immediately asked if I thought this could be the first book in a series. What was I going to say, no?

Q. *How much of your protagonist is in you—or vice versa? Or are you and Ben Kincaid not even remotely alike?*

A. Well, I doubt if Ben and I are precisely the same—for starters, I'm a much better lawyer. Still, I did put Ben in an environment that I understood. How else could I write the things? When I created Ben, I tried not so much to create someone like me as to create someone whom I would like—figuring that if I liked him perhaps others would, too. In many ways, particularly with his strong sense of what's right and his dogged pursuit of justice, Ben is an ideal to which I can aspire.

Q. *To what extent does your real-life law practice enter into the novels?*

A. I don't think I've ever written a courtroom scene that was not grounded in some actual event—either something that happened to me or something a friend told me about. And that includes the "mini-trials" at the start of several of the *Justice* novels that are often humorous, if not outrageous. People have no idea what really goes on in courtrooms! Occasionally a reviewer will write that such-and-such scene was funny, "but of course this could never happen in real life." They have no clue! If anything, I usually have to tone the scenes down, to make them more "realistic."

Q. *Are your novels platforms for your own personal agendas—political, societal, governmental—or do you envision yourself as a storyteller only?*

A. Well, "political agenda" is a bit strong, but I have been fortunate enough to find a large audience for my books, and it seems to me that if all those people are going to be reading, maybe I ought to give them something worth reading about. All of my books have involved real-world issues, but it was in my fourth, *Perfect Justice*, that I really tried to write a more ambitious book, and to tackle a more complex subject. That book dealt with militias and similar hate groups—and was published more than a year before the tragedy in Oklahoma City. *Naked Justice* dealt with the effects of heavy media coverage on the justice system, and my latest, *Dark Justice*, has a strong environmental theme. This is a book I've been wanting to write for some time. One of my closest friends is the Director of the Nature Conservancy here in Oklahoma, and I've worked with her on several projects. Needless to say, I had no trouble getting information for the book.

Q. *The blank page—the one that ultimately becomes page one of a new novel—how do you fill it? How do you start the process of creating a novel? And have you adhered to a particular writing regimen . . . or has that changed?*

A. Certainly my writing regimen changed three years ago when I stopped practicing law. I enjoyed many aspects of my practice, but it is wonderful to be able to write first thing in the morning, when I'm fresh and eager, rather than late at night after the kids go to bed, when I'm tired and would much rather just go to sleep.

I always give my books a great deal of advance planning, so that by the time I sit down to write page one I pretty well know what's going to be on it. I don't try to cover every little detail in advance, but I work out the plot enough that I don't spend all morning sitting around wondering what happens next. Besides, if you want a plot that's full of twists, turns, and surprises (and I do), then you have to do some advance planning. Those things just don't happen by accident.

Q. *What would you like to say to whet readers' appetites for your latest hardcover,* Dark Justice?

A. In the previous book, *Extreme Justice*, Ben became not only a lawyer but an author—he sold his first book, a true crime account of one of his cases. In *Dark Justice*, Ben is "on tour" in the Pacific Northwest when he becomes embroiled in a violent conflict between a logging community and Green Rage, an extreme eco-terrorist group. One of the Green Ragers, a former Kincaid client, is accused of murdering a prominent local logger, and Ben reluctantly finds himself drawn into the fray. He soon learns, however, that all is not what it seems, that the stakes are higher than he ever imagined, that the battle lines have been drawn, and that everyone is in danger—including Ben Kincaid.

I've started putting my e-mail address (willbern@ mindspring.com) in the back of my books, and that has given me a wonderful opportunity to hear from more of my readers. One comment I heard again and again was that readers wanted to see the relationship between Ben and his legal assistant, Christina, develop. Well, if you're interested in what's happening with those two—you will definitely want to read *Dark Justice*.

Q. *Finally, what's next for Ben Kincaid—and Bill Bernhardt?*

A. *Dark Justice* is the main event on my horizon; I expect to be signing and touring my way through February. I've written a Christmas "holiday thriller" which was just published: *The Midnight Before Christmas*. All my life I've worked crossword puzzles, but after I left the firm, I decided to try my hand at making them. My first two puzzles were published recently in *The New York Times*. I'm working on a young adult book, I have an unfinished historical novel in my word processor, and I've just finished a book that could launch a new series. I like to stay busy.

Oh, yes, I also have a family. My wife is a lawyer who works at the Public Defender's office, and we have two children. My six-year-old boy is working on his own novel. He's written over three hundred pages, although I must admit the narrative tends to wander a bit. My three-year-old girl insists that I play Kerplunk! on a daily basis and hold her hand while she watches her favorite TV show—*Buffy the Vampire Slayer*. I know, you probably think it's horrible that I let her watch this (I do sometimes have to edit the episodes in advance), but I was pleased to see her get interested in a role model who was a little tougher than Barbie, or more career-oriented than all those Disney heroines whose lives revolve around marrying some undeserving dweeb prince.

—This interview originally appeared in a slightly different form in *Murder on the Internet* (www.randomhouse.com/BB/MOTI).